Large Print
Wilson, F. Paul
Mirage

MIRAGE

F. PAUL WILSON

AND

MATTHEW J. COSTELLO

G.K. Hall & Co.
Thorndike, Maine

Published in 1997 by arrangement with Warner Books, Inc.

G.K. Hall Large Print Mystery Collection.

The text of this Large Print edition is unabridged.
Other aspects of the book may vary from the original edition.

 Set in 16 pt. Bookman Old Style.

Printed in the United States on permanent paper.

Library of Congress Cataloging in Publication Data

Wilson, F. Paul (Francis Paul)
    Mirage / F. Paul Wilson and Matthew J. Costello.
      p.   cm.
      ISBN 0-7838-2022-4 (lg. print : hc)
      1. Large type books. I. Costello, Matthew J. II. Title.
    [PS3573.I45695M5   1997]
      813′.54—dc21   96-44452

To
Liza Landsman
(for keeping the faith)

Acknowledgments

To *Jo Fletcher,* whose Howdale Farm is around the bend from the imaginary Oakwood. Whatever seems real in our version of the Yorkshire coast and countryside is due to her generous help with firsthand descriptions, books, maps, and photos from her personal album. Any inaccuracies are our doing.

To *Betsy Mitchell* for her enthusiasm, support, and keen editorial eye. No theme is too large, no modifier too small to escape her scrutiny.

To *Al Zuckerman, Steven Spruill,* and *Bill Massey* for their input and generous support.

Thank you, one and all.

One

Memory is not written in stone; it's highly susceptible to reconstruction. So much of what we remember of our own pasts is nothing more than a . . . mirage.
— Random notes: Julia Gordon

1

Julie careened into her office. "Check my voice mail for me, will you?"

She was running late again, but what else was new. The department had six people doing the work of twelve.

"Already did," Cindy said, and handed her a handwritten sheet.

Julie scanned it. Nothing special there. Mostly interdepartmental minutiae. Return calls she could make later, tomorrow, whenever. . . .

And then she came to the last item: *Your Uncle Ethan — call him. Urgent.* Cindy had misspelled Eathan's name, but everybody

7

did that. A number followed, but Julie didn't recognize the country code. Not the usual 44 for Great Britain. Was Eathan on vacation?

"My uncle — did he say where he was calling from?"

"No," Cindy said. "But that's a Paris number."

Julie stared at her secretary. "Paris? How do you know that?"

"I knew *you'd* want to know so I looked it up." Cindy grinned and batted her big blue eyes. "Aren't I wonderful?"

"You're the best," Julie said, and meant it.

Cindy was the most efficient secretary she'd ever had, possessing that rarest of secretarial talents — anticipation. And she was neat. Julie detested clutter.

Cindy's only drawback was her looks. She was a pert little blonde with a pixie haircut and a knockout figure. She was engaged to a computer technician at Exxon and would be a married woman in three months. Julie dreaded the day Cindy might walk in and announce she was pregnant and was going to stay home to be a mommy. That was what her last secretary had done. The whole idea baffled Julie. This was the most exciting work in the world. How could anyone leave it to stay home?

"Did he say what he meant by 'urgent'?"

Cindy shook her head. "Nope. Just said, 'Call me back at once. It's urgent.' Then he left the number. But his voice did sound a little strained, or maybe tired. Want me to dial him?"

Why did Cindy seem so anxious to connect her? Then Julie realized that this was probably the first personal call Cindy had ever taken for her. And Cindy always seemed overly concerned about Julie's lack of a "life" — no friends, no lovers, just the project.

So maybe she didn't have much of what Cindy and a number of others in the department considered a "life."

But if I like it that way, why should they care?

Julie stuffed the note in her pocket. "No time right now." She glanced at her watch. "It's what — four P.M. over there? I'll call him after the demonstration."

"But he said —"

"You don't know my uncle Eathan. *Everything's* urgent to Uncle Eathan. But right here, right now, this demonstration is truly urgent. How do I look?"

Cindy stood and reached over the desk to straighten Julie's lab coat, then stepped back and considered her.

"How about some lipstick?"

"Forget it."

"Maybe just run the brush through your hair."

Julie pulled a brush from her pocketbook and stepped over to the eight-by-ten mirror Cindy kept on the back of the office door. She straightened some of the flyaway strands caused by the wind-tunnel effects in the subway and checked herself out.

She looked pale. Why not? She was fair, a blonde — not as blond as Cindy, but her color was all her own — and she hadn't spent any time outdoors in years. She thought she looked okay, though. Her short, blunt-cut hair was all in place now. Her skin, pale as it was, was clear. And her blue eyes sparkled despite only four hours of sleep last night. Her lips were full but pale. Maybe she did need some lipstick, but she had none with her. Never bothered with it.

What they see is what I've got.

She tried a smile. Not a great smile, but not a bad one. Had to practice that smile for the Bruchmeyer man this morning.

She turned back to Cindy. "Wish me luck."

Cindy grinned and held up two sets of crossed fingers. "You wouldn't believe how hard it is to type like this."

Julie laughed. "Right. Probably slows you down to ninety words a minute."

"Seriously," Cindy said, her smile fading.

"Good luck, Dr. Gordon."

"Thanks," she said, waving as she headed for the hall. "I'll need it."

Yeah, she thought, all but trotting for the lab. Loads of it.

The Maria Bruchmeyer Foundation had tons of money to spend. When Heinrich Bruchmeyer's wife died of Alzheimer's disease, he set up the well-funded foundation to finance research into the causes of and possible cures for Alzheimer's. After months of barraging the foundation with phone calls, letters, reprints, and abstracts of her journal articles, Julie had finally persuaded a member of the Bruchmeyer board to trek downtown for a demonstration.

Today was the day. The demo was scheduled for 10:00 A.M. — twenty minutes ago. God! Why today of all days?

She rounded a corner and saw Dr. Mordecai Siegal pacing the hall outside the lab. Spotting her, he waddled toward her, his hands fluttering in the air before him like meaty butterflies.

Don't we look spiffy, she thought, giving her superior the once-over. Clean lab coat — open as ever because he couldn't button it around his girth — thinning gray hair combed and parted, pressed pants, shined shoes, and could that really be Old Spice she smelled? Mordecai Siegal, M.D., Ph.D.,

11

world-renowned guru of memory mapping, was trying to look the part today.

Must have been hard for him to get himself so together without Bernice's help. Hard? She would have thought it impossible. He'd lost a lifelong companion just two months ago, but somehow he was holding on.

"He's here, Julie! He's waiting. You're late and he got here early! Where have you been?"

"I had a heavy date last night and was out partying till dawn. Just got in."

He looked at her over the tops of his glasses. "I sincerely doubt that."

"Okay, I was down at the mainframe running one more debug on that new chunk of code we added last week. Won't do to have our software get temperamental this morning."

"Please, God, no," he said, clasping his hands before him and glancing at the ceiling. They both knew a system crash would be a disaster. "But he's been *waiting* for you. I managed to kill some time with chitchat and the nondisclosure forms, but I ran out of gas."

"Well, we don't want to appear *too* anxious, do we. And I didn't exactly have anyone else I could send down to the mainframe, did I."

"Touché," he said. "Maybe if we impress

the Bruchmeyer man, we'll be able to hire our own propeller head to attend to the programming. Give you a break."

"Wouldn't that be nice."

"Speaking of nice," he said, touching her arm, "please be patient with this man, Julie."

She feigned shock. "*Moi?* You're insinuating that I could be anything less than patient?"

"Well, you do have a tendency to be abrupt with people who don't catch on right away. Just remember, no one else in the world is doing what we're doing, so it takes time even for knowledgeable people to catch on. This man may not be . . . well, knowledgeable."

"But he's got deep pockets."

"Right. Very deep." He gave her a shy smile and dropped into a Yiddish dialect. "So a little charm vouldn't hoit."

"Gotcha. I'll send Cindy out to Victoria's Secret for a see-through peignoir —"

"You know what I mean, Julie."

"Yeah, I know."

She straightened his tie. She liked Dr. Siegal. A lot. Not only was he a brilliant theorist and a great boss, he was a decent human being. Too bad he was thirty years older. All the good ones were either too old or too married.

He'd practically adopted her when he

13

learned that she had no family here in the States. Sometimes he was more father than boss, and she had to remind herself every so often that he was director of this department.

"Are we ready?" she said.

He took a deep breath. "Ready if you are."

"All right. Showtime."

Julie slipped past him and stepped up to the door. MEMORY MAPPING was stenciled on the frosted glass. She grabbed the knob, pulled, and stepped inside.

2

Julie flipped the helmet's goggles over Mr. Henderson's eyes and adjusted the black rubber seals around his orbits.

"Comfortable?"

He nodded. "As comfortable as can be expected."

An honest answer, she guessed. Henderson looked like an overgrown kid at the mall ready to play VR Troopers. The helmet was heavy and clunky. The user's neck would begin to ache after twenty or thirty minutes. A research tool, with no attempt to pretty it up for commercial use. The wire-riddled metal helmet was stereoscopic and stereophonic, supporting 3-D binocular goggles with a separate monitor for each eye, and a pair of deep-range headphones.

And the gear didn't fit Mr. Henderson's head too well. He was tall and gaunt, with an elongated skull that wasn't made for headwear — especially *this* headwear. But somehow they'd got it on him.

Great, she thought. I say send me someone so I can demonstrate the equipment, and they send Lurch from the Addams Family.

But he seemed knowledgeable about her research — apparently he'd read all the articles she'd sent — and genuinely interested. She appreciated that. And he was bright. That made it easier. She sensed that if she brought off this demonstration they had a good chance of getting a meaningful grant.

If the system didn't crash.

And as soon as the first check cleared she wanted to find a larger space for the lab. This place had a comfortable occupancy limit of three. Five people plus an extra console were crammed in here now. She wanted more space, more staff, a hot new Silicon Graphics computer just for image processing. . . . She was dreaming.

Money — it had become a constant chase. With funding to the National Science Foundation being cut again, the project's primary source of federal grants was iffy for next year. And NYU was cutting its contribution by a third. The whole project was in danger of collapse. Desperate, they'd gone to the private sector. So hard to get pure research dollars out of bottom-line-obsessed bean counters. Everybody found the memoryscape fascinating, but how much would it return on the dollar?

Couldn't they see? This project was opening up the seat of consciousness, of personality. It was going to change the way the world looked at the mind.

But not without many more trials and lots more time to tweak the software. And that took *money.*

She glanced around. Good thing she wasn't claustrophobic. Dr. S. stood near the door, arms folded across his chest, looking anxious. The subject, Lorraine Deering, one of their regular volunteers, lay on the bed with her head encased in a smaller, tighter-fitting helmet lined with scalp electrodes and pickups; she snored softly in diazepam-induced sleep. Teresa Gomez, the nurse anesthetist, sat between the bed and Julie's recliner.

Then there was Mr. Henderson, seated on the second recliner they'd squeezed in; all in a ten-by-fourteen cubicle. The expression "cheek by jowl" took on new meaning.

Fortunately all the computing hardware — the university's mainframe — was in the basement. All Julie needed to run the show was her terminal on its rolling cart. She could tell from Mr. Henderson's initial expression that he was ready to be un-impressed. Where was all the sci-fi gadgetry he'd been expecting? But when she pulled out the VR helmets, his eyes had lit.

"Now the headphones," she said. "These are specially constructed to block out external noise. From now on I'll be speaking to you through my microphone. You'll have your own mike for any questions. Okay?"

He nodded again. "By the way, are you British?"

"No. American."

"Your accent —"

People always asked her about that. Funny, she didn't think she had any accent at all.

"Born in New York State, raised in York, England."

"Ah. That explains it."

She flipped the oversized headphones down over his ears. A little fuzz and they'd look like earmuffs.

She pulled her wire microphone up in front of her lips.

"Can you hear me?"

An abrupt nod. Mr. Henderson looked impatient to get on with it. Julie wanted to knock his socks off. She took a deep breath.

"Great. Okay, now we're going to recline your chair until you're almost horizontal —

just to make you more comfortable with the headgear."

Dr. Siegal helped Julie ease the chair backward. For most people it conjured up images of a visit to the dentist. When they finally had him in position with his ankles crossed and his hands folded on his abdomen, Julie looked up at Dr. Siegal. She turned off her mike and spoke in a stage whisper.

"Nice enough?"

His eyes widened as he jammed his index finger against his lips.

Just then a knock on the door. Dr. Siegal squeezed back and edged the door open. Cindy poked her head through the opening.

"Dr. Gordon?"

"Yes?"

"I'm sorry. It's your uncle again. He's on the line. Says he must speak to you."

Julie felt her annoyance rising. Cindy should know better than this.

"Didn't you tell him I was busy?"

"Of course. I told him you were running an important demonstration and couldn't be disturbed — but he won't get off the line. He says it's extremely urgent."

Julie bit her lip. She knew how insistent her uncle Eathan could be. And maybe this was truly urgent. But whatever it was would have to wait until after the demonstration. No way could she leave the Bruchmeyer Foundation man with his head locked in that uncomfortable rig while she talked to her uncle . . .

. . . and watched the grant fly away.

"Tell him you spoke to me and I said I'll call him as soon as I can but that it's impossible for me to speak to him now. Take his number, and then hang up."

Cindy's eyes widened. "Really?"

"Really. Otherwise you'll spend the rest of the morning on the phone with him."

"Okay," Cindy said, but she looked uncomfortable as she ducked out.

Dr. Siegal looked at Julie questioningly as he shut the door. "You think maybe you should — ?"

Julie shook her head. She owed Uncle Eathan — owed him big time — but he could be a real pest. Still, interrupting her in a meeting, that was a bit much, even for him. What could he possibly want?

She shook off the uncertainty. First things first, and getting this grant came first.

Flipping the mike back on, she donned her own headgear.

"All right, Mr. Henderson. Sorry for the delay. We're just about ready to enter Lorraine's memory. As I told you, it can be disorienting at first, and you may even feel a little vertigo until I adjust the visuals, so hold on to the armrests of your recliner until you're comfortable."

She watched him grab hold, then flipped down her own headphones. Julie's gear was different. Her helmet was equipped with electrodes similar to Lorraine's. She pulled the VR glove onto her right hand, then adjusted her goggles with her left.

Inside the goggles, a thin four-button bar with ENTER — EXIT — WARNING — WINDOW ran along the top of the twin screens; a physiological readout ribbon showing Lorraine's EKG along with her EEG, pulse, and respiratory rates ran along the bottom. All the space between was a blank pale blue, like a cloudless winter sky.

Julie checked Lorraine's EKG — a normal QRS with a rate of 72. Respirations were 8. EEG running at 10 Hertz. Good. All normal.

She leaned back in her own recliner.

"Ready, Mr. Henderson?"

"More than ready."

"I like that attitude. Here we go."

She moved her glove and the motion was transmitted to the computer, which generated an image of a hand with a pointing index finger on the screen. She guided the fingertip icon over to the Enter button on the bar at the top of the screen and clicked it.

Two

We're all so cavalier about memory. No one considers the veritable flood of information that gushes from our five senses into our brains every second of the waking day, and how our brains divide up and store this endless flow of perception into banks of information that we can tap into and access in nanoseconds.
— Random notes: Julia Gordon

You see a couple of vertical rolls on the goggle screens, then the video stabilizes. Wisps of cloud appear in the blue. The breeze sighs, birds twitter below.

As usual, it's a beautiful day in Lorraineville.

You angle the hand icon downward. The clouds rotate out of sight. A sensation of falling — maybe too fast — and then the green horizon comes into view.

Henderson's voice sounds in your headphones. *"Wow. Just like Flight Simulator!"*

Good. Already he's enjoying this.

"A little bit, except we don't use a joystick.

21

And you won't find any enemy fighters out there. What I'm going to do is take you on a little tour of Lorraine's memoryscape."

You point ahead and you begin to move forward, gliding over rolling green hills and perfectly shaped trees. Quaint villages dot the landscape. But the grassy surfaces are not flat. They appear to be crisscrossed with linear mounds, as if a tangled network of pipes has been overlaid with sod.

"Looks like she's got a bad case of moles in her lawn down there," Henderson says.

You smile. A good analogy. "Not mole burrows," you say, "but they are tunnels of a sort. That's the memory-link network. It forms the infrastructure of the memoryscape."

"Is this her past? Looks like computer-generated images."

You bite back a sharp remark. What else did he expect?

Calmly, evenly, you say, "Because that's exactly what they are. Lorraine is a bright, well-adjusted graduate student who's helping us with our research and getting paid as an experimental subject. The computer is sorting a wide array of impulses from her cortex, arranging them into images, mingling them with impulses from me, feeding the mixes back to her, rereading them, feeding them back again, and so on in a continuous loop that allows us to interact with her memoryscape."

"Interact? You mean, change her memories?"

"No. We seem to be able to trigger memories by our presence, but we can only move among them, view them from different angles. We cannot change the memoryscape. I've explored Lorraine's memoryscape many, many times, and it's always the same."

"Always?"

"Yes. This is who she is. Spread out below us is the sum total of Lorraine's available life experiences. And you *are* your memories. Without your memories you have no past, no family, no friends, no experiences. You haven't been anywhere or seen anything or met anyone. You are defined by the accumulation of your day-to-day experiences. With no memory of those experiences, who are you? You're a cipher."

"Which is why our foundation finds your research so intriguing. But surely not every memoryscape looks like this."

"Absolutely not. Lorraine had a fairly prosaic upbringing. I've been in 'scapes where it's not so sunny and there aren't any white picket fences —"

"Like a ghetto?"

"Right. But even subjects with a ghetto background have these rolling, well-organized, wide-angle landscapes. It's just that the empty areas tend to look like vacant lots and the buildings look like tenements."

"Might have been more interesting to visit one of those."

You feel your jaw muscles bunch. You're taking this man on a tour that only a handful of people in the world have experienced, and already he's grousing.

" 'One of those' wasn't available — at least not one who'd allow a stranger to open the book of her life."

"But they let you —"

"Only after they get to know and trust me. Lorraine trusts me implicitly. And she doesn't feel she has anything to hide."

"Everybody's got something to hide."

You can't argue with that, so you say, "Let's go take a closer look, shall we? Pick any structure you want."

You rotate the visual field, giving a panoramic view of the memoryscape. A gallimaufry of structures dots the terrain below: ranch-style tract homes, the brick edifices of public grammar and high schools, churches, fast-food joints, college dorms, taverns, movie houses, soccer fields, the Eiffel Tower, Big Ben, and, towering over everything, a huge white two-story colonial house.

"Why the landmarks?"

"Lorraine spent her junior year abroad in Europe. Don't forget, the memoryscape doesn't exist in her head; it's a symbolic virtual environment — computer generated. Lorraine's mind determines what's important, the computer simply accesses that hierarchy and fashions an environment — her personal

24

memoryscape — from it. Every significant person, place, and event in her life is down there."

"And the not so significant?"

"Down there too. Usually tucked away in and around the big ones. You just have to know where to look. The presence of adrenaline or noradrenaline in your system at the time of the event embeds those important moments more firmly in your memory."

"Well, if big equals important here, let's have a look at that huge white house."

"Good choice. That's where she grew up. Lots of memories there. Hang on."

You work the glove, pointing, banking right and swooping down to ground level. After so many visits to Lorraineville, you've become Top Gun navigating the memoryscape. It's fun showing off. Sometimes you feel more at home here than in the real world.

The white colonial looms ahead, towering above you. Yet as you approach, it seems to shrink, continuing to diminish until, by the time you reach the front steps, it's been reduced to normal size. You're used to this phenomenon, but your passenger is not.

"What happened?" Henderson sounds alarmed.

"Size can be whimsical in the memoryscape. As the saying goes: You ain't seen nothin' yet."

As you approach the front door you push on it and it swings open. You step inside and look around. The foyer is huge; the ceiling towers twenty or thirty feet above you. It never fails to remind you of the Yorkshire manor that was your childhood home.

And for a second you flash on your uncle Eathan's "urgent" call. You hope it's not *that* urgent.

"Good lord! The perspective's all wrong."

"Not if you're a child, and we're obviously in a child's perspective. If we turned around and reentered, we'd — Here, I'll show you."

You back onto the porch, pull the door closed, then push it open again. You move forward and the foyer seems normal size now.

"Now we're viewing the environment from an older perspective, possibly a teenager's. This is one of the unpredictables within the memoryscape. Time is elastic here. If the subject spent many years in an environment — or decades, in the case of this house — you can never be sure from which time frame you'll be viewing it. We're not too sure what determines the hierarchy of memories. But we think it has to do with the subject's most current experiences . . . and how they relate to the past."

"Was she ever an adult in this house?"

"Not in a real sense. She visited for weeks at a time during her college years, but didn't really live here then."

You glide into the living room. It's dark except for the TV. By its light you can see a couple locked in an embrace on the couch. The boy is sneaking his hand under the girl's sweater and the girl is pushing it away.

"This looks interesting," Henderson says.

Typical voyeuristic male, you think. You bite your tongue.

"That's her first steady boyfriend. He lasted about four months. She never let him get much beyond what you see here."

You move into the dining room. Seventeen-year-old Lorraine, her brother, and her parents sit around the table in stiff silence. You can almost smell the tension in the air. You remember plenty of similar scenes like this from your own teen years — although you were never the cause.

"Uh-oh. This doesn't look like a happy group."

"Want to know why? I'll show you."

You return to the living room, where it's night and all the lights are on. It's packed with teenagers now, many of them drunk or stoned as Bruce Springsteen shouts about how he was born in the USA. A Saturday night in the summer. Lorraine's parents are away for the weekend — you caught the parental good-byes and warnings to Lorraine in an earlier visit. The cats are away, and now it's Lorraine's time to party.

As you weave through the crowd a fight breaks out. A lamp is knocked over and smashes on the floor. Lorraine screams for them to stop but the fight only gets worse.

"This is fascinating," Henderson whispers. *"Utterly fascinating!"*

You pass into the kitchen, where you find

27

Lorraine standing by the sink looking defiant while her mother sits at the kitchen table and cries. Lorraine's formerly long and glossy chestnut hair has been chopped to a two-inch length, dyed bright orange, and moussed into a dozen spikes.

"The rebellious years. We all had them," you say, but you don't remember rebelling like this.

That was your sister's department.

"Where's the regular day-to-day life? Everything here seems so emotionally charged."

"Adrenaline, remember? Strong emotions flood the bloodstream with adrenaline and noradrenaline. They activate the amygdala, which in turn makes the cortex more receptive to memory. As a result, emotionally charged events — happy, sad, frightening — are more deeply and firmly embedded in our memories than the routine incidents. If we hang around long enough we'll see some of those, too, but they're faint. Your memory edits for you. Do you really need to file away the details of the ten-thousandth time you passed through the living room on your way to the kitchen?"

"Where's that go?" Henderson asks as you pass a closed door.

"The basement, but you can't go there."

"Why not?"

"Because it's locked and we don't have the key. Lorraine doesn't go there herself and so she doesn't want us going there either."

"Ah! Repressed memories."

"Not repressed so much as tucked away. They're unpleasant and so she keeps them out of sight. Truly repressed memories — if such things exist — would be deeply buried; even the subject wouldn't know where they were. And once you located them you'd really have to dig to reach them."

"So you've never been down to the basement."

"I haven't found the key."

A lie. You did find the key. You always were good at finding things. It's folded within the pages of the scrapbook in Lorraine's bedroom, rammed through the photo of Johnny Kozik. Because among other things in the basement is the fuzzy memory of the loss of Lorraine's virginity to good ol' Johnny. They'd call it date rape now.

Johnny, two years older and light-years more experienced, came over with a bottle of Southern Comfort one night when her parents were out, got her drunk, began undressing her. Lorraine, feeling more sick than amorous, tried to push him away, but he became angry and began pushing her around. He frightened her and she was too groggy to put up much of a struggle. You couldn't watch. You had to turn away as she let him do what he wanted to do.

It gives you the creeps to know that the same date rape is playing in an endless loop below your feet. Even now . . .

You've never returned to the basement, and

you sure as hell aren't taking a stranger down there.

"What's upstairs?"

"The usual — bedrooms and bathrooms. We can —"

You are interrupted by the Warning button flashing red. You check the readout ribbon. The EKG retains a normal QRS pattern but the pulse rate is up to 120 and respirations are 14.

"What's wrong?"

"Nothing. For reasons we've yet to explain, we're limited to how long we can stay in the memoryscape without causing physiological reactions. The limit varies from subject to subject, but rising pulse and respiratory rates are the first signs. Part of it has to do with a diminution of the diazepam effect, so as that wears off, the reactions begin. But even with extra doses, once the reaction starts, it progresses."

"What will happen if we ignore the warning and stay here?"

"We can't. It's a failsafe in the program. If we don't exit, it will exit for us. I've no desire to find out what would happen if we push it. It may be harmful, it may not. Why risk it? We can always go back in later."

"Then let's exit immediately. I'm not here to cause this young woman harm."

As you move the fingertip of the hand to the Exit button and click it, the genuine concern in Henderson's voice causes a pang of guilt.

You had Gomez give Lorraine a light dose to guarantee a short session.

No matter. You've given him a tour. Dragging it out would only be repetitious. Because you have no intention of revealing any of Lorraine's secrets. You promised her.

The screens go blank. You reach for your goggles.

Three

*I'm often asked if the memoryscape pro-
grams could be useful in criminal cases.
Sure, you could go into the head of a
guy who says he was out of town when
his wife was murdered. In the memoryscape you could watch him slashing
his wife's throat, and have every detail
of the crime scene right there for all to
see. But what guilty accused is going to
let you do that?*
— Random notes: Julia Gordon

1

Julie rubbed her eyes, then lifted her helmet. Across from her she saw Dr. Siegal
helping Henderson off with his. Henderson
sat up and stared at her, then at Siegal.
His eyes were wide with wonder as he
searched for the right words to say.

"That was . . . incredible. Do you people
have any idea what you've got here? Why

haven't you gone to the media with this?"

"Because it's not a parlor game," Julie snapped and caught a warning look from Dr. Siegal.

Easy, girl, she thought. So far, so good. Don't blow it now.

"What Dr. Gordon means," Dr. S. said quickly, "is that we don't want this technology exploited in an unseemly fashion. It's not the latest high-tech toy for thrill seekers or talk shows. It makes vulnerable the most private moments of an individual's life. Just imagine abducting someone, sedating them, and then invading their mind. What a tool for blackmailers. Or industrial espionage."

"Or for the courts," Henderson said. "Looks to me like the ultimate lie detector."

"Yes and no. A memory is not necessarily an accurate reflection of reality. It's a recording of a perception, colored by emotion, and often influenced by intervening events. Someday, after endless court battles, this might be accepted as a legal tool. But as a method for exploring memory itself, dealing with the loss of memory —"

"That's where Alzheimer's might come in, I should think." Henderson turned to Julie. "Have you ever visited an Alzheimer's patient's memoryscape?"

"No. I'd very much like to, but I'm willing to bet it wouldn't be too startlingly different from Lorraine's on the surface — at least not until actual organic degeneration of the cortex takes place."

"Why do you say that? Their memories are shot. I'd expect a desert, a barren wasteland."

"That's because you're confusing the existence of memories and the ability to access them," Julie said. "All memories are fragmented, with bits and pieces scattered all over the brain. Take the memory of a chocolate-chip cookie, for instance: Its smell is encoded and stored in the olfactory cortex, the look of the cookie is in the visual cortex, the soft warm feel of it in your hand is in the tactile cortex, and the taste in the gustatory cortex. So when your olfactory nerve picks up the smell of a freshly baked Toll House cookie, the convergence systems of your brain assemble all the pieces . . . and your mouth begins to water. But if your brain *can't* find the links and access those memories — even though all the components of the cookie memory are still intact — the odor means nothing to you. It's not a cookie — it's just a smell."

"Of what benefit would this be to Alzheimer's patients?" Henderson said.

Julie hesitated.

"Come on," he said. "This is a magnificent breakthrough. I want the Bruchmeyer Foundation to be a part of it. But the board of directors will not part with a dime unless they feel it will ultimately benefit Alzheimer's patients."

Julie spoke slowly, carefully, trying to keep her tone casual. They'd hooked him; now they had to land him.

She glanced over at Dr. Siegal. As crucial as this was to her, it was absolutely vital to him. He'd already lost his wife; Julie was not going to let him lose his project.

"I don't want to make promises we can't keep, but broken memory links can be restored via the memoryscape."

Henderson rose to his feet. "Is that theory or has it been done?"

"It's been done," Julie said, trying to hide her excitement. Yes, it had been done. But by only one person, on one isolated case. "It's damn hard, but I've done it." She held up a hand. "But not in an Alzheimer's patient."

"But I thought the memoryscape was purely symbolic."

Julie nodded. "It *is* symbolic, but not as purely symbolic as we originally thought. We can't change memories, but reestablishing links in the memoryscape appears to carry over into real-life function. The thing is, we don't know *why* it works. That's why I was hesitant to mention it."

Henderson looked like he wanted to pace but there was no room for it. "But wait a second — if we supplied you with funds and brought you Alzheimer's sufferers as volunteers — you'd know soon enough, wouldn't you?"

Julie nodded. "I imagine we would."

"Excellent!" He bounded to the coat hook on the wall, grabbed his Burberry, and turned to them. "This is wonderful! I'm going straight to Mr. Bruchmeyer himself — today. He'll want to know about this immediately. He'll be *very* interested."

"How interested?"

"You mean in dollars and cents? Well, the Bruchmeyer Foundation never lends halfhearted support. If it's a go, we'll back you all the way. Of course we'll need a detailed experimental protocol to place before the board. How soon can you have that?"

"Two weeks?" Dr. Siegal said, glancing Julie's way.

Julie nodded, using all her willpower to keep from screaming Yes! and pumping her fist into the air. "That sounds doable."

"We'll be waiting to hear from you," Henderson said, opening the door. "End of the month at the latest."

As soon as he stepped out the door, Dr. Siegal flung his arms around her. He laughed aloud and spun her around.

"We did it!" he cried. "We're going to get a grant!"

"Let's not count the money yet." She never allowed herself to be too optimistic. Things had a way of backfiring when you became complacent. The Bruchmeyer board would be scrutinizing the documentation very carefully. Everything would have to be perfect.

"Julie, you were wonderful!"

"Nothing to it," she said, enjoying his elation. So good to see him happy again.

"Oh, right," he said, pushing her back to arms' length. "As if there weren't a couple of moments there when —"

"I was in control — total, complete control. Except when I wanted to —"

"What's going on?" said a voice behind them.

Julie turned. Lorraine was sitting up on the bed, looking groggy and slightly befuddled.

"How'd I do?" she said.

Dr. Siegal rushed over and wrapped an arm around her shoulders. "My dear, we did fine! And you were magnificent — at least your memoryscape was!"

Julie watched them. She wished she could show her gratitude to Lorraine like Dr. Siegal had — hugging and clasping Lorraine's hand. But that wasn't her style. Something always held her back. She felt glued to the spot.

"You done good, kid," she said.

2

"What are you doing for lunch?" Dr. Siegal said as he followed her into her office.

Julie glanced at Cindy's empty desk and then at her watch. 12:05. That explained where Cindy was.

"Lunch? Who's got time for lunch? I'm *days* behind now."

"And I know what you're going to do first."

"No. Not lunch. I don't do —"

"I'm not talking about food. I'm talking about your uncle. Weren't you going to call him?"

Uncle Eathan! Damn! He'd completely slipped her mind.

"The number . . . where is it?" She pawed through her lab-coat pockets. "I had it right — here it is."

"Good," Dr. Siegal said, pointing to her inner office, set off by gray room dividers. "You call, I'll wait out here. Then we'll do lunch."

She gave him a look. "Dr. Siegal . . ." Truly she didn't have time for lunch, but he wasn't going to quit. "All right. This will only take a minute."

She punched in the number, waited through a few rings, then heard *"Bonjour."*

Julie recognized the voice. "Eathan. It's Julie."

"Julie! Thank God! I've been going crazy trying to reach you! Didn't you get my messages?"

She realized from his frazzled tone that something was seriously wrong. This wasn't Eathan being the oversolicitous uncle. He sounded scared, frantic, and now a sense of foreboding enveloped her. Damn! She should have called sooner. She hoped he was okay.

"I'm sorry. It was impossible for me to get away until now. What's wrong?"

"It's Samantha."

"Oh." Julie felt a sudden cold seep through her. She bit back adding *Is that all?* and let out a breath she hadn't realized she was holding. *What else is new?*

"What is it this time?"

"I don't know. Nobody knows. Not yet, anyway. That's why I'm calling you."

"Well, she's disappeared before and popped back up again after everyone went crazy looking —"

"She isn't missing. She was found unconscious in her studio."

"Great," Julie muttered. "Another overdose. What's the hot new drug in Paris these days?"

"Please, Julie. This is serious. She's been

comatose for two weeks."

"Two *weeks?*"

"I just found out about it yesterday. I rushed to Paris immediately. She's a very sick girl. And it's *not* drugs — all the toxicology tests were negative."

"Then what — ?"

"I spoke to the hospital chief of staff. No one knows what's wrong. Every test they do comes back negative."

"She's been checked for encephalitis? Meningitis? Did they look for any sign of a blow to the head? A fall?"

"Yes, yes. And all the possible metabolic causes. It's a public hospital but they were very thorough. They say they can't do anything else for her."

"There's got to be something. Every coma has a cause — it's not a state the body goes into just for the hell of it."

"I'm having Dr. Elliot fly over to consult."

"The neurologist? From Oxford?"

"Yes. He's supposed to be the top man in coma."

"He is." Julie knew his reputation. "No one even comes close. He'll find out what happened."

As usual, Uncle Eathan was pulling out all stops for Sam. Of course, Julie knew he'd do the same for her, but it always seemed to be Sam who needed rescuing.

"If Dr. Elliot agrees with the others —

that we'll just have to wait — then I'll have Samantha moved to a nursing home where we'll . . . just . . . wait."

"Well, I hope he can help her."

"God, so do I. Samantha's been through so much."

Julie didn't respond to that. The correct way to say it was that Samantha had put *herself* through so much.

A pause, then Eathan spoke: "When are you coming over?"

"To Europe?" Oh, no. He didn't expect her to . . . "I — I can't. I'm right in the middle of something very important. That memory project I've been telling you about."

"Oh." He sounded crushed. "I thought maybe you could help."

"Me? You're the M.D."

"I haven't practiced for almost a quarter century — you know that."

"But I'm not a medical doctor; I'm a Ph.D."

"In neurophysiology. Anything you can add . . ."

"I can't add anything to Dr. Elliot. He's world class. Look, you know that if there was something I could do, I'd be heading for the airport now. But I can't. And I'm stuck here. The work is at a critical juncture." She waited a beat. "You can do without me there, but I'm needed here."

"Julie . . . I know you and Sam haven't

been getting along . . ."

Getting along? she thought. We haven't *spoken* in years.

"That's not it. And I promise I'll come over as soon as I can get free. I mean it."

"Please do. The *instant* you're free. This is very serious."

"Keep me informed of any changes, all right? I'll call you tomorrow. I'll stay in touch. I promise."

"Very well." She could hear the disappointment in his voice. "I'll be at this number."

Julie said good-bye and hung up.

Damn. Here she was, twenty-eight years old and still allowing her uncle to make her feel guilty. Or did she feel guilty because of Sam?

"Everything all right?"

Julie looked up and saw Dr. Siegal standing in the doorway.

"Family problems," she said. She felt almost embarrassed telling him.

"Anything I can do?"

"No. It's my sister. Nobody could ever do much with my sister."

"The sister you never talk about?"

She nodded. "My evil twin."

"A twin? How fascinating. You mean there's two of you?"

"Hardly. She's the most unidentical identical twin you could ever imagine."

"She's in some sort of trouble?"

Julie summarized what Uncle Eathan had told her, and he asked most of the same questions she'd asked Eathan.

"Don't you worry about a thing," Dr. Siegal said. "I'll keep things running here. You just get over there first flight that you can. Go. Be with your family. Take as long as —"

"Oh, I'm not going anywhere."

Dr. Siegal's eyes were wide, incredulous. "Your sister — your *twin* — is in a coma and you're not going to her side?"

"I've got too much to do here, especially with the Bruchmeyer protocol. And besides, she's in good hands."

He stared at her strangely for a moment, then stepped forward and took her arm. He pulled her toward the door.

"Come. No argument. If you don't want to have lunch, then we'll have something else."

"What?"

"A talk. About priorities."

3

A warm, sunny October day, with the trees in Washington Square starting to change color. The park was crowded with people eating their lunch, drinking their lunch, smoking or snorting their lunch, or trying to bum change off the rest so they could buy some lunch.

Julie let Dr. Siegal drag her along the littered walks until they found an empty half of a park bench next to an entwined couple who appeared to be having each other for lunch. They sat down.

In true New York fashion Julie and Dr. S. ignored the amorous couple. Harder to ignore were the scattered papers and empty bottles and cans and fast-food containers that dotted the park. An unusual amount of litter, Julie thought. Even the parks were suffering from cutbacks.

"Is this talk really necessary?" Julie said. As much as she liked him, she couldn't help feeling annoyed. This was wasted time.

"That's what I mean by priorities," he said. "Nothing is as important as family. Work is simply work. We're not saving mankind here, Julie."

"I'm convinced we might be — and I know you feel the same. Besides, I don't have a family. You know that."

"Except for an uncle and a black-sheep sister you now tell me is your twin. You told me your parents are gone. Did they die when you were young?"

For a moment she resented his probing, then remembered sitting beside him in that stuffy little room in Saint Vincent's Hospital, watching him clutch his dying wife's hand as if he could keep her from slipping away.

Maybe this was important to him.

"Yes. When we were five."

"I'm sorry. An accident?"

"A fire. Our house burned to the ground."

"Oh, Lord. You were there?"

Julie nodded. "We both were."

"Why didn't you ever tell me? That must have been terrible."

"It was." She said it flatly, looking at the trees, trying to take some pleasure from the golden colors against the blue sky. Such a perfect New York day — but she was beginning to feel trapped.

She stared at the bright red leaves. . . .

And then bright, clear memories of the fire flashed through her mind: choking smoke, searing heat and flame, paralyzing fear. Then she remembered her father's strong arms around her, the way he scooped up Sam and her and carried them from the house, dropping them on the grass, then dashing back into the flames to find their mother. She could feel her own arms around Sam as they huddled on the dew-wet grass, clutching each other, chilled by the night air but feeling the heat of the fire from so far away. She remembered screaming, waiting for Daddy to bring Mommy out of the fire . . . waiting

. . . and waiting. . . .

The nearest she got to seeing her parents again was at the closed-coffin funeral.

A trio of pigeons flew down from the nearby Washington Square arch and began pecking the ground only feet away.

"Eathan Gordon — Uncle Eathan — was my father's brother. After the fire he took us in and raised us like his own."

"He must be very special to you."

Julie smiled. "He was. I mean he is. I just don't think of him as part of my life any longer. Back then, he was an internist and a bachelor, living in the same town as my parents. After the fire he closed his practice, dropped everything, moved us all to England. He devoted his life to raising us."

Had there been anything else in his life during our childhood? He could have hired nannies but he personally took on the daunting task of playing father and mother to two little girls. A full-time job. Of course there'd been Glyndebourne and the opera season, and he loved his gardens — he became the *compleat* Brit — but "personal" relationships? If he'd had any, he hid them well.

"England . . . you did mention you were raised there. But why England, do you think?"

"I asked him later on. He said we were both so traumatized by witnessing the fire

46

that killed our parents that he felt we'd never be right if we stayed in a place where we'd be reminded all the time. And truthfully, I think he wanted to move himself away from the area too. He and my dad were very close." Julie smiled. "So he got us as far away as he could."

Car horns started blaring behind Julie, and she looked over her shoulder to see a line of frenzied cabs blocked by a delivery truck.

The park seemed like a peaceful island, alive with people enjoying the day, oblivious to the trash. Moms pushed their kids on swings and dog owners sat and talked while their pets ran free in the fenced-in dog run.

"Where'd this fire happen?"

"Up in Putnam County. A sleepy town called Millburn."

"For a complete change of scenery he could have taken you to California. I still don't —"

"Eathan didn't think much of American culture. Still doesn't. Whenever he's compelled to put the words *American* and *culture* together, he inevitably divides them with *soi-disant.*"

Dr. Siegal pursed his lips. "A snob, in other words."

"Yes, but a very good, decent snob. He was an Anglophile. And he couldn't have been more supportive as we were growing up. *Too* supportive sometimes, I think."

"Ah," Dr. Siegal said, and leaned forward. "I have a feeling we've arrived at the matter of your twin. Do I take it he tended to favor her?"

"Not a bit. He was remarkably even-handed, I'd say. But he didn't know how to be a parent. He wasn't cut out for it, and I think he knew that. Thus his bachelorhood. But we were thrust upon him and he did the best job he could. He made an excellent guardian, but a lousy parent. He should have reeled Sam in when she was little. But he didn't know how. He tried counselors and psychiatrists and special schools, but nothing worked. She was a first-order flake. Eventually she turned self-destructive."

"And toward others?"

Julie laughed bitterly. "Oh, I'm sure she's hurt a lot of people."

Dr. Siegal was looking at her and Julie realized that she was revealing more than she intended. She spotted a hot-dog stand at the corner of University Place and Waverly.

"You hungry? There's the Sabrett's man."

Dr. S. shook his head, catching her attempt to shift the discussion.

"No. So tell me, how does one as bright and focused as you have an identical twin who's a flake? How could Samantha be so different?"

"I wish I knew. You know all this right-brained and left-brained stuff? Sam is definitely right-brained. She's even left-handed. Enormously talented but can't focus on anything practical long enough to become good at it. First she was going to be a dancer, then a singer, then a writer, then an actress, then a painter, then back to a singer again. God, it was a merry-go-round. She started with the boys early on — word got around the village pretty quick that" — Julie heard her voice slip easily into a thick Yorkshire accent — "the American bird, Sammi Gordon, was a right sure thing for a bit o' the ol' in an' out."

"Certainly not the first teenage girl to be generous with her favors."

"Damn lucky she didn't wind up pregnant, although she might have had a dozen abortions for all I know. After a while Uncle Eathan kept her secrets, and he was always saving her butt one way or another. And then it was anorexia, then bulimia. And mixed in with everything was booze and drugs. She's had overdoses, she's had disastrous affairs. . . ."

Julie leaned back and took a breath. She was getting worked up just talking about it. Even thinking about Sam put her on edge. Why? It was long gone, done, over, finis. So why the hell was her adrenaline flowing?

"You were never close?" Dr. Siegal said.

"Never."

"Do you hate her?"

Julie hesitated. It was a question she'd often asked herself. She answered truthfully. "No. Of course not."

"Do you love her?"

Julie opened her mouth, then closed it again. Sam was her sister. You're supposed to love your sister. You don't have to *like* her, but somewhere, somehow, it's generally assumed that you love her.

Did she love Sam? How could she love someone she'd never understood, never had anything in common with beyond DNA and disaster?

"I sense indecision here," Dr. Siegal said. "Tell me, Julie: Do you love anyone?"

"Yes. Of course. I — I love my uncle Eathan."

"I won't contest that, and he certainly sounds like a wonderful man, but gratitude is often mistaken for love."

"I love my work."

"Yes! I'm so glad you said that. No question about it. You do love your work. And that, I fear, is the rub. You see, your work is incapable of loving you back. And it appears to these old eyes that you love your work to the exclusion of everything else in life."

That wasn't fair. "Not true. I swim or jog

every day, I sail in the summer —"

"All solitary pursuits. Good pragmatic exercise. Do you have any friends?"

"Of course."

"*Close* friends?"

"Well . . ."

"How about a fellow? A young man? Are you seriously involved with anyone?"

Julie began to feel more uncomfortable. She didn't like these questions. Where was all this leading? What was he getting at? Julie had rummaged through the intimate corners of other people's minds, but just talking about her own memories, her feelings, made her want to jump out of her skin.

On cue, for comic relief, an old man/ woman — hard to tell which — came rolling by pushing a supermarket cart filled with soda and beer cans, singing a garbled version of "I'm Too Sexy."

She loved this city.

"No," she said. "No 'fellows' at the moment. I'm fresh out of young swains. But there's been —"

Dr. Siegal waved his hand between them. "I'm not asking for names, but what happened between you and the young men that you're no longer together now, hmm? Do you break it off or do they? What makes it go wrong?"

Now she was really uncomfortable. She

glanced at the entwined couple sucking face on the other half of the bench and thought of Todd, of how, against her better judgment, she'd let him move into her one-bedroom co-op in the East Seventies, how they'd lived together for three months . . . and how one day she'd come home from the lab — late as usual — to find he'd moved out, leaving a note that accused her of, among other things, being a cold fish.

Truthfully, she'd been glad to see him go.

I've got my apartment back, she'd thought at the time.

And there'd been others before Todd, none of whom lasted very long.

"It's usually just a . . . combination of things. I don't think I want to get into it much deeper than that." She grinned. "This is the nineties. Relationships are tough."

"Fine, fine. I'm not looking for details. I'm just trying to establish a pattern."

"A pattern? Of what?"

"Of . . ." He grasped her right hand and held it between both of his. "Julie, dear, I've been watching you since you came to work for me, and you are the most brilliant theoretician I've ever seen. You've got a mind like a steel trap. You're heading for world fame, maybe even a Nobel Prize. The work you'll eventually do will change lives. Someday people will go to sleep blessing your name."

She never blushed, but if she did, she'd be blushing now.

"I bet you say that to all the girls."

"I'm quite serious," he said. "But amid all that approbation, I fear you won't be happy. I fear you'll *never* be happy. Because you don't connect with people, Julie. You won't have anyone to share the honors with, to tell of your latest victory, to share the wonderful glow of success well earned. No, you'll sit there alone in your hotel room after the ceremony and wonder, Is this it? Is this all there is? Where's the rest of it?"

Being alone never bothered her. Was that something she should worry about?

"You're a wonderful scientist, Julie, but you're only living half a life. You get results because you're not only brilliant, you're a workaholic. There's a piece missing, my dear. You need to balance your professional life with your personal life. It's a lesson I've learned over the years and it's stood me in good stead. And a big part of that personal life is family."

"I told you —"

He squeezed her hand. "Yes, I know. You say you don't have a family. But you *do.* You have a sister who needs you right now, and a loving uncle who could probably use someone to lean on a little. He was there for you. Now you could be there for him. This is part of life, Julie — go to them."

"I can't. I've got to stay with the project. You know as well as I do what a crucial juncture we're at."

"We'll survive — at least for a while. You won't be gone that long. We'll get the paperwork started without you, and you'll be back to finish it up. Besides, I'm not giving you a choice: I insist that you go. Visit your sister. Even if you can't do anything definitive to help her, be there for her. Let her hear your voice. Find a way to renew an old bond or forge a new one. Make contact with *someone, Julie.*"

Reach out and touch someone? she thought, then instantly regretted it . . . because the sarcasm only confirmed what Dr. Siegal was saying. She did live in an emotional vacuum. Relationships took a backseat to . . . everything.

But dammit, it's not like I'm just punching a clock to collect a paycheck. This isn't just a job. This is a career. More than a career, it's a vision, a quest.

She'd have plenty of time for relationships later, when things slowed down, plenty of time.

But she didn't believe that either.

"You're going to Paris, my dear," Dr. Siegal was saying. "You're going to burn some of that accumulated vacation time you never use and you're going to unwind and try to be someone who's not working on a research project, try to find that other part of you. At least for a while."

Paris, she thought. She hadn't been there since the year she'd spent at the Institut de Science, in the Physics Department. Paris was beautiful in the fall. Maybe she should go. She hadn't seen Uncle Eathan for a while. He sounded lost, scared, so unlike Eathan. And Sam . . . well, they'd never had much to say to each other even when they both were conscious.

What was wrong with Sam anyway? If it wasn't drugs, what could it be?

The more she thought about it, the more the question intrigued her.

But Dr. Siegal's suggestion struck a sour note deep inside: . . . *unwind and try to be someone who's not working on a research project, try to find that other part of you.*

What if there *is* no other part of me? she thought. What if, when I stop being Dr. Julia Gordon, stop being Ms. High-Powered Researcher, there's no one there?

What if I simply vanish into thin air?

Four

People have started picturing the brain as a computer, and memory as its hard drive. Bad analogy. A hard drive merely copies the lumps of data sent to it. The memory mechanism of the brain divides input into its component parts and stores the components separately.
— Random notes: Julia Gordon

1

Julie watched the taxis swarming in the early morning rain outside the international terminal at Orly Airport. She stood just outside the doors, protected by an overhang. She could have taken a cab to the nursing home, but Uncle Eathan had insisted on picking her up.

Her eyes felt like hot coals and her limbs like lead. It was early morning here, and everyone around her seemed wide awake and ready to start a new day. Not her.

Thinking it would help her doze off, she'd drunk some extra wine on the plane. But sleep hadn't come, and now it was somewhere around 3:00 A.M. according to her internal clock. She was still fuzzy from the wine, and she wished all these perky people jabbering in French would go away.

All this preceded by two solid days of nonstop hustle on the Bruchmeyer protocol and still things hadn't been settled enough for her to feel comfortable leaving it. Dr. Siegal had wanted her to leave directly from their park bench in Washington Square, but she simply had not been able to do that.

Not as if this was an emergency; Sam had been out of it for two weeks already. What was the rush?

She saw a big black Saab pull up and a tall, trim, dark-haired man in his midfifties step out onto the pavement. Two passing women looked back over their shoulders and whispered to each other.

No, ladies, Julie wanted to say. That's not Gregory Peck hiding behind that beard. It's only Uncle Eathan.

A little grayer since she'd last seen him, especially in the beard, but still trim. At six two, with an almost military bearing, he cut an imposing figure. Eathan was more than a handsome man; he radiated a strength, a solidity that Julie found instantly comforting. It was hard not to lean against such a tall tree in times of crisis, even if that tree now might need support.

Wheeling her suitcase behind her, she stepped toward him and waved. Eathan smiled and hurried forward to give her a brief hug and a quick peck on the cheek. He'd always had trouble showing affection.

Like me . . .

"Julie." His voice was rich and dark, like coffee. He held her at arms' length and grinned through his beard. Close up he looked tired and strained. "God, it's so good to see you again."

"Good to see you too, Eathan. Been a long time."

Another smile. "Too long." Eathan took her arm. "I'm just sorry that it takes something like this to bring us together."

Minutes later her suitcase and carry-on were in the trunk and they were on their way toward the airport exit.

"Any change in Sam?" Julie asked.

Eathan shook his head. "Not a bit. Dr. Elliot gave her a thorough examination, reviewed all the lab work and test results, and said he can't find any evidence of an organic etiology. There's nothing there — no structural damage, no evidence of a metabolic cause, no signs of a toxin. He thinks it's psychological."

"Psychological? What's that supposed to mean? Post-traumatic shock? Schizophrenic catatonia? What?"

Eathan shrugged. "He couldn't say. Or wouldn't say. He's a neurologist, not a psychiatrist. There's no physical evidence of trauma. No sign that she was attacked, brutalized." Eathan took a breath. "Or raped. It's so strange, Julie. She was found on the floor of her studio, unconscious."

Psychological. Julie leaned back and mulled that. Maybe that was the problem all along. Maybe there was a reason behind Sam's erratic behavior all these years. Perhaps Sam had spent most of her life on the verge of schizophrenia. And finally the dam broke.

That would explain so much.

"Poor Sam." She noticed Eathan looking at her strangely. "What?"

"You don't know what it means to hear you say that. For years I've been hoping for some sort of rapprochement between you two."

"Well, I've been angry at her for all these years for acting like a jerk . . . but if it's all been due to some form of incipient schizophrenia, well, how can you be angry at someone whose neurochemicals are screwed up?"

"Dr. Elliot had that idea too. But she's not responding to the antipsychotics — they've tried Thorazine, thiothixene, loxapine, even clozapine, all to no avail."

"But a psychogenic catatonia . . ."

"Not a catatonia," Eathan said. "She's not conscious. She doesn't respond to anything but painful stimuli, and even then the avoidance response is sluggish." He looked out the window, into the wet, gray morning. Julie could see how much this upset him. Maybe he did have a favorite. Sam might as well be his own daughter. "Sometimes . . . I'm afraid that she's gone forever."

"This doesn't add up," Julie said.

Eathan turned back to her. "Exactly what Dr. Elliot said."

She touched his arm. "And what about you? How are you holding up?"

"Pretty well, I guess. They moved me up to assistant professor at Edinburgh."

"Congratulations. You're becoming quite the academician."

"But I've taken a leave until Sam is better."

She'd been glad to see that he'd found something to fill his days after she and Sam had moved out. She hadn't liked the thought of him wandering like a ghost through the empty halls of his Yorkshire manor. After so many years away from practice, he'd claimed his medical skills and knowledge were too rusty to pass a licensing procedure in Britain. And besides, he didn't want to be another cog in the wheels of Britain's National Health Service.

Fortunately a position had opened in the Science Department at Edinburgh University and they'd been delighted to have an M.D. teaching basic science to their pre-med classes.

"I like working with young minds, shaping them. It keeps me young."

Julie watched the brown fields and golden trees and swirling green cypresses of the French countryside slide past outside the window. The sky had lightened, the rain stopped. Then as they turned east the morning sun broke through and filled her with a strange urgency.

"I want to see her."

"Of course. That's why you came."

"I mean now."

Julie was puzzled by this sudden, almost overwhelming desire to see her sister. She'd waited days before flying over. Why couldn't she wait a few more hours?

"I have a room for you at an inn where I'm staying. I thought you'd —"

"I need to see her now. Is it far?"

"No. That's why I advised you to fly into Orly. De Gaulle is on the wrong side of Paris. The nursing home is just outside the town of Palaiseau."

"Good. Let's go."

2

Julie found the Sainte Gabrielle Home a pleasant surprise: a modern, compact, single-story, skilled nursing facility only a half hour outside of Paris but surrounded by century-old oaks. With the sun pouring in, it looked to be the *Les Invalides* of extended care.

The interior was brightly lit, clean, and fresh smelling. The receptionist waved them through with a warm smile for Eathan. He obviously had worked his spell on the staff.

They were halfway down the hall of the east wing when —

"Mon Dieu!"

Breakfast plates, cups, and saucers slid off the aide's tray as she stopped short and stared bug-eyed at Julie.

"No-no," Eathan said, stepping forward and steadying the woman's tray. "This is not Mam'selle Samantha. This is her sister. *Sa soeur, vous comprenez?"*

The girl's eyes danced between Eathan and Julie. Finally she smiled and nodded. *"Ah. Sa soeur. Oui."*

"What's her problem?" Julie said as they walked on.

"Think about it. She probably left Sam flat on her back and unresponsive a few minutes ago. Now she comes out of a room and who does she see walking down the hall?"

"Me?"

"No!" He laughed. "Samantha!"

"Oh, come on. We don't look *that* much alike."

"Not to each other. Not even to me. But to people who haven't spent years with you, you're mirror images — even with your shorter hair."

Julie had trouble buying that. She wasn't anything like Sam; she found the idea irksome, but let it go.

Eathan led her to the last door on the left at the end of the hallway.

"This is it," he said, and stepped aside to let her precede him.

Julie stopped on the threshold, momentarily afraid to step across. For as little as they'd had in common, for all the cold silences and screaming fits they'd suffered, for all the resentment she'd built up against the sister who'd put their well-meaning uncle through hell, Julie didn't want to see Samantha like this. It was close to seeing Sam dead.

"Julia?" Eathan's voice behind her.

She nodded and stepped into the room. As she approached the bed she kept her eyes averted, looked everywhere except at the form between the sheets. She saw the

IV drip, the dull, dead screen of a TV hanging on the wall, the curtains open to show the great woods outside.

A nice room, private, carpeted, morning sun pouring through sheers behind floor-length drapes, upholstered chairs, a recliner . . .

. . . a hospital bed.

And in that bed, Sam.

Julie felt her breath catch at the sight of her.

Pale, so pale that if the sheets weren't pink she'd be invisible. She lay flat on her back. One of the aides had braided her long blond hair so that a girlish pigtail hung over each shoulder. It made Sam look even more vulnerable.

Her arms lay at her sides atop the sheet that had been folded back at the level of her breasts and snugged around her. She might have been Sleeping Beauty — except for the feeding tube, and the catheter bag, and the IV.

Suddenly Julie was afraid. Of what, she couldn't say. She was just —

Oh, Sam — what have they done to you?

Startled, Julie stiffened. Where'd that come from? Almost as if the thought had leaped between them. Why think anything had been done to Sam? No evidence of trauma, no attempted rape, no assault, nothing . . . yet.

She shook off the strange feeling. If anything, Sam had probably done something to herself.

Still, Julie felt a little weak. The extra wine and too little sleep didn't help. She would have loved to sink into one of the chairs, but she had to touch Sam, convince herself that she was real, that she was alive, that this was really her sister.

She reached out and laid her fingers on Sam's arm. The skin was cool, smooth, soft, coated with a fine film of moisturizing lotion. She knew that the nursing staff would be bathing her, turning her on her side, making sure her inert body didn't develop bedsores.

And if Sam didn't come out of her coma, that kind of care would go on forever, until Sleeping Beauty slowly turned into an old hag.

She moved closer to her sister.

"Sam?" Absurd as it was, she could not resist the urge to shake her arm, the feeling that this was all it would take to make Sam open her eyes. "Sam, it's Julie. Wake up."

No response, of course. Julie leaned over Sam and lifted one of Sam's eyelids. The pale blue iris tightened around the pupil in response to the morning light. She lifted the other lid. The pupil there was already constricted.

"Her . . ." Julie's voice caught an instant

in her throat. "Her third nerve seems okay."

"All the cranial nerves are intact," Eathan said. "All the reflexes — corneal, deep tendon, abdominal, Babinski — intact as well. It's given me some . . . hope."

"Are her medical records here?"

"Yes. I had them sent along when she was moved from the Paris hospital."

"Can I see them?"

"Of course, but Julie — you can do that later." She felt Eathan's hand rest gently on her shoulder. "You look done in. I'll get you over to the inn, and after you've had some rest you can spend all the time you want with them. And believe me, you'll need time. There's quite a stack."

Julie knew nothing short of some IV diazepam was going to let her sleep now, and maybe not even that.

"Just a quick look, okay? Just to get some sort of handle on this."

"Okay. I understand. I'll have the nurse bring them in." He squeezed her shoulder. "I'm so glad you're here."

3

They went over the records together. Julie began with the EEGs, the electrical signature of the brain. She found half a dozen fat, fan-folded recordings in the pile.

She spread out the long pink-and-white-gridded sheets on the floor of Sam's room and crouched over them, scanning them blip by blue blip.

She knew she wasn't a physician, didn't want to pretend to be. But she did know the human nervous system more extensively and intimately than most M.D.s, so that was where she focused her attention.

"Damn!" she said an hour or so later as she straightened and stretched her cramping back. "They're all normal."

"I could have told you that," Eathan said. "Dr. Elliot went over them too."

"I know. But nobody's perfect. He might have missed something."

But he hadn't. The overall pattern in all the EEGs was normal — eight- to thirteen-Hertz activity. She could see that from across the room. What she'd been looking for were bilateral, synchronous, paroxysmal bursts of slow waves in the one- to three-Hertz range — a sure sign of metabolic disease, or a toxin, or a drug effect. She'd also been looking for unilateral slow activity that might indicate a structural lesion.

Nothing.

Normal eight- to thirteen-Hertz all the way.

Julie stared at Eathan, sitting across

the room with a pile of reports on his lap, watching her.

"This doesn't make sense," she said.

"Exactly what Dr. Elliot said. He was very intrigued. In fact, he wants to come back and examine her again."

"I can understand that. And he's ruled out alpha coma and locked-in syndrome, I gather?"

Eathan nodded. "He says it must be psychogenic."

"But I don't get it. Catatonics are awake. Their eyes are open. They sit up. They chew and swallow. . . ."

Eathan said, "I see here in one of Dr. Elliot's notes that he calls it 'catatonic coma.' Coma is described as unarousable unresponsiveness, and Sam certainly meets that criterion, yet she's neurologically perfect, which she shouldn't be. He says he's never seen anything like it. Which is why he's willing to fly back from London to reexamine her if she doesn't show any changes by next week."

Julie rose and approached the bed again. She stared down at her sister. Her MRI and spinal tap were normal — no stroke, no tumor, no hemorrhage, no damage, no toxins. Her cortex and brain stem were both functioning absolutely perfectly.

Sam, Sam, she thought. Always an enigma — even when you're unconscious.

She felt baffled and helpless. Neither was a comfortable fit.

"What if we — ?"

"Pardon?"

She turned and saw a middle-aged woman in white. Her name tag said ELAINE MONCEAU.

"*Oui?*" said Eathan.

"*Monsieur, il me faut manipuler la demoiselle.*"

Eathan said, "*Ce n'est pas possible d'attendre quelques minutes?*"

The woman obviously needed to check Sam. Julie's French was atrophied from long disuse, but she managed to grasp that Elaine was a physical therapist and was here to give Sam her daily massage and range-of-motion exercises.

"Let's leave her to her work," Julie said, stooping to refold the EEGs. When all the reports were back in their respective folders, she picked up an armful.

"Can we take these back to the inn?"

Eathan hesitated. "They probably want to keep them here, but I'll see what I can do."

Ten minutes and a few release forms later, they were driving away with all Sam's records in the trunk.

4

The inn, Le Bois Farrand, a two-story stucco affair with a slate roof and vines climbing the walls, managed to be luxurious while retaining a quaint country charm.

Like an inn out of a storybook, Julie thought.

Eathan had reserved her a bright, airy room with a four-poster bed and an enormous down comforter. She went to the pair of French doors — of course — that opened onto a small balcony and stared out at the poplar-lined road that led to the inn.

The bed looked inviting but, tired as she was, Julie felt too wired to sleep. Besides, if she could last until after dinner, she could crash for the night and be a good way toward resetting her body's clock to Greenwich Mean Time.

She wondered how things were going back in New York, then realized it wasn't even dawn there yet. She tried not to think about the Bruchmeyer grant. Sam's mysterious coma was the important thing here. Julie was baffled and challenged by the puzzle. She needed more pieces, and she thought she knew a good place to look.

She crossed the hall and knocked on

Eathan's door. He appeared in shirtsleeves with a towel in his hand. His beard was damp. For a moment he looked oddly different with his beard matted to his cheek. Almost like the old pictures of her father.

He blotted droplets of water from his face. "Something wrong?"

"I'd like to go into Paris."

"Oh, Julie, come on. You're not too tired?"

"No. I'll do better if I try to reset my clock in one day. But I'm too bleary-eyed to read any more medical reports."

His smile was sympathetic. "I understand. Anyplace special you want to go?"

She chewed her lip.

"Sam's apartment. Do you have the address?"

Five

Marcel Proust: "The bonds that unite another person to ourself exist only in our mind. Memory as it grows fainter relaxes them. . . ."
— Random notes: Julia Gordon

1

Uncle Eathan had insisted on driving her himself. The Latin Quarter was not the safest section of the city, he'd said. And besides, he'd met Sam's landlady a number of times already; Julie would have an easier time getting in if he was with her.

Julie hadn't argued. Actually she was glad to have someone familiar with the territory along.

So now they were fighting the midday traffic along the busy boulevard that followed the serpentine path of the Seine. And despite everything, Julie had to admire the beauty of Paris. The *bateaux mouches,* the

72

sight-seeing boats, were already ferrying tourists up and down the river, while the dozens of bridges that spanned the murky river were filled with Parisians hustling to and fro, moving urgently from Left Bank to Right, or Right to Left.

"A lot's changed since you've been here."

"Yes, when did they stick that glass pyramid in front of the Louvre?"

"Don't like it? A lot of Parisians consider it an eyesore. Your sister loved it."

"That figures."

They took a curve and ahead Julie spotted Notre Dame and the Île de la Cité. On her first visit, years ago, she had gone to the top of the cathedral and stood by the gargoyles who leered out at the city. A young couple had asked her to take their photograph, posed with a horned monster between them. Then they in turn asked Julie if she wanted to be photographed.

The idea seemed funny to Julie. By myself? With a monster?

She shook her head.

"You never liked Paris?" Eathan said.

"Oh, it's beautiful enough. I guess I found the mood, the air of the place too frivolous. And maybe because Paris was always Sam's city."

She looked over to see whether she'd offended Eathan, but he showed no reaction.

He made a right and Julie saw that they were on the Boulevard Saint-Germain. In a few minutes, they passed the entrance to the giant Jardin du Luxembourg.

"Ever been in there?"

"No. Too busy when I came for that conference."

"You should take some time —"

"And smell the roses?"

Eathan laughed. "Your sister's studio is just off the Boulevard Saint-Michel, the 'boul Mich.' It's a lot like your New York SoHo, I imagine."

Eathan turned down a narrow *rue*, passing a street cleaner in a green uniform wiping the pavement with a mop. Through her open window, Julie sniffed the pungent smell of the wet cobblestones.

The smells and sights of Paris . . .

Now it felt exactly as she remembered it from her year at the Institut de Science. That was the nice thing about European cities — you could return after years of absence and, outside of some new monstrosity erected by a minister of "culture," everything would be pretty much as you left it.

The closer to Sam's studio, the quieter Eathan got. Then —

"When do you think it began to go wrong for Samantha?" Eathan said.

"*Began?* I can't remember when she was ever *right*."

"You're too hard on her. Always have been."

Here we go again, she thought. The old *why-can't-you-two-be-friends* routine. Why couldn't he ever bring himself to blame Sam?

You've always been too damn *easy* on her, she wanted to say, but bit it back. She'd noticed new worry lines on Eathan's face. Maybe he was already blaming himself.

"Maybe you're right," she said, not believing it. "But she was always so emotional about everything, always frightened of something. As she got older, she changed, almost seemed to *embrace* anything dangerous, but when we were kids, there was *always* something under her bed. Even Bugs Bunny cartoons scared her. And remember that scene in Harrods when we were Christmas shopping? How old were we then? Ten?"

"I believe so. But do you remember what set her off?"

"No."

"It was by the Christmas village Harrods had constructed on the children's floor. You were standing right beside her. Are you sure you don't remember?"

Julie thought back. They'd been leaning over the railing, watching the miniature train chug through the snow-covered English village that had been rendered in amazing detail, even down to the smoke puffing from the tiny chimneys. Suddenly Sam had stiffened beside her and begun screaming at the top of her lungs as if terrified for her life.

"I don't think I ever knew what set her off. She just went hysterical for no reason. I was used to it by then."

"I found out," Eathan said. "Later. She told her therapist at that time that she'd seen one of the village houses on fire and it had frightened her."

"There was no house on fire," Julie said. "I was there. I know I'd have noticed that."

"I went back and checked, and you're right. There was no little house on fire. But I did notice that the chimney on one of the models was blocked, and the smoke that was supposed to be going up the chimney was coming out the windows instead, making it look as if the little house was on fire."

"Right. I remember that now. And I remember thinking it was strange looking."

Another turn onto an even narrower road. They passed a shop with a giant ceramic horsehead outside. For lovers of "la viande du cheval." Julie didn't eat much red meat, and the thought of eating Trigger . . .

"It didn't upset you? Didn't remind you of another fire?"

"Not at all. It looked like a clogged chimney and that was that."

Halfway down the block there was a café tabac, and a few rumpled, leathery-skinned workers — Algerian, maybe — sat outside, smoking cigarettes, as if waiting for a parade.

"So you don't think about that fire?" He was staring at her intently. "Ever?"

"When someone mentions it, yes. Witnessing that fire was a terrible thing, but it was twenty-three years ago. I wish it hadn't happened, but it did. And it's over. That was then, this is now. You keep going."

Eathan stopped at the corner. A woman led her toddler across the street. In her free hand she carried a three-foot-long baguette, diapered around its middle with a single sheet of white paper. The bread, Julie had forgotten the bread, baked fresh three or four times a day. Her mouth watered.

"You're very lucky to be able to put it in perspective like that. Sam never could put it behind her. That was her problem. All the therapists, the special schools, nothing could heal the terrible wounds of that night. I kept trying to get you two to talk about it. Wounds need air to heal. Lock them up and they only fester."

Julie remembered how Eathan would sit them down at regular intervals and make them talk about the night of the fire, all the details they could remember. "Ventilate," he'd say. "Get it out. Let it go." It had worked for her, she supposed, but obviously not for Sam.

"If Sam had only had a friend to confide in," he said — pointedly, she thought.

Julie was *not* going to let him start this.

"Her 'friend' would have had to be as reckless as Sam. Don't forget all the drinking and drugs. How many schools kicked her out for violent behavior? Three, wasn't it? I don't see how you can blame the fire or lack of a 'friend.' None of that ever happened to me. We're twins. We witnessed the same horrific tragedy. Could it have affected us so differently?"

Eathan nodded as they kept on along the small *rue.* "You're two different people. Your father was a scientist, a chemist; your mother was artsy, in a way. You and Sam have the same genotype, but obviously you express those genes differently. You've always been the rational one, steady as a rock, while Samantha took everything to heart and seemed bent on self-destruction. I wish you could have . . ."

"What?"

"Nothing."

"Watched over her? Looked out for her? I was growing up too, you know. And not having such an easy time myself."

Julie didn't like thinking of her adolescent years, being considered one of the class nerds because of her grades, never having more than one friend, always feeling different, always "out" with the "in" crowd. She liked to think she'd put all that pain behind her.

"I know," Eathan said. "I'm sorry. I shouldn't have said that. I know you had problems too. But somehow I always knew you'd pull through. Sam . . . I doubt she'd have made it even this far if not for her art. I think that's the only thing that saved her from self-destructing before she got out of her teens."

Sam's art. Julie had to admit she'd had a real talent for it since day one. She began painting seriously in secondary school and whenever the class would put on an art show, Sam's display would always draw the most attention. Nobody would be standing too close, of course. More like a crowd around an accident. The violent, disturbing images that ran through her paintings fascinated as much as they repelled.

She dabbled in everything "artistic," but painting seemed to be her real love. So much so that she enrolled in a London art school instead of a university, but just as she was beginning to gain some recognition — an art columnist had given her favorable mention in the *Times* — she dropped out and fled to the Continent.

Self-sabotage, another of Sam's fortes.

"If you remember," Julie said, "her art almost got her killed. If that theater director's wife hadn't been so drunk, her aim might have been better and we'd have lost Sam then and there."

Eathan's smile was rueful. "She didn't need me to deal with that particular angry spouse, but there were others."

Even Julie was forced to smile. Incorrigible, insatiable Sam; she went through men like a drunk goes through beers.

"Lots of angry wives over the years, I imagine."

He nodded. "And once, a very angry husband."

Julie felt her jaw drop as the meaning registered. "You don't mean . . . ?"

He shrugged. "I've probably said too much already. Let's just say that your sister's tastes are, um, eclectic, and leave it at that."

When am I going to learn never to be shocked by Sam? she thought.

"Sounds like you've spent a lot of time running around the Continent putting out Sam's fires. Why? Don't you think that might have contributed to the problem?"

"You mean am I — what's the fashionable term — an 'enabler'? I don't like to think so. I certainly didn't think so at the time. I was mostly concerned with keeping her out of trouble and making sure she had enough money for food and rent so she could continue her work."

"Money? What about her trust fund?"

"Well, as you know, your trusts pay out in stages, a certain percentage every year until —"

"We're thirty-five. I know."

That gave Julie a little over $100,000 a year, disbursed every January 2. At thirty-five she'd get the rest of her trust in a lump: three million at last count. She'd be able to fund the memoryscape project herself then. But that was seven years away. It was this year that was do or die for the project.

"Sam ran through her last installment by midsummer. Like most of the installments before it."

"What does she *do* with it?"

"I can only guess. But I didn't want lack of funds to stop her from painting. We both know she's enormously talented. I want her to be recognized for that talent. I want her to be famous."

Famous. How many times had they heard that growing up? Fame had always been one of Uncle Eathan's hang-ups. He'd supported both of them in every endeavor, but it never seemed to be enough that they merely succeeded in life. He wanted them to be recognized for their work, revered — *famous.* And that didn't quite go with his low-key, almost reclusive lifestyle. He didn't crave the limelight for himself, but he certainly wanted it for his nieces.

Maybe it was a vicarious thing — he'd feel famous through them. It was curious.

"Sounds like you were always on call."

He shrugged. "I got used to that during my years as an internist. But it's become more of a problem since I took the position at the university. The department head has been generous with leaves, but I can push him only so far. I've made a point of keeping tabs on her, dropping in on her regularly, helping her out when she needed it, giving her encouragement when she got into one of her funks. And when she agreed to therapy, I helped find the right person. You, on the other hand . . ." He reached over and patted her hand. "I've never had to worry about you. You're the self-starter of the pair. But I hope you don't feel neglected."

"Not at all," she said, and meant it. She didn't want anybody, even her dear uncle Eathan, looking over her shoulder all the time. "Sam's always been the squeaky wheel."

Then Eathan slowed.

"We're here?"

"Almost . . . I'm not too sure we can park on this block."

Julie looked right and saw a man with

82

jet-black eyes and a sinister mustache looking at her. She pushed the lock button on the door.

In the middle of the *rue* was a cluster of gray-stone apartments, standing shoulder to shoulder, leaning over the narrow sidewalk.

"This is where she lived?"

"She wanted to be near the galleries up on Montparnasse. I never liked that she lived here."

Then Eathan pulled in behind some cars parked on the left.

"This looks okay. . . ."

He killed the ignition and got out. Julie sat there a moment, reluctant to leave the car. Why? Scared of the neighborhood? Worried about what she might see inside? Or was it just fatigue?

Why did she want to come here? What did she expect to find? She supposed she wanted to see Sam's latest version of herself. Sam was constantly redefining herself. Maybe the apartment would give a clue to the latest iteration . . . and maybe a clue to the cause of the coma. Maybe even her paintings would have something to say about what was wrong with Sam.

She followed Eathan up the three steps to the front door. He rang a bell labeled DUPONT and waited. A moment later, a middle-aged woman with a worn apron around her middle and her hair in a scarf opened the door. A little girl with dark hair and dark eyes, determinedly chewing gum, hovered behind her.

The woman nodded to Eathan, addressed him as "Dr. Gordon." Then she looked at Julie and cried out. She threw her arms around Julie's neck and sobbed as she hugged her, crying, "Samantha! Samantha!"

It took Eathan a while to pry her off Julie and convince the woman that this was Samantha's sister. Mme. DuPont seemed crushed. Julie struggled to understand her as she inquired in rapid French how his other daughter was doing. Eathan's French was much easier to understand as he corrected the woman regarding his relationship with Sam and Julie and told her there'd been, *tant pis, pas de change.*

He asked if Sam's sister might see her apartment.

"Mais oui," was the reply as she pulled a key ring from her apron and led them to the third floor.

Stocky Mme. DuPont was panting by the time she reached the final landing. She waited a moment to catch her breath, then went to the door on the left. Julie noticed that the doorjamb was unpainted and the lock looked shiny and new.

"Mon Dieu!" the woman cried as the

door swung open.

Hands on hips, she stormed into the apartment and began shouting in machine-gun French far too rapid for Julie's unpracticed ear. Julie stepped inside and froze as she realized what Mme. DuPont was shouting about.

Sam's studio had been ransacked, though from what Julie remembered of Sam's room when they were kids, this was not too far from the usual state of her sister's living quarters. Sam thrived on disorder.

But the landlady was running around, hands to her face, pointing at the open drawers, the papers on the floor —

Eathan hurried to calm Mme. DuPont while Julie drifted through Sam's space.

And that's what it was — a space. A single open room with a window at the far end and a huge, dingy skylight in the slanted roof. An empty easel in the center of the room, unframed canvases on all the walls and stacked on the floor, an unmade bed in the corner, and a single dresser. An *empty* dresser. All the drawers had been pulled out and dumped onto the floor. Bras and panties, some shirts, crumpled bits of paper, matchbooks.

No syringes, at least, Julie thought.

She poked at one of the piles with the toe of her shoe and saw a metallic flash. She stooped and pushed a tangle of bras aside. A gold chain lay on the wooden planks. She picked it up and examined it. No pendant, just a fine herringbone chain of good quality, possibly twenty-four karat. She poked around some more and found a gold ring set with a ruby. She pocketed both as she rose. The jewelry bothered her.

Obviously whoever had ransacked the place had something other than robbery in mind.

Was there a connection between this and Sam's present condition?

She turned to say something to Eathan and found herself inches away from one of Sam's paintings, a brilliant mass of orange and red. She stepped back for a better look.

More abstract than what Julie remembered of Sam's work. No recognizable images. She was struck by the ferocity of the colors and the brush strokes, as if Sam had been slashing at the canvas. The painting radiated danger and heat. She sensed that if Sam's brush had been a knife, she'd be looking at shredded canvas now.

She felt as if she were staring into the heart of the sun — about to go nova.

Not a painting I'd want in my apartment.

Julie moved to the next canvas, this one all blues and blacks, with a heart of darkness, seemingly fueled more by fear and hopelessness than anger.

And on to the next, and the next; the emotional intensity of the series was almost overwhelming. These canvases more than spoke to Julie; they reached out and grabbed her by the throat and yanked her in. By the time she'd made a circuit of the room, she felt exhausted by their power.

"Ah — it's that boyfriend of hers," she heard Mme. DuPont saying. She seemed calmer now and was speaking slowly enough for Julie to understand.

"Boyfriend?" Julie said. "What boy-friend?"

"Oh, he was about all the time, practically lived here until the week before she became sick. Then she wouldn't let him in. I heard him yelling at her."

"They had a fight?" Julie said.

She gave a Gallic shrug. "Possibly. I do not know. She would not let anyone in during that last week. She kept the door locked and would only open it when I brought food to her room and insisted that she eat. I was worried about her. But at least she ate the food."

Julie caught Eathan's eye. "Sounds like a breakdown," she said in English. Then in halting French to Mme. DuPont: "Do you know what she was doing in here all that time?"

"Of course! She was painting. Yes, her hands were always *full* of paint, dripping

87

with color. And — and I saw a large canvas on her easel. But Mademoiselle Samantha looked sick. Very pale. Her eyes were strange. Her hair was not combed. And I must tell you: She was not bathing. I thought she was going mad."

Maybe Sam truly had been going mad, Julie thought. Why hadn't this woman called someone? Maybe she didn't know anyone to call.

"But about this boyfriend — was he here?"

"He came every day — many times a day. Banging on her door so *loudly.* But she had it bolted from the other side and would not let him in. He was very angry. Many times I picked up the phone to call the police — but he always left."

"What was his name?"

"Jimmy . . . she called him Jimmy Walsh."

"Where does he live?"

Another Gallic shrug. "I do not know." She swept her arm toward the empty bureau and its scattered contents. "But even though I have changed the lock, I am sure that he did this."

"Then he could have been in and out without your knowing it?"

"Of course. I have six tenants. I can't keep track of all their comings and goings. But I knew when he was here that final night."

She pointed to the new lock and doorjamb. "He broke the door."

Julie shivered at the violence done to the wood. "He didn't hurt her, did he?"

"I don't know. I don't think so. I heard the crash and was on my way upstairs when he came racing down shouting that Samantha was sick, unconscious. Already I was worried about her because she hadn't answered when I last knocked. I went up and saw that she was lying on the floor before her easel . . . then I called for an ambulance. As soon as it arrived, her young man fled."

"Have you seen him since then?"

She shook her head. "No. But I bet he did this, I bet he's been back. I know it. And I'm going to call the police."

"Do you really think that is necessary?" Eathan asked, touching the woman's shoulder. "I wish you wouldn't."

Julie was struck by the request. Why didn't he want the police involved? Then Eathan shot Julie a look that said, *I'll explain later.*

"No, I'm sorry," she said, heading out the door onto the landing. "I cannot have strange men coming into my house."

As she started down the stairs, Julie turned to Eathan.

"Why not call the police?"

Eathan glanced out into the hall, then

gently shut the door.

"Because . . . I know who this Jimmy Walsh is," he said in a low voice. "And that's not his name. His real name is Liam O'Donnell and he's wanted by Scotland Yard."

"Oh, great. Can Sam pick them or what. What's he wanted for? Drugs?"

"I almost wish."

Julie stiffened. "What, then?"

"Terrorism. They want him in connection with a number of IRA fire bombings in London and Belfast. Even now before the cease-fire they say he's an arsonist."

"Oh, God! Did Sam know?"

He nodded slowly. "Yes."

Julie was shocked speechless for a moment. What on earth had Sam got herself into?

"That's why I didn't want the gendarmes called in. If they find out who this fellow is they'll come asking about Samantha. It could be dangerous for her. She's not protected here. I think she's got enough trouble at the moment."

"How did you find out about him?"

"I ran into him here on one of my visits. After only a few moments of conversation I felt sure that he was hiding something. I hired a detective to run a check on him. I tried to warn Sam. . . ."

"Ever the guardian angel."

He sighed. "In Samantha's case, somebody has to be."

"Do you think this O'Donnell had anything to do with her coma?"

"I don't know. From the way Mme. DuPont tells it, it doesn't sound like he had time to do anything, and there were no marks on Sam's body. But who knows?"

Julie looked around. Sam's studio suddenly had a terribly sinister feel to it . . . filled with the presence of whoever did this. Julie tried to shake off the feeling. She looked around the studio. . . .

What had happened here? What had gone on in Sam's life, in her mind, during that week of seclusion before her coma? What had she been painting when she locked herself away?

"What about all this?" she said, looking at the paintings. "What will happen to them?"

"They stay right here. I've paid the rent in advance till the end of the year and nothing will be touched. When Sam comes back I want it to look just as she left it. I want her to be able to resume her life . . . her art."

She turned and looked at Eathan. "What did we ever do to deserve you?"

"Don't be silly," he said, looking uncomfortable. "I'm just doing what your father would do."

On the way out Julie stopped at Mme.

DuPont's apartment.

"Madame?" she said as the woman opened the door. "Which painting was my sister's last? You said that you saw her working on a big canvas."

"Ah yes, but I do not know," she said. "The easel was empty when I found her."

Six

So what is consciousness, after all? How does that three-and-a-half-pound lump of gray cheese inside our skulls produce a mind? The philosophical debate gets politicized, but scientifically, we're closing in on the nuts and bolts of the process. And it does appear to be a process rather than a state. The latest work from Llinás and others points to a 40 cps binding wave moving front to back across the cortex — one pass every 0.025 seconds — that links up all the areas of the cortex and conveys their information to the thalamus.

— Random notes: Julia Gordon

1

As soon as she got back to the inn, Julie placed a call to New York. It was a little after eight there now. They should all be hard at work. She was glad to hear Dr. Siegal's voice.

"Yes, yes. The proposal and protocol are coming along fine, just as you laid them out. Now, tell me about your sister."

He was sympathetic and as baffled as everyone else after she filled him in on the medical details of Sam's condition.

"I don't understand. You're sure there's no toxin?" he said.

"They ran a complete toxicology screen — all negative."

"Julie, no toxicology screen is complete. They can't possibly screen for everything. They screen for the usual."

"But even if there is some unknown toxin at work, if it's potent enough to put her in a coma, wouldn't it affect the EEG?"

"Not necessarily. The EEG registers cortical activity. So what if your sister has been exposed to a toxin that affects subcortical activity?"

"I hadn't thought of that. Is there such a thing?"

"What do I know from toxins? Nothing. But I do know from unconscious. And with an unusual case like your sister's, maybe we should go back to basics and ask ourselves, What is consciousness? Neurologically speaking, of course. We're not interested in epistemology at the moment, so maybe I should rephrase: What does the brain require to be conscious?"

"A functioning cortex, of course," Julie said. "And the arousal mechanisms of the reticular activating system . . ."

"And *communication* between the cortex and the RAS."

Julie considered that. The reticular activating system wasn't an anatomically discrete organ; it was a functional unit spread out through the upper brain stem. So there was no single connection.

She said, "So what if Sam's cortex and RAS aren't communicating — no anatomical lesion, just a functional block between the two? What sort of clinical picture would you have?"

"You'd have an unarousable, unresponsive person with a completely normal neurological exam."

"Right! Which describes Sam perfectly," Julie said. They were onto something. She could feel excitement beginning to percolate through her. "How do we confirm it?"

"I haven't the foggiest," Dr. Siegal said. "It's a hypothetical condition. If you had some history, someone who was with her before she passed into unconsciousness . . ."

"No good. She locked herself in her room."

"Then I'm afraid you'll have to wait until she wakes up to ask her."

"No one's sure she *will* wake up. She . . ."

Julie's voice trailed off as an idea burst in her brain with the force of a bomb.

"Julie?" Dr. Siegal said. "Are you still — ?"

"Ask her!" she cried. "God, I'll *ask* Samantha!"

"That's the spirit. She should come around soon and —"

"No-no. In her memoryscape. I can go into her memoryscape and find out what happened during that lost week."

She couldn't remember being this excited in years. It was so obvious, and so simple. All she had to do was —

"No." Dr. Siegal's voice was firm, almost angry. "Absolutely not. I'm sorry. I won't allow it."

Julie felt as if someone had dashed ice water in her face.

"Why on earth not? We only use it on unconscious subjects. Sam is unconscious with a vengeance. This will be an actual clinical application of the technology. This could be a huge breakthrough."

"No. We're not ready for that. I'd have strong reservations even if she weren't your sister."

"What does being my sister have to do with it?"

"You've heard the maxim that a doctor shouldn't treat a member of his own family? Well, that holds doubly true here."

"I'm not a physician and I wouldn't be treating her."

"The bond is too intimate. She's your sister. You'll be entering a memoryscape in which you are a participant. You're *in* there, Julie. Have you thought of that?"

"Well, no . . ."

Truthfully, Julie hadn't. It was a disturbing thought.

"You'll be running into yourself, not necessarily as you were, but as your sister perceived you. Since you tell me you two had a stormy relationship, that might not be too pleasant."

"I can handle it."

"Knowing you, I'd say you probably can. But there's another factor that concerns me even more."

"What's that?"

"The genetic factor. You did tell me she's your identical twin?"

"Yes."

"So you share not only a history, but an identical set of genes as well. That's an unpredictable and possibly dangerous combination."

"I don't see that."

"Think about it, Julie. The memoryscape software works by interfacing your brain waves with the subject's. So far the computer has had no difficulty differentiating between experimenter and subject. But it's never been challenged with a pair of identical twins. What if your brain-wave patterns are so similar that it can't separate them? What if you leave some of yourself with Sam and take some of her back with you?"

"Don't tell me you really think that's possible. It sounds too far-fetched."

"So does the memoryscape program. But it works, doesn't it? I can't imagine it tangling brain waves under normal circumstances, but with identical twins . . . I don't know. The results could be merely inconvenient, or they could be devastating — to both of you."

Julie suppressed a shudder. The possibility was unsettling, but it was no more than that — a possibility. And a remote one at that. She wasn't going to let it stop her.

"It's a moot point anyway," Dr. Siegal was saying. "You don't have access to sufficient computer power there, and you don't have the software or the hardware."

"What about the Internet? I could access the mainframe that way."

"Uh-uh. Not enough bandwidth."

"All right, then we'll use the satellite link — same as we did when we demoed the memoryscape for the NSF down in D.C."

"Forget it, Julie. You're not going in there. I'm not allowing it."

Anger flared in her. "Just a goddamn

minute here. I'm part of this project too. Don't I have any say?" She caught herself.

Dr. Siegal paused. "Of course you do. But I'm still the head of the project and I won't risk my number one researcher — my number one *brain,* about whom I happen to care very much, by the way — in such a dangerous and reckless experiment."

"It's not reckless. This means a lot to me, Mordecai."

Silence on the other end. She never called him by his first name — never even thought of him by his first name.

"A *lot* to me," she continued. "More than you can imagine."

She had to do this. Julie knew she wouldn't be able to rest until she'd seen Sam's memoryscape.

"Maybe we can find somebody else to go in. . . ."

"There *is* nobody else. I'm the best and you know it."

"That's why I won't risk you."

Julie fumed silently for a moment. Finally . . .

"Then I resign."

She heard him gasp. "You don't mean that!"

Maybe I do and maybe I don't, she thought. This wasn't a good time to be offering an ultimatum. She was tired, hungry, angry, and frustrated enough to hurl the phone through the window.

But now that she'd said it, she wasn't backing down. She only prayed he wouldn't call her on it.

"I do," she said. "If my wishes — my *needs* — mean so little, then there's no point in my continuing with the project. You told me to come over here, get back in touch with my family, get *involved,* and that's what I'm doing. I *am* involved. And here I have the knowledge and the experience to perhaps save my sister's life, or at least her consciousness, and you're turning your back on me."

"I'm *not* turning my back!"

"That's how I see it. And look, I'm not going to beg. I've presented my case. You have my number. If you change your mind, let me know. Otherwise, good-bye, Dr. Siegal."

"Julie!"

She hung up.

And felt weak.

I've got to be crazy!

The memoryscape project was the most important thing in her life. She'd poured everything she had — her brain, her heart, her *soul,* dammit — into it, and now she was risking it all on a whim.

But Dr. Siegal was important to her too. She could lose him as well.

She went to the window and stared out at the countryside without actually seeing it. Then she turned and paced the room, trying not to look at the phone.

He'll call back. She rubbed her fingers together. They felt cold and clammy. *He'll call in five minutes, maybe ten. He's got to call back.*

Doesn't he?

She was the core of his team. He'd have to go back to square one — or at the very least, square two — without her.

But what if she'd pushed Dr. S. too far? He'd seemed adamant in his opposition.

"Come on," she said, finally facing the silent phone, glaring at it, willing it to ring. "Come *on!*"

The sudden jangle of its bell startled her. She stared at it in wonder. She resisted the impulse to snatch it up. Biting her lip, she let it ring once again . . . and again.

Finally she reached for it, thinking, If this is Eathan, I'll scream.

"Hello?"

"Are you really serious about resigning?"

Dr. Siegal's voice. Rubber-kneed with relief, she slumped onto the bed.

"I'm not in the habit of saying things I don't mean," she said, avoiding a direct answer.

"I know that. That's why I'm calling back. Is there no way I can reason with you?"

"None."

"I don't like ultimatums and I don't like

blackmail, but you're not giving me much choice."

"I don't like this either," she said, and that certainly was true. She hated putting him in this position, but she had to *do* this. "But I'm in a situation where I can help my sister and break new ground at the same time. I can't accept no for an answer."

"Are you trying to help your sister? Truly? Or is this simply something new to try?"

A good question: Was she doing this for Sam or for herself? It made her uncomfortable. So she didn't answer it.

"Give me a little credit, will you?"

A long pause on the other end, then a deep sigh.

"Very well. I don't like it. I want to go on record that I oppose the whole thing, and I will allow it only on the condition that I can monitor you via the satellite hookup whenever you're in your sister's memoryscape."

"I can live with that," Julie said.

"I'm not so sure, but I certainly hope so."

Now that she'd forced him to give in, she felt guilty.

"Don't sound so ominous, Dr. Siegal. I'll be fine. When can you send everything over?"

"I don't know. I'll have to get the materials together — do you have access to a satellite dish over there?"

"I'm sure I can get one. Can I expect a delivery tomorrow?"

"Tomorrow? Impossible!"

"The next day then. I want to get moving on this. We don't know the cause of this coma, or what may be going on in her brain. There could be progressive damage. She could *die*, Dr. S. Every day we delay —"

"All right, all right. I'll try DHL and see if they can get it to you day after tomorrow."

"Excellent."

They discussed details of delivery and ended on a fairly agreeable note. Already Dr. Siegal was loosening up. Julie expected him to become an enthusiastic participant once he got over his initial resistance.

Now the next hurdle: Uncle Eathan. And that would be a big one.

2

But jet lag pounced on Julie in the afternoon before she could broach the subject to Eathan, and it was all she could do to hang on through a light dinner before she headed to bed. She'd tackle her uncle in the morning when she was fresh.

She should have slept like the dead. Instead she found herself awake half a dozen times during the night.

The couple next door didn't help. The

Bois Farrand had sturdy walls, but these two were really going at it. Maybe the myth about *l'amour* and the French was true. The neighboring headboard was banging against the wall inches from Julie's head — *whack, whack, whack* — and the woman was positively operatic.

Julie couldn't make out her words, but her moans and cries of passion needed no translation. And then she climaxed — at least Julie assumed that was what her long, high-pitched scream of ecstasy signaled — and was still.

About time.

But even after the X-rated sound effects were over, Julie couldn't sleep. She lay in the dark and wondered, What was that like? To climax, to orgasm, to feel such overwhelming ecstasy that you howl into the night? She'd never even come close. Was it because she feared the lack of control? That probably was part of it. She found sex occasionally enjoyable. Todd had been what most women would consider an excellent, giving lover, but even then there were no stars, no explosions. And many times it was — annoying. And often inconvenient. And ultimately messy.

What was the big deal? Why was the human race so obsessed with it? Why did so many people think with their gonads instead of their minds?

The mind — *that* was where the real action lay, the real excitement.

Throughout that night, when Julie found herself awake, her thoughts turned to Sam. That terrible last week, the last painting, the broken door . . .

Sam. It was one thing if her twin was the victim of something like schizophrenia, or even if she'd done this to herself. Julie could accept that — she'd hate it, but she could get on with her life.

But if someone else had a hand in this . . .

That was something else entirely.

The possibility disturbed her. And, surprisingly, angered her.

3

She awoke late and found Eathan sitting in the sunny dining room of the Bois Farrand having a light breakfast of croissants and *café au lait.* He looked dashing in a cranberry sweater, gray slacks, and a tweed hunting jacket. He nearly ruined that look when his oversized coffee cup slipped from his fingers as Julie told him what she wanted to do.

Eathan was already familiar with her research and had told her time and again how proud he was of her.

Even so, she'd expected his reaction and was prepared for it.

"You want to use your sister as a guinea pig?" he said in a hushed tone as he blotted the spilled coffee from the tablecloth.

"What's the alternative? Sit around and watch her rot?"

"We simply have to hope that she'll come out of it."

"Has there been any indication of that?"

"No. Not yet. But —"

"But what? Look, I've done this hundreds of times back in New York with never the slightest harm to anyone."

"But were they sick?"

"No, but —"

"There! That's what I'm saying! It's possible you could make her worse, isn't it?"

"I don't see how."

He leaned forward, enunciating carefully and forcefully. "A possibility of exacerbating her condition — yes or no?"

Julie thought about that. She didn't know what she'd find in Sam's memoryscape, couldn't be sure if her very presence might further upset the imbalances within.

"I can't give you a black-and-white answer. We've not had a single instance of any harm either to subject or to researcher."

He stiffened. "To *researcher?* You mean there's a chance of danger to *you?* Lord, then you can forget about it. I have one niece in a coma; I won't risk having two."

"That will never happen."

"At least we can agree on that: It will never happen because I've got power of attorney for Samantha and no one can touch her without my permission." He wiped his mouth and tossed his napkin onto his plate. "And my permission, Julia, is expressly denied."

"I can *help* her, Eathan!" she said, grabbing his arm as he started to rise. He pulled away. "I might be able to bring her back!" She doubted that very much, but she was getting desperate. "And if I can, I'll be the first person in history to do it." She pulled out her ace card here. "I can name my ticket after that. I'll be famous. Sam and I will *both* be famous. When the art world hears about what Sam's been through, they'll be clamoring for a look at her work."

"I only want Sam better. What matters fame?"

"You always wanted us to do something amazing, wonderful. . . ."

Eathan settled back into his seat, studying her. Finally, his voice hoarse, he said, "But tell me this . . . do you really think you can bring her back?"

"I honestly don't know. It may be an impenetrable jumble in there. The first time I go in I might see that it's hopeless. But if

I can travel her memoryscape, if I can see her memories, put the puzzle together, I might be able to figure out what happened to her during that last week. If someone did poison her, I might be able to find out who. And if we know who, then we're on our way to finding out what he used . . . and how to get her better."

"Don't be so sure it was a *he*. As you know, your sister littered the Continent with angry wives."

"He, she, it, what does it matter? At least we'll have a direction. Right now we're just floundering."

Another silence, longer this time. Eathan's eyes were troubled, almost tortured, his expression grim. He pulled the napkin off his plate and began twisting it in his hands.

"I'm not at all comfortable with this, Julie," he said finally. "I love you both. I couldn't bear losing you, too. . . . But how can I turn my back on what may be Sam's only chance for recovery? Especially when her own sister will be in charge?"

Julie reached across the table and gripped one of his hands to save the napkin from further abuse.

"Don't worry. This is the right thing to do. It can't hurt her — it can only help her."

"And what about you?"

"I'll be fine." I *hope.*

"I must impose one condition, however."

Another condition? Dr. Siegal had to have one, now Eathan was insisting on one.

"What's that?"

He leaned forward, his expression grim. "I will be watching everything very closely. At the first sign of any — *any* — ill effects whatsoever to *either* of you, I will call a halt to the procedure."

She leaned back and stared at him, offended.

"And you think *I* wouldn't?"

"If you had the slightest suspicion that Sam's condition might be deteriorating — of course you would. But I'm not so sure you'd stop if you thought *you* were being affected. I can see you ignoring the warning signs and pushing on." He squeezed her hand and gave her a smile. "You're still young, Julie. All you young people think you're immortal."

"Not me," she said, giving him a level stare. "I stopped believing in immortality at age five."

4

DHL did its part: The hardware was delivered right on time.

Setting it up and getting it working was another story. Despite his reservations,

Eathan threw his support behind her and became indispensable, running interference for her with the nursing home and dealing with its medical director, who was understandably upset at all this strange equipment being set up on his turf. Eathan soothed him, assured him that nothing invasive was being done, convinced him that this was little more than a supersophisticated EEG. Eathan signed a stack of releases absolving the Sainte Gabrielle Home of all liability. He helped Julie hire workmen to set up the dish on the roof and run the cable to Sam's room.

Finally all was ready.

Three of them in Sam's room: Julie, Eathan, and Sam — no anesthetist needed. Gloomy, with late afternoon light fading behind the drawn curtains. The room was only slightly crowded with the extra hardware, which Julie had kept to a minimum: two headsets and a VR glove, a monitor, a terminal, a VCR to record the monitor feed, and wires, *lots* of wires.

They'd spent all day making the final preparations, testing the equipment, the satellite feed — everything was go now. Julie realized she needed sleep, but with the time difference, it had to be this afternoon or wait until tomorrow.

No way could she wait.

Sam lay in her bed with the Medusa-like

headpiece snug around her scalp. Julie looked across the room at Eathan, seated before a monitor where he'd be able to watch a monoscopic feed of what would play in Julie's goggles. He'd be passive — no chance to interact.

"Comfortable?" she said.

He tried a smile. It looked awful. He looked as if he was about to be sick.

"Absolutely not."

"Relax," she said. "This is a trial run. We'll make it short and sweet."

"I hope so."

She tried to look calm, but inside she was wound as tight as an armature coil. Her underarms felt soggy, and her fingers trembled as she adjusted her headphones. She had to radiate confidence for these two men: Eathan here and Dr. S. on-line in New York. Either one could call this whole procedure to a halt at any time.

And for the thousandth time, she questioned her motives. Did helping Sam play any part in this? Or was she recklessly venturing into her sister's memoryscape merely because no one had done it before? Or were her true motives even more base? Was she playing voyeur with her sister's past?

Whatever the truth, she'd have to reflect on it later. Right now she had someplace to go.

She pulled on the data glove. Something so medieval about this — like suiting up to do battle with demons and dragons. She wriggled the fingers. The hand icon danced on the screen.

Next, she grabbed the headset and lowered that onto her head. She pushed back her hair to keep it off her face. My helmet, she thought.

The headset was a clunky item, heavy, and though padded all around, you never forgot that your head was encased in plastic.

She adjusted the headphones and clicked the goggles into place.

Sky-blue emptiness ahead of her. She moved her hand. The icon skated across the blue. She clicked the Window button on the upper bar. A small block of sky in the upper right corner under the button wavered and Dr. Siegal's face appeared.

"All set on your end, Dr. Siegal?" she said.

He nodded. "All set. But I'd like to make one more plea —"

"Thank you," she said, cutting him off. "We're ready to go."

He sighed. "Very well. Remember, there'll be a slightly sluggish feel to the program due to the satellite delay. Be patient. I'm available when you need me. And I'll be watching."

"I appreciate that," she said, and clicked the Window button again. Dr. Siegal disappeared.

Everybody's watching me, she thought. Let's hope everything goes as smoothly as I've promised.

She pressed the Enter button with her virtual finger, held her breath, and watched the blue fade to black.

Seven

"I think, therefore I am," doesn't quite make it. "I remember, therefore I am" is more like it.
— Random notes: Julia Gordon

Something is wrong.

You're in a closet, and the lights are out. Or you're sealed in a cave, buried alive. Dark like a womb, but absent its warmth. Maybe a glitch in the satellite link: no visuals, no sound — nothing.

You should pull out and contact Dr. Siegal.

And then you notice the sparks. Tiny dull pinpricks of light out there, ahead somewhere. Are they close enough for you to touch or are they on the other end of the universe? There's no way for you to tell. No scale here, no way to gauge distance.

You lick your lips.

The wetness is a reassuringly real sensation.

You reach out and see your smooth, realistic virtual hand as it magically draws you on. If you had feet you'd be stumbling about like a blind man on an obstacle course. But you glide like an angel through the haze of smoke and fog. Somewhere above — far above — you see a faint blob of light, a moon of sorts, or a moribund sun, but it adds no worthwhile illumination to this scorched wasteland.

The other lights seem closer, or at least they've grown larger. As your eyes adjust to the cavelike darkness, you begin to see.

The tiny lights sputter like small fires dotting a bomb site. You make out twisted shapes, indeterminate structures like bombed-out buildings catching the faint glow. You turn left to see how far this, this . . . *devastation* goes. And it's everywhere, as far as you can see. . . .

Everywhere. You pull back your hand — and pause.

"My God!"

Your own voice startles you. It's the only sound you've heard since you entered this borderland of hell.

You search for something to compare it to. Hiroshima. Dresden after the fire. Yet even in those horrors, people survived, life struggled out of the rubble. But here, nothing is moving here.

And so intensely lonely, so unrelievedly bleak; a knot tightens in your chest. You want to leave. This is nothing like what you imagined you'd see. Yes, you want to leave, if for no other reason than to make sure that you *can* leave. You want to rip off the headset and scream for light: *Give me some light!*

But you calm yourself. You know this is merely a memoryscape, as harmless as Lorraine's, with the same underlying architecture: neural links connecting the memory nodes. Somewhere below, Sam's neural pathways weave and interconnect, linking events and experiences along the pathways that used to carry Sam's emotions and feelings and information to her consciousness.

But you see nothing moving here.

You've entered the land of the dead.

Suddenly the Window button begins to blink. You click it. The window drops down and there's Dr. Siegal. He looks frazzled.

"Julie! Julie, get out of there!"

"Why?" You know damn well why, but you want to hear someone else tell you.

"The devastation. It's — it's unimaginable. And it can't help affecting you as well."

"You don't know that."

"I don't want to argue, Julie. This is far worse than either of us expected in our worst nightmares. Get out, Julie. Get out now!"

You're ready to agree, ready to click the Exit button and return to the real world of warmth and light and life, when you notice a blue glow somewhere near the center of the twisted structures that dot the memoryscape. A pale blue light, cool fire, small, flickering, like a pilot light on a stove.

"In a minute," you tell Dr. S. "There's something I want to check out first."

"Julie, please —"

You click the Window button and Dr. Siegal disappears.

You take a breath and reach out your hand. The glove feels heavy. The act is a decisive one. The hand drags you toward the blue glow, drifting over the razed nodes. You trace the gopher-trail connections leading from one structure to the next. Most look broken, shattered here and there along their lengths like ruptured water mains.

You look down at them, expecting to see something scurry out, some ratlike creature that can thrive among these ruins.

If you had arms you'd rub them to drive off the chill. . . .

Chill? Why are you chilled? Certainly not from Sam's memoryscape. You can't feel anything in a memoryscape — you can only observe it. Probably an emotional response to the desolation. Or perhaps someone left a door open in the nursing home and cool air is seeping into Sam's room. But no sensations from the memoryscape itself. That simply can't be.

Your eyes are fully adjusted to the darkness now, and you see dimly glowing mounds dotting the ruined horizon. They shine with a warmer light than the blue glow before you, almost inviting.

Memory nodes maybe? Is there still life in this place?

You look ahead and now you're close to the blue glow. This doesn't resemble a bombed-out building. No Eiffel Tower here, no house with a picket fence. Just this cool blue sphere.

You pull back for a moment and watch the blue orb. You've seen nothing else like it in this barren landscape. If you're to learn anything here, perhaps this is where you must begin.

You raise the glove and it looks as if your hand is reaching out to touch the blue sphere, perhaps to grasp it.

You begin falling into it, the blue light ready to swallow you. Too late to pull back. An instant of panic, of featureless cold blue fire. You hear a noise. A door opening, the jangle of keys, and then the blue light is gone and you're in a room.

In an art studio.

Sam's studio. You were here last week. You look around. The floor is clean. Samantha's bureau is intact, the drawers all closed. The studio looks unrealistically neat. No sign of anyone breaking in. Nothing like what you saw then.

You turn to your left and see the paintings. One canvas is all slashing blue and black streaks, a violent piece of work, similar to the one you saw in the real-world studio. You raise your hand to it and you're closer.

The paint glows. It looks like alien lava dripping off the canvas. The painting is changing before your eyes. It seems alive. Is Sam's unconscious trying to finish the work? Or trying to destroy it?

You wait, but nothing intelligible emerges from the swirling streaks.

You turn farther left. There's a delay, as if your command to look left has to be processed. Which of course it does. Another painting leans against the wall but this looks like one of the old masters, a Brueghel. Villagers at harvest time. Women in their starched linens, men in baggy trousers with sheaves of wheat strapped on their shoulders.

You know you're in Sam's studio, her workplace. And yet here is a painting that's clearly not hers. Or perhaps it is; perhaps one she painted and sold during all those years you barely spoke. There could be hundreds of those.

And this one moves too. You look in the upper right corner and see a tiny red demon with a pitchfork. The demon moves closer to the villagers. He carries his pitchfork with determination, with purpose.

The demon pounces upon a villager and spears the hapless man with a vicious jab. The bumpkin writhes on the end of the fork as a fiery pit opens in the sward and he's tossed into the flames.

"No!"

Your own voice startles you again, not because it pierces the silence, but because of the sudden surge of horror that forced you to cry out. Why should this crudely animated image disturb you so? It's not even a real painting.

And yet, as you watch the poor man tumble backward into hellfire, you want to reach for him, help him, and it breaks your heart that you can't.

He vanishes, and then . . .

It starts all over. Like a loop, the painting is back the way it was, the happy villagers, the demon up in the right, beginning his grim resolute march.

You pull back, turn away, searching out the other paintings in this studio, anything but that one.

You find a large canvas hanging way to the left where the walls of this studio come together in a V, an impossibly sharp corner. The large canvas is empty.

But no, you must have missed it. A moon hangs in the upper right corner of the canvas, a nearly full moon floating near the top of the canvas. A yellow, sleepy moon . . .

You think: *sleepy moon.* And that means something to you. *Sleepy moon.*

This canvas, too, is disturbing. *Sleepy moon.* Why does that seem important?

How long have you been in here?

You hear something behind you. A crackling sound. Something that sounds like a fireplace. Shakily, warily, you raise your hand, the dis-embodied appendage that stands in for the

120

rest of your body. You make it glide right.

Another canvas. A lion with a mane of fire stands proudly in an elegant Venetian gondola painted red and gold along its railing. The fiery head sizzles and crackles as it burns. Your fingers reach toward the painting and you drift closer. Is this one of Sam's, another work completed and sold in the lost years between you?

You turn around.

Something on the floor, standing out amid the immense empty expanse of virtual wood.

A palette knife, still thick with crusty blue paint, as if it had been dropped in the rush of the moment.

Move closer to it, gliding soundlessly as if *you* are the ghost, and not all these images. Reach down. There's no dexterity involved in picking up the knife. The program fills in the appropriate gestures, linking the objects. Your virtual hand closes on the palette knife, tidying the room by picking up this lone stray object.

You hold it, wondering why Sam dropped it. And it *was* dropped. You sense that.

A door slams behind you, startling you. It sounds like a gunshot in this dead place and you almost cry out. Someone laughs drunkenly. You turn around.

And see your sister.

Then — you *are* your sister, speaking:

"They told me bad things about you. . . ."

Samantha watches Liam enter her studio, catlike, looking around, nervous and unsure. His longish, wavy red hair is tucked behind his ears; his sharp, quick, bright eyes dart here and there. This is unknown terrain, an alien world for him. Sam finds his disorientation amusing.

A few feet into the studio, he stops.

"Isn't this room a wee bit dark for a studio?" he says.

She smiles and leans against the wall. Liam is just a dark shape in her apartment. How old is he, thirty? Thirty-five? Hard to tell. He has deep lines cut into his face. A weathered face. Sam imagines that it is a face cut by pain.

She enjoys the feelings she now has, the fear mixed with excitement —

"I have skylights. I can make it very cheery during the day. If I want to, that is. If ever I want the place 'cheery.' "

She kicks the door shut.

The sound echoes in the room. Sam reaches out and touches Liam's broad shoulder. He turns to her.

"I didn't bring you here to see my studio," she says.

His grin flashes back at her in the darkness.

"Didn't you now?"

And then he comes close, pressing Samantha to the wall, pushing her tight, snug

against the rough boards. His lips cover hers and slowly, deliberately, he moves against her.

She moans into his mouth, and the sound is a trigger.

She feels his hands on her, strong hands traveling up her body, over her hips, her breasts, up to her neck, when —

You see nothing. Your sister, the man — gone. Both vanished like ghosts.

What just happened here? Somehow you slipped into the memory. No, *slipped* isn't the word. You were ripped from your observer status and hurtled headlong into participation. You felt his lips on yours, his hands moving over your —

Christ, you *felt* things. You can't let Dr. Siegal know.

How did this happen? It's not supposed to happen. It *can't* happen. Unless . . .

Dr. Siegal's warning comes back to you: *You share not only a history, but an identical set of genes as well. That's an unpredictable and possibly dangerous combination.*

Well, he was right about the unpredictable. Hopefully he was wrong about the dangerous part.

But what happened to the rest of the scene?

Did something make it end? Was *that* the event that triggered Sam's comatose state. So many questions . . .

You glance again at the black-and-blue painting — or what used to be the painting. The canvas is blank, the pigment puddled on the floor, the painting gone.

Which means this dead memoryscape has changed — at least this part of it. And not necessarily for the better.

You have a thought: If things are changing in here, could something be changing outside? Are you helping or hurting in here? Mostly it seems like you're stumbling around.

You have no idea of time. But before you leave you want another look outside. Maybe you could catch the rest of Sam's memory with Liam. Idle curiosity? Careful, this is a high-order invasion of privacy.

And for the first time the possibility of witnessing what happened to Sam — what was done to her — frightens you. Can you stand to see it?

You turn and move to the studio door. You glide back into the night world of the memoryscape. It all looks pretty much the same: the ruptured axons, the twisted structures at the nodes, like violent modern sculptures. Nothing has changed here — or has it? You can't be sure, but it strikes you that there might be fewer glowing mounds on the horizon.

You see a not-so-distant node lit by a warm glow instead of the faint sputtering light of the others. You glide toward it. Along the way you think you see someone standing below. You approach cautiously. For an instant you think it's Sam and then you realize that it's only a doll made to look like Sam — a very *dumpy* doll of Sam. Actually, it looks like Sam's image painted on a giant, five-foot gourd. Like one of those toy boxing dummies.

You touch it with the glove icon and it begins rocking back and forth. And as it rocks it splits around the middle. The top half pops off and there's another doll inside, only this one looks like you. You realize it's a giant matrioshka doll, one doll nesting inside another. Sam loved these as a little girl. The matrioshka — open it up and there's a smaller doll inside. Open that and there's another one, and on and on until you get to the center, where the tiniest doll lives, the last doll that can't be opened.

The last doll, the one with no secrets.

You touch the new doll and that one splits, too, popping its top half off to reveal another Sam, identical to the first except one-third the size. You touch this one but nothing happens. That's it. No more dolls.

Sam, Julie, Sam. Why? Is it supposed to mean something? Or is it just . . . here?

Baffled, you move on, leaving the little Sam doll sitting in the lower half of the Julie doll, sitting in the lower half of the Sam doll, rocking back and forth, rocking. . . .

You reach the glow and see an enormous house, a squat and monstrously large estate. A mammoth stone dollhouse sitting in the war zone of Sam's memory. It almost looks like Eathan's Yorkshire manor, Oakwood, but it's impossibly large, larger even than Versailles, stretching for thousands of yards.

And yet this *could* still be Eathan's manor. It's only Sam's memory, after all, and if it's a childhood memory, size and scale mean absolutely nothing. The house *would* be impossibly huge.

You're closer, and the front doors to the mansion do look familiar, the dark oak with cut glass veiled by a heavy curtain. You reach out for the giant brass doorknob and feel like Alice in Wonderland, the scale is *that* exploded. Surely you'll find oversized chairs inside, massive mirrors, and a plate of cookies with a card that says *Eat me.*

You expect the doorknob to be locked, but it turns with a silkily smooth action. The twin oaken doors glide open.

And you see a little girl. You know her. She's you — or she's Sam. Always a challenge for people to tell you apart; even you have difficulty in some of the old pictures.

But then the little girl raises something in her hands. A statue. A Greek-looking figure standing on a base.

You remember this. You remember the day little Sammi threw the —

The statue smashes onto the marble steps, and shatters into a hundred pieces. The pieces quickly melt like chunks of ice on a hot skillet.

And Sammi screams: "I *hate* you! You ruin everything! You're stupid, Julie!"

Then you see yourself, racing up the stairs, chasing Sammi.

But why aren't you *in* Samantha like before? Is it because the younger you is here as well? Does that keep you out?

So much to learn here.

You follow, chasing your young self. You remember this day too well, remember the rage. You hear yourself yelling at Sammi, a cold, bloodthirsty sound: "I'm going to *kill* you."

But something's different. You remember this, and yet you don't. Why so angry? That wasn't *your* statue she broke. Why should you even care?

Up the staircase, not floating now, but pounding up the heavily carpeted steps. But when you reach the top — no one there. The second-floor hallway stretches right and left; like train tracks, the hallway seems to stretch forever.

You hear banging. A steady, thumping noise. You follow little Julie to the right, moving past doors and paintings and tables with flowers on them. You'd like to look at the paintings. They may be important. But the thumping draws you on, to a looming closet door.

You stop and hear the banging, the terrible pounding against the door. It can't be a little girl making all that noise.

You know what happens next.

You remember.

Little Julie stands outside the hall-closet door. She hears yelling coming from the other side, the dark, locked-in side.

"Let me out, Julie. Let me out! I don't like it in here!"

The little you moves closer to the door.

"Then I guess you shouldn't have hid in there, brat."

"Julie!"

Naked terror in that voice. Panic at being locked in someplace dark and strange. The feeling of being trapped.

You watch little Julie turn and walk away.

The scene happens again. Then again and again, a loop, the little girl turning away from her pleading sister.

"Julieeeeeee!"

A light begins flashing.

The warning light in the readout ribbon. You check the vital signs — pulse, respirations, EKG, EEG — all normal. The built-in time limit is up. So soon? Damn. There's so much more to see. What happened to Sam and Liam? Are there any further changes in the memoryscape? What are these paintings on the wall? What secrets do the hundred rooms of this fantasy house hold?

You don't want to leave, but staying past the limit might be damaging to you and your twin. Your brain waves are linked, more intimately than you or Dr. Siegal ever could have imagined. So you will leave the way you came: through the door. You want one last look at Sam's memoryscape.

You drift into the shattered night that was once your sister's life. A deep, unaccountable melancholy seeps through you.

What happened here?

You click on the Exit button.

Eight

The more I learn about the fragility of memory, the less disturbed I am by the innumerable distortions that occur, and more dumbfounded by the fact that we can remember anything accurately at all.

— Random notes: Julia Gordon

1

Julie pulled off the helmet. She looked at the monitor a few feet away, empty now except for the words *Session Terminated. Please Name File for Saving.*

The cursor blinked patiently but Julie did not — could not — move.

Sam's bombed-out memoryscape had left her rattled, confused. The unimaginable devastation — and the two memories she'd been able to access — had only added to the mystery. Why?

"Julie?" A hand touched her shoulder,

startling her. "Julie, are you all right?"

Eathan. She'd forgot about him, sitting here through it all, watching everything. She turned to him. His face was pale, stricken.

"You saw?"

He nodded. "It looks . . . terrible. Does everyone's — what do you call it — mindscape — ?"

"Memoryscape."

"Do they all look like that?"

"No. Sam has the Hiroshima of memory-scapes. I'm not too sure what I'll be able to find . . . or see."

"You're upset."

Julie sighed. "I suppose I am. But I'm also intrigued, and confused: Why *these* memories? What makes them so damn im-portant?"

She looked away.

"You never saw yourself fighting with your sister. I'm afraid that's something that happened quite often."

"Yeah, I know that. But —"

"It's what you said to Sam that concerns you, isn't it?"

Julie turned to her uncle. He was like a rock. She wondered why Sam ever needed a shrink with someone like Eathan to lean on. With all his concern and unflagging support, he was more than an uncle.

She nodded. "It certainly wasn't great

hearing myself say 'I'm going to kill you' to my sister. Kind of unsettling to stumble upon that as one of her key memories. And there was something different about it. That statue . . . I don't remember that."

"I don't recall what started the fight, but I remember the incident well. Samantha smashed your microscope on the floor — *that's* why you were so mad."

"Of course!" It all rushed back in a flash. Julie had accidentally stepped on a collage Sam had been making and refused to apologize because Sam had left it in the middle of the floor. Retaliations escalated, culminating in the smashing of Julie's microscope. "Then why isn't the microscope in the memory?"

"I'm afraid that's your area of expertise. I can tell you with fair certainty that the statue was Cellini's *Perseus.* And I can assure you without a doubt that we never owned one."

"Then what — ?"

"Well, you tried," he said, taking her hand and giving it a gentle squeeze. "It was a brave attempt, but now I think it's time to let the medical experts take over."

Julie shook her head. "I've only just started, Eathan. There's so much to be learned in there — about Sam, about what happened to her. You just saw her with that man who's supposed to be a terrorist. God, watching it I was scared for her."

"But what is this going to do for Sam?"

She took a breath. "I don't know. I've only scratched the surface in there. I'd planned on going in, learning what I needed, and getting out. One-two-three. But now . . . well, you saw what it's like in there. This is going to take a long time."

A knock on the door. Eathan said, *"Oui?"*

A nurse entered carrying a dozen crimson roses in a vase.

"Ces fleurs sont pour Mademoiselle Samantha."

She placed them on the nightstand and left.

"For Sam?" Julie said. "From you?"

Eathan shook his head, his expression grave. "Not from me. Is there a card?"

Julie spotted a corner of white among the dark green of the stems and plucked the card from the thorns. A chill crept over her as she read it aloud.

" 'For my Sammi. Don't worry. I won't let them hurt you.' "

"No name?" Eathan said.

She flipped the card over. No name. She shook her head.

Eathan shot to his feet. "It's from O'Donnell. Damn him! Why can't he leave her alone!"

"You don't know that," Julie said, alarmed by his reaction.

"No, you're right," he said, calming. "But who else would send her roses with a message that sounds like a warning."

"To us?"

"Doesn't that sound like a threat?"

Julie had to admit it did.

A high-pitched beep sounded behind her. She glanced around at the equipment monitoring Samantha, but everything was fine. She checked the monitor and saw that a small window opened in the corner of the screen showing a camera icon.

Julie swung around in her chair.

"What's that?" Eathan said.

"It's Dr. Siegal. He wants to talk."

"Your mentor. I hope he advises you to stop this. Meanwhile, I'm going to make some calls — see if I can find out who sent these. Wait for me. We'll have something to eat later."

"Sounds good," Julie said, but didn't mean it. The experience in Sam's memoryscape and the mysterious roses had stolen her appetite.

As Eathan slipped out, Julie used the mouse to click on the icon. Dr. Siegal's troubled face filled the screen.

"Julie . . . can you see me?"

"Yes — fine."

He smiled uncertainly. "Well, I can't see *you*, of course. You don't have a camera feed there, do you?"

"No, I didn't think it was important." She

hesitated, staring at his tense features. "Well, what do you think?"

Dr. Siegal looked around, as if uncomfortable with being seen.

"It's just as I warned you. *You* are in those memories. You are part of that memory-scape and whatever wrought such havoc in her may somehow pass to you."

Julie shook her head. "I disagree. Sure, I'm in those memories but —"

"Julie, you're being pigheaded again. This is not a sound procedure. If you were a heart surgeon you wouldn't operate on your own brother or sister."

She wanted to shout at him but took a breath instead. She wanted to discuss what she saw, not defend her actions. Probably a good thing Dr. S. couldn't see her exasperation. If she really cared for anyone in this world it was Dr. Siegal. He and Eathan, the twin rocks of her life.

Two men guiding her — pretty funny, she thought, considering her batting average with men.

"I would if I was the only surgeon with sufficient experience in the needed procedure. And" — she leaned close to the monitor — "I *am* the most experienced."

Dr. S. rubbed his chin. He looked up to the camera. "This won't leave you unaffected, Julie."

"I know that."

"There could be transference, shock, any number of effects on you. Your memoryscape could wind up as burned out as Sam's."

"Doubtful. But life is full of risks."

"I could still order you to stop."

"But you won't."

She hoped.

The risks he had mentioned were real. Julie knew that now, she accepted that. But this was too incredible to back away from. A single venture into Sam's ruined memoryscape was not enough. This was terra incognita, a whole new experience. The things she could learn in there — and help Sam, too, of course.

She watched Dr. Siegal's face as he considered his reply.

I'm hooked — and so is he.

"Very well," he said softly. "But at the first sign of physical distress from you, you're out."

"Agreed. Now, there are a couple of things I want to discuss."

"Go on."

"The point of view in Sam's memoryscape . . . I mean, you saw it. One moment it's the usual — like watching a movie. The next, I became her. . . . I saw the event through her eyes, I —"

Julie hesitated.

"Yes?"

Julie had almost let slip about feeling things, how it was more than a mental movie she was watching, that she *felt* whatever her sister felt.

But he'd pull the plug immediately if he knew that.

"I don't understand how I'm seeing the memories from her perspective."

"Yes, that's unexpected. But I think that's the genetic link between you two."

"But it didn't happen with both memories."

"It may depend on the memories themselves, how deep they go, the types of feelings attached to them. Or maybe it has to do with the other memories they lead to. Or perhaps it can't happen if you're *present* in that memory. Whatever the reason, Julie, you'd better prepare yourself for some upsetting experiences in there. But remember, memories aren't photographs. They're not reality. They are stored perceptions colored by emotions and revised by time and intervening experience. They get embellished, changed, merged —"

"I know that."

"Of course you do. And you mustn't forget it. You must remain objective in your sister's memoryscape — because everything you see is *subj*ective."

Julie nodded. Then, remembering that

Dr. Siegal couldn't see her, she said, "Got it, Dr. S."

His expression became stern. "And one thing I insist upon, Julie: Do not go into that memoryscape alone. I must be on-line during every excursion."

"Do you really think that's necessary? The time difference makes —"

"Nonnegotiable, Julie. If you get in trouble in there, I want to be on-line to help you out of it."

Yielding to an infantile impulse, she stuck her tongue out at his image. She didn't want to make a promise she might not keep, so she simply said, "I understand."

He smiled. "Now — I'm late for a class. So good-bye." He waved, and the little video window disappeared.

2

A light rain started just as they took their table at the bistro. Julie looked around the cramped Le Chien Qui Fume. Checkered tablecloths, wire-back chairs, everything looking like castoffs from a traveling company of *La Bohème*. She guessed it was not the type of place Eathan frequented. More Samantha's kind of joint, oozing local color. Julie gestured around her.

"One of your discoveries?"

He smiled. "Actually I heard about it from —"

Julie nodded. "Sam? Yeah, it reeks of Bohemia."

Eathan looked concerned. "We could go somewhere else."

Julie shrugged. "No. It's fine." She took a breath. "You must think I'm made of stone."

"No. Not at all."

Eathan pushed back his glasses. They kept slipping down, giving his already thoughtful face an even more avuncular expression.

He was made to be a professor.

He reached out and patted her hand. "No, you're not stone. I long ago accepted the fact that you and your sister were quite different." A small smile played on his lips. "Couldn't be more different."

The waiter appeared at Eathan's shoulder.

"Julia?" Eathan said, raising his eyebrows.

She searched her memory for the words.

"Un citron pressé, s'il vous plaît," she said to the waiter.

"Nothing to eat?" Eathan said.

She shook her head.

Eathan ordered a *café au lait* and onion soup.

"Your sister told me that the soup here is 'to die for.' But back to differences . . ."

"Yes, we're different, okay. But Sam's difficult to care about. She's so damned self-destructive."

A blue Gauloises truck passed by, belching smoke from its rear. The exhaust drifted in through the open doors of the bistro.

"No one's judging you, Julie. You don't have to attack Sam."

Julie smiled. "Oh, yes. Someone is judging me. I am." She wanted to change the subject. "Did you learn anything about the roses?"

He shook his head. "No. Paid for in cash by a man no one remembers. It's a busy florist. But the Sainte Gabrielle security man told me some disturbing news: They've had a prowler."

Julie tensed. "A break-in?"

"No. Just someone spotted on the grounds at night, sneaking around, peeking in windows."

"Maybe it's just a peeping Tom."

Eathan looked away. "He's been seen consistently near the south wing on Sam's side."

Now she was uneasy. "You think it might be this Liam O'Donnell?"

"I'd be willing to bet money on it."

The waiter returned with their order. Julie glanced up and caught the skinny man looking her over, exerting his French-man's prerogative.

"Tell me, Julie — what do you think about what you saw in Sam's memoryscape? Any clues about what happened?"

Julie sipped her lemonade. She looked left, feeling eyes on her. The bony waiter was standing next to another garçon, both now eyeing her. Julie wondered if she should stare the creep down or perhaps get up and —

Temper, temper, she told herself. I could never live in this country.

She took a breath. "Clues?"

"About what did this to Samantha."

"None. At least not yet. But I've only scratched the surface."

Eathan pushed his glasses back. He took a sip of his coffee. His face looked grim, terribly concerned.

"Could it have been rape? We saw her with that man, Liam."

Julie sighed. "There's no way to tell. It will take a lot more work. I want to go in again and —"

"What did your mentor think of all this?"

No sense in bringing Eathan into her ongoing debate with Dr. S. She chose her words carefully, opting for obliquity. "I'm going to continue."

Eathan shook his head. "I'm not sure that's a good idea, Julie. I want to find out what happened as much as you do, you know that, but —"

Julie leaned close to her uncle. "I need more time in there. If I —"

Eathan raised a hand and stared at her. He had piercing eyes that seemed to see right through her. Julie always suspected that Eathan could read her like a book. She could have no secrets from him. And yet he always understood and forgave whatever his twin nieces did.

Not that *I* ever gave him that much trouble, Julie thought.

Eathan shook his head. "Julie, I saw the devastation. It looks hopeless. You have a life to live. I'll take care of Sam; I'll get the best care, and —"

"No!" The force behind the word surprised Julie. "I mean, I'm not giving up. There are accessible memories. You saw Oakwood —"

"Is that why you want to go back in? Because thoughts and memories about you were there when this happened?"

This was something she wanted to discuss with Eathan. Why did Sam have this old memory of their fighting in the mansion? Why was Sam's memory of her young sister so close to the surface?

And why had it been altered?

"What was that sculpture again?" she asked. "You said it was —"

"Cellini's *Perseus*. As I remember,

Perseus slew Medusa. Cut off her head and delivered it to someone or other. I forget, myself."

Strange, so strange. She had to go in and probe further.

And again, that unsettling question: How much of this drive to push on was being fueled by concern for Sam, how much by mere scientific curiosity, and how much by the sheer voyeuristic thrill of reassembling the shattered pieces of her sister's life?

"I've got to see more," she said.

Eathan's nod was slow and reluctant. He always recognized her resolve. Like the time Julie insisted that she was going to New York University, across the ocean — as far away from Sam and Eathan as possible. No amount of discussion would change her mind.

"Very well," he said through a sigh. "I understand that this is something you need to do. I just hope it is the right thing — and for the right reasons."

The waiter returned, wiping his hands on a serviette sashed to his belt.

"Quelque chose plus, Monsieur?"

Eathan looked at Julie, who shook her head. Then he asked for the check.

Julie looked outside and saw the glow of the bistro's neon sign, a squat dog with a cigarette in his mouth, reflecting on the pavement.

She wanted to hurry back to the hospital. Back to her sleeping sister, a tainted fairy princess now locked away in her own mental dungeon.

I'm locked in there too, Julie thought. A piece of me — as a little girl. And who else, what else?

"Ready?" Eathan said.

Julie stood up and followed her uncle toward the door of the smoky bistro.

More than ready.

3

As they passed through the front entrance of the nursing home, Eathan said, "I need to make some calls regarding Samantha."

"About what?"

"About her future disposition. I'm concerned about security here. It shouldn't take too long. Do you want to wait?"

"I've got some odds and ends to take care of in Sam's room. Need to shut down the system for the night. That'll take a while."

"Okay. I'll meet you here when you're through."

Julie checked the computer as soon as she entered the room. She was worried that the night nurses had fiddled with the buttons and accidentally changed the settings, or that the mysterious prowler might have got in, but all was as it should be.

She reached for the power switch to turn it off, then hesitated. She looked at Sam, sister Sleeping Beauty, and thought about the nightscape within.

Another look . . . she needed another look.

But alone. She knew it was safer, more sensible to have someone on-line with her, but she wasn't keen on the idea of dear old Dr. S. looking over her shoulder while she explored. After all, it was her life in there too.

She fitted the subject helmet on Sam's head, donned her own headset, then picked up the glove. Funny, the data glove was such a clunky thing in real life, a giant robot appendage with dozens of wires running off it. But in the virtual world of the memoryscape it became a sleek, graceful hand guiding her into alien terrain.

Julie flipped down the goggles and looked at the twin screens. Now she was truly alone with Samantha.

"Okay, kiddo," she said. "It's just me and you again." Julie hit the Enter key and the program started. "Just the way we started out."

She checked the readouts in the bottom ribbon bar. Pulse and respiration were normal.

It's been only a few hours. Is this too soon to be going back in? she wondered. Probably won't have any effect on Sam. But what effect will it have on me?

She chewed at her lip, once again guiltily aware that it was not Samantha she was concerned with.

The screen darkened to night.

And she was *back.*

Nine

Recall — the act of memory — should not be viewed as merely opening a mental drawer and pulling out a memory. Recall is a reconstructive act — the various pieces of that memory must be located, gathered together, and reassembled for inspection.
　　　　　　— Random notes: Julia Gordon

The nightscape draws you back, like a gravity well sucking you in. You retract your hand, and, like hitting a brake, you stop.

You look around. You're prepared now, ready for the broken web of twisted structures and scorched earth. Still, it shocks you.

You search for the blue glow of the gallery. There — you find it. A landmark. You're oriented now. And beyond that, the glow of Eathan's Oakwood. But dimmer now, flickering.

Oh, no. Is that dying too?

You approach it and see something beyond it, something you didn't notice last time when Oakwood was brighter, something that looks like a pile of pure white sugar, a giant white hill.

Cocaine, perhaps? That certainly might occupy a place in Sam's memory. Any substance that stretched her mind was fair game. Anything to feed the frenzy that was Samantha.

You hear a noise, a scuffling sound, and turn around. A possum. Something is alive here!

You watch its naked prehensile tail thrashing madly back and forth as it paws under a pile of debris. It pulls something free and begins gnawing on it. Curious, you move closer and it backs away, guarding its prize. You lean closer; you aren't going to steal it away, but you're curious what it's got there. It turns toward you and —

You jerk back. A hand — the possum has a severed human hand clamped between its jaws. You turn away, sickened, as it begins to gnaw on a finger.

You raise your glove toward the hill. You want to get out of here.

You float over the memoryscape, a clinical angel calmly inspecting the damage below as you near the white hill.

Soon you see it's not sugar, not cocaine. No, it's a snow-capped hill. As you near you see that the peak is flattened. Suddenly on your left a huge wave rears up out of nowhere, its foamy edges reaching for you like white-clawed hands. You dart back and the wave freezes, framing the far-off mountain.

And now you know that mountain: It's Fuji. And somehow you're in Hokusai's *The Great Wave off Kanagawa.*

Well, what did you expect in your sister's memoryscape? You could have guessed it would be lousy with art.

That was another thing you never agreed on. You're drawn to artists like Georges de la Tour. You adore his *The Penitent Magdalen* — the light, the shadows, the clarity. You love the representational schools; Sam loves everything but.

But now you're part of Hokusai's *Great Wave,* and it's okay as art, but it's in your way. You dart past the wave, ducking through its trough, and continue toward the mountain.

When you look back, the wave remains as you left it, frozen, waiting to tumble toward a beach that doesn't exist.

Ahead, you notice tiny people on a snowy mountain that's no longer Fuji. They glide back and forth, skiing under a brilliant blue sky —

Samantha pushes the goggles higher off her face. The man with her is older, with sharp, dark eyes and a grin that glints like the snow.

Karl Tennstedt is director of Berlin's Bertolt Brecht Theater. He's been Sam's boss, and now wants to be her mentor and lover. All through the production of *Galileo* he's been putting moves on her, hinting about

149

other productions . . . and their working together.

But his wife is crazy, and so insanely jealous it's scary. . . . Who knows what she'll do if she finds out.

"Let me tell you what to expect on this slope," Tennstedt says.

Sam shakes her head. Why listen, why experience the slope in words before experiencing it in life? How boring.

"Don't worry. I'll be fine."

The man's smile changes.

"This isn't some baby run, Samantha. This is *Die Grosse* 'Edge.' This is a professional alpine run."

Sam pulls down her goggles.

"Good." She pushes away, close to the edge of the run. She looks down, and the sight takes her breath away. It's not a sheer drop, but it is an incredible expanse of white, sloping sharply at a forty-five-degree angle.

She sees skiers cutting left and right, controlling their speed by weaving back and forth.

"The run turns," Tennstedt says. "Halfway down, the run narrows and —"

Tennstedt is too old. Acting like a father, so worried and concerned. All that, and he wants to get into Sam's pants. That's what this little ski holiday is all about. He's boring her.

But this slope isn't.

Tennstedt still jabbers at her. She feels his apprehension and that adds to the excitement.

She pushes off the edge and hits the slope already moving fast, taking the downhill dead-on. She pulls her poles tight to her body, crouching.

Look at me. I'm a downhill racer.

Faster, and faster, the thin layer of powdery snow does little to slow her. She flies past other skiers trying to tackle the steep slope in measured assaults. Such caution, such an accounting approach to life. Tiny crystals of snow in the air bite her cheeks. The goggles paint everything with a warm yellow tint.

It's dreamlike, wonderful.

The run begins to narrow.

What had been a giant tablecloth of white funnels into a narrow gap.

Now Sam realizes that her speed is out of control. With the gray granite walls closing in from the sides, she knows she's got to do something to slow herself.

This is the way it's always been for her.

Test the limits. Heed no warning. Take no prisoners.

She starts awkwardly schussing back and forth, trying to dig her ski edges into the snow to slow her. The effect is pitiful. Then her right ski edge tries to dig into an exposed icy patch but skids over it.

She feels her balance go.

The cold on her face is matched now by terror. She fights to regain control. She can only glance at the slope, ever narrower, the stone walls closing in on her. Then — with a last sickening glance — she sees the run turn sharply to the right.

Her left leg, trying to counterbalance her wobbling, gives way.

And she falls, tumbling into the snow, a biting spray flying into her face. She begins rolling, screaming, banging — and . . .

And you *feel* it.

The snow shooting into your face, filling your mouth.

You feel your limbs smashing against the ice, rolling, flopping around.

You moan. You feel this. But that's not supposed to happen. You're just an observer here.

You need to think about this, but how can you think while you're falling down a mountain, experiencing your sister's memory with your body feeling every electric jolt, every sensation?

You moan again.

Or is that Sam? Why can't you tell?

Sam opens her eyes.

She's aware that the movement has stopped. She feels the snow on her lips and knows she is facedown.

A sharp pain arcs from below, a dull, throbbing message from miles away. She tries to reach down and see what's hurting so much.

She raises her head off the snow and twists around to look at the source of the pain.

It seems amazing that the sky is still blue, with the sun a brilliant yellow hanging low in the sky. Nothing has changed. Except —

She raises her head higher and sees the red stain, so dark, almost black against the white snow. From miles away, she understands. There's blood down there.

Then another delayed realization.

It's mine.

Suddenly all movement on the mountain stops.

You've done nothing, but now you're gliding back from the brilliant white of the slope, leaving the antlike speck of Sam stranded on the mountain. Farther back until you see the whole snow-covered mountain.

Rippling, undulating slowly.

The white is moving.

Closer now, again without your doing anything. You remind yourself that this is a memory. More like a dream, the way it cuts back and forth, mixing one scene with the next, making surreal jumps.

You watch, hooked by this drama of your

twin, opening up her life to you in a way that never could have happened when she was conscious.

You see a bed. A white sheet.

The sheet moving. Sam, her head in bandages, moves under the sheet. Someone stands nearby, a dark figure. The director?

The figure moves closer to the bed and puts a hand on Sam.

Eathan!

Is this happening now, or then? You feel completely disoriented.

You see Eathan touch Sam's brow. He looks younger. This was five, six years ago. You remember this, and you don't want to be here.

You feel yourself being drawn into Sam. You don't want to be inside her because you know what happens here:

> "I've called your sister."
>
> Sam nods, but the pain makes her wince.
>
> "I left a message about the accident . . . your loss of blood."
>
> He gently touches her head. No matter what Sam does to herself, Eathan is always there to pick up the pieces.
>
> I'm like Humpty Dumpty, Sam thinks. Except one of these days all the King's men won't be able to put me back together again.
>
> Then Sam sees something on the small side

table. Was it there before or did Eathan bring it?

A matrioshka with Gorbachev as its outer skin.

The phone rings. One long ring that fills the room.

Sam watches Eathan pick up the receiver. She listens.

"Yes, Julia. She's in Grenoble. Yes, the Universitaire Hospital. It's very good."

Eathan smiles at Samantha.

The doll is gone from the table. Vanished. She must have imagined it.

"Yes, a compound fracture with arterial damage . . . yes, a lot of blood before they got to her. Julie. I was hoping . . ."

Another smile from Eathan for Sam.

Thinking about Julie in New York. Stopping her busy New York life, listening to the news of sister Sam's latest disaster.

You remember the call. You remember how you felt.

The words you said.

"So what did Sam do this time?"

You asked about the hospital. "We're AB positive — that's compatible with just about any donor. There's got to be other ways to get blood to her. She doesn't need me."

Did you really say that? Yes . . . yes, you did. You remember those words.

She doesn't need me.

You wanted the tie to be cut. You wanted Eathan to know that you weren't going to be part of Sam's rescue squad. You had your own life, your own work —

And Eathan said . . . he said:

"I understand. Yes. I'm sure we can get enough blood here. I just thought — right, Julie."

The receiver clicks down with a terrible finality.

Sam looks away . . . up to the ceiling, the off-white ceiling that seems so far away.

She knows what Julie said. She didn't hear the actual words but she's got a very good idea of the content. She feels a pressure in her chest. She doesn't want to cry, not simply because of the pain it will cause in her broken ribs, but because she swore years ago that Julie would never make her cry again. So she won't cry. She *won't*, dammit!

But a sob breaks through, and pain stabs from her right side. And she cries harder, huge, wracking sobs.

Damn Julie. She did it again.

You can't stand this. The pain — the emotional pain — is too much. You click the Exit button and watch the scene fade.

Ten

Joseph Conrad: "Vanity plays lurid tricks with our memory."
— Random notes: Julia Gordon

Julie yanked the data glove off her hand. Its sweaty insides stuck to her skin. Then she pulled off her headset and wiped her eyes.

Tears! she thought. My God, I'm crying! She never cried.

But it really wasn't Julie crying. These were Sam's tears. Somehow Sam's emotions and her physical response had transferred to Julie.

She took a deep, shuddering breath and stared at her silent, unresponsive sister. She almost expected to see Sam all bandaged, still recovering from her ski accident. But Sam's face was unmarked now, and she slept, quite beautiful, her shiny blond hair picking up the muted light in the room.

Oh, Sam. I always knew you bruised easily, always took things hard, but I never really appreciated, I mean, I never knew *how* hard. God! Is that how I made you feel?

Julie sniffed. The tears had stopped; the aching hurt was fading, but traces of it remained.

Soon I'll be all me again, she thought.

She wiped her eyes one last time and began removing Sam's headgear — she didn't want Eathan to know she'd made another foray into her memoryscape.

She smoothed Sam's hair.

I never meant to hurt you, Sam.

God, I lost patience with you all the time, raged at you, but I never — ever — wanted to cause the kind of pain I just experienced. Never knew I could.

Do they make sisters any colder?

I don't think so.

And yet that wasn't completely fair. If positions had been reversed — if it had been Julie in the bed in New York and Sam on the phone from Europe — it would have made perfect sense to Julie for Sam to say it wasn't necessary for her to make a transatlantic trip when there was so much AB positive–compatible blood available. She'd have understood completely.

But to Sam it was another stab in the back, another brick in the wall.

Julie tried to shrug it off, but couldn't. She'd felt physical sensations: tasted the snow, felt the slope slam against her body.

She rubbed her leg, half expecting to feel the beginnings of a bruise.

Nothing showed, of course.

But now, emotions — someone *else's* emotions. That was scary.

And other disconcerting things as well: the dimming of the Oakwood memory node. Was there ongoing deterioration in Sam's memoryscape?

The door to the room opened. A woman dressed in a starched white dress came in.

"Mademoiselle, voulez-vous un café?"

Julie nodded. *"Oui."* Then remembering the niceties of French etiquette, she quickly added, *"Merci, Madame."*

Remember the niceties, Julie.

She was just about through with the shutdown procedure when the door opened. Julie turned, expecting to see the nurse with a steaming mug of coffee.

But Eathan was there.

"Sorry," he said. "I didn't mean to leave you alone for so long."

Eathan seemed distant, preoccupied. Was something wrong?

On impulse, she decided to tell him.

"I made a quick trip back into Sam's memoryscape."

He stiffened. "Alone? Don't you think —"

"I saw Sam's ski accident . . . from her point of view."

Eathan made a face. They had never

discussed Julie's reaction to her sister's accident. Eathan had never criticized Julie's refusal to come to Sam's side, to donate blood.

"Your sister careens from crisis to crisis." He pulled a chair close to the computer console and sat next to Julie. "That was only broken bones. This is far worse."

The large windows that faced the quiet rue de Bourgogne were now tinged with a filmy light. The full moon was slowly rising in the east.

"I gather you didn't stay in too long."

"No. I . . ." No, she couldn't tell him about the tears. "I just took a quick look."

"And it's still devastated?"

She nodded.

"I guess it's hopeless, eh?"

Julie shook her head. "Not at all. I'm convinced I can learn something."

"But you *didn't* see what happened to Samantha?"

"No. Not even close. Just an old, painful memory . . . about me."

Eathan put a hand on her shoulder. "Julia, one of the calls I made was to Samantha's doctor. I asked him if I could arrange to bring Samantha back to Oak- wood."

Julie shook her head. "What? No — I mean, I want to go on with this."

"I can get Samantha the absolute best

care at the estate. I already have my personal physician lining up a U.K. team of neurological specialists. Though no one feels that there's any chance —"

"But —"

"And it's more than that."

The pasty white top of the moon had slid free of the houses across the street. Now it was a giant light shining in on them. Julie looked at it, and for some reason it chilled her. The moon, she thought. That dopey, dumb, grinning face. Always the same dopey face . . .

She turned back to Eathan.

"I think there may be danger here, Julia. If someone did something to her to cause this . . . Sam could still be in jeopardy. If she knows something and were to come back to consciousness, that could be dangerous. For all of us, but especially her."

"You think this man, this Liam — ?"

Eathan raised a hand. "I don't know. But the roses, the prowler they've spotted — I only know that it would be safer for Samantha if she came back to Oakwood. She'd be out of the country and away from O'Donnell."

Julie hesitated. Oakwood. She remembered hearing the name for the first time as a little girl. After the fire, their uncle had purchased an English estate, a secluded manor on the North Yorkshire coast.

Julie had never liked it there, too big, too many secret places, too isolated —

"I want to come."

Eathan shook his head. "Julia, you have your work. You've seen inside your sister's mind. There's no hope. Let it go."

"I can't."

She saw Eathan make a face. The lopsided grimace of the moon was now fully in the window, watching her plead for this chance.

I don't want to go to Oakwood, she thought. But if Sam's going, then that's what I'll do. She reached out and took Eathan's hand.

"Let me come. As you said, Oakwood is safe, secluded. I can make real progress there."

Eathan looked at her. She tried to fathom what he was thinking. Was it concern for her, or for Sam, or did he lack faith in her new technology? Or would Eathan find what happened to Samantha too painful?

"I don't know, Julia. I —"

"Please. I've never asked for much."

A stinging remark. Leaving out the unsaid words, *Not like Samantha. I haven't been a problem.*

"All right," he said. "You're always welcome, of course. You know that. Call it a homecoming of sorts. Oakwood has been terribly quiet since the two of you left." He stood. "I've arranged for Samantha to be flown out of Orly tomorrow morning. I'll be accompanying her. Should I make arrangements for you?"

Julie shook her head. "I'll see to that. But could you arrange for the satellite dish to be installed before I arrive? I have to see to getting my equipment packed."

"I'll call ahead. If I can't find someone in Bay, I'm sure I can get someone from Leeds."

Julie watched Eathan move to the door. She stood and again grabbed his hand, squeezed it. Eathan squeezed back.

"You two always could talk me into nearly anything."

Julie grinned. "I always knew Sam could."

"Maybe you two are more similar than I thought."

He opened the door.

"Eathan," she said. "Thank you."

And Eathan nodded.

Eleven

Cahill's research indicates that fear or other strong emotions act as memory boosters. The adrenal surge of epinephrine and norepinephrine in a stressful or threatening situation activates the amygdala to stimulate the cortex to give this particular occurrence a prominent place in the memory banks. The adaptive advantage is obvious.
— Random notes: Julia Gordon

1

Julie spent the next day rushing to pack her equipment for overnight delivery. Eathan made all the arrangements with DHL, and the fragile electronics were waiting at the hospital desk for pickup.

Her few clothes were already packed. Her flight was still hours away.

There's time, she thought.

She wanted to see Sam's studio again,

Sam's *real* studio, before she reentered the surreal virtual studio of Sam's mind. She may have missed a clue.

Taking her bag with her, she caught a cab to the 6th Arrondissement, back to the last place Sam was conscious.

2

Madame DuPont, the landlady, recognized Julie and, with one of her Gallic shrugs, let her into the room. The top floor was chilly. A storm was coming in, and the skies over Paris had turned a nasty gray.

The woman stayed at the door for a moment. Then she said, *"Il me faut préparer le dîner. . . ."* It was the dinner hour.

Julie raised a hand. *"Merci, Madame,"* she said. The woman turned and left.

And Julie was alone in the room.

She walked the floor, stepping on the dried splatters of paint, the remnants of Sam's last work. This had been Sam's world. Now it was an empty, shadowy space, keeping its secrets.

Julie looked around. The fresh colors on the floor were a bright orange and a dark, blackish blue.

Julie pondered the paintings, wondering if there was an order to them. Did they get progressively darker, the images more bent and twisted?

She stopped before one that showed a deformed face as though distorted by a fun-house mirror. The mouth hung open in a frozen scream. A disturbing work, and it gave her the creeps to be standing here alone with it.

She bent closer, looking at the open mouth . . .

And spotted a detail she hadn't noticed. Inside the mouth, at the back of the tongue, were tiny figures, a family sitting in a quaint 1960s living room. A mother, a father, two children — two girls. The father was carving a roast. Julie leaned closer. No, not a roast . . .

She jerked back.

. . . a human hand.

I'm so dense, she thought.

She'd looked at this painting on her first visit, but hadn't seen this. A severed hand. She'd seen one in the memoryscape. Twice now. It must mean something to Sam . . . but what?

What else am I missing?

I wish . . . I wish the missing painting were here.

She moved on, retracing Sam's memory of coming into this studio with Liam. Reality and memory, the line was becoming blurred.

A floorboard creaked behind her.

She turned.

A girl stood there, ten or eleven years old, watching her. Mme. DuPont's daughter. She snapped her gum.

Julie stumbled to say something in French. "Er, *qu'est ce —*"

"Mama says you are Mademoiselle Samantha's sister."

The girl's English was perfect, with just a delightful hint of an accent.

"Yes. I was. I mean, I am —"

"She's not better?"

"No. Not better. But she's going . . . home." The word didn't come easy. Was Oakwood home anymore?

The girl took a step into the studio. "That's good. Because I think —" She looked out into the dark hallway. "Because I think that the man might come back."

A chill trickled down Julie's spine like a bead of ice water. She thought of the roses, and the prowler the Sainte Gabrielle staff had seen near Samantha's window. This is real, she thought. I'm not in my sister's head now. This girl is standing here, telling me —

"It was raining. And the man, he came wearing a hat and an overcoat. I told Mama —"

"Yes?" Julie said gently.

"I told her that I couldn't see his face.

167

But after he left, I knew something had happened."

"Do you think it was her boyfriend?"

"I do not know. I liked your sister. She was nice. She always gave me gum. She —"

"Cecile!"

A voice yelled from below, the landlady summoning her daughter. *"Cecile, viens ici!"*

A stranger, Julie thought, but the child didn't see the face. Just a figure in a coat, a hat. Still, Julie should make sure that the French police came and spoke to Cecile.

And maybe it wasn't such a good idea to stay here, alone.

She took one last look around the room and left.

3

Julie had to race to Orly Airport.

A particularly nasty thunderstorm hit Paris at the peak of rush hour, slowing traffic to a crawl. She kept checking her watch. She gripped the back of the cabbie's seat as if she could urge the driver to find some magical shortcut.

The driver whistled and happily chewed on a sausage, oblivious to the precious minutes slipping away.

But once out of the center of the city,

traffic finally began to flow. Julie sat back, telling herself to accept her fate if she missed the plane.

More mayhem at the airport as the wind whipped the rain sideways, creating giant puddles.

Julie handed the driver a stack of franc notes and dashed out into the maelstrom with her bag held tight. She thought of her hardware, all padded and crated, and hoped it was protected from the storm.

The British Airways counter line curled back and forth a dozen times. Julie looked up to the monitor and saw that her departure was "On Schedule."

Why was there never a delay when you needed one?

She ran over to the customer service desk and showed her ticket to an airline representative; the woman immediately saw the urgency and brought Julie to a side desk. In minutes Julie was easing into her coach seat on the near-empty flight to Manchester.

Shortly after takeoff, she dozed, thinking of Oakwood.

She never could bring herself to describe the old stone manor as "home." No, home was the place that burned in upstate New York, a place she and Sam never would return to. In her mind that house was in eternal flames, her father bravely rescuing her and Sam, setting them on the grass, saying "Stay here. I'm going back for your mother," then rushing back into the fire.

Never to return.

That was home.

Oakwood was always something else, a strange old place; protective, almost castlelike, filled with halls and hiding places.

But never home.

Julie closed her eyes. And slipped into a dream . . .

. . . of another rainy night, with terrible thunder outside and the brilliant lightning flashing long shadows onto the carpeted floor of the great library of Oakwood, filled with fine leather-bound books and over-stuffed chairs.

She was playing hide-and-seek with Sam, calling out for the sister who always hid too well. Sam knew secret places.

Julie crept up the stairs and walked down the long hallway, calling Sam's name.

Until she came to a room.

A locked room.

Like in a fairy tale. You may enter any room, save one. This *one* room you must not enter.

Like Beauty and the Beast.

She touched the door. Uncle Eathan's study. He kept all his private papers in there. He didn't want his nieces playing in such an important room.

Only now, the always-locked door *opened.* The click of the turning handle was deafening.

And inside, she saw Samantha at their uncle's desk.

Trying to open a drawer.

"I — I found you," Julie said.

The game was over, hide-and-seek ended. But Sam shook her head. *That* game had ended.

Sam's face . . . so grim, so determined.

Through the library windows came a blinding flash of light, followed by a floor-shaking crash of thunder. Julie closed her eyes. She covered her ears . . .

. . . and woke up.

I don't dream, she thought. God — I can't remember the last time I dreamed. What could have made me dream? And why about Eathan's office?

Or maybe it wasn't a dream. Perhaps it was a memory. But Julie couldn't remember that incident. Did it ever happen? Or had she carried it back from Sam?

Now *there* was an unsettling thought.

Then the plane rocked, a jittery rattle more appropriate to a heap of a car coughing out its last gasp. Then another sickening bounce.

Julie heard a discreet chime above the rattle as the seat-belt light came on.

Only turbulence, she thought.

Her modus operandi when flying was to ignore any potential threat to the flight: rain, snow, storms, whatever. The only way to fly: You go up and you come down. That was all she needed to know. Statistics were on her side.

Another rattle. Somewhere a baby started wailing. Julie heard the pilot's voice through her headset, the English accent calm, reassuring.

"Folks, er, we appear to have hit a bit of that storm front. Not much we can do about it, I'm afraid, since it's with us all the way to —"

Another rattle, worse than before. Julie saw a flash at the window. *Was that a lightning bolt out there? We're smack in the middle of the damn storm system.*

She shifted in her seat, grabbed an arm-rest. The portly executive sitting next to her was as perfectly upright as he could be, as if he could somehow guide the plane that way. His bulbous eyes were locked on the back of the seat in front of him.

Julie didn't like this.

She liked to think she was in control of her life. But in a plane you were an egg in a flying carton. And you never get to see who's carrying the eggs.

". . . all the way to Manchester," the pilot continued. "We'll try to find some quiet altitude but I think we're in for a bumpy flight. So please stay in your seats —"

An even brighter flash lit the window.

Julie heard the gasps and "ooh"s of the passengers as they saw the lightning.

The baby was crying louder now.

The reassuring pilot's voice had disappeared.

The plane tilted right. We're just hitting a thermal, Julie told herself. We're a little speedboat bobbing up and down on the choppy surf. That's all that's happening.

But the more she struggled to fight back the uneasiness, the stronger it became, feeding on the brilliant flashes at the window, growing with the lurches left and right. Julie now had a sickening, giddy, weightless feeling each time the plane dipped.

A dozen call lights were on, people searching for a stewardess or the lone male steward.

But they weren't around.

The plane tilted sharply left — *whee* — and some passengers moaned. They were getting their money's worth.

And Julie, as much as she tried to avoid it, was forced to think of what . . . mattered to her.

If I die now, what would be lost?

Who'd miss me? Dr. S.? Yes, he'd be very sad.

And Eathan. Julie never questioned his love.

How about Sam? Well, even if her twin were functioning, no real loss for Sam.

That kind of love had never existed between them.

The plane went up another invisible roller-coaster hill, then down.

No, the real loss for Julie would be that she never would find out what happened to Samantha.

"Shit," she whispered. She felt the fleshy businessman looking at her, his bulbous eyes fixed in their horror.

If she was going to put up with this bouncing, heaving crap, the least the flight crew could do was hand out those nifty little bottles of Glenfiddich.

She grinned at her gallows humor.

Would the staff at the memoryscape project miss her? Not right away, maybe, but after a week or two . . .

Would Dr. S. be able to land the Bruchmeyer grant without her? Good question.

She closed her eyes, and in the rattling freight car of the plane's cabin, she waited for the landing, or whatever the hell fate was going to throw at her.

It seemed like an eternity, but twenty minutes later the plane touched down, miraculously, out of the rainy England night sky onto a slick-black runway.

People walked off on wobbly legs to waiting relatives and faceless taxi drivers.

Julie wasn't going far. She'd made arrangements to sleep at the local Hilton. She'd rented a Ford Fiesta at the airport for the next day's drive to Oakwood.

She was so glad she didn't have to face that tonight.

And glad too that the hotel room had a well-stocked minibar.

But despite a couple of stiff scotches, sleep wouldn't come.

Just as well. She didn't want to dream again.

Twelve

The ultimate horror, I think, would be having no memories and no ability to form them. You'd have no past, no data to use as reference points. You wouldn't know who you were, where you were, or why you were there. You'd have no sense of time because that requires memory of a previous event. You'd be a person without a past, without a future, lacking even rudimentary self-aware-ness, existing only in the moment in an endlessly alien environment peopled entirely with strangers.
— Random notes: Julia Gordon

1

A crisp, blue October sky domed the morning — about as un-British as Julie could imagine. The countryside seemed alive with the pulse-quickening chill of fall.

Cramped in her Fiesta, Julie headed east,

aiming for the North Sea through the heart of Yorkshire. She felt pangs of nostalgia as she passed giant, empty fields of recently cut corn and rape, and bundles of harvested hay, ancient signs of people preparing for winter. Sheep and cattle dotted the rolling hills. And then she was flying through Fylingdales Moor, its heather all dry and brown now, but she remembered Augusts when it was alive with mauve blossoms as far as the eye could see.

Oakwood stood on a high sea cliff between Whitby and Scarborough. The elegant gentleman's estate was testimony to Eathan's financial acumen. He'd taken the keen mind that had made him such an excellent diagnostician and applied it to the financial markets with enviable success. His professorship at Edinburgh University was for the soul rather than for sustenance.

Picturesque Robin Hood's Bay was nearby, though its charm was lost on Julie . . . a bit too determinedly quaint for her taste. She remembered when Sam threw a tantrum in the dining room of the Bay Hotel and had to be carried out by an embarrassed Uncle Eathan.

Then she had a thought about Sam. She was getting ideas about what she wanted to do once she went back inside her sister's memoryscape.

She picked up her micro tape recorder.

177

"Keep watching for fever . . . maybe get some more blood work done." She clicked the Off button. She had an idea, not something to put a lot of faith in, but there was the possibility that Samantha had picked up some kind of unknown slow virus that attacked the brain's reticular activating system. If that was the case, other symptoms might manifest themselves soon.

If Sam's problem was due to infection instead of trauma or toxin, she'd find no meaning in the chaos of the memoryscape — no hidden memories, no traumatic secrets.

She doubted that was the case, but it was worth a check.

She drove a few more miles, then she scooped up the recorder again.

"Ask Eathan to contact the Paris police. . . . Have them talk to Madame DuPont's daughter."

The girl had said she hadn't seen what the man looked like, but maybe something might come back to her. Memory could be funny that way.

The road grew narrower, barely two lanes now as Julie passed through Robin Hood's Bay — just "Bay" to the locals — with its stone and brick houses stacked higgledy-piggledy along the cliff edge. Oakwood wasn't far.

The ideas, the memos, stopped.

Strange to be coming home like this . . .

To a place that had never felt like home.

Trees lined the long, winding lane that left the road and climbed to where Oakwood crouched near the cliffs overlooking the North Sea. The lane swerved left and right, each time providing a glimpse of the manor through the trees.

The trees had always seemed like a fence when she was a little girl, a wall sealing them off from the rest of the world.

And here we are again.

Then the trees ended and the house hove into view: a large, very straightforward Georgian manor, a rectangular block of a building, built of dressed stone laid in a herringbone pattern.

Julie instinctively looked left, to the sunken gardens, once a favored place to play. The luxuriant flowers and herbs there were Eathan's pride and joy. Sam especially had taken pleasure in playing there, paying no attention to Eathan's warnings to watch out for *this* flower, don't step on *that* delicate plant.

Always too tolerant of her.

A small circular driveway curved in front of the house, then wound around to a parking area in the back near the toolshed and garage. But since Julie felt like a guest, she pulled to a stop in front of the house, grabbed her small bag, and got out.

Was anyone here? Sam already should be settled inside, silent and immobile, unaware that her mind, her memories, were a South Bronx of the cerebrum. Where was Eathan? Over by his flowers, planting bulbs for next spring?

"Julia."

The voice from behind startled her.

She turned and saw Eathan striding toward her.

He was dressed in the relaxed garb of a country squire, all tweed and expensive leather boots. Every time they'd spoken since she left for the States, he'd asked her to come and visit. *Do the holidays at Oakwood, spend some summer vacation there.* She always found an excuse to put him off.

Now she was here.

She shifted the bag in her hand. "I'd forgotten how beautiful it was."

Eathan turned and looked around at the house. "Oakwood? I haven't done much inside, of course. Kept it clean. Kept your rooms pretty much as they were."

Eathan had never married. The very idea of her uncle Eathan married seemed strange. He was perhaps the most self-sufficient of men. No room for a woman in this picture.

But that was before she had left. Had things changed?

He reached out and took her bag, and

started walking toward the house.

"Is Sam — ?"

"Yes, I had an ambulance bring her here yesterday afternoon. She's in her old bedroom. Dr. Evans thinks it best she be in familiar surroundings."

"Who's Dr. Evans?"

"Samantha's psychiatrist."

"Psychiatrist? I didn't know —"

"You'll learn all about it later. I had to move some things out of Samantha's room to make space for the monitoring equipment. I hired a trio of nurses who are rotating coverage, plus physical therapists . . . all very good people."

Julie nodded. They were on the steps that led to the giant oak doors.

"I'd like to start right away," she said. "I thought I saw some further deterioration before we left. I'd hate to think that's continuing."

"Yes. Well, anything you want I'll arrange for. Oh — I've already had the satellite dish installed on the roof, and they tell me our present phone line will handle the — what's it called?"

"Modem?"

Eathan smiled. "Right. A modem."

Julie knew he preferred old-fashioned forms of communication. Her descriptions of the wonders of the Internet had always fallen on politely deaf ears.

"Anyway, the lines are all set. You should be able to connect to your Dr. Siegal in New York."

Eathan pushed open the front door. Julie entered the foyer, all polished wood — the oak from which the manor took its name — and saw the staircase leading to the second floor. It still seemed terribly large.

She thought of the scene she'd relived in Sam's memoryscape, the two of them playing right here. And she remembered that the memory had been altered. Why had the nonexistent Perseus sculpture been substituted for the real-life microscope? It bothered her that she couldn't find an answer.

"Would you like to freshen up, perhaps some lunch?"

Julie smiled at Eathan. She saw his concern for her, always worried that she didn't get enough rest, that she didn't eat enough food.

She shook her head. "No. Let me get started."

"Very well. I'll put your bag in your old room. You know where Samantha's room is. The nurse is there. . . ."

Julie reached out and touched Eathan's arm. "Thanks. I'll be fine."

Julie walked up the great carpeted staircase, her hand trailing on the smooth grooves of the walnut handrail. She knew those grooves, remembered chasing Sam up and down these stairs countless times.

Ten years since she'd lived here, and with each step, more memories of her childhood seeped from the walls and stalked her all the way to her room.

2

Her bedroom looked more like a guest room. She'd pretty much cleaned it out when she moved to the States, leaving no sign that anyone had grown up here. As she dropped her bags next to the bed she realized she was hungry after all.

Downstairs in the large, anachronistically modern kitchen she found some sliced turkey and Diet Coke in the fridge. The cook, an apple-cheeked matron with a warm, friendly smile, came in and insisted on making her a turkey sandwich on heavy whole-wheat bread from the bakery in Bay. She remembered this bread, dark, heavy, a meal by itself. She wolfed it down and headed for Sam's room.

On the way she stopped off in the library. It looked much the same as it had during her school days when she used to come here to check out something in the encyclopedia. Smelled the same too — that rich mixture of old paper in good leather bindings. She inhaled and sighed. This had always been her favorite place, with its bookshelves stretching all the way up to the ceiling, crammed with tomes of all shapes, colors, sizes, and bindings. The old *Britannica* set still occupied its spot on the shelves immediately to the right. Julie moved to her left, found the library's book on Greek mythology, and looked up Perseus.

A pretty busy fellow in his day, it seemed, but Perseus's major accomplishment was killing Medusa, the snake-haired horror whose visage turned men to stone. He did it by not looking directly at her, but watching her in the polished surface of his shield as he walked backward. To fool Medusa about his backward approach, he'd worn a mask on the back of his head.

Right. The Perseus sculpture Samantha broke in the memoryscape had some sort of face on the back of its helmet.

Whatever, the trick worked: Perseus got close enough to cut off Medusa's head.

But why was Perseus substituted for the microscope in Sam's memory? What was the point? The mask? The shield mirror? Looking backward? *Not* looking backward?

Was there a point?

Frustrated, Julie jammed the book back into its slot on the shelf and went upstairs to Sam's bedroom.

She stopped on the threshold. White curtains were drawn against the morning light.

A woman in a starched nurse's uniform swiveled in her chair, her reading glasses perched precariously on her nose. She started at the sight of her, glanced quickly at her patient, then back to Julie.

Yeah, we're twins.

Julie raised a hand to the nurse, indicating that there was no need to get up.

Sam's room — but different.

Toward the end, before she ran off to Europe, Sam had started filling her walls with art, her own bizarre sketches and strange drawings from the other students at art school, along with garish images ripped from punk-rock magazines, all haphazardly taped to the wall.

Most of them were gone. This wasn't Sam's room anymore.

Only one painting remained on the wall now, something Sam did when she was young. A country house in a meadow, sitting under a perfect blue sky. Unusual for Sam's work, even at that early age. The only giveaway that Sam did the painting was the windows in the house. They were all black, dark ugly smudges dotting the carefully rendered clapboard.

Julie's eyes always were drawn to those black holes, to the secrets inside the house.

The nurse was still looking up.

"Miss, would you like a few minutes alone?"

She had a thick Manchester accent; she spoke in a hushed tone as if this were a wake.

Which it may very well be, thought Julie.

Julie shook her head. "No, thank you."

She walked around the bed to the make-shift computer table holding her equipment. Everything looked in good order. She'd have to check the connections, of course, then do some tests to see if the satellite link was operational.

She flicked a switch. The computer beeped, and ran through its diagnostic check.

She looked at Sam, half expecting her to react to the noise.

But she lay there, immobile. Her skin smooth, her face relaxed, giving no hint of the chaos within. She looked free. At peace.

Julie looked around for another chair and saw an oak straight-back against the wall. Sam used to sit in it and pretend to do homework, all the while filling sketchbook after sketchbook.

Julie pulled the chair to the console and sat down.

3

It took most of the afternoon to initialize the system and set up the protocols with the satellite link.

When everything was up and running, she asked the nurse to call Eathan into the room.

"I think I'm all ready," she said when he arrived.

"You're going in *now?* Can't you wait until after dinner?"

Julie shook her head. "No. Time is important, I think. I told you, I'm concerned about progressive deterioration. Besides, Dr. Siegal is on-line and waiting. Is something wrong?"

"I have to go to Leeds, to pick up someone at the airport."

She turned. "Really? Who?"

"Someone who may help. Someone who you'll want to meet. But that's *my* secret until dinner."

She smiled. "Thanks for letting me do this. I know you don't agree. . . ."

Eathan raised a finger.

"Just be careful."

"Not to worry. Dr. Siegal will be monitoring me all the way."

This time, anyway.

"The wonders of modern technology. Oh — what about the nurse?"

"She'd better wait outside. What I'm doing is about as deep an invasion as one can make. I'd like to show some respect for Sam's privacy."

"Consider it done."

As Eathan and the nurse left, Julie donned her helmet, then slipped the data glove onto her right hand.

She opened and shut the fingers, double-checking that her guide, the glove, was in good working condition.

She spoke softly. "Okay, Sam — let's see what you've been up to while I was away."

Julie used the glove to press icons on the screen, initializing the programs, establishing the link, checking the feedback system. A green light at the bottom told her that the feed was going out to Dr. S.

"Here we go," Julie said.

She leaned forward; it had been days since her last visit. She licked her dry lips. Would there be anything left?

Thirteen

Memories die. If the brain loses synaptic connections to a memory, it's gone forever — the event cannot be reconstructed by the brain's convergence systems, at least not without help.
— Random notes: Julia Gordon

You see it immediately.

It's different.

Sam's memoryscape is even more of a disaster zone, more of a post-apocalyptic nightmare. There's been change, deterioration.

You recognize the nodes that you visited previously, barely glowing in the deepening gloom. The dollhouse estate appears to be sinking into the scorched surface of the 'scape as though it were quicksand, taking its childhood memories with it.

Some of the glowing mounds you saw on the horizon during your first visit have disappeared completely, and the remaining others are like scattered blooms in the desert.

This is bad. If you had any doubts about the progressive deterioration of Sam's memoryscape, this confirms them. Her mind — her life, her *self* — are disappearing before your eyes.

But wait . . . the studio is still glowing. Have the paintings within changed? The studio is key, you're convinced of it.

But you keep turning, farther to your right. And there on the horizon, something still glows, pulsating with life. Excitement bubbles within you as you point the glove and sail toward it.

Along the way, you notice a white ball — glaringly white — rolling along the ground on a path diagonal to yours. Your paths will intersect ahead. You look beyond it for someplace from which it could have sprung but you see nothing, no one. It appears to be moving under its own power. You pause, waiting for it to come within reach, and when it does, you touch it. The ball stops. Its glowing white surface shimmers as a seam forms along its equator. It splits open and the northern hemisphere flips back, revealing its contents.

A cube, as black as the charred surface of the 'scape. You touch it and it splits open, revealing another glaringly white sphere. You touch the sphere and nothing happens. Nothing else nests within.

Another crazy matrioshka doll. First Sam in Julie in Sam, now this. Is there a reason for only three nested dolls? God, is it important? And why are two of the dolls always the same? What does it mean?

Your growing frustration tempts you to boot the whole mess across the memoryscape. But before you can do anything, the black cube snaps closed on the smaller sphere, and the outer sphere closes over the cube. The ball begins rolling again, rolling away, origin and destination unknown.

You watch it for a moment, then continue on toward the pulsating light. As you near it you see a vast plain. Odd figures stand here and there, a man on his knees, a girl holding a bird skeleton in her hands. A multicolored cube swirls, oozing color as though alive.

The figures cast long, black shadows . . . and now you remember seeing this painting. You laugh. You *know* this strange place. It's a Salvador Dali, one of his whimsical surreal landscapes: *The First Days of Spring*. You prefer his earlier, more realistic work. This is dumb. But to Sam this was a disturbing painting, sad, overwhelming. You didn't get it.

So much about art you never got. All those extra courses you took in Saint Martha's School, determined to show Sam you could be as artsy-fartsy as she. All it took was a little effort.

Not. Even with a lot of effort, you never *got* it. But you have an excellent memory. You can see a painting and name the artist, the work, and even the year it was painted. But as to what it means or what it does for you?

Usually nothing.

But now to *enter* the painting, to see the figures move, the shadows stretch to the horizon, the colors pulsate . . . it's wonderful. Incredibly beautiful.

And then you see something else. A new structure, not in the painting.

A house.

You stop. Something terribly familiar about that house.

You don't move any closer. You want an answer first. *Whose house is it?*

You look down at the ribbon bar showing Sam's respiration and pulse. Both have picked up. Because you're here? Or because — ?

The house. You know what it is now. It's the house in Putnam County, in Millburn. *Your* house — before the fire, before it burned and took your mother and father away.

A pang of loss hits you like a blow, surprising you. Funny, you thought you were over that.

You hesitate.

You've pictured the house before, even thought about it, but always in flames. Always with the fire in the basement racing to the first floor, quickly dancing up to the roof. Always with your father rushing back in, running, hurrying to save your mother.

You never imagine the house like this: peaceful and intact, small and inviting, with a front porch with an old-fashioned glider, the clapboard siding painted eggshell white with rose trim.

They're in there, you think.

Your mother, your father, captured by Sam's memory, looking the way they did.

Still, you don't move. It's too much for you.

And yet, how can you turn away? How can you *not* go in?

You point your glove at the old Victorian house and begin to glide toward it, up to the front door. It opens and . . .

. . . the smells waft around you — the rich, sharp tang of the crackling fireplace competing with the aroma of the dinner in the oven, a roast of some kind. The light-bedizened balsam in the corner adds a pine scent to the mix.

A man comes out of the kitchen. Dark hair, thick, dark mustache, and piercing eyes.

Daddy.

The word, the concept, so ancient, so primal. Your heart stops. Time stops. You want to run to him, throw your arms around him, but you can't. You're not here. You're Scrooge and this is Christmas Past. You can only watch.

You watch Daddy stop at the fireplace and stare at it. He crouches and grabs a poker. He jabs at the wood, stabbing it, forcing it to burn hotter, brighter.

Little Julie and Sammi are crouching too, huddled together on the stairs. So small, just past toddler age, two girls in matching Dr.

Denton's. No way to tell them apart, no way to keep them apart. They heard the shouting and have come down to see.

Someone else comes out of the kitchen, wiping her hands on a flowered apron. It's Mom. Her blond hair in a Brady Bunch shag, and her smile so fragile, as if ready to crumble at any second. Except when she looks at you.

Mom . . . as if it were yesterday.

"Nathan," she says. "Nathan, we have to talk."

Daddy continues his assault on the wood, unable to leave the fireplace, to turn to the woman.

Finally, he stands up, slowly leaning the poker against the red brick hearth.

"And what exactly did you want to talk about?"

Mom comes closer. Another wipe of the hands on the apron. Struggling to clean them, to make the stain go away.

"Nathan, what I said, I didn't mean."

"Oh, you didn't? That wasn't what you meant? Why the hell *else* would you say something like that?"

Mom doesn't move. She stands her ground. She shakes her head. "Because we have no *life*. You and your work, this obsession with your theories. You're never here. And when you are . . ." She glances toward the stairs and sees the two forms crouched there. "Never mind."

"No, Lucy, I won't 'never mind.' I care more about our family than you can imagine." He takes a step toward his wife. "But who do *you* care about? Who do *you* love?"

Why is he asking her that? And like that?

Mom shakes her head. She looks like she's about to cry. The two girls are frozen on the stairs, an audience watching everything, understanding none of it.

"I — I —"

Another step, and he's in her face, yelling. "Answer me! Who the hell do *you* love? Who the hell do *you* care about?"

And Mom turns away — except she turns slowly — like a wind-up ballerina. Her gaze falls on the two girls.

There's an answer there. Through the yelling, the jumble of smells and emotions . . . an answer.

And then a knock on the door. Ignoring it, Daddy turns back to the fire and stabs at the logs again. Mommy hesitates, then goes to the door and opens it.

It's Uncle Eathan, looking incredibly *young*, with longer hair and a much fuller beard than he wears now. The girls are so glad to see him. Even Mommy forces a smile.

"What's up, doc?" she says.

You pull back. Too abruptly, and you're out of the house. No door slams behind you.

Did the memory end, or was there more to see?

The feelings overwhelm you. And you think: I don't get overwhelmed by feelings. Christ, that's not *me*. And then there's a more important question: What is this memory doing here?

At least some part of the memoryscape is alive and you should be glad about that.

But it's starting to feel like a minefield. And you've got so many unanswered questions.

You click on the Window button and a few seconds later Dr. Siegal appears.

"Yes, Julie? Ready to come out?"

"Not yet."

Can there be anything this compelling in the real world? you think. It's like a drug. I can't pull away.

"That was a pretty tense scene. Was your father always so ill-tempered?"

Instantly you resent the implication.

"Frankly, I don't know if that was real."

"You were present in the memory as a child."

"But I don't remember that scene. I don't remember my parents fighting, or my dad having a temper like that."

"You were awfully young. Perhaps that memory is gone."

"But not for Sam. And she was just as young."

"Different people retain different memories."

"But why am I encountering these memories? Is it a random process? Or have these particular memories surfaced for a reason? And if so, what's behind them?"

"Not what," Dr. Siegal says. *"Who. Who could it be but your sister?"*

You think he might be onto something.

"Could some residue of Sam's consciousness — or maybe her subconscious — have forced these memories to the surface?" The thought jolts you, excites you. "Good God — is Sam trying to tell me something?"

"That sounds a little far-fetched, Julie," he says, ever the conservative theoretician. *"But it might indicate that there could be more than one level to Sam's memoryscape."*

Your excitement grows. Multiple levels to the memoryscape — it's not a new concept, but you've never seen evidence of it in anyone else's 'scape. It's not impossible. These memories struggling to stay alive could be mere tracers, telltales of the real secrets buried deeper, perhaps levels down in this construct of Sam's mind.

Lord, what do *those* levels look like?

"Thanks," you say. "I'm going to keep looking."

You float higher, searching. The scorched bleakness of the 'scape is relieved only by the dim glow of a half-dozen nodes.

"Your sister's memoryscape appears to be collapsing. You have to find a way to get to the deeper levels."

"Right. But how? Dig a hole?"

197

"No. Look for a portal, maybe a common nexus point for all the levels."

You drift past the sinking Oakwood to the cliffs overlooking the sea.

A flash of white in the water.

"Did you see that?"

Then another flash near the dark shore below.

Maybe it's another piece of the message from Sam.

"I'm going to take a look."

You click the window shut and drop down the hundred or so feet to something that looks like a boat floating in the dark sea. A giddy white froth of waves churning. The rise and fall of a choppy ocean.

No, not a boat. Now you see that it's a bed. With two people in it. Sam and Liam, rolling on the sheets, laughing, naked.

You turn away. You shouldn't be here. This is too much of an invasion of Sam's privacy. And you're not alone here. Dr. Siegal is watching. And there's a videotape running. Other people will see this.

But that will only matter to Sam if she comes out of this. And she won't come out of this unless . . .

You raise your hand and pull yourself closer, floating toward the bed, floating right over it and —

Sam laughs, running her fingers through

Liam's red hair.

"Now, why don't you tell me who you really are."

He laughs too, but then he looks at the ceiling.

"And haven't I been telling you?" he says. "I'm here representing a bloody Irish import-export company." He turns back to Sam, a warm, disarming smile on his face.

But Sam doesn't believe him. No, she believes what her flamboyant friend Edmund, owner of the Galeries Nouveau, told her.

He's very bad news, Samantha, though I certainly see why you like him. But I'm sure, even after the IRA cease-fire, he's still a criminal. Don't even think about playing with him.

But that's what makes this so attractive. And besides, she loves his brogue.

Slowly she lets her hand wander down Liam's chest, playing with the curly hair. Liam is old enough to have a wife and kids somewhere. Probably does. And that doesn't bother Sam at all.

"I should go. . . ." he says gently.

Sam shakes her head. "No. I don't want you to."

Now his hand, a big rough hand, a strong, perhaps dangerous hand, reaches out and caresses her. It trails haphazardly over her breasts. Such big hands, playing so gently, toying with her.

"I have work to do in the morning," he says.

"You have no work." She laughs. "No *real* work." And then she's serious. "Can you pick a lock?"

His offended look is exaggerated. "You wouldn't be calling me a thief now, would you?"

"No. I just want to know if you know how to pick a lock."

"And why would you be wanting to know such a thing?"

"Maybe I have a lock that needs picking."

He glances around the studio. "Here?"

"No . . . in England. In my uncle's house."

"The uncle who's always looking after you? He already gives you everything. Why would you be wanting to steal from him?"

"My uncle's hiding something."

Liam looks at the ceiling again. "I'm waiting for the day I meet someone who's not."

"He's hiding lots of things, I think. And I know just where he's hiding them. There's a huge locked wall cabinet in his study. If you could get it open for me —"

His grin is tight. "I could get it open for sure, but not by picking."

"Super! Next time he's away, we'll fly over and —"

"Oh, no, we won't. I'll not be flying to Merry Olde anytime soon."

Samantha rolls on top of him, drawing up her knees beside his chest. She reaches down and grabs his wrists, playing at imprisoning him.

"Yes, you will. I'll make you."

"You think you can?"

She bends down and kisses him hard, punishingly.

"Wait and see," she whispers.

Then another kiss, gentler now, trying to rekindle the fire. Feeling him grow hard, she loses herself in those kisses, until he kisses back and she can release his wrists.

His arms encircle her and hold her tight. He pulls her close until her breasts press against his chest.

And slowly, Sam straightens out, sliding her legs beside Liam, feeling him ready.

"But if you have something better to do . . ." she says, mischievously. "Then . . . go. . . ."

Liam answers by turning her over. In one smooth move he rolls her onto her back. Now it is her wrists that are pinned. A fierce glow lights Liam's eyes.

Samantha wets her lips, watching Liam lower his head, arching her back as he starts licking her. . . .

You wet your own lips.
They feel full, rubbery. As if —
And there's more. Christ, you feel your nip-

ples harden — as if you were standing in a draft after a shower. You're chilled, then there's a warmth.

You take a breath. Another.

You're responding to what's happening here.

You're there, inside Samantha's mind, inside her body, sharing the feelings washing over her. In other nodes you've shared her physical pain, and even her emotional pain. But this goes further. Your body is reacting; you're having a physiological response to what's happening in the memory.

You should leave. Yes, you know you should leave . . . but God it feels good. You shift in your recliner, the warmth spreading. . . . So good . . .

Samantha reaches down and imprisons Liam's head between her thighs, locking it in place with her hands. "Yessss," she says. Then louder.

She moans. The sounds could be cries of pain, the cries of a little girl who scraped her knee and came to Daddy for help.

Except this is bliss. It makes everything else go away. There is no room, no studio filled with paintings that surround the bed. No dark canvases that won't let Sam go.

Liam comes up and now he's a machine as he kisses her mouth, her eyes, while he enters her and begins a steady, forceful rock.

The kisses continue while the dance drives everything away. It's wonderful. It's oblivion. It's heat. The burning of the two bodies, growing sweaty, almost desperate.

Then there's something else in the bed.

Fire. The bed in flames. The white sheets turn orange and red.

Samantha's eyes open.

She looks up at Liam.

He smiles cruelly as if this was a plan, to trap her body, to consume her with heat and flames.

He speaks, and somehow it soothes her.

"Now," he says to her, the rocking accelerating, the flames somehow magically receding. Another kiss, and he whispers in her ear.

"Now!"

Now.

The word is a trigger. You feel as if you're in a dark, locked room with a heavy wooden door. The room is on fire and you're standing at its center. The word echoes in that room, and somehow that door clicks open.

And water rushes in, a tidal wave that knocks you down but doesn't extinguish the fire.

It pushes you around the room, swirling into

a whirlpool that catches you and spins you, dragging you down.

Now.

The word is stunning in its simplicity, its directness. Not later, not yesterday, not tomorrow when you can, when it might be convenient. But right here, right now.

You breathe out, and you gasp as waves of pleasure shudder through your body. You've no control at this moment. There is nothing but the pleasure, intense, fierce, all-encompassing.

Your back is arched, your eyes are shut, your ears are roaring, your teeth are clenched to keep from screaming. But a little moan struggles free.

A chime reaches you as the roaring fades and your muscles relax.

You open your eyes and see the Window button blinking. You reach out a shaky hand and click it. Dr. Siegal drops down.

"Julie — are you all right?"

"Yes." You struggle to clear the hoarseness from your voice. "I'm fine."

"Then what — ?"

"I'm exiting the 'scape now."

You click the window closed and hit the Exit button. Before the screen fades to blue you see the bed — empty.

It looks like a still life, you think.

You feel loss, emptiness. You know what just happened to you, and you don't know how to

respond, what to think.
Sam is gone.
Liam is gone. The bed remains.
An empty boat on a dark and empty sea.

Fourteen

We don't realize how fragile memories are. Memories decay if they're not accessed regularly. We've got a finite number of neurons in our brains, so older memories get shunted around to make space for the constant flow of new ones.

— Random notes: Julia Gordon

Julie pulled off the headset and quickly glanced around.

Alone. Eathan hadn't returned. No one had seen her. Thank God.

She slumped back in the recliner and closed her eyes, drew a deep, shuddering breath. She was weak, she was damp.

My God! My . . . God!

So that's what it's like!

Now Julie knew why Sam had always been so hot for the boys. How different her own attitude — hell, her whole life — might be if she could respond like that.

She stared at her sister. Sleeping Beauty was still breathing softly, her cardiac moni-

206

tor ticking along at a steady seventy-two beats a minute. No sign that she'd relived the moment Julie had just experienced.

But as Julie's own racing heart slowed, as her jumbled thoughts reorganized, Sam's pillow talk came back to her.

My uncle's hiding something.

What was that supposed to mean? Hiding what?

A beep from the monitor made her jump. The camera icon blinked insistently from the blank screen. Dr. S. wanted to talk.

Talk was the last thing she wanted to do right now. She just wanted to close her eyes and luxuriate in this strange, peaceful feeling.

Another beep.

"Okay, okay." She found the mouse and clicked the icon. Dr. Siegal's face appeared.

"Julie? Are you there?"

"Yes, Dr. S. I'm here."

"Are you all right? You quit the memoryscape so abruptly."

"It was time to go, don't you think? I mean, that was an intimate moment."

"You didn't have to stay in that particular node. You could have gone elsewhere in the memoryscape. Julie . . ." His eyes narrowed as if he were staring at her through the screen. "Is there something you're not telling me?"

Thank God the video ran only one way.

She felt the warmth of her flushed cheeks. One look at her and he'd know.

But she had to come up with a plausible answer. Probably the best tack was a little righteous indignation. She found it easy to sound angry.

"It disturbed me to see my sister screwing the man who might be responsible for her present condition. All right? Is that up close and personal enough for you?"

"I — I'm sorry, Julie," he said. "I didn't mean —"

"I know you didn't," she said, softly this time. "It's just . . . can we talk about this later?"

"Of course. I'll be here."

"Fine. I'll get back to you."

She broke the connection and his face faded. She felt like a rat for jumping ugly like that, but she couldn't risk a lengthy discussion with him now. And she couldn't risk too many more sessions in Sam's memoryscape with Dr. S. looking over her shoulder. Sooner or later he'd put it all together and realize she was having sensory participation in the 'scape. And then he'd pull the plug. No question about it.

Julie turned off the monitor and called the nurse, who slipped back in with a funereal air. Julie nodded to the woman and then headed for her own room. She needed a shower.

On the way down the hall she passed Eathan's study.

She slowed, the message from the memoryscape reverberating through her. She stopped, turned back, and stood outside the closed door.

My uncle's hiding something. . . . He's hiding lots of things, I think. And I know just where he's hiding them. There's a huge locked wall cabinet in his study.

What could Eathan be hiding? Or, more likely, what could Sam have *imagined* Eathan was hiding? He'd always kept his study locked when they were children, and that had provided a great source of mystery and intrigue. But as they grew older, that need for privacy, to protect one's valuables, became perfectly understandable to Julie. Especially with someone like Sam foraging through the house in perpetual search of material for her endless stream of collages. A rare first edition could end up cut into a hundred pieces, adorning a crazy quilt of scrap paper, ticket stubs, and photos cut into fragments.

Many a time Julie had opened one of her magazines — *Astronomy* had always been one of Sam's favorite sources — to find photos of nebulae or distant galaxies ripped out. She'd run to Sam's room to find them glued to a board amid a meaningless — to Julie at least — hodgepodge of other scraps of paper.

But now, with the manor all to himself, was there any reason for Eathan to keep his study locked?

She reached out and turned the handle. The door opened.

I guess not.

She stepped inside. Not the first time she'd been in here. She and Sam had charged in on occasions when Eathan was working at his desk, sneaked in on other occasions when he'd forgotten to lock the door. But they'd never been able to stay long. Eathan always appeared to scoot them away gently.

Oak-paneled walls between the bookshelves, heavy green drapes on the windows overlooking the front gardens, dark green carpet matching the drapes; a huge oak parson's desk gleamed in the light from the windows. All very staid, very solid, very British, very beautiful.

But overwhelming all else in the room was the imposing bulk of the massive oak cabinet that dominated the north wall.

Julie felt herself drawn to the cabinet. She fought it, moving instead to the bookshelves. A set of half a dozen tall paper spines stood out among the first editions. She pulled one out: *The Journal of Neurochemistry.* She checked the date: 1968. All six were from the late 1960s. Odd. She quick-scanned the contents page and came to an abrupt halt at the name of one of the contributors: Nathan Gordon, Ph.D.

Dad.

Good God — research articles by her father. Her heart pounded. She hadn't known he'd published. She wanted to sit down and read these. Now. But how could she? She wasn't even supposed to be in here.

Later. She'd find a way to pop in while Eathan was here and "find" them.

After she replaced the journals in their spot, her feet seemed to move her toward the wall cabinet of their own accord. And then she was standing before it, gazing up at its towering height, staring at the intricate grainy swirls within the glossy surfaces of the massive pair of doors that guarded its contents from the outside world. The two handles were antique brass, but there was nothing antique about the sturdy Medeco lock plate that stared at her from above the right handle.

She reached out and tugged on one of the handles. She'd never seen the inside before.

Locked. Still locked. No one in the house but Eathan, the cook, and the maid . . . and still locked.

My uncle's hiding something.

Julie turned and started for the door.

Eathan's business was just that: Eathan's business. If he wanted to keep his cabinet locked —

The desk. The huge oak desk caught her eye. If he didn't carry the cabinet key on him, where would be the logical place to leave it?

She veered toward the desk but passed it without slowing. Instead she went to the windows and stared out at the front gardens. Eathan wasn't back from the airport yet.

He's . . . I'm here. . . . There's time. . . .

Abruptly she turned and approached the desk. She couldn't allow herself to think too much about this, because there was nothing rational about what she was doing. This was a blatant invasion of privacy.

But then she seemed to be making a habit of that lately, didn't she? She needed to eliminate Sam's paranoid idea.

Eathan always told them to go out and do what they had to do to get what they wanted. Well, she was following his advice.

She started with the top middle drawer and found no need to go further. A brass key with MEDECO stamped across its bow lay in the pencil tray.

Julie chewed her lip. She shouldn't do this. It wasn't right. If only she hadn't heard Sam say that.

She turned away and stepped back to the

window, almost hoping she'd see Eathan's car approaching. But no, the driveway was empty.

That did it.

She snatched up the key and hurried over to the cabinet. The key wobbled in her fingers as she shoved it into the lock and turned. She hesitated before pulling the doors open. What if they were alarmed?

Don't be ridiculous.

She yanked on the handles and swung the doors open a few inches. No sirens, no bells and whistles, just a puff of cool air redolent of musty old paper. She threw them wide.

And staggered back.

In a space almost like a small room, bigger, deeper than she'd imagined, half a dozen file cabinets sat in a neat row, the handles of their drawers arching toward her. But what she saw around them made Julie feel as if her entire life were flashing before her.

To her left the inside of the wall cabinet was decorated with the oversized scholastic awards or certificates of merit she'd won as a child — and she'd won plenty — along with prizes and ribbons for research papers and science projects; even some of the old science projects themselves, carefully wrapped in plastic and settled on shelves.

The right side was devoted to Sam, a dazzling array of old paintings and collages, from childhood through high school, even some of her surviving papier-mâché sculptures.

Julie gaped. Uncle Eathan . . . it looked as if he'd saved just about everything of theirs he'd been able to lay his hands on. But why hide it away like this? Was he afraid to show that he cared this much for them?

And why don't I feel touched? she thought.

She stepped up and tugged on one of the file-cabinet drawers. It slid open, revealing a row of hanging folders. The first was unmarked but each after that was tagged in succession: *Julia: Age 6 . . . Julia: Age 7 . . .* and so on.

Her heart beat a little faster as she reached into the drawer. What was all this?

She pulled out the first folder, the unmarked one. It contained a number of folded newspaper pages, stiff and yellowed with age. Julie carefully unfolded one of the sheets and found herself staring at page one of *The Millburn Express*. An ominous feeling crept over her when she saw the issue date of March 7, 1972. She knew that date. No need to look for the story. The banner headline told it all:

COUPLE DIES IN FIRE — CHILDREN MISSING

And below it:

Millburn: Shortly after midnight, fire gutted the home of Nathan and Lucinda Gordon in the western hill section . . .

Julie couldn't bring herself to read any further. And she could barely do more than glance at the grainy photo of the charred ruins that had once been her home.

Pretty damn morbid keeping that in here.

She carefully refolded it and tucked it back where she'd found it. Enough hard news. What was the rest?

She pulled out the *Age 6* folder and opened it. The first thing she saw was her primary school picture at the Saint John School in Whitby. She saw her six-year-old face staring unsmilingly at the camera. Sam stood close behind her, practically spooned against her, looking no more happy to be there than her sister. A pretty grim time for them: their mom and dad dead only a year before, placed in the care of their uncle Eathan, who'd moved them to England, where all the other kids thought they talked funny.

Someone — Eathan, she assumed — had circled a *J* and pointed an arrow to her. But why no arrow to Sam?

She flipped through the rest of the file: report cards, penmanship lessons, spelling and addition tests. All hers. Why no Sam? Unless . . .

She pulled open the top drawer on the neighboring file cabinet. And there she was: *Samantha: Age 6 . . . Samantha: Age 7 . . .*

A quick peek in Sam's *Age 6* folder revealed the same class picture, only this time a circled S pointed to Sam. And along with Sam's report cards was some of her early crayon art. Typical of Sam, she never bothered to stay within the lines. A rebel even then.

Julie pulled open more drawers and saw that the *Age* cards went all the way up to *30* for each of them, even though they were only twenty-eight. Obviously intended as an ongoing project.

And equally obvious why the folders started at six: Everything up to age five had been consumed in the fire. The newspaper in that first, unmarked file was like a black stripe scorched across their timelines, marking the starting point of their recorded history.

But why? Why such a detailed chronicle of their lives? Even the most devoted parents weren't this obsessive. It was almost scary.

But then again, Uncle Eathan had to be one of the most meticulous people she'd ever met. Maybe this was just his way. It certainly showed how much he loved them.

But why keep it locked?

The last cabinet was a different make than the others, a little wider, a little taller, and much older. She tugged on the top handle but the drawer wouldn't budge. And then she noticed a four-digit combination lock on the facing above the drawer.

Great. A locked file within a locked cabinet. What did Eathan have in here? Another, smaller, locked cabinet?

Julie jumped as a car door slammed somewhere out front. She darted to the window and saw Eathan getting out of his Bentley, but couldn't see who was in the passenger seat.

Oh God! He's back!

Quickly she closed the open file drawers. They banged shut.

"Damn!" she said, annoyed at her clumsiness.

More gingerly, but still hurrying, she shut the doors, relocked the cabinet, then returned the key to Eathan's desk drawer.

Trying to look as casual as possible, Julie strolled out into the hall.

A quick glance left and right: empty.

She released the breath she'd been holding and hurried toward her room.

My uncle's hiding something.

Yeah, Sam, she thought. You're right

about that. Eathan is hiding something. But nothing bad. That was pretty obvious.

It could have been worse. She could have found a collection of whips and chains and B-and-D sex toys. Or the bones of missing children. Or — she had to smile — a closetful of women's clothing, all in Eathan's size.

Instead she'd found . . . their lives. Every event recorded, labeled, and filed away. How strange. A labor of love worthy of the most dutiful parent. And hardly sinister.

But what about the file cabinet with the combination lock? Whose life was kept in there?

None of my damn business.

She may have grown up here, but she'd overstepped her bounds just now in Eathan's study. That was his private sanctum. She'd just paid her first and last visit to his cabinet. From now on she'd concentrate on what she'd come here for: to explore Sam's memoryscape.

She slowed as she passed the top of the stairs. Dinner was cooking. Smelled delicious.

She wondered who Eathan's mystery guest was.

Fifteen

Memory storage is highly organized. Words, for instance: Nouns are stored along the left temporal lobe, but they're not all lumped together. At least 20 specific areas have been identified for fruits, animals, numbers, colors, body parts, plants, etc. Verbs are stored near the motor cortex. How elegant . . . since verbs involve doing.
— Random notes: Julia Gordon

1

"Ah Julia, I'd like you to meet Dr. Alma Evans."

A dark, compact, middle-aged woman stood beside Eathan by the bar at the far end of the drawing room. She stepped forward, smiling and switching her drink to her left hand — the one with the cigarette — and extending her right, as Julie entered.

"Dr. Gordon. I'd have known you anywhere. You look exactly like your sister. I've heard so much about you from your uncle."

"Call me Julie, please," she said, taking the woman's hand. It was cold from the ice in her drink.

"Only if you call me Alma."

"Deal."

Alma Evans had dark hair and bright brown eyes. A nice smile, even if the teeth were a little crooked and slightly nicotine stained. Her accent was strictly upper-class British lockjaw.

Eathan said, "We're trying a fifty-year-old single-malt scotch I picked up outside Edinburgh last month. Care to try some?"

"Fifty years old? Is it still drinkable?"

"Eminently so," Alma said, holding up a short crystal tumbler. "It's sinfully smooth. . . ."

Julie accepted a couple of fingers' worth neat. Usually she took hers on the rocks with a splash of soda, but diluting fifty-year-old scotch seemed a capital crime.

She raised her glass. "Cheers." And sipped.

It was heaven — smooth, rich, with a smoky, peaty tang.

"I'll take a case," she said. She sipped again. "Make that two cases."

Eathan laughed. "If you knew what this one bottle cost, I think you'd cut your order."

They discussed the various wonders of single-malt scotches until they'd beaten the subject to death, and then it was time for dinner.

As they headed for the dining room, Eathan drew her aside.

"Are you all right? You look a bit frazzled."

"I'm fine."

"Is it the memoryscape? Did you see something?"

It's not what I *saw*, she thought.

"Nothing that made much sense."

"I hope to change that," he said.

2

Rack of lamb was served with a vintage bordeaux. The fine cuisine of Oakwood's succession of chefs was wasted on Julie and her sister growing up — but she certainly could appreciate it now.

Eathan raised his glass.

"While we're feasting down here, let us not forget Samantha upstairs. To her quick recovery."

"Hear, hear!" said Alma Evans. "Poor thing . . ."

"How well do you know Sam?" Julie said.

Eathan said, "Alma has been Samantha's psychiatrist for a number of years."

"Really?" Julie wasn't terribly surprised. Eathan's mention of a psychiatrist this morning, and then a mystery guest for dinner. She'd half suspected it. "I'm amazed she'd agree to any sort of therapy."

"After the Venice incident she decided maybe she should try something," Alma said.

Julie shot Eathan a look. "Venice? What happened in Venice?"

Eathan looked away. "A suicide attempt. She didn't want anyone to know — especially you."

"Especially me." Julie thought, Why am I not surprised at that, either? "She's overdosed before. You're sure this Venice incident was intentional?"

Eathan nodded. "She left a note. But that's all in the past. With Alma's help she got over what it was that made her so desperate. She actually seemed to be straightening out. Then this . . . coma. I brought Alma here to meet you tonight because she knows probably better than anyone what's been going on inside of Sam lately."

"This puts me in somewhat of an awkward ethical position, as you can imagine," Alma said. "But in weighing patient privilege against patient survival, I see no choice but to come down on the side of survival."

"I'm sure I appreciate your help," Julie

222

said. "Every day we seem to be losing more of Sam, but I don't see —"

"I've asked Alma to stay over for a few days," Eathan said. "I thought she might be able to give us some insight into Samantha's dreams."

"Dreams?"

"Yes. Those things, those" — he waved his hand in the air — "fantasies you see when you go into her memory."

"They're not dreams. They're memories."

"But they're not *accurate* memories," Eathan said. "They're distorted. That statue of Perseus was a good example. I don't know yet what you saw today, but maybe Alma can interpret the symbolism."

Julie didn't like this. For one thing, she didn't want Eathan or anyone else talking up the new memory technology. For another, it was bad enough to have Eathan and Dr. S. looking over her shoulder; now to have this stranger . . .

But if she could answer some questions . . .

Julie turned to Alma. "My uncle told you about the statue being substituted for the microscope?"

She nodded. "Yes. This memory process you've developed sounds absolutely astounding. I must see it in action."

Julie nodded. She didn't know how she felt about that. It was one thing to share

Sam's past with her therapist . . .

But I'm in there too.

"You will. But the distorted memory Eathan told you about: What's your take on that? Any idea what it could mean?"

"I really couldn't say," Alma said. "I'd have to see more of these experiences before I'd even attempt to come up with an interpretation. It seems symbolic. . . ." Alma looked over to Eathan, then back to Julie. "But of what?"

Well, at least she hadn't offered some facile garbage for an answer. Julie was leery of any sort of instant analysis. Dr. Evans had just taken a step up in her estimation. She respected any supposed expert who had the courage to say "I don't know."

"Julie, my plan was to have Alma review the videotapes you've made so far of your 'memory' trips. Perhaps she might draw some conclusions, give us all a little guidance."

Julie stiffened as she remembered today's videotape.

The VCR attached to the monitor feed had recorded this afternoon's journey into Sam's memoryscape: the lovemaking . . . and Sam's suspicions.

My uncle's hiding something. . . . He's hiding lots of things, I think.

She knew he was hiding a collection of their artifacts, but was that all?

Sam's suspicions might hurt Eathan. And might put him on his guard, make him even more dubious about letting Julie continue. She wished to avoid both.

Because, she thought, because — someday I might want to learn what's in that locked file cabinet.

She took a deep breath, then a sip of the bordeaux.

She'd have to hide the tape as soon as she got upstairs. Later she'd say she forgot to start the recorder before the session.

"Yes. Of course. I wouldn't show them to just anyone. They're intensely personal. But since Alma is her psychiatrist . . ."

"Excellent!" Eathan said. "The more heads we put together, the sooner we can resolve this mess and return Samantha to consciousness." Eathan's smile faded. "That is . . . if she *can* return to consciousness."

3

After a dessert of lemon glacé, they retired to the drawing room, where Alma lit a cigarette. Eathan passed out glasses of port, then ignited a thick, dark cigar. Julie felt as if she were in a *Masterpiece Theatre* episode. What was next — talk of the "Great War"? Trouble with the help?

"Since when do you smoke?" Julie said, fanning her hand in the air before her. She wanted to tell him how his stogie stank, but it was his house.

"I've picked it up over the last few years. Only cigars, and only rarely. One or two a week at most." He smiled. "I'm not a nicotine fiend."

Alma laughed. "Your uncle is learning to enjoy life a little. You Americans — so terribly abstemious about the good things in life. Smoke-free planes and restaurants, low-fat this, no-cal that, light, lighter, lightest. What a joyless existence. Please don't take this personally, but most of us over here think you're all quite mad."

Julie coughed. She couldn't take much more of this smoke. It was like the house was on fire.

"Yes. Utterly mad. Obviously." She turned to Eathan. She wanted the answer to one question before she hightailed it for the fresher air of the second floor. "I didn't know my father was a neurochemist. And that he'd published. Why didn't you tell me?"

He puffed out a plume of blue smoke. "Of course you knew — at least you knew he was a neurochemist. I thought that's why you wound up in neurology yourself."

"I knew he was a *chemist,* but not a

226

*neuro*chemist. I had no idea."

"How'd you find out?"

She rolled out her prepared answer, hoping it didn't sound too glib.

"I was doing a computer search and noticed an abstract from an old article by someone named Nathan Gordon, Ph.D. — from way back in the sixties. I downloaded it and was shocked to realize I was reading my father's work."

Eathan smiled. "Nathan published sporadically. His theories on the developing brain weren't widely accepted at the time. Too bad he didn't live long enough to pursue them. He was a brilliant, brilliant man. He'd be a giant in the field of developmental neurology today if he'd had time to complete his work. As it was, with all his papers lost in the fire, no one could pick up where he'd left off."

Alma cleared her throat. "Probably you've simply forgotten that you knew he was a neurochemist. But the knowledge may have influenced you subliminally."

Julie wanted to say that she knew all about memory and subliminals. But she had to admit it no doubt was more than coincidence that she, the daughter of a neurochemist, wound up with a doctorate in neurophysiology.

"Perhaps," she said.

Another question popped into her head.

"Tell me, Eathan: Did Dad have a bad temper?"

"What makes you ask that?"

"One of Sam's memories I saw today. He was arguing with our mom and seemed to be on the verge of a violent outburst."

Eathan stared at the glowing tip of his cigar. "Your father was a visionary. He saw the world differently and sometimes reacted to it in an unorthodox fashion. He was a good man, and he absolutely adored you and Samantha. I remember him talking endlessly about the two of you, how absolutely fascinated he was that identical twins could be so different. He fostered those differences, nourished them whenever possible. And as I'm sure you've realized, I've tried to do the same in his absence."

Eathan tapped his ash into an oversized tray on an end table, then looked back at Julie.

"But he had his faults too. He was often too wrapped up in his work for social niceties. People often mistook Nathan's preoccupied state for aloofness or even rudeness. I think you can empathize with that, can't you, Julia?"

Julie gave him a sheepish smile. She'd been misunderstood more than her share of times, people thinking she'd snubbed them when in fact she hadn't even been aware of their presence.

"Yeah . . . I suppose I can, but —"

Eathan raised a hand. "You know, I've been giving the scorched appearance of Samantha's memoryscape a lot of thought," he said, "and I was wondering if it might relate symbolically to this Liam O'Donnell fellow she was seeing. I mean, he is a known arsonist, reportedly a firebomb specialist."

"Oh, dear," Alma said. "Arsonists? Firebombs? I don't think I like the sound of this."

"Oh, don't worry about O'Donnell," Eathan said. "I've learned that Scotland Yard has a standing warrant for his arrest. He'll be avoiding British soil at all costs — which is one of the reasons I wanted Samantha brought back here."

Julie felt a flush creep into her cheeks at the memory of the man's lips on her, his tongue, the feel of him inside —

No, not me — Sam! He was inside Sam. *And don't forget it!*

Taking a deep breath, she said, "But if all that's said of him is true and he wanted to get rid of Sam, what would be the reason? And wouldn't his preferred method be fire?"

Eathan shrugged. "Maybe she knew something about him. Or maybe it wasn't him. Maybe it was the people he works for. Maybe he has nothing at all to do with any of it. I don't know. It's just that everything inside there seems to have been burnt to the ground and . . ." He rubbed a trembling hand across his eyes and his voice broke as he stared at the floor. "Oh, Lord, I don't think she's ever coming back to us."

Julie's heart went out to Eathan. He'd always been able to protect Sam, to shield her from the consequences of her recklessness. Now he was helpless and it was eating him alive.

She took a step toward him, but Alma got there first.

"There, there, Eathan," she said gently, putting a hand on his shoulder.

What's this? Julie thought. She hadn't assumed Uncle Eathan was living a monklike existence, but a relationship with Sam's therapist? If true, that was a little surprising.

"Don't you worry," Alma was saying. "We'll find some way to help Samantha. You've got a brilliant niece working on it, and I'll do anything I can to help. You know that."

"I do know that," he said, straightening and looking at Alma, then at Julie. "But I fear that it's hopeless."

"Don't count me out yet," Julie said, trying to imbue her smile with more confidence than she felt. "I've only begun to fight."

She was impressed by Alma. She seemed to have genuine empathy for Sam. She was a practicing psychiatrist, she knew Sam's psyche, and the different perspective she offered could help.

Julie glanced at her watch. Almost nine o'clock. That meant it was midafternoon back in New York. She could call Dr. Siegal. . . .

"And speaking of which, I think it's safe now to make another foray into Sam's memoryscape. Alma, would you like to monitor me?"

Her eyes lit. "Really? I'd be thrilled."

"Good. By the time you two finish polluting the air down here, I should be ready up there."

4

When Julie reached Sam's room she told the nurse she could take a break. Then she popped out the videotape of her last session and stared at it. She didn't want Eathan to know this existed, but wanted it available for review should the need arise. She put a small X in a corner of the label, slipped it back in among the blank cassettes, and pulled out a fresh one.

She had everything ready — including Dr. S. on-line — by the time Eathan and

Alma arrived. They settled before the monitor as Julie donned her headset and glove.

"Alma, before we start I must get a verbal nondisclosure agreement from you. This equipment is proprietary. Patents are pending. You may tell no one anything about what you're about to see. Do you agree to that?"

"I understand and I agree," she said. "I'll lock this away in the patient-privilege drawer and forget it."

Oh, I don't think you'll forget this, Julie thought. Especially if we catch Sam and Liam going at it again.

She snapped her goggles down, clicked the Enter button, and she was on her way.

Sixteen

John Kotre: "As a maker of myth, the self leaves its handiwork everywhere in memory. With the passing of time, the good guys in our lives get a little better and the bad guys a little worse. The speeds get faster, the fish get bigger, the Depression tougher."
— Random notes: Julia Gordon

You're almost used to the darkness and devastation now.

You stand outside the glowing "studio" and scan the ruined vista. You notice even fewer pockets of light, evidence of lost bits of memory sinking through the seared crust of the 'scape. Signs of life persist, but not enough. Nowhere near enough. The sky remains as dark as ever, and the perpetual pall of smoke still hangs in the air.

A sense of hopelessness, of utter futility, assails you. You can't make this work. The devastation is too extensive, and worsening. What does it mean? Are those sinking bits of memory lost forever? Or is there a way to

233

revive them? You wish there was a guidebook to this chaos. If this destruction represents a similar process in her mind, then everything that was Sam will be gone forever.

You're losing her. You've *got* to find another way.

And then you notice a dark figure standing near the studio.

"Hello?" you call, but the figure doesn't move, doesn't respond in any way. Something wrong here.

You step closer and realize with a shock that it's your father, standing there shrouded in a long black cloak. But he looks different. His face is pale and his hairline seems to have developed a widow's peak.

"Daddy?"

Suddenly he smiles and you recoil from the sharp white fangs he reveals. Then he spreads his arms and his cape and, like a scene out of a corny old horror movie, metamorphoses into a bat that squeals and flies in dizzying loops before disappearing into the studio.

Hesitantly you follow him into the gallery and stop inside the entrance. It's empty. No bat . . . and no paintings; they're gone.

You push forward, searching for the large canvas, the one with the slowly emerging painting. That's gone too.

You feel the first stirrings of panic. As hopeless as it had seemed a moment ago, at least you had the paintings. Now . . .

You catch a flash of color in the corner. A mix of yellow and orange. You rush to it.

Not all the paintings are gone. One of Sam's originals, the lion with the flaming mane, riding the gondola, remains. But it's been moved to the rear of the gallery. Why? Why are all the others except this one gone?

You touch the fiery mane and jerk back. Hot! But how — ?

And then you see that the mane is truly aflame now. And the fire is spreading, the flames licking at the canvas around the lion's head. Within seconds it eats a hole through and begins spreading in an ever-widening circle of fire. Before you can do anything the fire has consumed the painting, leaving only smoldering embers along the inner margin of the frame.

Beyond the flame is blackness. Not the gallery wall, not an opening to the outside memoryscape. Simply an opening. A void. A black hole.

You move closer and peer through this rent in the fabric of Sam's inner reality. Utter blackness lies beyond.

And it beckons.

Entranced, you move even closer, but the blinking Window button distracts you. You click it and Dr. S. appears. You know what he's going to say.

"I'm going in, Dr. Siegal."

"Now wait a minute, Julie. Now let's just wait a

minute and give this some thought. You don't know what —"

"I can click EXIT and end the session when-ever I want."

"Yes, but there may be more to it than that. We discussed —"

You click the Window button and Dr. S. disappears.

Rude, yes, but you sensed he was going to warn you again about the risks inherent in your personal and genetic links to Sam. You'd have listened politely if you were alone with Sam. But you can't risk alarming Eathan, who's watching the monitor and listening to every word. If he thinks there's the slightest risk to you, he'll withdraw permission and shut you out of the memoryscape altogether.

Before Dr. S. can interrupt you again, you dart through the frame —

And fall.

No wind in your face, no sense of plung-ing in gravity's grip, yet you know you're falling because a look behind reveals the glow-ing rectangle of the picture frame receding above you like the hatch of a plane from which you've leaped.

You look ahead. At least you *think* it's ahead. This utter blackness is disorienting. You're los-ing your sense of up and down. You feel your chair against your back but the vertigo over-whelms you. There's no sense of reality here, only your virtual fall. Hopefully the program will keep you oriented. You might well be panicking now if not for that comforting, ever-ready Exit button on the bar across the top of your visual field.

And now you see something: a faint, lacy pattern of blue-white light in the Stygian blackness far below. You're falling — skydiving — toward it. As you near, the pattern reminds you of a silver filigree, but you need another moment or two before you appreciate the scope of what you see. The silver is water, and the openings in the filigree are islands. You are falling toward a vast, moonlit archipelago.

Finally your descent slows and you find yourself hovering a few feet above the craggy surface of one of the larger islands in the center of the group. You glance up for the source of the light and see a crescent moon, a narrow sliver of milky light but impossibly huge, hanging impossibly close in the clear, starless sky.

No, not hanging. You can see it falling down the sky, a glowing fingernail clipping from a careless god.

You lower your perspective and study your surroundings. You realize this is not the peaceful archipelago it appeared to be from on high. Instead, you are surrounded by another vista of unimaginable devastation. But this time the engine of destruction was water instead of fire. A deluge of forty years instead of forty days. These clumps of land around you are not islands — they're hilltops. The ground beneath your virtual feet could be a peak in the Rockies, or the Appalachians. Or Mount Ararat, perhaps, waiting for the Ark to come to rest on one of its crags. This may be a deeper level of Sam's memoryscape, but it is just as wasted as its companion above.

You land on the largest of the islands and stare at the water. It looked so clean and clear from up there. Now, close up, you see oily rainbows drifting across its moonlit surface. Black water. And nothing ripples that dark surface from below or settles upon it from above. Truly this is a dead sea.

Dead . . . does this represent a dead area of her mind, lost forever, or is this only symbolic? But no one is here to give you answers. You're the first explorer in this strange netherworld.

You turn and freeze.

Behind you is a giant black nautilus shell, an onyx mass gleaming in the moonlight. How did it get here?

Never mind. The rules of the outside world mean nothing here. What matters is the light seeping from inside, inviting you in from the wet and cold of this postdiluvian wasteland. You accept.

Inside, you realize this is another gallery. New paintings decorate the walls. Only one is familiar, and even that is changed: The gondola still plies the Venetian canal in the magically restored canvas from the upper-level gallery, but no flaming lion rides in its bow.

And the large work in progress is back as well. You approach it and see that new details have been added: more trees, and a fuller moon, the familiar moon you've seen all your life, not the alien behemoth lumbering across the sky in this place.

You return to the outside. Motion to the right catches your eye. A dark shape gliding along the water, moving closer . . .

A gondola. So strange in this lifeless sea. No lion with flaming mane is passenger in this one. It's simply an empty gondola. It gently floats to the bank before you and crunches softly against the slimy rock. And waits.

"Okay," you say. "I guess I'm supposed to go for a ride."

You expect another warning from Dr. S. but his window is quiet.

So, reminding yourself again that you can exit anytime you wish, you step aboard. It doesn't rock under your weight like a real gondola. Good thing too, since you've never done well on ships or boats of any size.

As soon as you seat yourself, the craft drifts from shore. You need no Charon to guide you upon this Styx of the soul as your craft carries you along the polluted channels, winding around and between devastated islands of rock that once housed memories.

It's dead here, deader than the scorched level above. The only light is in the gallery dwindling behind you and the overbearing sliver of moon above. The crescent has fallen closer to the horizon. Soon it will set and you fear the darkness will be absolute. Perhaps you should go back.

You admit something to yourself: You're scared here.

And then ahead . . . something bobbing upright on the surface, like a softly glowing buoy. As you near you make out details . . . and realize it's a giant plastic glow-in-the-dark dashboard Jesus. You pass within a few feet of it, and as the buoy comes abeam, it becomes flesh. Suddenly Jesus is standing on the water, staring at you. He holds up a pierced palm in greeting.

"The blood is the life," he says, then turns and strides away . . . across the water.

"Blood," you whisper. "Dad as a vampire, and now Jesus. Are you still after me for that transfusion, Sam?"

You scan the horizon and see a larger glow. Yes! A memory node, no doubt, a survivor of the deluge. That, you guess, is the reason for the gondola. To take you to it. So you wait.

The water moves past the gondola at perhaps three knots, yet you approach the glow at something like fifty. And soon you recognize it.

Venice. Not the Venice you remember from your trip to the old city three years ago. This is the stylized Venice from Sam's painting. Gone are the strings of lights and crowds of colorful people. Darkness, the great equalizer, has stolen them. You sail the city's black waterways, cruise beneath its empty footbridges, glide past the stuccoed fronts of its narrow houses with their empty black windows.

Or perhaps not so empty. Who knows what waits and watches behind those panes? But the gondola doesn't stop.

Ahead you notice something hanging from one of the bridges, something furry, dangling upside down. A monkey? No . . . as you near you see it's a possum, hanging and watching you with a big, bright Cheshire Cat grin. The same possum from the upper level — the one with the hand? You wait for him to do something but he only grins at you as you pass. Soon he falls behind and the shadows swallow him, but the grin remains.

And above and beyond him you spy the giant moon crescent scything into the horizon. Thankfully there's some light in this benighted city. You catch glimpses of it seeping between the buildings, glinting off the black mirrors of its dead canals. You sense you are heading for the source. You feel your fear receding.

But then you hear a noise, a ratcheting sound, soft and rapid. You look up and see a dark-haired boy in ragged clothes sitting on the railing of another of the many bridges, his bare feet dangling over the edge at midspan. He clutches a fishing pole in his hands and works the reel furiously, winding in the taut line from the inky water. You shake your head. As if anyone could fish these polluted waters.

You watch the still surface as you pass, curious to see what he's caught, but he keeps winding and winding. He must have miles of line out. Endless winding, as you pass under his bridge and the next curve takes you out of sight. Yet still you hear his reel . . . winding . . . winding . . .

And then you round another bend and forget about him, for the night is suddenly aglow. You recognize the place. It doesn't belong here; this is not the way it really is, but you know the building.

The Venice Opera House. *Teatro la Fenice.*

You're no fan of the opera, but you looked at its façade when you came to Venice. Sam once did sets here for an avant-garde production of . . . you forget the opera.

And then you see a familiar figure.

The lion with the flaming mane sits regally on the quay, waiting. Music wafts from inside, the sound of an orchestra tuning up.

The gondola noses against the bulkhead and stops. You know what you're supposed to do. The lion turns and watches you debark and climb the steps. Will the lion say anything? you wonder. But then it fades away. . . .

You look at the marquee. It reads OTELLO, but the front doors are shut, apparently locked, since they don't respond to your virtual grasp.

You move around to the side, to the open stage door. You enter there. And you see Sam:

She weaves her way through the cramped backstage area. Outside, where the audience sits, it's sumptuous and luxurious.

La Fenice. The Phoenix, a theater reborn from the ashes of a great fire in 1774. The jewel of Venice. Royalty have enjoyed its blue-and-cream interior for centuries. Mary Shelley wrote home to England about its beauty.

But here, backstage, it's a madhouse, bedlam.

Sam loves it.

And what an opportunity. The youngest-ever art director for a major production at *La Fenice*. And though her taste runs more to Nirvana and Pearl Jam, Sam finds herself drawn to Verdi's thunderous music, the extravagance, the lush color, and the gaudy pomp.

A young nobleman walks by, bellowing basso vocal exercises. The chunky mezzo who plays Emilia is complaining to the stage manager about something. Mezzos are never happy.

Nor is the prima donna, Katia Mareau.

The star, the Desdemona, of this *Otello*.

Sam carefully steps over the ropes and flats all in place for the last act of this dress rehearsal. Katia Mareau will be killed, as she will be for the next two weeks while well-heeled patrons arrive by gondola to see Verdi's take on Shakespeare's tragedy.

Opera. A silly, comic world, yet somehow wonderful. Larger than life; it obliterates life.

Sam walks up to the door with the carefully calligraphied gilt name — *Katia Mareau* — then below it, in slightly smaller letters, *Desdemona.*

Sam knocks once.

No response, so she knocks again.

And the voice inside sings a greeting.

"Sì, entrare!"

Sam goes in and finds Mareau in front of her makeup table, studying her image surrounded by a legion of lightbulbs. She doesn't even glance at Sam.

"Oh. Samantha, puh-lease close the door. I feel a chill. So damn moist here."

Sam turns and dutifully shuts the door. Mareau certainly felt worse chills growing up on a big ranch in Wyoming.

"You've seen the set?" Sam says.

"For Act Four? Yes, my dear, and the bed's too small." Still not looking at Sam. "But I told you that, didn't I. Well, we'll see how it plays out."

Sam nods. It's the bed that this Desdemona will die in, night after night. Diva Mareau wants a grander stage for her swan song.

"The director told me that the blocking is fine, that —"

"He's an ass. A silly, stupid man. Couldn't stage a yard sale."

Now, finally, Mareau stops and looks at Sam.

"Have you been eating, sweetheart?"

So strange for Sam to be so much in the spell of this woman. Mareau feels like a giant elemental force, whether singing . . . or not.

Mareau stands. "I worry about you, you know."

Sam nods. Mareau is a tall figure, with dark brown eyes and lustrous black hair that cascades to her shoulders. She's wearing the Act IV nightgown, a pale blue item, sere and iridescent. She takes a step to Sam.

"An important day, eh, Samantha?"

The first dress rehearsal was always the make-it-or-break-it point. After it's over, they will know whether all the confused elements of the opera — the sets, the singers, the orchestra, the blocking — have come together.

Mareau moves closer.

"You look like a frail bird, Samantha. Have you given absolutely everything to our production . . . with nothing" — Mareau touches Sam's cheek. The singer's hand is warm, comforting. Practiced. She traces a finger over Sam's lips — "left for me?"

Sam knows this is crazy. How she fell into

this — relationship — is beyond even her. Is it the sheer force of Mareau's personality, her charisma, her power — or some stupid weakness? She doesn't know.

The singer's other hand comes up to Sam's left cheek, holding her head, like a mother examining a schoolgirl's first makeup.

You recoil.

For a moment, you consider hitting the Exit button. Because what you think you will see will challenge even what you thought you knew about your sister. Was there nothing she wouldn't try, nothing she wouldn't experiment with?

And yet Sam seems so quiet here, so subdued . . . a little girl.

You brace yourself.

Mareau leans forward and kisses Sam, a strong, passionate kiss.

For a moment Sam stands there, letting herself be engulfed by this woman. Then her hands go up and encircle Mareau, touching the pale, silky blue material. And Sam is dizzy with the smell of the perfume, the taste of those full lips, the glare of the makeup lights hitting the mirror, filling the tiny dressing room with warm, yellow light.

It's Mareau who breaks off the kiss. Too abruptly, as if all she wanted was a quick confirmation of Sam's devotion.

"That *was* sweet. But I have a bit of bad news."

Samantha nods. The schoolgirl, listening to —

"Tonight. After the rehearsal, I won't be able to" — a hesitation — "meet you. Some old friends from the Met are here."

"And after that?" Sam doesn't keep the disappointment from her voice.

"Dearies, after that I'm going right to sleep. I won't have time" — she smiles — "for anything."

Another brush of Sam's cheek, and it's over. Dismissed. Love given and withdrawn. The promise of other times, other embraces.

The room feels as if it's spinning.

A knock on the door. *"Presto, Signora."*

"Presto, right — as if anything happens in this damn country *'presto.'* But let's see if I was right about the bed, eh?"

Sam's mouth opens. She wants to say something. But the only thing there, at the tip of her tongue, is corny, stupid, embarrassing. Something like *I love you.*

So she says nothing.

Mareau turns away, and fires off a few high practice trills that are deafening in the small room.

Then, slipping into a "New Yawker" accent, Mareau says, "Let's go let the Moor kill me, eh, kiddo?"

And she leaves the dressing room.

You feel the emotions washing over Sam: the confusion, the pain, and finally the emptiness.

Is there more to this? There has to be. It must be important, but why?

You follow Sam out to the backstage area, to Act IV of *Otello*.

She stands in the wings. Her sketches and paintings have been brought to life.

And this is no traditional *Otello*. The medieval Venetian castle and the king's bedroom have been rendered as if the action is taking place on a spaceship, with a silvery bed that glistens like a fiery jewel.

A great wall mural in the back of the stage is all metallic silver and red. On the mural, the lion of Venice stands thirty feet tall, holding fistfuls of people in his gripping claws. This is a "political" *Otello*.

The production will surely cause an incident, a *cause célèbre*. Which is why they came to Sam to begin with.

And damn, she's proud of herself.

But now — for the first time — she's watching the costumed singers move through her Act IV stage design. The floor is red metallic girders, more appropriate to a power plant. A golden glow filters up from below. The glow will turn orange, then red, before —

Sam looks back to Mareau, finishing her big solo. Desdemona's "Ave Maria" ends. Now she waits, terrified of her husband, the insanely jealous Moor, Otello.

Otello, a tenor in blackface, barges into the bedroom.

He launches yet another accusation. "Where is the handkerchief I gave you?" he demands.

Mareau looks genuinely frightened. She squirms on the silvery bed.

It *is* too small.

Perhaps we can —

But Sam freezes. Otello is singing out his rage in Italian. Pointing at Desdemona, yelling, "You love another . . . You love . . . Cassio!"

Sam's Italian is perfunctory at best. But she knows what happens. Otello tells Desdemona that Cassio is dead. And you — you, my wife, are lying on *your* deathbed.

Sam grips one of the curtain flies, twisting the heavy brocade material. She feels dizzy.

Mareau — Desdemona — looks scared. The drama is too powerful, too intense. The music swells, roaring along with Otello's rage.

Desdemona begs for her life, for just this night, for an hour, for the moment, but Otello leaps onto the bed, encircles her throat, and begins to strangle her.

And then — and then — Mareau looks

over to Sam, her eyes bulbous, terrified.

Sam releases the curtain. She takes a step out of the wings, and then another.

The scene continues, Desdemona writhing, pleading.

"No," Sam mutters. Another step.

The light is changing from the metalwork below. Golden, to orange, to —

Samantha is on the stage, but no one stops her. Perhaps she's checking something.

The thundering power of the orchestra is overwhelming. Cymbals crash, the drums rumble.

Then Desdemona is dead.

"No!" Sam screams.

She runs to the bed, pulling at Otello, yanking on the actor's costume. His blue eyes flash in the surrounding black makeup.

Sam is shrieking, her own screams joining the orchestra, which only now starts to peter out, as if the conductor has lost his way.

"You must . . . not . . . kill her!"

She pushes Otello away, then cradles Mareau's head, not seeing the woman's open eyes, her shocked face.

Not seeing anything because she's rocking and crying, whimpering over and over: "No . . . no . . . no."

A tear falls to the metal girders below, glistening there. Before slipping even lower, to the fire below.

And then you're at the stage door. Locked out. You try the latch but you sense the theater has no more to show you.

You feel so empty, so hopeless. You wonder: Is this what Sam felt then? Was this behind Sam's suicide attempt?

Reluctantly you glide back to the front of *La Fenice*, to the entrance. And there the gondola awaits.

You hurry down the empty steps. The opera is over. You're supposed to leave.

Presto, presto . . .

And for the first time, you feel compassion for your sister. It was as if she had created a fantasy image so powerful that it brought her to her knees.

But what was this all about? Her love for another woman? Then seeing her killed? Did it have to do with that self-inflicted fiery glow?

You need to know so much more, but now the only thing you want is to get out of here.

The gondola takes a meandering path, leading far away from here, you hope.

Above the buildings you see the knife-point edge of the rising moon as it begins climbing the sky on the far side of the memoryscape. You barely notice the passing bridges and buildings. You want only to be away from this place, to sit alone and sort out these feelings, to disentangle Sam's emotions from your own, to rid yourself of Sam's strange love for that woman and this overwhelming sense of loss and desolation.

But you can't leave the memoryscape. Not yet. You have to get out among the islands again and see what else awaits you among the drowned memories.

And then you hear a familiar sound. The soft, rapid ratcheting of a fishing reel. You look up and see the little boy again. You realize this is a different bridge, but he's still reeling in his line. Who is this child, this street urchin with a fishing pole? And what does he mean to Sam? Suddenly there's a splash as his catch breaks the water.

Finally! You lean over the edge to see what he's caught and recoil with revulsion when you realize it's a severed hand, hooked through the webbing of the thumb. It drips and wobbles as the child reels it higher and clutches the line to land it.

What is it with this image? This is the third time you've seen it: once in the real world and now twice in the memoryscape. What's Sam trying to tell you — if she's trying to tell you anything at all?

You watch silently, waiting for him to recognize his catch for what it is and toss it back. But his eyes light as he grabs the hand and places it on the railing. With a single swift motion he unhooks it from the line, raises it to his mouth, and bites into the fleshy heel of the palm.

"No!" you shout, but he ignores you and continues to tear at the hand with his bright, sharp teeth.

Sickened, you turn away. Now, more than ever, you want to leave this place, but that's the last bridge up ahead. No sign of the Cheshire possum. Soon the last turn is negotiated and you are once again sailing the open waterways. You search the horizon but find no signs of life. No glow of memory nodes clinging to the surface of this black, oily sea.

This world is all but dead.

Is that all there is here — the Venice memory? There's got to be more to this vast, wet wasteland than a single node. But even if there are more nodes, this one has so drained you that you lack the will to go on.

And why this particular memory? Has it anything to do with the fact that you were discussing it with Sam's psychiatrist shortly before entering the memoryscape? Are you bringing things with you? Are you in some way shaping the memoryscape? Programming it? Is whatever's left of Sam's subconscious somehow responding to what's in your mind as you enter?

Or is it just coincidence?

Too damn many questions.

God, you wish this wasn't such an infant science. If only you knew more. If only you could —

Suddenly the boat rocks as something

scrapes against its keel. A rock? A reef? Are you entering shallow water?

Another scrape. That wasn't rock. Too soft for rock. Almost . . . leathery. The gondola had been steady but now it weaves on the water.

Exit button or *no* Exit button, you don't want to fall in.

And then a splash to port. You whirl. Something black and shiny has broken the surface. It glistens for an instant in the moonlight, and then it's gone, leaving only spreading ripples to mark its passing.

You shiver. Guess you should be encouraged to know that these waters aren't completely dead. At least some sort of life exists here, but you can't help having a creepy feeling not knowing what *kind* of life is moving beneath you.

But you make it back to the isle where your trip began with no further scrapes or splashes.

You reenter the gallery and it's pretty much as you left it, except the flame-maned lion has returned to his gondola. And the painting on the easel has more detail in the trees, but little else has changed. Three steps ahead, two back.

You feel depression seeping through you. Your own emotion or Sam's? Could be either. This certainly seems hopeless. The devastation seems worse on this level than above. How are you going to learn anything here when everything is drowned?

"Shit," you say — simply to hear your own human voice.

Before the feeling can overwhelm you, you click EXIT and get out.

Seventeen

People shouldn't compare memory to a videocamera, either. No way is a memory an objective recording of an event. Memory is an extension of perception, and stored as outcomes of perceptual analysis. It's colored by our feelings about the event, our emotional state, hell, probably even our blood-sugar level at the time.
— Random notes: Julia Gordon

1

Julie removed the headset and glanced to where Eathan and Alma sat before the monitor.

Eathan stood up and rubbed his hands on his thighs. "I'm very uncomfortable with this," he said. "Very. I really don't want to know this much about Sam's personal life. I never realized everything she went through. I . . ."

Words failed him.

Julie understood. She, too, was beginning to appreciate the depth of her sister's torment, but the fact remained that Sam was ultimately responsible for all the messes she created for herself. The question was, Why did she create them? What were the demons that drove her into these situations?

Demons . . . she thought of the Brueghel picture and its demon.

Quickly Julie signed off with Dr. S., then noticed Alma, still sitting before the monitor, gazing at it as if mesmerized. Sensing Julie's scrutiny, she shook herself and looked up.

"I . . . I'm speechless," she said. "This is the most phenomenal . . . the most revolutionary . . ."

Julie knew all that. She wanted Alma to tell her something she didn't know.

"But did you learn anything?" she said.

Alma nodded vigorously. "Oh, yes. Your sister was always so vague about certain details. Now I know exactly what happened. I mean, I — saw it."

"Don't be too sure of that," Julie said. "I've learned never to accept what I see in there as objective truth. It's Sam's take on reality. It's colored by fears, dreams, fantasies. . . ."

"I realize that," Alma said. "And that's my point. This may not be what actually happened, but it's how Sam remembers it, how she *feels* about it — and to a psychiatrist that's always more important than objective truth."

Julie nodded, encouraged. No doubt about it, Alma was on the ball. But could she add anything?

"What do you think? What about all that water? Post-holocaust on the first level, post-deluge on the second. Any significance to that?"

Alma rubbed her chin. "Water is always mysterious. You never know what lurks beneath the surface."

Well, thanks for that news flash, Julie thought. "What about my father as a vampire and the floating Jesus?"

"Blood imagery, perhaps?"

"And the severed hand?"

"Now *that* was disturbing. Quite grotesque and completely out of place."

"But it's not the first time I've seen it." She told Alma about the possum gnawing the hand on the first level and the father carving a hand for his family in the painting in Sam's apartment. "If I'd seen it only once, I could ignore it. But it's a recurring theme. It has to be important."

"Yes," Alma said slowly, leaning back and closing her eyes. "Obviously it's important. The hand is a potent image — the Hand of Fate, the Hand of Death . . . we shake hands, touch each other — but in each instance in Sam's memories someone seems to be devouring the hand. I don't know —" She opened her eyes and straightened. "Biting the hand — *biting the hand that feeds you!*"

Julie felt a chill. Alma was close, but Julie sensed she didn't have it all. She looked up and saw Eathan staring into space, a queasy look on his face. The cannibalistic scene had obviously rattled him.

"I think you've almost got it," Julie said. "But what could it mean?"

"I don't know," Alma said. "I'd like to view the videotapes of your other sessions before I attempt to answer that."

"Fair enough. When will you have time?"

"How about right now? I am absolutely entranced by the wonders of your equipment. I wouldn't sleep a wink tonight knowing I'd have to wait until tomorrow to see more."

"Great. We'll take the tapes downstairs, plug them into the VCR in the family room, and leave you alone with your patient."

"I can't wait."

2

Eathan had already seen the first tape and didn't care to view it again. After her two

259

exhausting excursions into the memory-scape already today, neither did Julie. They left Alma entranced before the oversized screen of the family room's projection TV and retired to the drawing room.

As Eathan poured her another port, Julie said, "Isn't there anything left of my father's work besides his published papers?"

"I'm afraid not. The fire razed the house to the foundation."

"But didn't he have an office somewhere?"

"Up until about a year before the fire, he worked for GEM Pharma as a psychopharmacologist. The company's big R and D thrust back in the late sixties was for a new antidepressant drug. Nathan's knowledge of brain chemistries made him a valuable man. But he was more interested in pure basic research. He went before the GEM board and proposed a number of avenues he wished to follow in addition to the antidepressants."

Julie's interest leaped. "What were they? What was he into?"

Eathan shrugged. "I don't know. He rarely discussed his work — thought it would bore everybody but him. As you've probably guessed, the board saw little or no commercial potential in his proposals so they turned him down. He stayed with the company but eventually the product-oriented research and testing wore him down until he couldn't take any more. He quit and began applying for research grants. Didn't have much luck, I'm afraid. So all his papers and experimental journals were at home. They all were lost. Up in smoke. He had a dream. I don't know what it was, but he never got to make it real."

Julie's heart went out to the man she barely remembered. She felt a kinship with him that went beyond blood. What if she hadn't hooked up with Dr. Mordecai Siegal? She might be stuck in some deadly dull research job, bored, frustrated as hell, and climbing the walls. She might be thinking of quitting and hunting for research grants . . . just like her father.

"Poor Dad," she said. "I wish I had some idea of what he was working on." She gave out a hollow laugh. "Maybe I could find a way to complete it."

She looked up and caught Eathan staring at her. For an instant she thought he had tears in his eyes.

"What a wonderful thought," he said. "And what a loving gesture that would be, if only it were possible. But who knows? Perhaps you *are* carrying on his work and don't even know it."

"Now *that* would be creepy."

Eathan raised his glass. "To Nathan's dream — whatever it was."

Julie raised her own, then sipped. They stood in silence, savoring the moment of communion with someone long gone but dear to both of them.

And then Eathan turned away and reached for his cigar.

"I think I'll go out for a little walk around the gardens," she said as he began relighting it and fouling the air with plumes of smoke. "I could use a little air."

"It's dark out there. Be careful."

"I know the paths by heart. I can walk them with my eyes closed — unless you've changed the landscaping."

He smiled. "No changes. Everything is just as you left it."

Julie grabbed her Mets baseball jacket from the hall closet and stepped out the front door onto the steps.

It was cool, and the darkness out here reminded her of the bleakness inside Sam.

Still, as her eyes adjusted to the night she saw only a few familiar constellations: Orion, the Pleiades, the Big Dipper. They were old friends, reassuring.

She took in a deep lungful of the clean, briny air and let it out slowly. Clouds had moved in, obscuring the rest of the stars, and a fine mist was drifting in from the water. Soon it would be soup out here.

That's more like it, she thought. Now we're back to typically English weather.

She angled right across the driveway and followed a winding path that ambled among the gardens and along the manicured lawns, past the line of trees that bordered the grounds proper, and into the rough. The breeze against her face stiffened as she picked up the mutter of the North Sea at the base of the cliff ahead.

Chilled, she pulled the jacket more closely around her as she stopped at the fence that ran along the rocky edge.

Even though the cliffs had been a good walk from the house, Eathan had feared that one of them — Sam was the more likely candidate — would fall the hundred feet or so to the jagged rocks below, so he'd put up the fence when they first moved in.

Julie leaned against one of the posts and felt it sag under her weight. Apparently Eathan had let the fence go to rot. No sense in maintaining it nowadays. She remembered sneaking out here with Sam to look for fossils in the shale. The cliffs were supposedly loaded with them. Once they'd found the remnants of a prehistoric fern, tattooed into a slab of rock, another time a spiral ammonite that she'd treasured for years. She wondered where it was now. She smiled — maybe in Eathan's cabinet.

She was staring out at the darkness, listening to the waves on the rocks, letting wind fingers run through her hair, when she had a vague sensation that she was not alone.

She turned but saw no one. She could make out the high grass and heather in the rough, and the lights of the house through the trees, but no sign of anyone else.

She'd been out here long enough anyway.

She made her way back to the grounds, retracing her steps along the path until she came to the sunken gardens. Standing on the top step on the rim of the deep, bowl-shaped depression, she tried to remember how it looked when she and Sam used to play here. And they *had* played. In times of truce they were just like any other sisters — laughing, joking, playing make-believe with their dolls and toys. This was their special place where they shared their se-crets and hid from their uncle and ate the sweet-cakes they'd steal from the kitchen when cook wasn't looking.

But as the truces grew shorter and the battles longer and more fierce, the sunken garden became a war zone, to be occupied exclusively by only one combatant at a time.

In the end, it became Sam's place. To sketch, to brood, to do other things.

What a shame, Julie thought. We could have been friends . . . if only Sam had been different. And — maybe — if I had learned to lighten up . . . Trouble is, I still don't know how to do that.

She walked down the steps to the sunken center of the garden. She rested her hand on the marble pedestal of the sundial that used to be "home" in their games of tag.

Julie heard a sound behind her, a scrape. She turned but saw nothing moving in the darkness. Probably a dry leaf blown against the slate walk.

But as she walked around the pedestal, pivoting her finger on the point of the sundial, she caught a blur of motion to her right, movement that looked like something other than a shrub swaying in the breeze. She froze and stared but could see nothing out of the ordinary.

Time to head for the house. Could be her imagination was running in high gear after her most recent sortie into Sam's memoryscape, or could be someone else was out here in the sunken garden. Either way, she wanted out of here — now.

She turned and hurried up the steps.

She didn't make it to the third one before she was grabbed from behind. A leather-gloved hand clamped over her mouth, sealing off her cry of terror as a powerful arm snaked around her waist and lifted her off her feet.

Frantically, desperately, Julie kicked and struggled with all her strength. She jammed an elbow backward, but to no effect. Her heart raced, her breath whistled through her nostrils as she fought for more air. Visions of rape and death, memories of the Central Park jogger's fate, flashed through her brain, fueling her terror.

But here — at Oakwood? It was insane.

And then lips pressed against her ear and a voice whispered.

"Hush now, darlin', and be calm. I wouldn't be hurtin' you for all the world. I need your help. . . ."

That voice, that accent — oh, God, she knew who it was.

"Do y'hear me now?" he said, still whispering. "Do you understand? I'm sorry for frightening you like this, but it just wouldn't do to have you shouting and raising a fuss. I'm a friend of Sammi's. Do you understand? A friend . . . and I've got something to tell you."

Though her mouth was still covered, the pressure was less intense.

"If you promise not to yell, I'll let you go and we'll talk like regular people. Do I have your promise?"

And what if I don't promise?

Julie stopped struggling. She didn't have much choice. He was so much stronger than she. And if she kept fighting him, what would he do? If he let her go, she might have a chance to get away, to scream for help, to do something.

She nodded and he released her. Julie coughed and sucked in a couple of deep breaths, then turned to face him. He was all in black, from knitted watch cap to his shoes, his face a pale blur not two feet in front of her. And she loathed him. She swung a fist at his face with all her strength but he easily dodged it.

"Ooh! Right-handed, are we? Your sister's a lefty."

"You bastard!"

She swung again but this time he caught her wrist in midair.

"Now, now, love. None of that." He sounded amused and she hated that. "You promised."

She wished that she had done more than the introductory class of Tae Kwan Do. Her words hissed between her teeth as she wrenched her wrist free.

"I promised not to *yell!*"

"That you did. But I've no time for law-yerin' about it. I'm here to ask about Sammi — and warn you about your uncle."

"And what does Liam O'Donnell know about my uncle?"

That got him. His head snapped back as if her swing at him a moment ago had finally connected.

"Wh — what makes you think I'd be any such person?"

"Sam told me."

He grabbed her by both her upper arms and practically lifted her off the ground.

"Sammi! Sweet Jesus, she's awake? She's come 'round?"

Julie couldn't make out his expression and couldn't tell whether his whispered voice was hoarse with alarm or joy. But that wasn't what bothered her most. Julie felt herself responding to his touch. Warmth grew where his gloved fingers gripped her, spreading up her arms, into her chest, and downward. . . .

"No," she managed to say. "She's still out."

"Oh."

He released her and turned away.

The warmth receded, thank God. She needed all her wits about her to deal with this man. But that response — was it a leftover from Sam, or her own? After all, she'd been about as intimate with Liam as one could ever be . . . after a fashion.

He turned back to her. "But you said —"

"I knew this from before." *I know more than you can imagine.* "And I *know* Sam thinks our uncle is hiding something in his cabinet."

"But how?"

"I heard it from her own lips." That was certainly the truth. "And I can tell you he *is* hiding something in the cabinet, but it's nothing bad. . . ."

Liam's face seemed to disappear for an instant as he rubbed a black-gloved hand across it. "I don't understand this. Did she call you? She more'n once told me about you. No love lost between you."

"She told me. How doesn't matter. But tell *me:* Did you send her those roses?"

He hesitated, then, "Yes."

"Why?"

"If you're knowing anything, you know I love her."

"I know nothing of the sort. Only you know that. But the note: 'Don't worry. I won't let them hurt you'? Why send a threat?"

"Not a threat — Lord. Just a promise. And a warning. I'm damned if I knew what you were doing to her with all those contraptions you moved into her room. She seemed like a poor bugger of a lab animal."

"So *you* were the prowler they spotted on the Sainte Gabrielle grounds."

"I was. And I'm the prowler here, as well. Especially now that you've brought in that head-shrinking bitch. Sammi never trusted her. So you can count on me prowling about until Sammi's up and well again."

"Is that what you want?"

"And what else would I be wantin'?"

"My uncle found out all about you. And he thinks that maybe you caused her coma. Maybe she knows things about you . . . and maybe you don't want her 'up and about again' at all. And maybe you're prowling about so you'll be the first one to know if and when she is."

Surprised by her own intensity, she stepped back, unsure how he'd react, and afraid. Liam was a big man, powerful. And even if she did scream, she doubted whether anyone at the house would hear.

"You may be her twin," he said, shaking an angry fist in her face, "but you don't have half her heart, and not a tenth of her soul." He lowered his hand. "But you've got her guts, I'll give you that . . . accusing me of harming her. Christ, if you were a man —"

Julie retreated. "Okay — so maybe someone you work for, then. Someone who wants her out of the way."

"I don't work for anyone. I'm kinda freelance, an independent contractor."

"Yeah. Import and export. Right." She took a breath. "I know you're with the IRA."

"Oh? And who in bloody hell would be sayin' that?"

"My uncle says Scotland Yard is looking for you. Is that true?"

"Are you the type who's believing everything she hears?"

Julie ground her teeth. "Must you answer every question with another question?"

"Now what makes you think I'm doing

any such thing?"

Even in the darkness Julie caught the flash of his grin, and had to smile herself, though she did her best to hide it. He was a charmer, this one. Big, powerful . . . but charming. Better watch out for him.

And then his smile disappeared. "If I was you, I should be after looking out for me uncle," he said. "If Sammi said he was hiding something, hell, it's a damn good shot that he is. She says he's got all your da's papers tucked away somewhere."

Julie felt a chill worm its way through her coat. Or did it come from within?

"Wait. No, stop right there. That's wrong. Everything our father owned went up in smoke with the house."

"Ah, sure that's what you've been told. But Sammi didn't believe that. She said —"

"Julia! Are you still out here? Ju-lia!"

Julie whirled. Eathan's voice — calling from somewhere toward the mansion. He could be here in minutes.

Closer now: "Julia, where are you?"

She turned back to Liam but no one was there. She searched the darkness but he was gone. Shaken, she pulled her coat closer and hurried up the stone steps. The whole episode had an unreal feel to it. She had to check her bearings to make sure she wasn't back in Sam's memoryscape.

"Coming, Eathan!"

271

When she reached the top, he was on the driveway and coming her way.

"The sunken garden," he said. "I should have known. What were you doing?"

"Reminiscing," she said.

"Out loud? I thought I heard your voice."

Should she tell him about Liam? Damn, she hated secrets. But what if Sam was right about Dad's papers? What if they hadn't been burned? Why would Eathan hide them? Always so damn overprotective. Was there something in them? Some secret about their father?

Listen to me, she thought, taking the word of a known terrorist and Sam, that paragon of good sense and rationality.

But just in case . . .

"Sometimes I think out loud," she said. "One of the perils of living alone."

"Let's go inside," he said. "Alma seems to be missing a tape."

She followed him to the darkened family room, where the tape of tonight's session was playing on the big screen. It had to be near the end because the point of view was in the deeper-level gallery, resting on the painting of the lion in the gondola. Then it swung over to the unfinished painting on the easel. Then it faded to black.

Alma started as Eathan turned on the lights. "Oh! I didn't know you were there. I was so engrossed."

"Any insights?" Julie said.

Alma rose from her seat and turned to her. She held a yellow pad full of squiggles.

"Nothing that leaps out at me, but there's something there — *lots* there. I simply need more time, more viewings to put it all together. And didn't you say you ventured into Samantha's memory twice today? I seem to be missing the earlier one."

"That's because there isn't one. My fault — I forgot to turn on the VCR this afternoon."

Really racking up points in the deception category, aren't I, Julie thought.

"That's too bad. How much do you remember?"

Alma took furious notes as Julie described the glowing matrioshka ball, the argument between her parents, Sam and Liam making love . . . but left out Sam's suspicions about Eathan.

"Very good," she said as she scribbled her last note. "Very good. With that fresh in my mind, I want to review the tapes again."

"Tonight?"

"Yes. Immediately." Her eyes were bright, almost feverish. "I do believe Samantha is trying to tell us something."

Julie knew that look. She'd seen it before . . . every time she'd demonstrated the memoryscape. Dr. Alma Evans was hooked.

"Do you really think that's possible?"

Eathan said. "How could there be anything left — ?"

Alma nodded. "Her conscious mind is down — a massive voltage spike followed by a power outage is probably the best analogy as to what happened in there. But her subconscious mind could still be active."

" 'Could'?" Eathan said.

"Well, we don't know for sure. We don't know much for sure about the subconscious mind. We know it houses memories and functions that exist apart from the conscious mind. Habits, for example — all your habits, all your routine activities, exist in the subconscious mind. Take fingernail biting, for instance. You don't say to yourself, 'Let's chew on the left ring finger now.' But if you've got a nail-biting habit, you'll find yourself gnawing away on a finger, even if you don't want to, even if you're consciously trying to stop. But more, the subconscious knows things the conscious doesn't — it retains some of the garbage the conscious tosses out. It can make intuitive leaps the conscious wouldn't dare."

"But the subconscious is not as organized as the conscious mind," Julie added.

"Exactly!" Alma said. "It's nonlinear, nonlogical, nonverbal, and inherently symbolic.

And that's the problem here. These inchoate memories we're seeing appear to be random in nature —"

"How can you be sure they *aren't* random?" Eathan said.

"I can't. But if the subconscious is at work here — if it senses the presence of its twin and is trying to communicate — then eventually a pattern will emerge."

"How long is 'eventually'?" he said.

Alma shook her head. "That I don't know."

Julie didn't want to bring everybody down, but she had to say it.

" 'Eventually' had better not take too long, because we don't have forever. Deprived of stimulation and interplay with the conscious mind, the subconscious will become quiescent as well. And that's what worries me about the second level: We saw one very active memory node, but Venice was obviously a critical time in Sam's life. The rest of the level looks dead and drowned. I take that as an ominous sign. And if I can't find anything else there tomorrow . . . well, then, I'm afraid we might be in real trouble."

Eathan sighed and looked away. "You mean she's getting worse?"

"Memory nodes are disappearing, vanishing. . . . There's no question about it."

Alma grabbed her arm. "Then we've no

time to waste. Every minute counts. I want to rewind these tapes so I can watch them again immediately."

"Will it matter?" Eathan said.

"Who can say?" Alma was suddenly a ball of fire. "But if anyone can figure this out, it's me. I think I can safely say that I know Sam's psyche better than either of you."

You've got that right, Julie thought.

"But I want you both to sit with me. I need filling in on historical details so I can separate fact from fantasy as we go along."

"I don't know. . . ." Eathan said.

Alma touched his arm. "Please, Eathan. For Samantha."

He sighed. "Very well. But I really don't see how that's going to help."

"I do. Truly I do." She looked around. "Now . . . where's that first tape?"

3

Julie was about to slip into bed when she heard a gentle knock on the door. She opened it and found the maid.

"A phone call, miss. From New York. A Dr. Siegal."

Dr. S.? she thought as she hurried downstairs. Why would he be calling now? She glanced at the windows as she stepped into the drawing room. Could Liam be out there watching?

Shivering, she picked up the phone.

"Julie," Dr. Siegal said without preamble. "Mr. Bruchmeyer is so enthusiastic about the project that he's instructed the board to fast-track our proposal. You know what that means, don't you."

"You need me back there."

"As soon as you can get free. I hate to rush you. I know I encouraged you to be with your family. We can proceed a little further without you, but we'll need you here in a few more days."

"A few more days?"

Leave Sam? Strange . . . two weeks ago, nothing in the world mattered more than getting that Bruchmeyer grant. Now everything was changing. She still cared about the project — deeply — but it was no longer the only thing that mattered.

"Well," he said. "As soon as you possibly can."

"Okay. I'll let you know."

They discussed a few details about the proposal, and then said good night.

Julie drifted back upstairs. What's happening to me? she wondered. Why aren't I more stoked about the project being fast-tracked?

As she reached the top of the stairs she caught a flash of white at the end of

the hall. She turned in time to see a neg-
ligeed Alma slipping into Eathan's bedroom.

I guess she's not here just for my sister,
she thought.

Eighteen

Quantum consciousness. Various theorists, Roger Penrose most prominently, have tried to wed quantum mechanics to consciousness theory, and point to the brain cell's microtubules as the root of consciousness. Vibrations, traveling through these microtubules, insulated so that they're not forced to choose a single state, provide the code of consciousness. I don't buy it . . . at least not yet.

— Random notes: Julia Gordon

1

Julie awoke late, feeling groggy. She opened her eyes and bolted upright in bed when she recognized her childhood room. For a moment she felt frightened and disoriented, then remembered that she was back in Oakwood.

For a brief moment it had been as if she

were a little girl again.

Funny, how that scared her.

Yesterday had been a long, trying day: arriving here, two trips into Sam's 'scape, then staying up late watching memoryscape videos with Alma. Too much.

And her encounter with Liam. She should be frightened by his skulking about the grounds at night, but she wasn't. She'd sensed no threat from him. But then, neither had Sam, obviously, and look what had happened to her.

Perhaps she should tell Eathan this morning.

And tell him about what Liam had said about Eathan hiding Dad's papers, the ones supposedly destroyed in the fire?

It was probably garbage . . . all garbage.

But then what about that locked file in Eathan's cabinet?

Julie pulled a pillow over her face to block out the morning light. She wished she could block out reality as easily. Dr. Siegal's phone call last night — he was tugging her back to New York while part of her needed to stay here.

And Alma sneaking into Eathan's room. God! Everything was getting so complicated.

She threw off the pillow and the covers and rolled out of bed. One thing was certain: Early this afternoon, as soon as Dr.

S. was up and about in New York, she was heading back into Sam's 'scape. And hopefully she'd find a new memory to access.

Of something else she was not so certain.

What to do about the video from yesterday afternoon? Should she show it to Alma? The woman was devoting so much time and effort to solving the puzzle of Sam, was it right to withhold one of the pieces? Alma knew Sam's inner workings. Was Julie hurting Sam by keeping that tape secret?

Still pondering that, she headed for the shower.

2

By the time she was dressed and ready for breakfast, Julie had made up her mind: For Sam's sake, she had to let Alma see the video from yesterday afternoon. She'd make up a story about being mistaken about the VCR being on. It didn't matter how lame it was — Alma would be too overjoyed to get the video to ask many questions.

But she wondered if there was some way to spare Eathan the "My uncle is hiding something" part.

Eathan was just finishing his breakfast when Julie arrived in the dining room. Alma was nowhere about.

"Sorry I couldn't wait for you," Eathan said, glancing at his watch as he took a last sip of coffee, "but I want to catch one of the London commuter flights out of Leeds."

"Something medical?"

"Legal, I'm afraid. Regarding Sam. Guardianship, trust-fund matters, provisions for long-term care. I'll be spending most of the day with lawyers."

"I'm sorry to hear that."

His smile was wan. "Not as sorry as I." He patted her shoulder and kissed the top of her head as he passed. "Need anything from London? I can have someone pick it up while I'm with the lawyers."

"Thanks, but I'm pretty well set."

"Cheers, then," he said. "See you for dinner. And take good care of Sam while I'm gone."

"I will."

Cook brought her some scrambled eggs and muffins; Julie declined the kippers. She'd just started digging in when Alma arrived. She looked haggard and older than she had last night.

"God, I didn't sleep a wink," Alma said as she let cook pile her plate high with eggs, bangers, kippers, and potatoes.

Julie couldn't resist. "Really? Whatever kept you up seems to have left you with quite an appetite."

"Goodness, yes. I'm quite famished. My mind kept combing through those videos. Over and over . . . I couldn't stop it."

"Getting anywhere?"

"Yes," she said, nodding vigorously. She pointed to her head. "But I need more fodder for the mill. When are you going in again?"

"This afternoon."

"Good. I can run through the tapes once more by then."

"What about your practice? Don't you have other patients?"

"I've been limiting my practice, and I've taken on an associate who's covering for me this week. I'll have to be back in London by Monday, though."

"You have family there?" Julie didn't want to sound as if she was probing, but . . . "A husband?"

"Divorced, I'm afraid. Just my Jack. My son. He's a barrister. Doing very well. Maybe if you're in London sometime, I'll introduce you."

Julie smiled and decided to change the subject. She was about to inform Alma of the miraculous discovery of yesterday afternoon's tape when she heard the tires of Eathan's car crunch on the driveway as he headed for the airport.

And suddenly it hit her: Eathan was going to be in London for most of the day.

That gave her all morning to poke through his study.

Maybe she'd hold off on giving Alma that tape. Just a little longer.

3

By midmorning, Alma was camped in the family room with the door closed, the curtains drawn, and the VCR running.

Except for Sam and the nurse, Julie had the whole upstairs to herself. She went straight to the study, closed the door behind her, retrieved the key from Eathan's desk, and opened the big oak cabinet.

Again, she had that sensation of her life passing before her. The scholastic awards, the ribbons, Sam's old paintings and sculptures . . . they all engendered another feeling: guilt. Eathan's last words: *Take good care of Sam while I'm gone.*

So what was she doing instead? Snooping through his private study. Nice . . .

One tug on the handle of the locked file cabinet was enough to convince her that guilt was premature. If she found nothing, *then* she'd feel guilty. But if Sam was right and Eathan was hiding their father's papers, that was another story.

She looked at the four-digit combination. It read 9574. She wished it were a letter code instead of numbers. She knew from her computer-hacking days as a teenager that people were a lot more predictable when they had to choose a password as compared to a PIN code.

She tried Eathan's birthday: 12-1-41. Easy to remember because he always said he was born a week before Pearl Harbor. She tried all the four-digit permutations she could think of, tried adding a zero before the one, even tried putting the month second, British style. Nothing. The drawers wouldn't budge. She tried permutations of her own birthday. Same result.

And then, without warning, she heard the study door open behind her.

Julie froze, dreading the prospect of turning around and facing Eathan.

Oh, God! What am I going to say?

The door closed again and a now-familiar voice said, "And who would that be now, snooping through her uncle's private study?"

She whirled. "You!"

Liam grinned at her. "Himself."

He was dressed in jeans, sneakers, and a heavy white sweater. His gleaming smile sparkled, as did his blue eyes. With a cloth cap pulled snug over his long, red hair, he looked like one of the groundsmen.

"How on earth — ?"

"Oh, saw the uncle leave, I did, then saw

the cook head into the village. So I walked in the back door. I know you're out in the middle of nowhere, but you really do need better security here." He stared at the wall cabinet. "Look at this, will you. I grew up in a flat smaller than this."

As the shock wore off, anger flared in Julie. "Get out of here! Get out now or I'll call the police!"

"You'll be doing no such thing, and you won't be taking another swing at me either, I'm hoping." He gave the brim of his cap a mockingly deferential tug as he stepped past her. "Because you're as curious as I am, aren't you. Sammi as much as asked me to take a look for her. Said, 'You can do that kind of thing, can't you?' It was her last request before she locked herself away in her bloody room and wouldn't see anybody. And so I'm honoring it." He surveyed the cabinet. "Now what have we here?"

Julie's anger dissipated. She didn't feel afraid of the man. He easily could have gone to Sam's room if he'd wanted to, could have just as easily hurt Julie last night. She took a breath — and accepted the fact that he wasn't a danger. For the moment.

She also realized that Liam was the one person who could tell her about Sam's last days.

"What was she like that week? Did she say anything about being afraid of anyone?"

"Poor thing was afraid of her own shadow about then, and I don't know why. Don't think she did either. She went a little bit off. Maybe more than a little. All she wanted to do was work on that painting. Didn't sleep, didn't eat. Wouldn't give anyone even a peek at it, or let them near it."

He paused. "Now that I'm thinking of it, you could almost say it was the painting she was afraid of. Scared to death of it and yet she couldn't drag herself away from it. Does that make any sense?"

Julie shook her head. "Not a bit."

He shook his head. "I didn't think so."

"But what happened to it?"

He turned to her and stepped closer. "That's what *I'd* like to know. I'm the one who found her on the floor, right in front of her easel. And it was empty. Someone had been there and took the painting."

Julie met his gaze levelly. "Eathan thinks it was you. And frankly, so do I."

Did she really? She wasn't sure. . . .

"Not me. I swear to God."

"Who then?"

"Ask your uncle."

"Eathan? How can you say that?"

Liam turned and gestured to the display inside the wall cabinet. "He seems to be the world's foremost collector of Sammi's work."

Julie stood silent for an instant, stunned

by the implication. Then she shook it off.

"Yes, but if you'll notice, he's also a major collector of Sam's sister's work, as well."

"Well, you've maybe got a point there. A bit weird, though, don't you think?"

"Obsessive, perhaps. But Sam was right in a way. Our uncle has been hiding something. But it's all innocent. Just memorabilia. Benchmarks from our youth."

"You sure that's all?"

He began pulling open the filing-cabinet drawers. The sight of him pawing through the file folders offended Julie.

"Stay out of there. That's none of your business."

"If it concerns Sammi, it's my bloody business. Like I told you, she sent me here. She said —" He stopped as he tugged on one of the drawers of the locked file cabinet. "And what have we here? Locked, is it?"

"I was trying to figure out the combination when you barged in."

He turned to her and grinned. "*Slipped* in, love. On little cat's feet." He swung back to the locked file cabinet. "So what could he be hiding in here now, do you think? Maybe your da's papers?"

"I told you: They were all destroyed in the fire."

"Were they now? Well, why don't we get this open and see? What have you tried so far?"

She explained about using permutations of birth dates — Eathan's and Sam's and hers.

"Well, I'm thinking now, if this here cabinet hides your da's papers, why not try his birthday?"

That struck Julie as an excellent idea, except for one thing. One very embarrassing thing.

"I . . . I don't know my father's birthday."

Liam swung on her. "You don't *what?* Are you expecting me to believe that?"

"It's true. I don't know my mother's, either, come to think of it. Nor their anniversary date. We had no cause to. There were never any birthday parties or celebrations; we never had to buy them gifts." Julie hated having to explain herself to this man, but felt compelled to. "Dammit, we were five when they died."

Liam's frustration showed on his face. "All right then. How about his *death* date, then?"

"March seventh, nineteen seventy-two."

"You know the day he died," Liam said, staring at her, "but you don't —"

"It was the day that changed our lives." She stepped past him to the locked cabinet. "Let's try it."

She set the numbers to 3-7-7-2 and pulled on a handle.

The top drawer popped open.

A strange feeling shot through Julie's intestines, a little like pain, a little like nausea. Eathan had used the date of her parents' death as a code number on a lock. That wasn't right. Unless the contents were . . .

She spread the first of the hanging folders and ran her fingers across the tops of the papers within. She saw a letter addressed to Nathan Gordon, Ph.D., and something that said *Last Will and Testament.*

"Your da's papers, am I right?" Liam said.

Julie nodded, unable to speak.

Dad's papers. Here all this time. Eathan had been lying to them all these years. God, why?

She felt as if her whole world were unraveling.

"What did I tell you?" Liam was saying, oblivious to the turmoil inside her. "Now aren't you glad I stopped by? If I hadn't you'd still be here next year dialing numbers into that thing."

He reached toward the open drawer but Julie slammed it shut, just missing his fingers.

"You keep your hands out of there. *I'll* go through this cabinet, and if there's anything that concerns Sam, I may — *may* — let you see it."

"Now wait just a minute, darling. I'm the one —"

"No!" The ferocity she felt surprised her. She was going to protect these papers from Liam O'Donnell and anyone else who wanted to snoop through her father's life. "This is *my* call, do you hear? You either accept that or get out! Clear?"

Obviously taken aback by the outburst, he held up his hands, palms out.

"All right, all right. I know better than to get between a lioness and her cubs."

Julie pulled the drawer back open and returned to the first file. She removed the thickest document, a thick sheaf bound by an old rubber band that broke when she pulled on it. On top lay the *Last Will and Testament of Nathan Gordon.* Beneath that was the *Last Will and Testament of Lucinda Gordon.* And finally, *The Insurance Trust of Nathan Gordon and Lucinda Gordon.* She flipped through them, scanning the headings and some of the body.

"Anything important?" Liam said.

Julie shook her head. "Just wills," she said as she stuffed them back into the folder.

If the need arose, she could go over them in detail some other time, but she had a pretty good idea of how they ran: If Dad died first, everything went to Mom, and vice versa. Then if the surviving parent died, everything went into A and B trusts for the children. But if both died in the same accident, Dad would be considered the first death, then Mom, leaving everything in the trusts.

She pulled out another sheet. This one was a letter to Nathan Gordon dated November 28, 1970, from BankAmericard denying him the credit-limit increase he'd requested.

Odd. Why would they turn him down?

The next letter was from the Millburn State Bank, dated December 12, 1971. A loan officer was telling Dad that if he didn't pay something on his mortgage soon the bank would be forced to begin foreclosure proceedings.

Julie was stunned. Foreclosure? She'd had no idea Dad had been in financial straits. How was that possible when they'd been left with such generous trust funds?

She pulled out another sheet. This one was from the FDA, dated January 25, 1966. Specifically from a Jack Winslow, Ph.D., informing Dad that his request for approval of a clinical trial protocol for testing certain neurohormones (detailed in clinical application #F97674-02) was being denied. The reason for denial was the lack of sufficient primate trials required before moving up to human testing.

"So what's going on there, darling?" Liam said at her shoulder. "Anything that matters?"

"Mostly bad news," Julie said. "A whole file of bad news. Stuff I never knew."

Dad, it seemed, had had his share of problems.

She shoved the letters back in and closed the file. Maybe the next —

Suddenly she heard Alma's voice in the hall outside: "Have you seen Julia?"

Her heart pounding, Julie eased the drawer shut as quickly and as silently as she could while Alma listened to a muffled, unintelligible reply, probably from Sam's nurse.

Julie leaned close to Liam and whispered in his ear. "Grab that door. She could be coming in here!"

Outside, she heard Alma say, "Well, if you see her, please tell her I'm looking for her."

Julie had the right door, Liam the left; they were backed into the cabinet and pulling them closed as the latch on the study door turned.

She *is* coming in!

They stood there, cramped together in the darkness with the handles of the file drawers pressing against Julie's back. She felt Liam close to her, heard his breathing. She was surprised he didn't make a joke. Nothing seemed to scare him.

The only light came from the bright slit between the doors. Julie put her eye to it.

Alma was crossing the room. She went

to the windows that overlooked the gardens and stared out.

Looking for me?

"What's she doing?" Liam whispered. Liam's lips were close to her ears.

Julie didn't reply — it was reckless to say a single word in here. He was close. She could sense the warmth of him, feel his breath on her neck. So close. Almost like in the memoryscape . . .

And then she remembered: She'd left the key in the wall-cabinet lock. What if Alma saw it?

After a moment at the windows, Alma turned away and headed for the book-shelves. She found the book she wanted, pulled it out, and left, closing the door behind her.

She certainly seems to know her way around, Julie thought. How often does she stay here? Julie had never given much thought to the women in Eathan's life.

She pushed the doors open and turned to the file cabinet containing her father's papers. She rolled the numbers on the combination lock.

"Now why would you be doing that?" Liam said in a hushed voice.

"Because we're getting out of here."

"But we've only just started —"

"It's too dangerous. She could be back for another book or to return that one anytime. I don't want to get caught."

Liam said nothing as she closed the big doors again — this time with Julie and him on the outside — and locked them. But she pocketed the key instead of returning it to the desk. She didn't want Liam to know where to find it.

She turned to him. "How will you get out of the house?"

"Leave that to me. But before I do get out, I've got a favor to ask."

"What?"

"I want to see Sammi."

Julie felt herself tense as she realized that for a nanosecond she'd actually considered agreeing to it. How had she let herself fall under this man's spell? He was a prime suspect behind Sam's condition, and here they were, acting like co-conspirators against Eathan.

"Just for a moment," he added when she didn't reply.

"No. Absolutely not."

His fair skin reddened with anger. "Why the hell not? I love her. She means every-thing to me."

"Neither you nor anybody else is getting near Sam until I find out what happened to her."

He started toward the door. "Then I'll find her myself."

"There's a nurse with Sam whenever I'm

not. You go anywhere near her room and I'll be on the phone to Scotland Yard, telling them that Liam O'Donnell is in North York-shire."

He spun and faced her. "Bloody hell you will!"

"In a New York minute," she said levelly, meeting his glare.

He stood facing her, his jaw clenched, his hands opening and closing into fists. For an instant Julie was afraid she'd crossed an invisible line with him. He looked as if he were going to attack her.

But he didn't.

"Be damned, then," he said softly.

And then he was striding for the door. He opened it a crack, peeked out, then was gone.

Julie hurried after him into the hall. Empty. Suddenly frightened, she hurried down to Sam's room.

If he's there, she thought, if he harms her, I'll never forgive myself.

But only the nurse and Sam were there. Where had Liam gone?

She turned and saw Alma walking down the hall toward her. She had her yellow pad under her arm.

"Ah, Julie," she said pleasantly. "There you are. I've been looking all over for you. Where have you been hiding?"

"Just killing time until I can take another

look into the memoryscape." She glanced at her watch. "Still a couple of hours to go before the States are awake."

"I can hardly wait. But listen, I think I've come up with something on the Venice memory from last night. Venice isn't important. Neither is that diva — at least not of crucial importance. The key to the memory is the opera itself."

"*Otello?* Why?"

"I'm not exactly sure yet. Maybe the painting is the key. If the subconscious is trying to get a message out, it will do so using symbols. Just like in a dream. The lion in the gondola represents Otello. He was known as 'the Lion of Venice.' So that's the key." She laughed. "Key to what, though, I can't say."

Julie shrugged. "Maybe it's the other way around. Maybe the painting is just a key to get us to the Venice memory, which just happened to take place during a run of *Otello*."

"Could be," Alma said. "But I don't think so. Frightfully involved, isn't it. But I truly believe Otello himself is the key to that memory. Samantha is speaking to us through her own art and through the art that spoke to her during her life. We simply need to see more. We need more pieces of the picture she is trying to paint for us." She held a book up to Julie. "I found this in your uncle's study: 'Stories of the Great Operas.' Might be of some help."

Alma's enthusiasm was contagious, but Julie felt compelled to leaven it with a dose of reality.

"*If* indeed she's really trying to communicate with us, and *if* there's enough of her subconscious left to finish the job."

"I'm quite sure of the first; and I'm praying for the second. Let me know the instant you're ready to go back inside her. We must make the most of every possible opportunity."

Julie glanced at her watch again. Hours to go before Dr. S. would be in his office. Why wait that long? She'd visited Sam's memoryscape without him before. Why not do it again?

"To hell with New York," she told Alma. "What's wrong with right now?"

Nineteen

Maybe I should approach Sam's coma-tose memoryscape as a sort of dreamscape. During dream states, the body is paralyzed and the doors are shut on outer reality. Cholinergic neu-rons in the pontine-geniculate-occipital system fire erratically, sending bursts of waves throughout the higher areas of the brain. These PGO waves disrupt the cognitive networks of rational, orderly flows of information, allowing irrational, disorderly thoughts, emotions, and im-ages to swirl through the mind. At this point only the inner reality exists, and all the rules are off. A dream is the result of the poor cortex trying to make sense of the chaos.
    — Random notes: Julia Gordon

You enter the memoryscape where you left it — in the deeper-level gallery. Your heart sinks as you look about and see no new paintings on the walls. You had hoped for a change.

You drift outside the gallery.

Still a drowned world, a vast expanse of stagnant water broken by dark, scattered fragments of land. Low in the sky to your left, the giant crescent moon slouches down the eternal starless night, sinking into the horizon of the endless black sea.

No gondola waits at the shore this time. You guess that was a one-time-only ride. You scan the dead waters, looking for some sign of life. You see nothing, and your sense of hopelessness deepens.

The night grows deeper as the far waters drown the moon. You watch it disappear, and when it is gone you find yourself in a darkness so profound it swallows even the wan light leaking from the gallery behind you.

The darkness invades your soul, enveloping your will. You can see no reason to stay here, no hope of changing this watery wasteland.

Maybe — you think — you don't have the guts for this.

But as you reach for the Exit button, you hear a crunch behind you. Turning, you see the gondola, waiting. As before, no gondolier. Heartened but wary of expecting too much, you step aboard but remain standing as it begins its journey.

And then, far ahead in the distance, a spark. You squint toward it. An illusion? Wishful thinking?

No, it's there, it's real. But so far away and so faint you would have missed it had the moon been up.

A long trip across the trackless sea as the spark gradually becomes a blob of light — but high above the waterline. As you near it you see an island rearing sixty or seventy feet above the sea. You see dead trees clustered at its center and marble doorways cut into its flanks. You've seen this place before. In a painting: Arnold Böcklin's *Isle of the Dead.*

But now the light is a glowing rectangle atop the island. You leave the gondola and glide toward it. Soon you realize that this light is the window of a diner. A Phillies Cigars sign runs across its roof — ONLY 5¢ — and its window glass turns an impossible curve. The counterman, wearing a white paper cap, works under the wooden counter. It should be Formica, you think, but it looks more like oak or mahogany.

In the corner, near the two large chrome urns, a sharp-nosed man sits next to a woman in a red dress. They're smoking and drinking coffee. On this end of the counter, a lone man in a hat sits with his back to you.

You know this scene. It's Hopper's *Night-hawks.* A lonely painting, a city painting . . . an eerie painting.

Forgetting about Sam and why you're here, you hurry for the door. If you had feet you'd be running. You've always wondered who this couple was, where they were coming from or going to, what they were saying to each other. Now at last you can find out.

You pull on the handle but the door doesn't budge.

You rattle the latch. The couple at the counter turn and stare at you. The counterman leans over the counter and says something you can't hear. He points to the door, then points to his right. You back up a step and see a hand-printed sign taped to the glass.

ENTER THRU THEATER
AROUND CORNER

You nod, wave, and hurry around the side of the diner. It looks so warm and bright in there and you long to come in from the dark.

But the theater around the corner also looks closed. The marquee is dark and cluttered with a meaningless jumble of letters. You can see the name atop the marquee: THE PALLAS.

You wonder: Shouldn't it be "Palace"?

But never mind. That's not important. You approach the ticket booth. A small, naked bulb somewhere below the counter lights the interior but it's empty. You continue on, past torn and faded posters in their display cases, to the door. The hinges creak in agony as you push through.

Dark inside. But not completely. A dull glow leaks from behind the concession stand. You smell popcorn but the popper looks empty. The glass front of the counter is broken and the candy looted. Popcorn is strewn about. It crunches under your feet. The light fades as you move farther inside, until it's as dark as the moonless night outside. How are you supposed to get to the diner through here? It doesn't make sense.

Suddenly you see flickering light ahead, coming from the left. You move toward it, turn. . . .

You're in the back of a theater. An empty theater. Something is playing on the screen, loud, full of color and activity, but the picture is out of focus and the sound garbled. Then you notice that the theater is not quite empty. Two people sit in the very front row. Curious, you move down the aisle.

And as you near the screen it shrinks, becoming progressively smaller until it's the size of a thirteen-inch TV set. And seated before it are two little girls, ages seven or eight.

Sam and Julie . . .

"I'm going to kill the waaaaabbit!"

On the TV screen, Elmer Fudd, in armor and horned helmet, chases Bugs Bunny dressed as a golden-pigtailed Rhinemaiden across a fantastic Valhallan landscape.

"I don't think I like this show," Sam says, peeking out from behind the chair cushion she's begun holding in front of her face. "It's stupid."

"What — are you scared?" Julie says, her voice dripping with contempt. "It's only a

303

dumb cartoon! Not like they're real people or anything."

Siegfried Fudd again calls out his murderous promise — *"I'm going to kill the waaaaabbit!"* — and Sam ducks behind her cushion.

That does it for Julie. She's had it with Sammi's weirdness. One cartoon character threatening another — big deal. They do it all the time. And even if you're stupid enough to think they're real, they always bounce back, no matter what happens. Look what that coyote lives through.

"Stop being a baby, Sammi. Look at it."

A muffled "No!" from behind the cushion. "And no one can make me!"

"Oh, no?"

Incensed by the challenge, Julie grabs the cushion and tears it from Sammi's grasp.

Sammi cries, "No!" and turns away, burying her face in her arms.

Julie leaps on her and a wrestling match begins.

"No, Julie! No! Please don't make me look!"

But Sammi's pleas fall on deaf ears.

You want to grab hold of the little girl you were and shake some sense into her. Doesn't she see that her sister is frightened — truly frightened? Terrified of that noisy cartoon. But young Julie can only see that her sister is being

304

silly. Who can be afraid of drawings? She'll show Sammi there's nothing to be afraid of, whether she likes it or not.

But you know differently.

You've begun to see what colors and lines and pictures mean to Sam, how her perceptions, her view of life were so different from yours that, in a very real sense, she grew up on a different planet. A scarier planet.

And as much as you want to stop this replay, you can't. You can only watch helplessly as Julie steadily overpowers the sister who never had much will to fight, even to protect herself.

Julie manages to pull Sammi's face free of her arms. Panting, struggling, she gets her sister's head tilted up to face the TV screen. But Sammi keeps her eyes squeezed shut.

"Open your eyes, Sammi! *Open* them!"

"No! I don't want to see!"

Frustrated, seeing no way to get Sammi's eyes open, Julie glances at the TV screen and notices a lull in the cartoon. She tries another tack. She releases her sister from the headlock and rolls away from her.

"Oh, forget it," she says. "The stupid cartoon's over anyway."

With that, Sammi opens her eyes and looks at the screen. There, in Technicolor, Bugs Bunny lies splayed on a rock, eyes closed, limp arms akimbo, while a lone flower weeps over him.

Sammi lets out an ear-piercing screech and leaps to her feet. She stands and stares at the screen, crying, "He's dead! He's dead!"

And then she runs screaming from the room.

Little Julie stares after her, baffled.

"What's the big deal?" she says softly. "It's only a cartoon."

On the TV, Bugs raises his head and looks out from the screen. *"Well, what did you expect in an opera — a happy ending?"*

You turn away, disgusted with yourself, and wondering what Alma's making of all this. You know you're not being entirely fair to the younger Julie. She couldn't understand Sam — didn't have the tools even to try. And even now you doubt the older, wiser Julie has all the necessary tools.

Perhaps it's just the challenge, or perhaps it's something deeper, but you're trying. Trying like all hell.

You hunt around for a way into the diner, but find no exit doors. No way in or out except via the entrance. You hurry out, back to the street. But next to the ticket booth, blocking your way, is another matrioshka doll, this one in the shape of Bugs Bunny, rocking back and forth on its round base.

You've no time for this, yet you can't resist finding out what nests inside. You touch the doll and it splits across its middle. The top pops off and there's Elmer Fudd in hunter's gear, trying to look fierce as he clutches his shotgun to his chest. Another touch, another split, and Bugs is back again, carrot in hand, that insouciant, wiseacre grin on his face.

But as with all the preceding matrioshkas, this is as far as it will go. Bugs inside Elmer inside Bugs. What does it mean? Does it mean anything?

You hurry back to the darkened theater front and turn left. When you reach the welcoming light from inside the diner, you pull on the door again. Still locked. You start to knock on the glass but stop cold.

It's different inside. The couple at the far end of the counter by the urns — the woman in the red dress now wears your mother's face, and the man has become Eathan. Not a young Eathan, but Eathan as you know him now. And the man sitting alone — he's now your father. And the counterman, Liam. He looks up from whatever he's frying on the grill and grins at you.

Disturbed, frightened, you back away. This is too crazy, even by Sam's standards. You turn and flee, soaring off into the night. Forget the gondola. Just go.

The dripping moon is half-risen from the sea on the far side of this drowned world. You aim for it, sensing that is the way back to the gallery. As you glide you notice something rippling the surface of the moonlit water below. Could it be whatever brushed the hull of your gondola last night?

You swoop down, but by the time you reach the surface the ripples have spread and dissipated. You hover there, wondering what could live in these dead waters.

Suddenly a splash. You turn and see a tentacle as thick around as a man's thigh uncoiling from the surface. The black water rolls off its skin. Its suckered undersurface reaches for you, the puckered mouthlike pores ready to grab and hold you.

You cry out — your voice in the real world startles you. Then you dart away, leaving the thing to slide back into the sea.

What would it have done to you? Dragged you down to join Sam in her coma?

With your heart pounding you click on EXIT. You'll return to the gallery another time. Maybe.

Twenty

Not all memories are conscious. We have loads of nonconscious memories — they're called "habits."
— Random notes: Julia Gordon

1

Julie pulled off the headset and stared at Sam as she waited for her heart to slow. She knew the tentacle couldn't have really grabbed her — she had no physical presence in the memoryscape — yet it appeared to be trying. Maybe that was good. It seemed a sure sign that something inside Sam was aware of her presence. But why such a frightening and ugly manifestation? And why try to snare her like that?

Retaliation for the memory she'd just relived?

Julie squeezed her eyes shut against a stab of remorse.

Can't say I haven't got it coming.

She glanced over at Alma, who was scribbling furiously on her yellow pad.

"What was *that* all about?"

"Which 'that'?" Alma said, still scribbling. "The cartoon, the diner, or the kraken?"

"Kraken?"

"The tentacle. The kraken was a mythical creature that used to rise from the depths, grasp hapless ships, and drag them under."

"Why would she have a kraken in there?"

"I can't say just yet. Perhaps it's a manifestation of Samantha herself, or her subconscious. Something obviously *deep*."

"Could that be why it reached for me — a sign she's trying to reach me?"

Alma's head snapped up. "Now *there's* a possibility. A very intriguing thought." She went back to scribbling. "If only I could have seen that first session yesterday."

"But I described it to you."

"Not the same as seeing and hearing with my own eyes and ears. Those landscapes are simply *acrawl* with meaning and symbols." She sighed. "If only I'd taken an earlier flight."

Guiltily, Julie glanced at the videotape box. The cassette with the little X on its label, the tape of the session in question, sat within arm's reach among the blanks.

Why not? she thought. Eathan is hours away in London. Alma will have time enough to watch it any number of times before his return. And if I ask her to keep mum, for Eathan's sake . . .

Could she trust this woman who made nocturnal visits to Eathan's bedroom? Julie imagined Alma's hierarchy of loyalties as Eathan first, Sam second, and Julie last.

But she had to risk it, for Sam's sake.

She reached over and plucked the X tape from the box.

"Alma? I hope you'll understand why I did this. . . ."

"Did what, dear?"

"Held back the tape of yesterday's first session. I —"

Alma leaped to her feet and snatched it from Julie's fingers.

"You have it?" she said, staring at the blank label. "This is *it?*"

"Yes, I —"

But Alma was already headed for the hall. "I must see this immediately!"

"But —"

Julie hurried out after her and followed her downstairs to the family room, explaining her concerns about Eathan's reaction to the tape.

"I don't think you give your uncle enough credit," Alma said. "He's considerably more resilient than that. Consider what he's already absorbed from Samantha all these years."

Julie didn't want to mention her other

reason: losing access to the wall cabinet.

"Just don't tell him. I don't even want him to know the tape exists. I hope I've made that very clear."

Alma stopped and looked at her. "If that is what you want, my dear, then that is the way it shall be. Fair enough?"

"Fair enough."

"Smashing. Now I must see this at once!"

As Alma disappeared into the family room, Julie dug into her pocket for the key to the wall cabinet. Maybe she'd better do some more snooping while she still could.

And then she remembered: Hadn't she seen a locksmith shop in Robin Hood's Bay as she drove through yesterday? She had Eathan's key. Why not have a duplicate made?

She headed to the front closet for her coat.

2

When Julie returned with the duplicate key, she immediately checked on Alma in the family room. She found the psychiatrist sitting in the dark, utterly absorbed in the videotape playing before her.

The light from the open door reflected off her glasses as she glanced over at Julie. "I'm so glad you let me see this," she said.

"It adds so much!"

Julie left her there and went directly upstairs to the study. She wanted the original key back where it belonged before she did another thing.

After replacing it in the drawer, she took the duplicate to the wall cabinet and tried it in the lock. It worked. Good.

She debated whether to delve further into that locked file cabinet. She'd only scratched the surface there, only seen part of the top drawer. She was about to pull the doors open when she heard a timid tap on the study door.

Quickly she relocked the wall cabinet, pocketed the key, and said, "Yes?"

Clarice, the maid, opened the door. A little mouse of a woman, she gazed at Julie through thick glasses. "Pardon me, mum, but I wonder if I'd be disturbing you if I cleaned now."

"No-no," Julie said. "Come right in. I was just looking for something to read."

Damn. The maid must have seen her come in here. Hopefully she wouldn't think enough of it to mention it to Eathan. Clarice hadn't been here during their childhood, when the study was Eathan's sanctum sanctorum, and no one else was allowed.

As Clarice started dusting, Julie wandered over to the bookshelf where she'd seen the neurochemistry journals with the

Nathan Gordon articles. Just what sort of research had her "visionary" and "unorthodox" father been into?

3

Julie put off the day's second trip into Sam's memoryscape until Eathan returned from London.

After seeing the dunning notices in the locked file cabinet, she'd wanted to quiz him on Dad's financial problems. But now, having read her father's journal articles, she had far more pressing concerns.

Eathan arrived in the late afternoon. The skies were a battleship gray, the air cool and damp. Not too many more blue-sky days in store.

She let him freshen up, then tracked him to his study, where she found him seated at the desk unpacking his briefcase.

She was more than a little nervous as she stepped through the door.

"Welcome back," she said. She held up the journals — she'd decided to be up-front about the articles. "I'm returning these."

He looked up. "What are they?"

"Neurochem journals with some of Dad's articles. I was in here when Clarice was dusting and spotted them on the shelf. Hope you don't mind."

He glanced around at the shelves. "Here? I'm surprised you found them. Of course I don't mind. They're part of your legacy from Nathan. Frankly, I find them impenetrable. I tried to read them after the fire but couldn't make much of them. Too much chemical mumbo jumbo. Do they make any sense to you?"

Julie nodded. "Yes. Maybe too much."

"I'm sorry?"

Julie stacked the journals on his desk. "All his work — at least what's in these — seems to center around right-brained and left-brained aspects of intellect and personality. He didn't use those terms. He simply called them creative and analytical abilities."

"I know the theoretical basics — Nathan and I discussed them many times. He saw creative and analytical abilities occurring on a bell curve, with analytical on the left and creative on the right, and the optimum at the top of the curve, where both abilities were perfectly balanced. I forget what examples he used, something like Einstein on the left, Van Gogh on the right, and Frank Lloyd Wright atop the curve."

"That sounds about right. But it's kind of scary in these articles the way he talks about influencing someone's place on the curve by dosing them with various neurohormones during their developmental years

. . . making them more left-brained or more right-brained, whichever you wish."

"Just theory."

"But it's not just theory. He outlines ways to do it. It sounds like . . ."

Eathan smiled through his beard. "Social engineering?"

"Well, yes, that too. But . . ." Her mouth was suddenly dry. Dammit! How could she say this? "But Sam and I are identical twins and yet we're so different. I mean, who's more right-brained than Sam? And as for me —"

Eathan shot to his feet. "Julia, stop it! Stop it this instant! How can you even think such a thing? Your father loved you two! You were the lights of his life. He would never even consider experimenting on you! It's unthinkable!"

"No," Julie said, slowly, deliberately. "It's not unthinkable. You yourself said he wanted to prove his theories but was turned down for research grants. And then his wife bears a set of identical twins. What better experimental subjects? They're genetically matched. Dose them with different sets of neurohormones and see if their development follows the predicted paths."

Eathan's face reddened. "I will not stand here and allow anyone, even his own daughter, to slander my brother like that!"

"It's not slander, Eathan. It's a horrible

suspicion, and if Sam and I were more alike, it never would've occurred to me. But we're not, so it did. I don't *want* to believe it. Talk me out of it."

Eathan sighed. "What can I say except that Nathan and I grew up together and, unlike you and Samantha, we were very much alike. We had our disagreements, of course. All brothers do. But on the whole we were best friends throughout most of our lives. No one, not even your mother, knew him better than I. And tell me, would the man who risked his life to carry you two out of that burning house ever entertain the thought of experimenting on his own children?"

Julie saw the flames again, felt the heat, and that strong arm wrapping around her, lifting her, and carrying her through the smoke and flames to safety.

She took a breath. Eathan's words made sense. The man who ran back into that fire to save their mother would not risk harming his family.

"Deep inside I think I knew it couldn't be true, but I needed to hear you tell me. The idea latched onto me as I was reading the articles and I couldn't shake it." She smiled sheepishly. "Pretty silly, I guess."

Eathan didn't return her smile. "Ridiculous is more like it. And insulting to his memory. Imagine, thinking that of your own father." Finally he did smile, but only slightly. "Perhaps you and your sister aren't so far apart as you think. That's the sort of wild idea I'd expect from Samantha."

"You've got a point there. Sorry."

"I'm not the one you owe the apology to."

Eathan seemed tired. Perhaps things hadn't gone well with the lawyers.

As he went back to unpacking his briefcase, Julie considered the next area of her father's life that needed explaining: his financial problems. But she'd have to be more circumspect here.

"Was Dad well off financially?" she said.

"Why do you ask?"

"Well, you said he quit his job and went looking for research grants. . . . I was just wondering where all the money came from. You know, our trust funds and all that."

Eathan didn't look up. "Oh, it came from insurance. Nathan was anything but rich. He was going through especially tight times before the fire, and that made the insurance companies act very suspicious."

"Suspicious?" Julie felt her chest tighten inside. "Why would they be suspicious?"

"Note I said 'act' suspicious. The plain truth is they didn't want to pay out two million dollars to a pair of five-year-old orphans." He looked up now and this time his grin was tight and very real. "But I made them pay every dime they owed you."

"But what was their problem?"

"Your father and mother each carried a million-dollar accidental death policy on themselves. You see, when you're young and healthy — like yourself, for instance — the most common cause of death is an accident, so it was a smart, cost-effective way to provide for their children's future should anything happen to them. But if you think two million dollars is a lot now, it was an *enormous* sum in nineteen seventy-two. The insurance company tried every trick in its arsenal to keep from paying. It sent one investigative team after another to look for evidence of arson, or that the bodies were not Nathan and Lucy Gordon."

He leaned over the desk. "I tell you, Julia, it was infuriating. I'm glad you two were too young to realize what was going on. To suffer through that fire, and then the endless investigations, the repeat autopsies . . ." He shook his head in disgust. "But none of their investigators found anything suspicious. So finally they paid up. And then I took the bastards to court to force them to add the interest that would have accrued during the delay."

That single word, *bastards*, punched home the depth of Eathan's feelings on the episode. It was atypical of Eathan. Julie couldn't remember him cursing once during her childhood.

"But let's talk about the present," he said. "Any progress on Samantha?"

Julie described her memoryscape excursion earlier today — neglecting to mention the fact that Dr. S. hadn't been along to monitor her.

"I'm getting ready to go in again. Want to sit in?"

"Yes. I suppose I should. I just . . ." He shrugged.

Poor Eathan. He still couldn't get used to the idea of peering into his niece's mind.

"Good," Julie said. "I'll collect Alma, we'll get Dr. Siegal on the line, and we'll be ready to go."

"I wonder what we'll see this time?" he said softly.

Good question, Julie thought as she left him at his desk. Hopefully I can steer clear of whatever is lurking under the surface there.

Twenty-One

If a dream state is an accurate model for Sam's ruined memoryscape, maybe I'll encounter new insights there. The "undocking" process that results from the cholinergic PGO waves in sleep — the dissolution of cognitive associations formed by the awake brain — allows new, unconventional associations to form. Most of what we call "inspiration" is the result of this free-form, dissociative process. It's been shown that intense prayer or deep meditation can bring on a dreamlike cholinergic state. When this results in a solution to a thorny problem, usually God or a maharishi gets the credit, but real thanks should go to the brain's PGO waves.
— Random notes: Julia Gordon

You float in the center of the gallery. You wish you were alone, but Dr. S. is watching. Alma and Eathan are nearby, also watching. The gang's all here.

And everyone's got their secrets. You and

Alma share one. And Dr. Siegal doesn't know you've gone in without him. And you now know that Eathan has secrets: your father's papers in his locked file cabinet, papers Eathan said were destroyed.

You're torn between the desire to see your sister's memoryscape and to get back to Eathan's study.

You look about the gallery. Against a wall, the lion of Venice still roars, and, farther on, you see Sam's big painting. You go closer. More details have been added. As the memoryscape deteriorates, is the painting being reborn? Yellow-orange light flares from somewhere in the center of the painting. But the center is empty. A dark, oblong shape blocks the light source. But the shape remains a secret.

Another secret. You have ideas about the big secrets.

They're about your father, your mother. Their relationship, his work, his success, his failure. Eathan has always been so protective. Does he believe you need protection from the truth? Yes . . . if he thought it would hurt you.

And then, in another corner of the gallery, you spot a new canvas. You move to it, and it's the strangest of them all.

A bit like a Mondrian, with his stark lines and boxes, his abstract constructs that always seemed to you to be devoid of feeling. Except this painting — whether it's Mondrian's or

Sam's — is all jumbled. The lines are broken, disconnected. As if someone took scissors to the canvas and cut it up.

You notice something on the painting. You move closer.

It's you.

Or rather, a tiny paper-doll version of you — trapped between two lines. Part of the jumble. So eerie and disconcerting to see yourself reduced to a stiff paper figure.

You move the glove over your image. You let the virtual hand hover over the image a moment — and then you click.

The paper doll comes to life. You see the tiny image of yourself smile. But then the smile fades as the doll figure looks left and right, seeing that it's trapped.

Then, like a piece of bacon on a skillet, the Julie doll begins to brown and curl, twisting into a charred knot before vanishing in a tiny puff of smoke.

And without doing another thing, you seem to melt into the painting — *through* the painting — and then you're outside, hovering above the black sea.

It's still dark out here, still tomb-silent and desolate, but now you notice there are fewer islands, and the remaining ones have changed position. They've gathered closer, as if huddling together until they too slip below the surface.

You spot an island where the lines and

boxes of the painting are now real. A confused girderlike structure painted in garish primary colors stands on the shore. And at the bottom is an opening, a doorway.

You start toward it, then − like the paper doll − you're in the structure, in a long, featureless hallway.

I don't like this, you think.

You point the glove down the hallway and move.

The hallway goes on forever. You keep moving but there's no break in the monotony, no side paths, just this one endless hallway. And it's dark. Barely enough light to see the virtual walls on either side, and only a few feet ahead.

Then you hear sounds. People talking, voices overlapping. It's impossible to hear what's being said, who's saying it.

You stop moving. The sounds . . . off to your left. You look that way and see another corridor. You turn right and find still another corridor leading in the opposite direction.

Finally someplace to go, but where do all these bleak corridors lead?

The voices fill the space, so it doesn't seem to matter much where you go. You move the gloved hand left and begin gliding that way . . . and that hallway opens into a room with an enormous checkerboard floor surrounded by a dozen doors. A single red bulb glows on the ceiling, like a bubble light from a police car.

Except it's not flashing. No emergency now.

All these doors . . .

And they aren't all the same. Some look like heavy riveted metal, the type you might find leading to a loft apartment, while others have a rich wood finish, much like the doors at Oakwood.

They remind you of that line from Aldous Huxley: "The doors of perception lead everywhere."

How much perception can you handle?

Each door begs to be opened. Which to choose? You pick randomly: a dark wood door. You click the glove on it and it opens.

A black corridor stretches before you as a tremendous gust of wind propels you over the threshold, down the black corridor, into . . .

A great public garden.

Sam looks angry. Liam turns away.

"I told you, Sammi, I'll not hear any of that damn crap from you. You just have to accept who I am, how I live."

But Sam doesn't let him get off that easily. She circles around to his front. She ignores the French mothers strolling with their children in the early October morning. She and Liam have been up all night, making love, drinking wine. . . . This stroll was her idea.

And in the brilliant Paris sunlight, she decides to dig deep under the skin of Liam O'Donnell.

"I know what my uncle says about you."

"And what would that rich old fool be knowing?"

"He's no fool. He told me that you're a wanted man, a terrorist. He said you're wanted for arson."

Sam watches Liam turn slowly toward her. She felt safe accusing him here, in the sunlight with all the children and their mothers around. But now his dark eyes, his tight lips, vaporize that security.

"He knows nothing. And there's only one thing you need to know, my little crazy artist —"

"Don't call me crazy!"

The beginnings of a smile vanish.

"No? It wasn't you who asked me to break into your uncle's house, eh? Now what would he be saying if I told him that?"

Sam grabs Liam's arm. "You wouldn't."

Now Liam allows the grin to reclaim his face. And Sam feels the loss of her advantage.

"Sure an' I wouldn't do that. No more than you would tell anyone about me. We all need our secrets, eh love?"

Sam looks to the left, and sees a boy holding a balloon, a bright red balloon. Of course . . . a giant red balloon. Do they make any other kind here?

As she watches it she hears Liam's voice, his lips close to her ear.

"You need know only one thing . . . I love

326

you, Sammi. Love you to bits, I do. And I want to —"

The balloon . . . growing, brighter red. Impossibly big, swelling . . . except the boy . . . the boy is *not* a boy.

The balloon explodes, sending red everywhere over the scene, filling —

This black corridor is now red, a broad, painted red bar on the Mondrian canvas. A giant red corridor.

The bastard! a part of you shouts. *Liam did this. God, it's so clear!*

But another part of you believes Liam loves Sam.

You turn around and you're back in the big room, the room of doors with all its many faceless, clueless choices. It's Monty Hall to the tenth power. You move to a battered white door set in a far wall. It's not the entrance to a cheery home . . . more like something from an institution or —

You click on the door.

This time it opens slowly, and you see another black corridor beyond the threshold.

You enter, and half a minute later you come upon yourself sitting cross-legged on the basement floor behind the furnace . . . striking matches. You always loved to play with matches. Not that fire itself fascinated you. It was research. Daddy was always telling you you were too young for a chemistry set, so you

327

had to improvise. You were only five, but you'd learned how to strike a match without burning yourself, and that allowed you to set up your own experiments, seeing what caught fire and what didn't, what burned quickly and what burned slowly. You're careful. You always close the cover before striking.

You leave yourself behind and enter another room. And then the brilliant lights stab your eyes.

The man stands at a long lab table, papers spread out behind him. Important papers. Never touch Daddy's important papers, Sammi.

And little Samantha wonders: How could paper be that important?

She holds her mommy's hand. Tight. Mommy doesn't have papers. No important ones, anyhow.

Sammi's not crying anymore.

"Nathan . . ."

The man in the white coat turns, and you see Daddy. His eyes have that funny look, as though he's looking so far away, way past the room, looking out to forever. He rubs his chin.

"I told you that I was working." Daddy's voice gets louder. "I told you never ever disturb me when I'm —"

Mommy takes a step into the room, and she pulls you behind her. You have no choice:

328

Even though you don't want to disturb Daddy and his important papers, she pulls you in. You don't want Daddy mad. You love Daddy. You want him to love you.

"Nathan, you must stop this."

Did Daddy smile?

"Stop what?"

"What you're doing to the girls. You've scared Samantha . . . showing her all those paintings. . . ."

Another tug, and Mommy makes Sam go closer to him, to the shiny table and the papers. You look up to her. Doesn't she know that Daddy shouldn't be . . . shouldn't be — what's the word?

Disturbed.

And he seems disturbed now.

"I'm teaching them, exposing them to the ranges of their possibilities —"

"Give up these crazy ideas, Nathan. No one's interested. If they were you'd have landed at least one grant."

"Money? Is that all you care about?"

Money is important. Like the papers. They yell about money. A lot.

Daddy takes a step closer. His hands are clenched, balled up into fists.

"You're scaring the children," Mommy says.

Nathan stops. He stands there, his fists tight, like a little kid ready to start a fight.

"I want to maximize their potential, Lucy.

Is that so awful? They've got talents, enormous talents. To consider wasting them —"

"They need to be children!" Mommy says. "They need to have *fun!*"

"Fun? They've got their whole *lives* to have fun! It's now, when their minds are thirsty sponges, that they must establish patterns of behavior that will carry them through their lives!"

You blink. A flash, and —

Nathan freezes. And now he looks like a wax figure, a museum display. Sam is gone, Lucinda is gone. You hear something, a crackling noise, a hissing sound. The wax dummy doesn't move.

Then, from behind it, a tiny golden finger of fire, curling around the table. Another fiery finger leaps to the tabletop and, snakelike, begins ranging across the surface, touching each piece of paper, then moving on. Soon the stream of fire has left a trail of smoking, blackened curls in its wake.

It crawls down the table, joining the other finger. They move to the feet of the wax dummy, and travel up Nathan's pants leg.

He's not alive, you think. Otherwise he'd react. It's only a dummy. . . .

The flames go straight up Nathan's chest, and then encircle his neck, corkscrewing up to the face.

You start as he speaks.

330

"I always loved you the best. . . ."

Who? Sam, or *you?*

The jaws move horribly as the flames envelop them like a mask. He has more to say but you can't hear anything because . . . because . . .

Now the face is dripping, the waxy bits of flesh sliding off, falling to the ground, revealing something else just below the surface. What?

You look down and see a trail of flame snaking toward you. In fact, it's only a few feet away. Virtual flame in a virtual madhouse.

You don't move.

You know you must get out now. These flames aren't real, yet you feel their heat. And if you can feel the heat from this distance, what will happen if they catch you? Every instinct tells you to get out, but what about that melting face? It's teasing you, promising to reveal something important.

The jaw is moving up and down. You try to make out the words.

I . . . yes you can make out that word. *I . . . love . . . you.*

But who's saying that? Nathan? Or Sam? Or somebody else?

The flames are closer. Time to go. Really. You know you should hit that Exit button. You notice the Window button blinking and beeping furiously, and you know who that is and what he's going to say: *Get out, get out, get out!*

You raise your virtual glove and back away.

But your movement is stopped. The door is closed. All rules aren't suspended here. You still need to open and shut things. You bring the glove near the Exit button.

No. You feel linked to this scene, to this place, tied to your sister's memory. If you jump out now, it all may vanish.

You make a snap decision.

You bring your hand down from the Exit button, and − instead − open the door.

Back into the giant room of doors.

You spin around, fighting vertigo. The flame follows, slowly, patiently, as if it has all the time in the world.

Doors − which one did you come through?

You turn right and see a black door. Of course. That was the one. But will you be able to remember the turns coming in?

You move to the door. The steady hiss and crackle of the fire trails behind you, louder now, as if it's consuming this house of doors.

The black door flies open and you see the Stygian void beyond. You stumble through, and after the brilliant light of your father's lab, you might as well be blind.

You move along the corridor and come to a T. Which way do you go?

You could call Dr. S. and ask him to rewind the tape quickly, but you've no time for that. You look around − the fire is growing, the thin trickle is now a lava flow of flame, picking up speed, roaring toward you.

You turn right, and immediately sense that's wrong. You come to another turn, and it's anyone's guess. All you know is the fire is coming for you and you know it will hurt you.

But dammit, you can't quit yet. You know this maze has more to offer than what you've already seen. But those flames . . .

And then you remember those behavioral psychology courses from your undergrad days. How does the mouse get out of the maze? It picks one wall and follows it.

You pick the right wall and begin to take every turn offered.

Behind you, the roar grows louder.

What if the wall brings you full circle back to the flame?

That's when you'll hit the Exit button.

But then the roar fades, and you're making no decisions now, just gliding down the black corridors, flying, leaving the hungry fire behind.

Until another door looms before you and you barrel through —

To find yourself in an English pub. You spin around and see the drinkers at the bar, smell the sour tang of spilled beer and the pall of tobacco smoke in the air. You whirl to a stop before a table and see Liam and Sam. He's nursing a pint of bitter and she's sipping some white wine.

"I still don't know why you brought me

with you," Sam says. "Especially to England. Aren't you the one who told me he 'won't be going to Merry Olde too soon'?"

She's suspicious of Liam, who's been uncharacteristically tense and taciturn since their arrival. He's disappeared for hours at a time for "meetings" and now he's insisted they come here to this run-down Knightsbridge pub for a drink before dinner.

"It's business," Liam says. He glances at his watch. "And I wanted you along for company. I miss you when we're apart, Sammi."

She rolls her eyes. "It's just a short hop over to Ireland. Maybe you could kiss the Blarney stone again." Playfully, she slaps his hand as he steals another glance at his watch. He's been doing that since they left the hotel. "And what's with the clock-watching? It's not like we're going to miss a train or any —"

A teeth-rattling *boom!* shakes the glasses off the back of the bar. The patrons start shouting and, drinks in hand, crowd out onto the sidewalk. Liam and Sam follow.

"H'it's the bank!" someone shouts from the corner. "S'burnin' like it was tinder!"

The crowd hurries down the street, carrying Liam and Sam along. When they reach the corner she stops, arrested by the sight of the bright orange and yellow flames leaping into the sky, reaching for the high full moon. She feels an old terror rising within her.

Liam tugs on her arm. "C'mon, Sammi," he says, his eyes bright as the flames. "Let's take us a closer look."

She pulls free. No way she can take another step closer.

"You go. I'm not into burning buildings."

"Okay," he says. "I'll only be a minute."

She watches him wander up the street and mingle with the swelling crowd. He looks so casual, but she can't help wondering: *Is* he casual? Or is this professional interest?

Feeling suddenly weak, she sits on the curb and rests her head against her knees, breathing deeply. The flames . . . she feels so strange. When she looks up again she sees Liam walking back to her, coming closer, silhouetted in the glow of the fire.

And she wants to scream. . . .

And you want to scream too. You don't know why, but even as the scene fades and you're in an empty virtual hall again, the urge persists. It verges on panic. You want to run blindly through these empty halls, bouncing off the walls, but suddenly you're spinning, rising — you're free, airborne, and flying away from the giant Mondrian-like structure.

As you leave it behind you see that a few of its lines and bars have been realigned. The overall shape makes no more sense to you than before, and yet . . .

I've learned something, you think.

But what? And what does it have to do with Sam?

You can't exit the program soon enough.

Twenty-Two

When people question the malleability of memory, I tell them about the "barn" experiment. Volunteers were shown a film of a car accident where one car pulled out of an intersection and was hit by another. A week later, they were asked how fast they thought Car B was going when it passed the barn. 17% remembered the barn, and could give details about its shape and color.

There was no barn anywhere on the film.

— Random notes: Julia Gordon

1

Julie left the headset on and sat with her eyes closed. She could hear Eathan saying something, but it was muffled through the headphones. She wished she were alone. She didn't want to face Eathan and Alma in this emotional state. She felt as if she were unraveling before their eyes.

A few deep breaths, a couple of rubs of her moist palms against her jeans, and she pulled herself free.

"— no question about it!" Eathan was saying.

Julie looked up at him as he paced back and forth in the tiny bit of open space remaining in Sam's room.

"Pardon?"

"O'Donnell! He did it! No question about it! Samantha connected him with the fire — she could place him in the city, on the scene. He had to silence her."

"The bank?" Julie said. "The one in the 'scape?"

"Yes. The Branham Bank's Knightsbridge branch was firebombed last month. Something to do with its dealings with Ulster, I think — I don't keep up on all these political squabbles. But I remember some radical group taking credit for it."

A wave of nausea hit her. She didn't want to believe that — after all, she'd hidden in Eathan's wall cabinet with the man — but she'd seen Liam and the fire with her own eyes . . . or rather, with Sam's.

"Was anybody hurt?"

Eathan shook his head. "I don't think so. The explosion was after hours."

Julie glanced over at Alma, who still sat

white-faced before the monitor. "What do you think?"

"I don't know," she said softly. "I want to watch the tape a couple of times. I think it's clear this Liam O'Donnell is responsible for the Branham fire — or at least Sam believes so — but that's not the interesting part of this session." She shook her head sadly. "That poor girl. So many conflicts. I realize now that even with all my sessions with her, I barely scratched the surface."

"I just realized something myself," Eathan said. "That bank explosion — it occurred a week before Sam was found unconscious. *One week!*"

"Perhaps we should show this tape to Scotland Yard," Alma said.

"No," Julie said. "This is not evidence against anyone. And I don't want this process made public. At least not yet, and not in such a sensational way."

"But if he's a terrorist —"

"No. I can't allow it."

Alma shrugged. "As you wish. The tape is yours. But I do wish to study it."

"Please . . . study it all you want. But don't let it leave the house."

2

After dinner, Eathan stood in the second-floor hallway outside Julie's bedroom.

"Sure you don't want a cordial? It might relax you."

"The last thing I need is a drink. I'm pooped."

"Stress will do that to you. Your mind is calling for a time-out, a respite from the strain you've put yourself under. And the best respite is sleep."

They hadn't spoken about the rest of her experiences in the memoryscape today, what happened and what she saw.

She needed to mention it.

"I never knew they had a problem. My mother —"

"You don't know what you saw, Julia. It was memory, filtered through a very young girl. Who knows what layers of meaning Sam put on it through the years."

"And what about all those other doors?"

Eathan shook his head. "I'm sure they're burned down, consumed in the fire. You know —" He stood up. "Samantha never got over the fire . . . not like you."

I don't know that I'm over it, Julie thought.

"I think I'm going to call it a day," she

340

said. "But tomorrow I want to go back in
. . . see if any of those other doors remain."

Eathan walked in a small circle, staring
at the hall rug.

Something's wrong, Julie thought.

"Julia, do you remember that time you
went skating on the pond. . . ."

"We went skating a lot."

"Yes, but this time you fell. Sammi came
running up to the door, screaming about
all the blood."

Julia laughed. "Yes, I think Sammi enjoyed that."

Eathan didn't laugh. "You were crying,
though. It was a nasty gash. I ran down to
the ice, picked you up, and carried you here
. . . close to the fire."

"I remember the cocoa."

"I bandaged your leg. You didn't need
stitches. . . . You remember that, eh?"

"How could I forget."

"When you were little, I never wanted you
or Sammi to be hurt. And it's no different
now, Julia . . ." Eathan came close to her.
"I said . . . I said I'd call a halt if I thought
anything would happen to you."

"Nothing happened to me."

Eathan studied her. "You mean to tell me
that you weren't frightened when that fire
came for you . . . that — that you didn't
think you'd get hurt?" He took a breath.
"I'm sure your Dr. Siegal is concerned."

And how, she thought. She'd already had an argument with him this evening. The only reason he agreed to let her keep going was he didn't suspect she had sensory participation in Sam's 'scape. If he knew that, if either of them even guessed . . .

She'd been expecting a similar argument with Eathan, but she didn't want to engage him now. Better to wait till tomorrow. Right now she was wiped, completely drained.

"Eathan, I was never in danger. And even if I were, safety is always just a 'click' away. But can we discuss this tomorrow?"

"Of course. But I don't see why you have to go back in again. I mean, isn't it clear that O'Donnell is the one?"

Nothing's clear, she wanted to say. The more I see, the less I know.

"But how do you imagine he did this to Sam?"

"Maybe drugs, maybe something psychological. I don't know precisely. But I do know he was there."

"What does Alma think?" she said.

"Oh, she's still poking through the entrails of that tape."

"I wish she'd come up with something."

"If anyone can, she will. But you . . . you need rest."

"Right." She pushed off the railing and headed for her room. "Good night, Uncle Eathan."

I'm just like a little girl again, she thought.

"Good night, Julia. Oh, by the way. I'll be heading for Edinburgh at first light. I have to clear more time with my department head and take care of some paperwork. See you for dinner."

3

Julie took a shower and ran into Alma on the way back to her room.

"Have you found anything?"

"Hard to say," Alma said. "I'm getting bits and pieces. But I've been reviewing all the tapes, especially the last one. And, well, I think I'm onto something."

For an instant, Julie's fatigue slipped away.

"What is it? What did you find?"

"Well —" Alma seemed wound to the breaking point. "There are so many pieces, the fire, your sister's troubles, her relationship with Eathan, and now — well, your father and mother obviously had a problem."

Julie had a feeling she was holding something back.

"Is it Liam? Is he behind Sam's coma?"

"He's no doubt a big part of this. As I said, I don't have the whole picture yet, but the pieces are fitting together. I mean, I've seen things that neither Samantha nor Eathan would ever tell me."

Alma folded her arms across her chest. She rubbed her upper arms. How could she be chilled? It was warm in here.

"I'm sure we're only beginning. But you get your rest." She raised a finger to Julie. "And we're going to help your sister, you and I."

Julie smiled. "Good. I'm glad you're here."

She stepped into her room and shut the heavy door behind her. Then she fell into bed, completely exhausted.

Twenty-Three

We forget far more than we remember.
— Random notes: Julia Gordon

1

Morning. A murky sky waited beyond the thin curtains.

Julie stretched. She still felt tired, achy, as if she'd been working out after too long a break. She sat up in the bed and rubbed her eyes. She was hungry; she'd kill for a cup of coffee, maybe a piece of crumb cake.

Julie slid out of bed. She peeled off her flannel nightgown and dressed hastily in the jeans and turtleneck she'd dumped on a chair the night before. Her clothes felt cold and damp.

She opened the door and headed for the first floor.

The maid told her that Eathan had already left for Edinburgh. After two rolls and three cups of coffee — enough caffeine to make Julie feel nice and edgy — she decided to go for a walk.

She skipped the gardens. The strong salt wind drew her toward the sea, and she decided to take the path that led to the cliffs.

Above her, the clouds steadily darkened from pale whitish gray to a gunmetal color. The wind cut at her as she stepped over a fallen rail of the rotten fence.

When was the last time she'd visited the edge?

Sometime when she was a teenager, she guessed. Maybe when she was thinking about leaving Oakwood forever, and wanted another last look at the North Sea, the rocks, and the waves crashing below.

Even when she and Sam became teenagers, Eathan never failed to warn them: *Don't go near the cliffs. The rock is always crumbling. The cliffs are falling into the sea.*

And he'd been right, of course. Why, just a couple of years ago, only a few miles down the coast, a hotel in Scarborough — an *entire* hotel — had tumbled into the sea.

But Julie was always careful, and it was such a beautiful spot. She liked standing near the edge, looking out at the turbulent water, dreaming of all the other shores lapped by the sea waves.

Her right foot landed on some loose shale that gave way. In a flash she went down, smacking her knee hard against a rock.

"Damn!" she said. And she looked around. For a queer moment there she'd thought someone was behind her, trailing her.

She remembered how Liam had popped out last time. He wasn't going to leave, and as long as Julie kept his secret, why should he?

She looked back along the path but saw no one, just the brambles and heather and bits of scraggly bushes hugging the rocky crevices as the wind tried to pull them away.

Julie got up and dusted at her banged knee. Her jeans weren't ripped but her kneecap had taken a good shot.

Another glance down the trail.

"Nobody here but us ghosts," she said.

She tried to be more careful as she neared the cliff edge.

I'm not sixteen anymore, she thought.

But then the sea loomed ahead, a giant, dark expanse dotted with white pinpricks of churning surf. Smugglers and freebooters used to own these waters. And Dracula landed a short way up the coast from here in the novel.

She moved closer to get the complete, unfettered view and lost herself in the primal, exhilarating moment of attaining something wonderful, the whole North Sea spread out before her like a mural, a wonder of wonders.

She stopped a few meters from the edge. When she was a kid she'd taken small steps closer and closer to that edge, ignoring Eathan's warning.

Of course what Sam used to do made that seem timid.

Sam would run right up to the edge and giggle when the sand and shale began to crumble under her feet. She'd wave her arms back and forth like a giddy tightrope walker who couldn't care less that there was no net — unless you considered a cluster of jagged boulders a net.

Julie could almost picture Sam at the edge, daring her sensible, cautious sister, Julie of the Measured Steps: Come to the edge. Look down at the rocks, the surf. Hang here . . . and dare a good stiff gust to blow you off the edge.

Julie took another step closer to that edge. The sandy soil felt mushy.

A sudden blast of air pushed against her chest, as if trying to keep her from the precipice.

Why am I doing this?

Then she had an answer.

Too much unreality, too much time at play in an unreal world that seemed to be growing real and dangerous.

This was a corrective. A good, healthy bite

out of real experience.

Half a meter to the edge.

She had a wonderful view of the water. It felt as if she could spread her arms and the wind would lift her off her feet, a human albatross riding the thermals.

She inched a bit closer.

Then she remembered her feelings from before. The sensation of being followed, that she wasn't alone.

She turned around. She could see the top floor of Oakwood, a thin plume of smoke trailing from the chimney to be quickly carried off by the steady breeze. It looked small from here, like a dollhouse —

Kind of what it looked like in Sam's memoryscape.

She'd come out to the sea to think, to let the air blow on her face, to get away. But everywhere — even here — there were reminders of Sam.

Poor, lost Sam, stranded in her own sea of jumbled memories.

"And who the hell knows what they mean," she said aloud.

She turned back to the sea, and the idea of challenging the cliff lost its appeal.

The moment had passed. That sort of stunt was more suitable to Sam. She was the risk taker.

Still, she gazed at the sea for a few more moments, girding herself for the work to come, before she'd have to go back into the mine.

She wasn't quite at the edge. Yet her eye could trail down and catch the jagged rocks below, the waves crashing and —

Something among the rocks down there.

Perhaps a bit of driftwood, or a tire that got hung up on the rocks. She saw only a bit of color flapping about.

The cliff overhung the beach, jutting its edge into the wind like the prow of some great vessel. To see the rest of the rocks she'd have to go a little closer to the edge.

She inched forward, and even that little movement brought more of the object into view. Didn't seem to be a tire, no, and the things moving around were — were —

A bit closer . . .

The sand squirmed under her feet.

She saw the color, the shape; recognition came and she froze.

"Oh, God. Oh!"

The two things flopping around in the surf below, playfully whipped this way and that by the waves — they were legs. And hung up on a jagged V made by two massive chunks of rock, Julie saw a torso, facedown in the water, its arms wrapped around the rocks as if embracing them.

Sickened, she turned away. God! How awful! Some poor soul — a fisherman maybe? — washed up from the sea.

She lurched away from the edge. She'd have to call Bay — they had a crack lifeboat squad there. And then she stopped, drawn back to the edge.

She dropped to her knees — the right one was still tender — and leaned over for a better look.

Oh, no. That wasn't a fisherman. That was a woman. Julie couldn't see the face, but . . . her fingers dug spasmodically into the sand — Oh, God! — she recognized the color of the tweed skirt, the tan blouse.

Moaning, Julie crab-crawled backward and crouched with her face buried in her arms. She retched.

Alma . . . it was Alma down there.

An awful thought lanced through her mind like lightning.

Who pushed her?

No reason in the world for her to think that. The edge was treacherous and maybe Alma had been out here in the fog. An accident was the most likely explanation.

So why was her first thought of foul play, and her first suspect — ?

Julie bolted to sitting and turned, half expecting to see Liam standing there ready to hurl her down on the rocks too.

But she was alone.

She breathed easier.

And heard a crumbling sound. The world began to tilt backward. No, not the world, only this little piece of it. The overhang was collapsing.

Julie dove and rolled away from the sagging shale. Her forearm scraped along the razorlike near edge of the crack as the overhang broke away and slid out of sight. Seconds later she heard the splashing clatter as it hit the rocks below.

She lay in the dry grass, breathing fast, puffing like a maniac. Had the falling rock landed on Alma's body? Someone else would have to look and find out. Not her.

She got up on all fours and rapidly crawled away, like a frightened infant.

When she stood she could see only the sea, none of the rocks below, or Alma's terribly twisted body. She stood there until her breath sounded normal.

Alma had said, "I'm getting bits and pieces. . . ."

And now she was gone. Like Sam, only more permanently.

Julie turned onto the path and broke into a stumbling run back to Oakwood.

2

The police inspector from Whitby, a man named Stephens, looked as if he had seen too many detective shows. He wore his trench coat with the collar up, and he kept nodding to himself as Julie spoke.

Eathan sat beside her on the living-room couch. She'd called him at Edinburgh and he'd rushed back. Usually an oak, unflappable, he now appeared distracted, almost disoriented, and his eyes looked puffy. Had he been crying? She knew that he and Alma had more than a professional relationship. Of course, Eathan would never say anything about that.

Now Stephens pointed a pencil at her. "I'm sorry, miss. Excuse me, I may have forgotten . . . but you said you went up there to — ?"

"I just wanted to walk . . . get some air."

The inspector rubbed his jaw. This was potentially a big case for him, a moment in the sun.

"But you didn't know, then, that Dr. Evans had gone up there?"

"No, I didn't."

A uniformed policeman came into the room, leaned over and whispered something to the inspector, who nodded, listening, looking at Eathan and Julie.

As the policeman left, Stephens said, "And tell me about your sister."

Eathan briefly explained Sam's mysterious coma.

The inspector scribbled more notes. "And you suspect . . . foul play, eh?"

"We don't know," Eathan said.

Stephens stood up. "Right, then. I'll tell you what we're going to do here. I'm going to walk back to the cliff, make sure my blokes aren't missing anything. And while I'm doing that, perhaps you want to think about any enemies that Dr. Evans —"

Julie glanced at Eathan, with his red eyes and his drained look. And now — he had to listen to what Julie was going to say.

But how do I say this? And what don't I say?

"Th-there's something I have to tell you."

Stephens had already taken a step to the door. He turned, eyebrows lifted.

"Oh? And what's that?"

Already Alma had been recovered from the rocks below. Already the body was in the undertaker's van heading into town.

"There's been somebody here, somebody who may have —"

She felt Eathan turning, looking at her.

"There's a man — I believe" — she hazarded a look at Eathan — "I believe he's wanted. His name is Liam O'Donnell."

She felt Eathan's eyes locked on her, boring into her.

The inspector nodded. Leaving it to Eathan to speak.

"Julie, what on earth do you mean?"

Now, slowly, she turned to meet his gaze. When secrets are revealed, there's pain, she thought.

"He was here. Two nights ago he showed up. He surprised me outside. . . . He told me how much he loved Sam."

Was it Julie's imagination, or were Eathan's lips curling in disgust?

"O'Donnell was *here?* At Oakwood?"

Julie nodded. "He asked me to tell no one. . . . He told me he loved Sam, that he didn't —"

Eathan stood up. He walked away from the couch, rubbing his beard.

Julie turned back to the inspector, who called over one of his men and handed him a slip of paper.

"We'll check on him, miss. But what is your sister's connection to this man?"

Eathan spoke before Julie could answer. His voice sounded hollow as he filled the inspector in on Sam's relationship with O'Donnell . . . and his suspicions. And Julie couldn't feel more stupid, less worthy of trust. What could she have been thinking?

Stephens scribbled more notes furiously.

"If he's around, if he's still here, we'll pick him up." He looked at Julie. "Though I don't know why you didn't tell someone, miss."

Neither do I, Julie thought.

She kept picturing Alma Evans's body flopping around in the tidal tumult.

Eathan seemed to be keeping his distance from Julie, standing apart.

God, I should leave, Julie thought. Get

on a plane and get the hell out of here, for all the good I'm doing. Someone's dead, maybe because I was stupid.

And befuddled. What sort of spell had Liam cast over her?

She guessed that somehow — via Sam — he'd touched her. He'd made her feel . . . something she'd never experienced before, and that had compromised her judgment, left her vulnerable.

But why couldn't it have been a simple accident, just like what almost happened to me?

The inspector shut his notebook. "Well, we have some work to do here, eh? We'll keep you posted."

Eathan nodded absently as Stephens put a hand to his brow, and then turned and left the room.

Julie stood there in the lengthening silence, keeping her eyes on the door, not daring to look at Eathan. She wished he'd shout, scream, throw something, for God's sake. This silence was killing her.

Eathan could get mad, she knew. But she feared his disappointment more. Julie never wanted to disappoint him. He'd had more than enough of that from Sam.

She heard steps. Eathan leaving or —

And then he was close to her. She set her jaw.

Here it comes.

"Why, Julia?" His voice was low, thick, filled with pain. Worse than a shout. Much worse. "Why didn't you tell me about O'Donnell?"

"I — I wish I had an answer," she said, her voice as low as his.

"Why on earth would you keep something like that from me? A known terrorist, a threat to my niece, your sister, on my property." His voice rose. "What were you *thinking?*"

"I wasn't thinking. So stupid not to tell you, I —"

"What *else* haven't you told me?"

More secrets. Should she come clean? Admit she'd been digging in Eathan's secrets, that Sam wanted those secrets, had even asked Liam to — ?

She turned to him and opened her mouth. "I —"

No. She couldn't. Not with that wounded look in his eyes. He'd been battered enough today.

Or was she rationalizing again?

"If only I'd seen the things we saw yesterday sooner, I'd have turned him in immediately. But Sam seemed to trust him and —"

Eathan stiffened. "Do you think he knew what we saw yesterday?"

"I don't see how."

"Did you *tell* him?"

"No! Of course not!"

"Then why is Alma dead?"

Oh, God, I wish I knew. She groped for an answer.

"It could have been an accident. The cliffs are treacherous — you said so countless times as we were growing up."

"Yes, it could be, but it seems a little too convenient." He swiveled toward the door. "I wonder . . ."

Suddenly he was out in the foyer and heading for the family room. Julie followed.

When she got there he was rummaging through the stack of videocassettes.

"What are you doing?"

"Looking for the tape of that last session — the one where we saw him in London at the time of the Branham Bank fire. Where is it?"

"It should be right here. Alma had it —"

Eathan threw a cassette across the room. "It's gone! Not only has he been on my grounds, he's been in my *house!* Damn him!" He swung around and jabbed a finger at her. "*You'll* have to live with this!"

He stalked back out to the foyer. Julie followed, feeling as if she were on a leash.

"Where are you going?"

"I have to go into Bay and arrange for the body, for" — his words stumbled, revealing a glimpse of his pain — "Alma to be taken care of. She has a son in London. I'll have to contact him. I don't know when I'll be back."

Julie had never seen him so angry.

He opened a closet and took out a suede fall jacket. Not his usual style. He didn't look like Eathan in it.

Without another word, he left the house.

Julie stood alone in the foyer, reeling with guilt about Alma, feeling lost, confused . . . and lonely.

A strange feeling, lonely. She couldn't remember being lonely before. Ever. She'd always taken pride in being self-sufficient, self-contained. She'd joke about it: "I'm never lonely when I'm alone — I'm with me."

She heard Eathan's car pull out of the driveway. She walked over to the window and pushed aside the thin curtain. She saw the police cars parked to the side. Stephens was off retracing Alma's steps, checking the sand for other footprints.

Alone . . . and lonely. She didn't want to be alone with Julie at the moment. She wanted company.

And she knew whose.

Julie walked upstairs to Sam's room. The nurse looked up when she came to the door.

"You can take a break," Julie said.

The nurse was used to her visits by now and quietly excused herself from the room.

"Hello, Sam," she said as the computer

initialized the satellite feed and ran through the dozens of preconnect diagnostic programs. "Like it or not, your sister's dropping by for another visit. Without Eathan and without Dr. S." *And, God, without Alma.* "Just you and me."

Julie had to admit that she was a little uneasy about Sam's 'scape now. It seemed to be edging out of her control, increasingly involving Julie as a participant, not a mere observer. Dr. S.'s warnings echoed in her head.

But the 'scape was like a siren call, with a steadily thinning line separating Sam's fractured memories and Julie's reality now.

Even when I'm out here, I'm never really free of it.

Which meant, she was sure, that she wouldn't stop until she'd gone as far as she could.

She pulled on her headgear. Nothing to see in there now, just blank video blue as the program prepared to run.

The loneliness was fading. Sam's door was opening. . . .

A single vertical roll in the lenses of the headgear as they darkened, and then she was back.

And what she saw took her breath away.

Twenty-Four

I was asked to be on a panel with a bunch of memory-recovery therapists. Normally I keep to myself, but this time I went — and gave them hell! Memory-recovery therapy — it drives me up the wall. Never have I heard anything so bogus. And these therapists try to pass themselves off as scientific? They should be arrested. They're not recovering memories — they're manufacturing them!

— Random notes: Julia Gordon

Sam's studio is almost empty. The virtual wall space is bare. The lion in the gondola is gone. So is the faux Mondrian. The large unfinished canvas remains, along with a few others scattered haphazardly about.

One catches your eye: a painting of a boardwalk under a swirling fiery sky, beside the blue of water, a lake or the sea . . .

But no people.

A boardwalk. Something about this entices you, but you're drawn to the door, to see

361

what's happened to the watery wasteland overnight.

As you rise into the darkness you notice major changes in the 'scape. In the moonlight gleaming off the black water, you see that the Mondrian island is gone, swallowed by the sea. You won't be able to search the rooms behind those other doors. And the *Nighthawks* island — gone too.

You feel a rush of dread as you realize that only three other islands remain . . . moving closer together. They almost seem to be gathering into a single landmass.

As you glide over the coalescing islands, you spot the boardwalk on one, a cartoony promenade rendered in crayonlike colors. Almost a kid's drawing — but you *know* this picture. Something about it is so familiar, yet some crucial identifying element is missing.

You wonder momentarily about the thing that lurks beneath the surface, but maybe that's still over near Venice.

You land on the boardwalk. The wooden slats glow with a burnished orange.

A boardwalk with no one on it. Strange, this doesn't look like the beaches at Brighton where Eathan took you and Sam for summer vacations. Is this memory something from Sam's Côte d'Azur days? Do they even have boardwalks on the Riviera?

You turn around, searching for someone, something. . . .

An old fortune-telling machine sits alone, its back to the sea, its dimly lit glass case glowing like a beacon. Inside, an old plaster gypsy stares out at you with dark glass eyes. Eerie . . . but you move closer.

As soon as you reach the gypsy, her right arm starts to move, stiffly, just like a real arcade fortune-teller, moving as if dealing out a card.

But no card is dealt.

Her glass eyes blink. The plaster lips move.

You hear nothing, but in the front of the machine, a small sign lights.

WHAT SECRETS SHALL MADAME HANAMSAT REVEAL TO YOU?

Below the sign, three subject areas begin to blink: LIFE . . . LOVE . . . FORTUNE.

And below each of those, a button waits.

"Okay," you say. "Tell me about —"

You reach out and press LOVE.

The gypsy's arm moves and a card falls into the slot. You pick it up and read: *How can you ask about love when you have none?*

The card disappears.

The lights flash again: Ask another question. You realize you're annoyed at this glass-eyed gypsy.

You press LIFE.

The arm moves. Another card falls.

Life before . . . or after?

Before or after *what?* This machine could have been programmed by Liam: It answers every question with another question.

And now two new words blink, two new buttons wait: BEFORE and AFTER.

You press the button beneath BEFORE.

Again the arm moves, again a card falls.

This one says *The moon, the house, or the mask?*

Great. You've stumbled onto the Zen monk of fortune-telling machines. But at least it's given you some more choices. The moon, the house, the mask . . .

Three choices, three buttons.

Of all the things you've seen in Sam's 'scape, this machine most convinces you that she's trying to make contact.

You reach out and press the button under the word MASK.

The plaster gypsy looks up. And for the first time she smiles, a knowing leer, a death grimace, while the glassy eyes retain the same expression.

The head cracks open.

And Nathan is there, sitting at a table facing you, and you're four years old. . . .

Daddy wants to play the game again, always the same game every day. And it's fun . . . most times.

"Julia, are you ready?"

She nods. "Yes, Daddy."

He brings out the cards.

Multiplication and division. Easy stuff. So

364

simple. 3×3, 8×8, 7×6 . . . except he goes fast, then faster.

"Come on, come on, Julia. You're hesitating. Come on. You *know* these."

Julie curls her legs around each other, locking them together. She snaps off the answers as fast as she can.

"Twenty-four . . . fifty-one . . . sixty-three . . ."

But Daddy shakes his head, and only seems to go faster.

"Come on, come on. . . . This is rote stuff, only memory, Julia. That's all. No thinking here, none at all."

Faster and faster, until Julie feels as if she's riding a pony, holding on to its mane, galloping over the number cards like they're hurdles.

She sees him smile. She's doing well. Riding that pony well.

Until he gets to the end and she feels disappointed. Maybe he has other problems for her to do, like arranging the blocks, or looking at the triangles and counting them . . . all the triangles, so many different sizes.

"That's all for today, Julia. I have an important meeting."

He stands up. He's so big. He slips the cards into his pocket. He takes a step away from the simple wooden table.

"Daddy . . ."

He stops.

"Can't I do one? To you?"

"I'm really very —"

"You always let me do one. Just one problem."

He smiles, and it's a good smile, a nice smile. He loves her; she's sure of that.

"Okay. Fire away, missy."

"Okay, okay —" Now she has to search for a problem, something hard. She's supposed to know the answer . . . that's the way the game is played. But he's never, ever checked. Never.

"Ninety-nine times" — she tightens the curl of her legs even more — "sixteen."

His eyes narrow. He has to *think* about this. Then, he answers.

"One thousand five hundred and eighty-four." He isn't smiling anymore. "Is that the answer, Julia? Is that it?"

"I . . . I . . ."

She doesn't know, but now the game isn't fun. What's happening here? The game is always fun but now —

"Is that the *answer*, Julia?"

"I . . . I . . . don't —"

And then it happens. You see a thin line appear on Daddy's head, a line that runs right down the middle of his face, from his hair down to his nose, onto his mouth, his chin. Such a thin line. She wants to say something to him, when —

The line begins to widen . . . a cracking,

peeling sound as the line *opens*.

"Is that the answer, Julia?"

"Daddy, Daddy, I don't know —" She's crying, watching this line widen, the face crack open, like one of those nuts at Christmastime, opening up —

And suddenly it's Uncle Eathan in there, his dark beard not so full, his eyes glistening, repeating the same words, with the same tone, the same voice . . . as Daddy.

"Don't ever ask me a problem . . . unless you know the answer."

Julie nods. The cracked outer head has curled away, like a shed snakeskin. Uncle Eathan turns and walks away.

Then the girl is gone.

Your first thought: That isn't Sam's memory. It's yours. God, you've just seen one of *your* memories in here. And not only that, you barely remember the number game you used to play with your father. You knew he drilled you, did puzzles and problems with you.

But what you just saw didn't seem like a game.

Then you're aware of where you are — on that boardwalk that stretches to the horizon. You see a white dot at the impossibly far end. You didn't notice it before, and perhaps you should investigate, but you're too rattled to do anything more.

You turn around. . . .

And the rest of the boardwalk is gone, ending as if washed away in a great storm. You see something near the edge, just beyond where the jagged remnants of the broken boards jut like spears. An upright stone pokes up from the black water.

You move to it.

And as you move, you have another thought, confusing, disturbing. . . .

Eathan and Nathan . . . they looked so similar, the eyes, and the voices. Of course they were brothers, but the way they spoke, their eyes . . . so similar.

You're at the stone, a blank, meaningless piece of rock.

But is *anything* meaningless in this 'scape?

You lean over the edge, studying it. Directly below you, the black, oily water acts like a dark mirror, and —

You see yourself. *You.* The way you looked this morning. You see your shocked face studying your reflection.

"Oh . . . my . . . God!"

The reflection mouths the words along with you.

"What the hell is going on here?"

You think the obvious. You're losing your mind. The memory-mapping technology works fine except for one small, tiny drawback: It drives you insane.

No way your reflection can exist here unless —

A splash. Suddenly tense, you look up, glance around. Nothing should splash here.

Another splash — louder. Oh no. You look down just as the thick, living cable of tentacle shoots out of the water, out of the open mouth of your horrified reflection.

You scream and recoil, but the tentacle is fast. It swirls around your ankle. God, it's cold — and slimy. The suckers have hooks, and the hooks are digging into the soft flesh of your calf. You feel it tighten its grip and it *hurts.* This can't be happening. You're not part of Sam's 'scape. You're a ghost here. Nothing can *grab* you.

But something *has* grabbed you, and it's tugging you, pulling you by your trapped ankle, dragging you toward the water.

The Exit button. Got to hit it now.

As if sensing your thoughts, the kraken gives your ankle a harsh twist, rolling you off the edge of the boardwalk and into the water. It feels oily and cold. You bump against the rock and drag against its surface. The kraken — it's trying to tow you out to sea.

The Exit button — *now!*

But as you reach for it, the cinching pressure on your ankle lessens. The tentacle uncoils and slips away, leaving you treading water on the far side of the rock.

You look up.

The stone is within arms' reach, and you see now that it's a giant headstone. You read the names: NATHAN AND LUCINDA GORDON. Your parents' gravestone. Dates are carved below the names — the date of the fire, and the birth dates, Lucinda's — May 17, 1943 — and Nathan's . . .

December 1, 1941.

The same as Eathan's.

They looked so similar, the eyes, and the voices. . . .

The tentacle pulled you this far, then released you. Almost as if the kraken dragged you here so you could read it.

You reach out and touch the heavy headstone. Water from your fingers drips down its carved surface, settling in one of the dates.

December 1, 1941.

Is that true? Nathan and Eathan are twins, just like you and Sam? How could you not know that? But then they never looked alike, especially with Eathan's beard. And you never celebrated your parents' birthdays. . . .

And twins run in families, don't they.

You turn and look around. The kraken hovers submerged in the dark water under the dark sky, with only its glowing eyes above the surface, watching you.

You shiver. The cold water, or something else?

Whichever, you've got to get back to reality. Now.

Twenty-Five

From Macbeth: *"Memory, the warder of the brain."*
— Random notes: Julia Gordon

1

Julie sipped the hot tea, inhaling the aroma of lemon and honey. She had her legs curled up under her and a blanket over her shoulders. Trying to get warm.

Too much to think about. She wished she could share her latest memoryscape excursion with Dr. Siegal, but if she did, it would be her last. He'd pull the plug in a heartbeat. All he had to do was shut down the satellite feed and Julie would be shut out of the memoryscape.

God, if only she could tell him that she'd developed a virtual presence in Sam's 'scape. What would he say to that? It was unheard of, undreamed of, but somehow the system was interacting with her own brain waves and memories and using them to construct a virtual body for her.

And it meant that she was in Sam's mind in a much deeper way than she'd ever imagined possible.

That might explain the number-game memory. That was Julie's own memory. At least she supposed it was. She had a vague recollection of her father drilling Sam like that, but she doubted he did numbers with Sam.

Probably showed her Rothko paintings instead.

But Sam must have witnessed the number game hundreds of times, had to know all about it.

Why had she stuck it there, on the boardwalk . . .

. . . near the gravestone?

That was the real shocker. Nathan and Eathan: twins. Was it true? And if so, how come Sam knew and she didn't?

She glanced over at her sister. Sam looked beautiful, so at peace sleeping there, peaceful in a way she'd never been when she was up and about. No sign of the sinister fortune-tellers and krakens and desolate landscapes that filled the inside of her head. Just her pale beauty, and the gentle rise and fall of her chest with every breath.

Julie drained her cup, the tea cool now.

Secrets, Julie thought. That's what this is all about.

She reached down and rubbed her right leg. Sore. She gasped when she pulled up the cuff of her jeans and stared at something that shouldn't be there — couldn't be there — and yet it was: A bruise encircled her ankle and lower calf.

No! A physical injury — from the memoryscape!

If it can bruise me, hurt me, what else can it do?

Kill me?

She rubbed at the welt. *Maybe I should stop this.*

And then a car pulled onto the stone driveway below.

Eathan. Uncle Eathan. Dad's twin, or was that a memoryscape fantasy?

Julie expected Eathan to come upstairs and look in on Sam, but he stayed below.

The dinner hour came but no one called her down. Perhaps Eathan had told cook to skip dinner.

But she couldn't postpone a confrontation any longer. Julie walked downstairs. She checked the living room, but Eathan wasn't there. She could see into the kitchen, and it looked dark and quiet. Strange. He was home, but —

She heard a noise from across the foyer. She crossed it and peeked in the library.

She'd always loved this great room filled with books. Eathan's retreat, a world redolent of rich leather and aging paper. Now she felt like a stranger here.

Eathan sat in a high-backed leather chair in a pool of light from a single lamp. No book in his hands; instead he stared at the designs in the oriental rug at his feet. The effect was strange and morbid.

"Eathan —"

He looked up slowly, as though he'd somehow aged since this morning.

"Julia . . . I was going to come up. Going to apologize for overreacting earlier. I was just so upset —"

"And you had every right to be. I'm the one who should be apologizing. I'm truly sorry."

He nodded slowly. "I accept your apology. Let's put it behind us and move on, shall we. Just promise me . . . no more secrets."

No more secrets? she wanted to say. Look at what you've been keeping from me.

"You look tired," she said.

"I am. Getting poor Alma taken care of, consoling her son . . ."

She stepped closer.

He kept looking at her. "You've had some dinner, I assume. I told cook not to bother fixing me anything."

On the table to his right she spotted a half-empty brandy snifter sitting next to a crystal decanter. She noted his barely slurred words. Had she ever seen Eathan under the influence, even the slightest bit tipsy? She didn't think so.

"Has there been any word about O'Donnell?" she asked.

"Word? You mean have they caught him? No, and I very much doubt they will. Just as I doubt that he'll come back here."

"You don't think it might have been an accident?"

Eathan grunted. "And is what happened to your sister an accident too?"

She took another step.

"I have to tell you something . . . ask you something."

Eathan was staring forward again. He nodded. "More secrets?"

"As a matter of fact, yes. When you were gone . . . I went into the memoryscape again."

Eathan nodded, still looking blankly ahead. He didn't act surprised.

"And?"

She was about to tell him the memory of the game she and his brother had played, the math drill. But she stopped herself. That wasn't the important issue here.

"I saw a gravestone . . . for my mother and father."

She waited for him to say something but

he sat there, silent, staring. This was so hard.

"I saw my father's birth date."

Still no response. Was Eathan even awake?

"And it was the same as yours. In the memoryscape, the same date, meaning that —"

And now, like that fortune-teller, Eathan turned his head. "That your father and I were twins. So?"

"You mean it's true?"

"Of course it is. Identical twins, just like you and Samantha. Why are you so surprised?"

"I . . . well, I never knew."

"Of course you did. Everyone knows that. Or at least they knew it when it mattered — when we were both alive."

"Well, I didn't. Why didn't you tell me?"

He stared at her, and she saw the lips within his beard twist with impatience. His words took on an edge.

"For the same reason I don't go around reminding you that you and Samantha are twins. Why should I tell you what I assume you already know?"

The library felt alien. Here she stood, surrounded by great walls, by endless spines of books, and at the center, her uncle. And she wondered . . . if he shaved off his beard, would he look just like her father? Would it be like seeing her father again?

She took a breath in the stuffy room.

"You should have told me."

And then, bitterly, with his tongue tripping ever so slightly on the words, Eathan said, "And you should have told me about Liam."

Stung, Julie turned and left the room.

2

Julie slept fitfully. She awoke a number of times, and on each occasion she could taste the remnant of some bizarre dream. Once she was traveling on a train, never able to get off. Next she was in a store trying to buy something but all the clerks and checkers had blank faces, no mouths, no eyes.

Once she sat up, shivering in fear, like a little girl waking from a nightmare, feeling something coming for her, something dangerous.

She was tempted to get up and walk down to Sam's room. At least there'd be someone there, a nurse sitting at her bedside reading a book by a pale yellow light.

Funny, in life she'd had no use for Sam, but now she felt as if she needed her.

In life . . .

But she's not dead, Julie thought. Sam's not dead.

But she might as well be if I don't do something. It's all falling apart in there. Devolution, entropy, got to find an answer before her memoryscape flattens into an endless, featureless, lifeless sea.

Eventually Julie fell asleep again.

Twenty-Six

Dr. Elizabeth Loftus is doing fascinating work with false memory. She's been able to create false childhood memories in adults ranging in age from 18 to 63. Her subjects became genuinely convinced that they'd got lost in a particular store at a particular age; each embellished the false childhood memory with a host of personal details and emotions, but it never happened. Some were so adamant about the veracity of the memory they were willing to bet money on it.

— Random notes: Julia Gordon

1

Morning light filled her room. For a moment it seemed like another dream, but then she felt the cold, damp morning air, and the light in her eyes. What time was it?

She turned to the end table and saw the

small digital clock. 10:30. Way too late.

I'm sleeping too much, dreaming too much . . . chasing phantoms, chasing secrets.

I think I'm losing it.

She got up quickly. She needed a dose of reality — needed to talk to Eathan some more. She had to clear the air between them.

Downstairs, the maid informed her that Dr. Gordon had left, that he had business to attend to in Whitby.

Julie went into the dining room hoping for a note from Eathan, but found nothing except a pile of rolls and coffee. She picked up a roll and bit into it, savoring the taste as it crumbled in her mouth. Good to have a real sensation. She poured herself a cup of coffee, dosing it with milk and sugar. She gulped it down and poured another.

She had to get out of the house.

She finished the roll and found her jacket in the hall closet. She stepped out the front door and stood there, taking in the gently rolling hills that led to the high moors. A chilly morning, damp, rehearsing for an English winter. No police about this morning.

She went down the front steps and cut around the side, heading for the cliffs.

She took the path slowly, scanning left and right. What am I looking for? she wondered. A bit of fabric stuck to one of the brambles? A half-smoked Gauloises? A shoe-print?

And all the time she wondered: What if Liam had nothing to do with Alma Evans's death? What if she did fall? I mean, if a whole hotel can fall off one of these cliffs, why not a lone woman? It had almost happened to her.

Why the hell couldn't she accept that Liam had done this? He had motive: The missing tape of Sam's memoryscape placed him at the scene of the Branham Bank bombing. He had opportunity: He'd been on the grounds; maybe Alma had caught him stealing the tape and he disposed of her. It was all so plausible.

Resisting the obvious was irrational, so much more like Sam than Julie.

Maybe I'm not the girl I was.

She kept searching the trail, peering into the tiny crevices of the rocks. Surely good Inspector Stephens and his men would have found any clue that had been left behind. But it was important to Julie to look for herself.

The wind blew at her open jacket, and the mist dampened her skin.

Then she spotted something peeking out of a tiny crack between two rocks. A bit of white. But when she bent to reach for it, she found it was a tiny flower with three white petals. Pretty, hiding in the crevice, protected from the wind.

She kept walking until she reached the cliffs.

No need to go to the edge, she thought. Unless someone else was down on the rocks.

There was a grim thought.

Just yesterday morning she'd come up here to clear her head, to look over the edge — and all hell had broken loose.

Poor Alma.

She stared out at the water and watched the sea fret, as the locals called the fog that rolled in with the tide, make its way toward shore. Beautiful . . . and eerie. The fog bank seemed almost alive, moving like a living thing.

She turned around.

And saw that she wasn't alone.

Liam stood on the path, glaring at her. Julie was keenly aware that the cliff was behind her, and that below were the same rocks that had so roughly cradled Alma's body. She felt a tightening in her midsection.

Liam's eyes flashed. "You gave me the hell up!"

Julie tried to keep her voice calm. "You should know — th-that there are probably police here, watching —"

Liam took a step closer.

"Don't give me any of that crap! The

stupid locals couldn't find their own bloody shoelaces. But now the Yard and the rest of the damn country know I'm here."

Julie glanced over her shoulder. She could hear the sound of waves breaking on the rocks below . . . far below.

"What did you expect? Alma Evans is dead."

Liam looked away, raising his hands to the sky. "Ah, and you're thinking I did that? More likely it was your bloody uncle. Or maybe — just maybe — it was an accident. Did that little thought ever occur to you?"

The waves crashing, a steady tattoo.

"I —"

"But you wasted no time in telling 'em about me, did you now."

"She's dead. Eathan thought —"

Liam leaped forward and grabbed Julie. "I should push *you* off the bloody cliff!"

She let out a yell but the wind took it, and she was far too frightened to make another sound as he drove her back, closer and closer to the precipice, backing her up until her heels were on the edge and she could feel the sand and shale giving way beneath them.

"Why don't I give them another body to scrape off the rocks?" He shook her. *"Eh?"*

But then he yanked her back and shoved her roughly away from the edge.

"I didn't do a thing, love," he said, near

breathless with anger. "Not a blessed thing. I wanted to help Sammi. Christ, I wanted to help you, but now . . ."

He took a step back down the path.

"Well, you've fixed it so's I'd better be makin' meself scarce. It's too bad. I loved your sister . . . and" — he looked back at her with a flash of a smile — "I liked you."

Julie believed him. He could have thrown her off the cliff. And he easily could have sneaked into Oakwood and harmed Sam by now. But he hadn't.

"I tell you this," he shouted. "That uncle of yours has more secrets than those mementos of your childhood. Sammi suspected something about him. But you're all she's got now. Look after her well, sister Julie. And do this for me, will you?" He looked Julie right in the eye. "If she ever comes out of it, tell her that I never gave up on her." Another flash of a smile. "And tell her that if there's a way, I'll be back." His expression turned grim. "And you, sister Julie — you watch your back."

With that, Liam raced down the path.

2

Like a moth to the flame, Julie was drawn back to the study.

She wished she'd had more time with

Liam, time to get over the shock of his presence so she could ask him about the missing videotape. Had he seen it? Had he peered through a window while Alma was watching it?

What about that scene on the cliff? Was he really going away, or was he hoping she'd pass that on to the police while he stayed nearby, watching?

A thought struck her: If he'd been able to pilfer from the family room, why couldn't he have reached the study? He'd been so fascinated by the wall cabinet.

Julie stepped over to Eathan's desk and opened the top drawer.

The key was missing. Damn! Liam had been up here too.

She ran to the wall cabinet and unlocked it with her own key. She heard her breathing, deeper, huskier . . . almost hyperventilating. Got to keep cool, she thought.

She pulled open the doors, and with the nervy aplomb of a practiced safecracker, she ran through the combination for the file cabinet. She flubbed it once, and for a dreadful moment she feared the combination had been changed. But the second time through, the lock opened.

Inside, all the files hung in straight, neat rows, pretty much as she'd left them. She rifled through them, seeing the letters, the affidavits, the yellow and tattered clippings from decades ago.

They seemed to belong to someone else's life.

She went to the window. The driveway was clear, empty. I could have all the time in the world, she thought. Or just a few minutes.

A scene she'd witnessed in Sam's 'scape had hovered on the edge of her thoughts for the past two days, haunting her. Now it leaped front and center: little Julie, playing with matches behind the furnace.

She pawed to the back of the file and pulled out one of the old newspaper clippings. This one was dated later than the one in the unlocked file. She scanned the crumbly paper, forcing herself to read every word, numbing herself to the gruesome details of the fire: How the bodies of Lucinda and Nathan Gordon were found close together — "As if he was trying to get his wife out," a state trooper said — a fire of unknown origin, probably electrical, that started in the basement, and how it spread so quickly through the old house.

. . . started in the basement . . .

Julie felt sick. She leaned against the file cabinet.

Oh, God. Was it me? Eathan had always said it was an electrical fire that raged through the wooden house. *But was I the cause? Did I start the fire that killed my parents?*

She closed her eyes and felt the horror, the fiery terror of being trapped by the choking smoke and searing heat . . . no way out and surrounded by hungry flames.

She straightened and tried to shake it off. *I don't know. I'll never know. And I can't beat myself up about something I may have had nothing to do with.*

She kept reading.

The bodies were burned beyond recognition. Eathan Gordon, brother to Nathan, could not identify either corpse.

That's what they were, then. *Corpses.* Not people anymore.

But the dental records for both Lucinda and Nathan Gordon had confirmed exactly who the corpses were.

That was it, then. Two lives ended, two bodies reduced to charcoal, identified by their teeth, and buried. Nothing left but a headstone and some yellowed newspaper clippings.

And their children, of course. *Sam . . . and me.*

One of whom may have started the fire.

Her hands trembled as she replaced the article. But as she closed the hanging folder she spotted something she hadn't noticed before: a flat box of some sort, wedged far back in the long file drawer.

She pulled it out, no easy thing with the bulging files.

A metal box, letter-size — locked.

She pried at the lid but that sturdy little lock held it shut tight. She put the box on the table behind her and reached back into the drawer, feeling around its bottom, searching for a key. Nothing.

Julie turned and stared at the box sitting on the table. She thought of matrioshkas, all those nesting dolls in Sam's 'scape. And here in the real world: Inside the locked wall cabinet is a locked file cabinet, and inside the locked file cabinet is a locked box.

And inside *that?*

She picked it up and studied the lock more closely. She could break it open. It didn't look that strong.

She put it down again. *What am I thinking?* Hadn't she hurt Eathan enough already? *When am I going to stop?*

She had to put the box back.

She was reaching for it when she heard steps in the hall outside. She hurried to the door and peeked down the hallway. Clarice was heading this way.

Julie darted back to the file drawer and pushed it shut. She jumbled the numbers on the combination. Then she shut the wall-cabinet doors and locked them.

When she turned she saw the metal box

on the table behind her. Damn! She'd forgotten it. Or had she? Too late to reopen the wall cabinet. Only one thing to do.

Julie hurried to the nearest bookshelf and grabbed the first oversized volume her hand contacted. She tucked it under her arm and slipped the box behind it. She reached the door just as the maid entered.

Clarice jumped at the sight of her. "Oh Lord, mum, you gave me a start!"

"I'm sorry," Julie said. She hurried by her, keeping the book between Clarice and the box.

In Sam's room the nurse got up and excused herself as soon as Julie entered.

Julie went to her sister's closet — empty now except for bedding and medical supplies — and put the box on the top shelf, slipping it under a comforter. Later, after Clarice was gone, she'd return it to the locked file cabinet.

She turned back to her sister and moved to the bed.

"What's in the box, Sam? Any ideas?"

She turned to the computer terminal and its attached headgear, ominous now as the virtual reality it created became less virtual . . . and more real.

She stepped over to it and eased herself into the recliner.

"Am I going to be hurt some more, Sam?" She looked at her sister one more time before slipping on the headgear. "I want to know about the fire, Sam. I want to know if I had anything to do with starting it. Do you know? Can you help me?"

She slipped on the headgear, took a deep breath, and started the program.

Twenty-Seven

Source amnesia is the root of most false memories. The source of a memory — its context in time and place — is its most fragile aspect, and often the first to decay. Once that's gone, the memory is adrift, so to speak, and the brain can no longer distinguish whether the event it encoded was real or imagined.
— Random notes: Julia Gordon

You slowly turn around in the near-empty studio, and your eye is caught again by the tantalizingly familiar boardwalk painting. You remember the white dot you saw at its end after your brush with the thing in the sea.

Something still waits for you there.

But you don't fear the kraken now, at least not as much. It had you — and then let you go.

Behind it you find a jumbled painting unlike anything you've seen before, looking like a golden mirror that's been smashed and then clumsily pieced together again. The golden shards are arranged into something resembling *Nude Descending a Staircase*. You can't see yourself in these pieces, but you sense an image, a shape in the jumbled mass.

You look closer. Has this painting drawn you, or is it simply one oddity among many? The golden color — could that be fire, the fire you're searching for? Is there a method here, or only madness?

You must go see firsthand. You float out of the gallery and into the moonlit night above the dark islands of Sam's memory.

Your heart sinks as you survey the watery emptiness. Only two other islands remain. One displays a familiar orange-and-yellow ribbon of boardwalk, scene of your encounter with the kraken, but it looks smaller now.

A driving urgency fills you. By this time tomorrow it will all be gone.

You rush forward and as you near one of the islands you see the golden shards from the canvas scattered haphazardly on it, reflecting the moonlight from the black surface.

Which to go to?

The golden shards are closer, beckoning like fire. You tilt down and head toward the largest piece.

As you near you see faces on the shard, blurry images seen through ice. Your mother . . . you recognize her. And hiding nearby, little Samantha. Suddenly you are your sister. . . .

Sammi loves to play "boo" with Mommy. Loves to climb behind the big easy chair and wait, quiet as a mouse, to leap out and yell *"Boo!"*

As Mommy comes downstairs, Samantha is ready. Except Mommy opens the front door and Uncle Eathan is there. She says what she always says when she sees Uncle Eathan.

"What's up, doc?"

Uncle Eathan is a doctor for grown-ups, not like Dr. White that Sammi and Julie go to.

It's strange to see Uncle Eathan here when Mommy is usually cleaning or going shopping.

He comes into the living room and shuts the door behind him.

Samantha likes Uncle Eathan. He always has a smile, and he isn't always asking questions and showing her pictures and making her draw, like Daddy. And his beard tickles when he kisses her.

"That's what *I* want to know," he says. "What's up? You sounded upset on the phone. What's he done now?"

Sammi watches her mom look around, searching for her. But Sammi stays hidden. She can't jump out now.

"It was nothing, just another one of our stupid fights, over money, over the girls —"

"The girls — ?"

Sammi feels a bit of dust in her nose, the

393

beginning of a sneeze —

If I sneeze, they'll know I'm here, they'll know I've listened.

The bit of dust continues to tickle her nose.

"Just the same craziness, Julie with math problems, Samantha with paints and crayons. I wish you could say something."

"Since when does Nathan listen to anyone on the subject of his daughters? But I don't think he's harming them."

Mommy stiffens and turns to Uncle Eathan. It gets very quiet in the room.

"If for one instant I ever thought — even suspected — that, I'd be out of here. *With* the girls."

Quieter.

"Well," Uncle Eathan says, "you know where you can stay." He puts a hand on her arm. "It would be like old times."

Mommy pulls her arm away. "We promised to forget those 'old times,' didn't we. Let's keep that promise."

And just then the tickle in Sammi's nose grows worse, as if the sneeze knew what a bad time this was. The tickle suddenly seems to fill her nose with air, and even though Sammi reaches up to close her nose, squeeze it shut tightly, it explodes.

Uncle Eathan, Mommy . . . staring at her.

Sammi jumps up and says what she always says.

"Boo!"

Suddenly you're back outside in the 'scape, high above the island. You are disappointed — nothing there about the fire. Below you the shards begin to glow with a rich amber light. You watch in awe as they flow together, re-assembling, until you see that the glass collage in the gallery was once —

A family portrait: Mom, Dad, Sam, and you — shattered.

Shattered by what? An affair?

Eathan and Mom — was there something going on between them? Or *had* there been? Was that what "old times" meant?

If true, this changes everything.

You look around.

The boardwalk island still beckons from below. Maybe the kraken is gone. It did its job.

You're almost afraid to go. If you don't find an answer, a solution here, then what? There's no place else to look? What's left of Sam will sink beneath the waves, like Atlantis . . . gone forever.

You hurry to the boardwalk, the empty boardwalk with its burnished slats stretching impossibly far on the sinking island. And at the end, in the impossible distance, far past where the now-vanished fortune-teller sat, a white dot.

"I suppose that's where I'm supposed to go," you say aloud. "Please let me find the answer there."

No one's going to hold it against you that

you're talking to yourself here.

You'll go crazy if you don't.

You start traveling the boards, missing the creak of the wood and the squeals of summer — the distant sounds of people playing on the shrinking beach, frolicking in the encroaching surf. But this boardwalk is silent, and the only sounds you're likely to hear are your own.

You look up. Just like the last time, the sky here is a swirl of bright-colored ribbons, as though the boardwalk were located on Jupiter.

You look ahead and see that the white dot is much closer, and no longer a mere dot. Appropriately enough, it's a concession stand. Hot dogs and more. Finally you can read the sign.

NATHAN'S.

Sure, you're at the beach, at Coney Island maybe, so naturally there's a Nathan's stand.

Except you don't think Sam's ever been to Coney Island. Eathan took you south for summer vacations now and then, but you never saw a Nathan's stand in Brighton.

That question again: Whose memory is this?

Closer to the stand. Someone's waiting there, being served. On the sign you see colorful pictures of all the wonderful food items, the crinkle-cut fries, corn-on-the-cob dripping butter, clams on the half shell.

You're getting hungry.

What's it like to eat virtual food? you wonder.

The person ahead of you is short, dressed in a long, dark coat. Waiting here, you have a minute to study that cloak. It's black like the water but dabbed with spots of color, all swirls, just like the wood, the sky, the boardwalk.

You can't see the counterman, but you hear him.

"There you go, sir. There you are —"

And then the fellow in front of you turns, moving like slow-motion film, and as he faces you he's holding his head, a hand tight against each side of his face, squeezing his head, as he —

SCREAMS!

The sound is an animal howl emanating from the oval mouth in his lightbulb head with two thumb gouges for eyes.

He scurries away, his piercing, whistling scream echoing after him.

When he's gone you realize you *know* that guy. Everyone knows *The Scream* guy. You had a chance to ask him what he was screaming about . . . and blew it.

Is Sam getting whimsical here? Playing with you?

Your mind is dying, Sam. The clock is running out. No time for games.

"How ya doin' today?"

You look at the counterman and it's Nathan. Your father.

"Doin' okay?"

He's chewing gum, popping it, acting like a

counterman, wearing a silly white cap.

You wonder if your image can speak in the memoryscape.

You say, "Dad . . . Daddy. I —"

And suddenly you're a little girl again.

"Daddy —"

The counterman grins. "What'll it be? The special?"

What's the matter? Julie thinks. Doesn't he hear me? He's acting as though the words are lost, taken by the wind.

"Daddy, it's Julie. I'm — I'm your —"

But the counterman turns away. "Okay, then, that's it — you want the special, with the works. You're gonna like it." A quick glance over his shoulder. "No, you're gonna love it."

This talk — it's so confusing, the way he sounds like he's from Brooklyn. That's not your father.

"Daddy, it's me. Don't you see who it is? Please, I'm —"

But he's fixing "the special," scooping something off the grill, then slowly turning back to Julie.

"Here ya go!"

He hands her something. Julie reaches out and takes it.

"Daddy . . ."

Something in a bun. Something heavier than a hot dog. She looks down.

In the bun is a hand — grilled, scorched, its fingers twitching.

And now *she* screams —

The sound of your scream has to fill the manor, but you don't give a damn.

Another severed hand − what the hell does it mean?

You see your father looking at you, grinning. *"Want some mustard on that? Goes real well with mustard."*

Your stomach tightens with nausea as you drop the obscene thing on the counter and back away. The hand topples from the bun and lies on the counter. You wouldn't be surprised if it scurried away on its own.

Your father shoves it back into the bun and says, *"Not hungry?"*

He raises it to his lips and takes a big bite, then closes his eyes in gustatory ecstasy.

"Mmmmm! Delicious!"

You keep backing away until the boardwalk railing bumps against the small of your back. You hear splashing in the surf behind you.

Something else touches your back, something wet.

You jump and turn but suddenly your body is encircled, your arms pinned to your sides. Whatever's got you is cold and slimy and very strong. You don't have to look to know what it is but you turn your head anyway.

The kraken again, looming out of the black

water, its many tentacles ranging back and forth across the sand. You see one giant, glowing eye studying you with cold detachment.

It let you go the last time, but still . . .

The Exit button — you try to point to it but your real-world arms are as trapped as their virtual counterparts.

You thrash about, your heart racing, your pulse pounding in your brain as terror grips you as tightly as the tentacle. There's nothing virtual or simulated about your fear. It's as real as anything you've ever experienced.

You feel the slimy suckers squirm against your skin as they open their mouthlike appendages to free the small hooks. A hundred needles pierce your skin, slowly, digging in. You yelp in pain but there's no one to hear. You're all alone with this thing.

"Sam . . . God, Sam — !"

And then you're moving, being dragged along the sand. You try to dig your heels in but the sand doesn't hold. You hear loud splashing behind you and know the black water is closer. You twist your head around and see the kraken sliding, jellylike, off the shore and into the deeps.

"Sam!" you scream. "I know you must have hated me at times, but I'm here to help! Don't do this, Sam! Please!"

You feel that icy, oily water swallowing your lower half, then your chest, and — all too fast — your head.

You close your eyes against the slimy feel of the water against your face. You seal your lips, but still you can taste the thick foulness.

And you can't *breathe!*

Down, down, down, the pressure building.

You're going to drown! A part of your brain knows there's air all around you in Sam's room but you can't get any! Panic surges through you. Your heart hammers in your chest as the water pressure hammers against your ears. You'd scream for help but if you open your mouth that filthy water will fill it.

You open your eyes and see the glowing chains of phosphorescence running along the kraken's flank, swirling in intricate designs as it carries you ever deeper. Almost beautiful.

You look back toward the surface — all dark — then below. A light below, bright, growing larger, burning like a quasar. The kraken drags you to it, pushes you toward it, thrusts you into the heat, the intolerable brightness.

And suddenly the water is gone. You gasp, cough, suck air. You can breathe again.

As the black water clears from your eyes, your surroundings swim into focus. No kraken. No black sea.

You're airborne.

You've been thrust into a new, deeper level, but one even more devastated than the previous two.

Below you stretch the remains of an endless forest that once must have been verdant and beautiful. But now the trees — *all* the trees — have been flattened. Stripped of every trace of green, they lie in concentric rings, all their denuded crowns facing away from the center of those rings.

You thought you'd be used to devastation by now, but this is truly appalling. You're reminded of photos you've seen of the mysterious Tunguska explosion in the early part of the century, or the hillsides around Mount St. Helens after it blew.

And in the center of these countless rings of millions of dead, uprooted trees sits a mountain. Or rather, half a mountain. Its top is gone, obliterated by an explosion of unimaginable force. A thin plume of smoke trails upward from the flattened, cratered top, and a small, ominous rivulet of golden lava, not much different from the color of the boardwalk you trod only moments ago, trickles down its craggy flank. And watching over it all, a dim full moon.

This is it, you realize. The last level. The source of all the damage sits before you. You see a rocky path leading up to the crater top.

That's where you'll find the answers.

Sam brought you here, she brought you down to this last level, to the smoking remnants of a mountain that must be climbed. You know that. And you're ready.

You're beginning your glide toward the mountain when you feel a tug on your shoulder. You gasp and spin around. No one there. Another tug, and a voice, muffled by your headphones.

Someone in the real world wants you.

Frustrated and annoyed, you click EXIT.

Twenty-Eight

Oliver Goldsmith: "O Memory! thou fond deceiver."
— Random notes: Julia Gordon

1

Julie lifted the goggles and looked around. Eathan's face hovered above her, his expression grim. He looked as though he'd been sleeping. His eyes were bloodshot, his normally handsome face drawn and haggard.

How long had he been there? Had he seen himself in that memory? Had he seen his brother's wife?

"Sorry. But I wanted to let you know that they almost captured O'Donnell."

"Liam?" she said, then caught herself. "Liam O'Donnell?"

"The one and only. They spotted him on Fylingdales Moor but he escaped."

"Then he's still nearby." He'd lied to her about leaving.

"Yes. I'm going down to the police station in Bay to post a reward for the bastard's capture. If I could just get my hands on him for two minutes . . ."

Julie laid a hand on his arm. "I know you cared for her."

He nodded. "I didn't have many people in my life besides you and Samantha. But after the two of you left, I . . ." He looked away. "Alma was special."

"I'm sorry."

He straightened. "Want to come into Bay with me?"

"No. No — I don't think so."

"We're going to get him," Eathan said, heading for the door. "I want to look this man in the eye and ask him what he did to Alma — and Samantha."

I've already done that, she thought. But she only nodded as he left the room.

Julie leaned back and stared at Sam's still form. Liam was still free and nearby. On the surface it meant one more danger to Sam.

But the real danger to Sam was inside, devouring her from within.

2

After making way for Sam's physical therapists to do their daily work, Julie retreated to her room and lay on the bed, pondering her next step with Sam.

The more she thought about it, the more she became convinced that something lay buried — maybe hopelessly so — in Sam's memoryscape. Sam's unconscious seemed to be reaching out, pulling her deeper and deeper.

Maybe the answer was inside the volcano.

The memory had to be so deeply buried that Julie would never find it by chance. She'd have to know exactly where to look.

What could it be? What memory could be so awful that Sam would bury it so deeply? Would it show her what Liam did to her — if anything? Or was it something else completely?

And again Julie thought of the mention in the newspaper article about the fire starting in the basement.

Had she been playing with matches that night?

Or had Sam tried to imitate her sister's experiments, setting the blaze? Was that what she'd repressed?

Shaken, Julie bolted upright and crossed the room to the door. She stepped into the hall, looking up and down its length, wondering where to go. She wanted to run. She almost wished she were a jogger. She could go out and find a path across Fylingdales and run across the moor until she forgot these gut-twisting thoughts. But she knew her lungs would give out long before her endorphins kicked in.

She thought of the box in Sam's closet. As much as she wanted to see its contents, she knew she'd need a screwdriver or the like to pry it open. She felt the key in her pocket and glanced down the hall to the closed door to Eathan's study.

Why not? What other treasures lay hidden in that locked file cabinet?

Maybe more information about the fire . . . maybe something to ease this gnawing fear. Eathan was still in the village, and she'd hear him drive up.

Minutes later she had her head in the second drawer. Much of it was correspondence from the early seventies with the life-insurance companies after the fire, plus the fire-insurance company, settling the mortgage, selling the property where the house had stood.

The collected minutiae of the aftermath of a tragedy. But why lock it up?

Unless he had nowhere else to put it.

Julie flipped through the rest of the hanging folders. More twenty-some-year-old correspondence. God, didn't Eathan throw anything away? A quick glance at the last folder — so thin she thought it might be empty — and she'd begin on the third and last drawer. A flash of white in the bottom caught her eye. She reached in and pulled out a double-folded piece of paper, sealed with a piece of ancient, yellowed Scotch tape.

She didn't hesitate. The tape practically fell off.

The first thing she saw when she opened it was the Millburn Valley Community Hospital heading. *Lab Report* was under that. Then the name Nathan Gordon and the words, "Sperm Analysis":

Sperm Count:	14,000,000 sperm per cc.
Motility:	20%
Viability:	20%
Morphologic Forms:	30% normal
Diagnosis:	Functionally sterile

Sterile? How could Nathan be sterile? He was the father of twins. This had to be wrong. You don't get a sperm count unless you're concerned about your fertility or you've just had a vasectomy. She checked for a date and stared in shock when she saw it.

A month before we were born!

Their father knew he wasn't sterile — his wife was pregnant with their first child — or in this case, children. Why would he have a vasectomy before his wife delivered?

Clearly he wouldn't. He'd wait until the pregnancy was over and the children delivered live and intact, and *then* he'd have the surgery. But never *during* pregnancy.

Unless . . .

Julie nearly dropped the report.

Unless he suspected someone else might be the father.

Oh, God no!

But if Nathan Gordon wasn't their father, who was?

Immediately a name popped into her mind.

3

Eathan's face went white as he stared down at the sheet of paper on his desk. Finally he looked up at her, his voice barely audible.

"Where . . . did you . . . get this?"

Julie stood on the far side of the desk, trembling inside. She'd agonized all afternoon over how to broach the subject with him. It meant confessing to trespassing in his most private sanctum, but she had to bring this out into the open. She had to *know.*

She pointed to the locked wall cabinet. "There."

"No!" Eathan slammed his fist down on

the desk, rattling his pen set and sending paper clips flying. And then both fists at once. "No!" His eyes blazed at her. "How could you? How could you break my trust like this? Sneak in here and rummage through my private files like a common thief? I . . ."

His fingers curled into claws, and for a moment Julie feared he might leap across the desk at her. She cringed and took a step back.

"I'm sorry," she said. It sounded dumb and lame but it was all she could manage right now.

"Sorry? You seem to be saying that a lot, lately. Well, sorry doesn't — what's the expression — cut it, Julia. In fact, nothing you can say will make up for this unconscionable invasion of privacy. I want you out of here. Out of Oakwood. Tonight."

"No, Eathan. You can't mean that. We're losing Sam. And if you were hiding this, I thought —"

He pounded his fist on the desk again. His face had lost its pallor and was now flushed with anger.

"I do mean it! I will not share my house with someone I cannot trust! Get out!"

"Eathan —"

"Out!" He pointed to the door. "Get *out!*" She had never seen him this angry. His fury was terrifying.

What could I have been thinking?

"All right," Julie said, moving toward the door. "I'll go. But I just want you to answer one question."

"No! Leave."

He wouldn't look at her. Did he know what she was going to say? Was that it?

"Are you my father?"

Eathan's arm dropped to his side.

He kept staring down at his desk, then dropped into his chair and buried his face in his hands.

Julie watched him a moment. He was frozen. Was it such a terrible thing? It would explain so much.

When he didn't move or say anything, she stepped closer.

"Eathan? Are you all right?"

He remained motionless, his face hidden by his hands. Julie moved around the desk until she stood over his shoulder.

"Is it true, Eathan? Are you my father?"

A long, agonizing pause, then he nodded into the sheltering hands.

Suddenly weak, Julie leaned against the desk for support. She'd guessed it, she'd felt it in her heart when she'd grasped the implications of that sperm count, but to stand here and have Eathan acknowledge it . . .

My uncle's hiding something. . . .

You had that right, Sam, she thought.

411

Everybody always said he raised us like his own children. . . .

She reached out a trembling hand and gently, almost gingerly, placed it on his shoulder.

"Hello . . . Dad."

Eathan took a deep, shuddering breath and pulled his hands away from his face. Without looking at her he reached up and covered her hand with one of his own.

"Julia . . . I'll tell you all about it," he said hoarsely. "But let's go downstairs. I need a drink."

4

"How can I toss you out because of a broken trust, after how I betrayed my own brother?"

They sat across from each other in the drawing room, sipping some of Eathan's fifty-year-old scotch. Julie barely touched hers. She was already numb. She didn't need any more anesthetic.

"You and my mother, I saw it in Sam's 'scape . . . it's hard to believe. How . . . ?"

Eathan's mouth curled in a funny way, as if the idea of Julie seeing them together was embarrassing. "Actually, Lucy and I were a bit of an item before Nathan even met her. Nothing terribly serious, so when

I went out to Stanford, to medical school, our relationship . . . well, I guess you might say it attenuated itself out of existence. That was when Nathan moved in. He was pursuing his doctorate at Cornell, so he was around all the time. Eventually they were married and it seemed like a good match. I still cared for Lucinda, but I didn't mind."

He took a sip. "Or so I thought. I didn't mind until Nathan got overinvolved in his work. He ran into financial and professional setbacks; he neglected Lucy. I was lonely too. We'd talk on the phone and I'd try to comfort her. Old feelings revived. We'd stop by and visit each other. We had a history, and before we knew what was happening . . ."

He sipped his scotch and looked away. Even now he seemed ashamed.

Julie imagined Eathan and her mother in the throes of passion. Not just a kiss, but making love.

And suddenly she felt sorry for her father — no, for Nathan Gordon, the man she's always *thought* of as her father — but she didn't *know* him. He was little more than a string of old memories.

Eathan, however — Eathan had been the guiding force in their lives, supportive of anything they attempted, and always there when they needed him. A real father.

"How long did the affair go on?" she asked.

"Oh, not long enough to qualify as a real affair. We were both too racked with guilt to continue it, so we scurried back to our prior existences and swore never to mention it again."

"Did you know we were . . ."

"My children?" He shook his head. "No. I think Lucy knew — I'm sure she must have known — but she never told me. Probably knew what it would do to me. No, I didn't have an inkling until after the fire when I was going through Nathan's papers. I almost passed out."

"But you said his papers were burned in the fire. How did you get them?"

Eathan sighed. "Nathan conned me into letting him move a filing cabinet into my basement. He said he didn't have room for it in his place and I believed him. His house was small, and with two little girls running around, there wasn't much room. I never guessed that the real reason he wanted those records out of the house was to make sure your mother never came across them. But after the fire, when I went through them, I . . . I was shocked."

"But, God, it means he knew. He knew right from the start that we weren't his. And yet he never said anything to you?"

"Never a word."

"Maybe he didn't know whose kids we were."

Eathan looked miserable. "Oh, I think he knew. But he kept mum and raised you as his own." He grunted as if in pain. "When I think about the countless times I dropped by and held you girls on my knee with him sitting there watching me, knowing all the while . . ."

And that image caused another pang in Julie.

"But why wouldn't he say anything? You were his brother."

"He had some strange ideas. I have a feeling he somehow convinced himself that you two really were his children."

"Oh, come now —"

"No. I'm quite serious. Because in a way you were. Genetically, at least."

Julie caught on immediately. "Because you two were identical twins?"

"Right. My genes were identical to his. And since he was sterile, you were the closest he would ever come to having children of his own."

"Amazing . . ." Julie said slowly. "Amazing that someone could rationalize to that point of view and live with it."

"Your father —" He caught himself. "My brother was an amazing man." He drained his glass and leaned forward. He stared into her eyes. "And now I have something to ask of you."

"Name it," Julie said.

"Your key to my wall cabinet. I assume you had a copy made."

Julie pulled it from her pocket and handed it to him.

"Now," she said. "Let me ask *you* for something: the key to that box you kept in the bottom drawer of the locked file cabinet."

"Kept?" Eathan said, visibly stiffening.

"I have it."

He shot to his feet. "Oh, no! You can't have that! You've got to give it back!"

"I need to see what's inside, Eathan. No more secrets, please. I can handle whatever it is. I deserve to know everything. It's taken over twenty years for me to learn who my real father is. . . ."

"There's nothing in there! Trust me!"

"No. You trust *me.* I need to know —"

Suddenly he was rushing from the room. Julie followed him as he pounded up the stairs and raced toward her room. He yanked open the door and disappeared inside.

By the time Julie reached her room he had half of her dresser drawers pulled open and was pawing through the topmost.

"Eathan — please! It's not here!"

He ignored her. He was out of control. It reminded her of that scene when Charles

Foster Kane rampages through his wife's bedroom.

"Eathan, stop . . . please!"

After finishing with her dresser drawers, he went to her closet and rifled through what little clothing she had hanging there. He checked the window seat — empty — then dropped to his knees and looked under the bed.

"Julia, get me that box. Give it back to me. Enough prying into the past!"

"It's my past, Eathan — mine and Sam's."

When he found nothing under the bed, he began tearing it apart, tossing the sheets and comforter onto the floor, pulling the mattress off the box spring.

Finally he stood amid the carnage, panting, turning a slow circle. His voice became plaintive.

"Where is it, Julia? Please . . . give it back."

"As soon as I find out what's in it."

For an instant his face changed, and for the second time tonight she feared he would attack her. She must be crazy to be pushing him like this. But he closed his eyes and took a deep breath. When he spoke his voice was flat, calm, cold.

"This is intolerable. I have the key and will not give it to you. I expect you to return that box to me before I leave for London tomorrow — for Alma's *wake*," he said pointedly. "If you do not, I will banish you from this house forever. Daughter or not, I will see you and all your electronic garbage out on the driveway before I depart tomorrow morning. Is that clear?"

Oh, no. Was she to gain her real father and lose him in the same night? She couldn't bear that.

"Eathan, be reasonable. I have a right —"

He jabbed a finger at her. "No! No, you have no right! What is in that box is my private business and has nothing to do with you! I want it back. In my office. *Now!* Otherwise, start packing."

He stalked past her and left her alone in the disheveled room.

Julie knew he wasn't bluffing. Eathan never bluffed. When he made a decision, that was it. If she didn't return the box, she'd be out of here.

And Sam would be gone . . . forever.

5

Julie latched the toolshed door behind her and turned on the flashlight. She pulled her coat tight around her. It had turned so cold.

No easy task sneaking out of the manor tonight. Eathan had sat up in the drawing room, as if on guard. But eventually he'd come upstairs. When she heard his shower running, she made her move to Sam's room and then out the kitchen door.

She crossed the shed and flicked the beam around until she found the splintery workbench. She placed the locked box on the scarred surface, then checked out the tools. A giant hammer hung on a rack behind the bench. She took that down. To her left sat a line of four screwdrivers. She picked the heaviest one.

It took a lot of hammering and made a godawful racket, but she finally managed to pry open the lid.

He'll never forgive this, she thought.

She opened the lid slowly.

A small manila folder lay inside. Her hands shook as she lifted it out. Inside was a report from the Putnam County coroner on the deaths of Lucy Gordon and Nathan Gordon. She sifted through it, glancing only briefly at the autopsy reports, the dental matchups. She gasped when the black-and-white photo of a charred corpse slipped into the light. Nathan Gordon's empty eye sockets stared at her. His blackened, half-open jaws seemed to be leering at her.

She told herself: That's not my father.

Julie shut the folder and shuddered. God! Why would Eathan keep something like that? She put it aside and saw what looked like three small notebooks or journals in the bottom of the box.

Could it be? Were these Nathan's experimental journals?

Her heart pounded madly against her ribs as she opened the top volume and began reading the crabbed handwriting.

Twenty-Nine

For a memory to stay fresh and vivid, or for a false memory to be reinforced, its synaptic connections must be periodically engaged — i.e., the memory must be reviewed — on a regular basis. Sort of the neurological equivalent of pulling the pieces of a memory from their various closets, reassembling it, dusting it off and polishing it up, checking it for wear and tear, and then putting it back on the shelf.
— Random notes: Julia Gordon

1

Barely aware of where she was but absolutely certain of where she was going, Julie stumbled along the dawnlit second-floor hall.

She felt dead inside, physically and emotionally drained.

She wanted nothing more than to crawl

into her bed, pull the covers over her head, and never show her face again — never *think* again. Her mind and body screamed for rest, for escape, but she would not, could not, permit it.

And so with Nathan Gordon's experimental notebooks clutched tightly against her chest, she forced herself to put one foot in front of the other until she reached her goal.

She'd spent the night poring over the journals. At first in a state of incredulous denial, flipping back and forth in a vain search for inconsistencies, for some evidence that this was a cruel hoax, and then with a slowly growing sick realization that it was . . . *all true.*

Days ago she had been accused of thinking the unthinkable by a man who had known the truth all along.

Julie entered Eathan's bedroom without knocking, throwing the door open and letting it bang against the wall.

Eathan stirred in his bed. "What? Who is it?"

The sound of his voice sparked something in Julie. Anger, resentment, rage — they fueled her, renewed her strength. She must have made a frightening apparition as she approached his bed through the gloom, for he struggled to a sitting position and raised a hand to her.

"Stop! Who *are* you?"

And again the sound of his voice stoked her fires. She raised the journals high above her head and then flung them at him with all her strength. He cried out in alarm as they fluttered and thudded against his chest and shoulders.

She didn't give a damn about banishment from Oakwood. She didn't give a damn about Eathan.

"Liar!" she screamed. "*Liar!* You've known about this all these years and you never told us! God, how could you *not* tell us?"

Eathan rolled away from her and reached for the lamp at his bedside. She heard the click and then the sudden gush of light blinded her for an instant.

As her vision cleared she saw Eathan, dressed in striped pajamas, sitting in the bed staring at the old journal he held in his hands. He looked vaguely ridiculous, but Julie wasn't in a laughing mood.

"Oh, no, Julia! Oh, no, you didn't! Please tell me you didn't!"

"Didn't *what?*" she said. "Didn't learn the truth you've been hiding from me all my life? Were you going to let me go to my grave not knowing Nathan, your brother, my 'father,' used Sam and me as lab rats?"

Eathan kept his head down, his face averted. He seemed to be trying to compose himself. When he finally raised his head, his expression was miserable.

"How could I tell you, Julia?"

"How could you *not?*"

"Tell *me* then," he said, a note of bitterness creeping into his voice. "Tell me the words I should have used to explain to you that your father — or at least the man we all thought was your father — experimented with your brains during your first years of life, inhibiting certain neurohormones while supplying an excess of others. Just how —"

"He made me all left-brained and Sam all right-brained. He warped our brains and personalities. He made us lopsided — *on purpose!*" She wanted to scream.

"And just how do you phrase that to a child, to a teenager, to a young adult woman going out into the world? What turn of phrase will keep her from feeling like a carnival freak, like a victim, like — as you put it a moment ago — a lab rat? Tell me how *you* would say it, Julia."

"We became adults. We had a right to know the truth," she said stubbornly. "It would have explained so much."

"And the truth was going to do what — set you free? Do you feel free now, Julia? Do you feel better about yourself? Has it boosted your self-esteem? Are you more ready to go out and tackle the problems of your career? Are you *happier* now that you know the gold-plated truth?"

Julie closed her eyes and spoke through her teeth. "I prefer dealing with a truth to living with a lie. Can I make it any clearer than that?"

"Maybe *you* could deal with it. But what about Samantha? How do you think she would have reacted? You know your sister. Imagine what the truth might have done to her. . . ."

"It might have given her some insight," Julie said, her eyes open again. "And me too. I've always analyzed everything to death — from math problems to relationships. Now I know why. Sam never analyzed anything. She *emoted* to every decision. But at least she could have understood what was behind that and maybe done something about it. Before it was too goddamn late."

Eathan pushed the journal away. He took a deep breath, and sighed.

"Yes. Or maybe it would have prompted her to be a little more efficient in her next suicide attempt."

"We never had a chance at normal lives, did we?" Julie said softly. "It's not fair."

"No, it's not fair. And, frankly, none of this has been very fair to me, either. I could have lived out my days quite happily not knowing any of this. Instead, I've been saddled with the knowledge of what my own brother did to *my* daughters, and then watching the effects of his experiment play out over the years in their lives. You dealt with it relatively well. But your sister always teetered on the edge of disaster."

"But why did you keep it hidden?"

"I certainly wasn't going to allow any of it to be published! Good Lord, the two of you would be tabloid freaks and Nathan would be portrayed as a monster."

"He *was* a monster, dammit."

"I thought so too, at first. But no man is a monster in his own mind. And as I read and reread those journals I became convinced that Nathan had no thought of harming you two. He seemed convinced, on paper at least, that the benefits far outweighed the risks. And I think the experiment succeeded far beyond his wildest expectations. His neurohormone treatment worked *too* well."

Julie stared at him. "I don't believe you! This man — and I can't see that it matters whether or not he was your twin — uses *your* children as guinea pigs, and you *don't* hate him? He knew they were your children and not his, that's why he treated us as disposable. You should *loathe* him, Eathan! You should want to scour the earth of every trace of his existence and never speak his name again!"

Now Eathan looked away, at the dull flow of daybreak at the windows of his bedroom.

"Perhaps. And I did feel that way at first, but when I considered his intentions —"

"I don't give a damn about his intentions. It's what he *did* that matters. And what he did to us was monstrous."

Eathan nodded mutely as he stared down at the journal in his hands.

"You must accept that I was only trying to protect you," he said. "Ever since you were teenagers you've accused me of being overprotective. Now you know why. Not just because I knew you were my own flesh and blood, but because I knew Nathan had played with your brains. So I was always on guard for some sign of instability, some warning of impending decompensation. With you there was never a worry. You had trouble with relationships but —"

"I *have* no relationships," Julie said.

"Perhaps, but you were functioning. Better than that — you were thriving, making great strides in your field. And Samantha . . . Samantha had such wonderful potential, but she always seemed to be teetering on the edge of self-destruction. I made it my mission in life to see to it that she lived long enough to achieve her potential."

"Well, you failed."

Julie immediately regretted the blunt words. Eathan was an innocent bystander. She saw that now. He hadn't asked for any of this. He'd thought he'd inherited a pair of nieces and then learned they were his daughters. And *then* learned that his own brother had tampered with their wiring. He'd been dealt a rotten hand and had played it as best he could. He didn't deserve her anger. If the positions were reversed, she couldn't say she'd have played it differently.

He looked up. "What are you saying?"

"I'm saying she's got very little chance of coming back. And it's Nathan's fault."

"How can you say that?"

"Because it's true. He sent her into the world with one leg and one arm, both on the same side. She had no balance. The slightest breeze tipped her over. It could be there's no single incident that sent her into her own black hole."

"But what about you?"

Julie stared at Eathan. And she held that stare for a few terrible seconds before saying, quietly, "Maybe I'm next."

She shuddered at the picture of herself immobile in a bed, her thoughts melting away like ice cream in the sun, until nothing was left.

One hell of a scary thought, but Julie wasn't going to turn away from it. It was a real possibility.

"I can't believe that. You're too sane."

"Am I? Who knows what will come along and fry my unbalanced circuits? Because that's what I now think is wrong with Sam. Her damage didn't come from outside. It came from within. She ran into something she couldn't handle, and the imbalance your brother created left her without the tools to handle it."

Eathan rubbed his palms against his face. "Damn."

"Or . . ."

Eathan looked at her. "Or what?"

"Or there's something else inside her that she couldn't deal with."

"What's that supposed to mean?"

"I'm not sure," Julie said. She rose to her feet and began walking about the room, aimlessly. "But I get the feeling Sam is both hiding something *and* drawing me deeper. Most of these memories feel like diversions, decoys to keep me from tapping into some other memory. Something she's scared of . . . something she's repressed."

"Repressed? What would Samantha have to repress?"

"I don't know," Julie said, turning toward him and fixing him with her stare. She'd been ready to mention the possibility of her starting the fire, but something else had just occurred to her. "Maybe neurohormone injections are just the tip of the abuse iceberg. Maybe dear old Nathan had his way with us in other areas as well."

She wanted to spark some rage in him,

see him shout and scream and hurl things against the wall.

But Eathan only sat there, staring at her.

"Listen here, young lady. Nathan may have lost perspective in the area of his research, but I knew my brother — he was no . . . no pedophile!"

Julie felt the poison rising in her. She didn't repress it. Instead, she drew it up and let it fly.

"With all due respect, Eathan, you didn't know shit about your brother." She spat the words. "How do you know he wasn't fucking with our little bodies while he was fucking with our little minds?"

"Don't talk like that. Nathan may have been many things, but he wasn't a sexual pervert."

"Damn it!" she cried. "Your brother was capable of *any*thing! Why not that? And why aren't you *angry* about any of this, damn you!"

Eathan looked away again. "Maybe — because I've lived with it for almost a quarter of a century." His voice sounded almost dead. "It took me years, but I'm past the anger. I've been more concerned with dealing with the consequences. And don't forget that he risked his life to save you two from the fire, even though he knew you weren't really his children. That was heroic. *I* haven't forgotten that. And don't forget this: His sacrifice gave me the chance to raise my two daughters."

The fire . . . in the shock and rage after reading the journals, Julie had almost forgotten about that. Maybe no man was all bad, but Nathan Gordon had come pretty damn close.

"One more thing," she said, "then I'll leave you alone. How did you get a copy of the coroner's file?"

"It wasn't easy. But I was a practicing physician in the area, remember? I had connections."

"Why would you want such a grisly thing?"

"I look through it every so often."

"But why?"

Eathan's eyes blazed as they bored into her, but his voice was wintry. "To make sure he's really dead. Every time Samantha would do something self-destructive I'd pull it out and look at those pictures just to assure myself that the man who altered my daughters' brains — *my* daughters, not his — wasn't out there somewhere laughing at me."

Julie nodded mutely. "I — I have to think about all this."

"We'll talk some more," Eathan said, but Julie hurried from the room.

And as she walked down the long hallway, she thought, Eathan isn't nearly as "past the anger" as he thinks.

That lightened her own load. Something comforting about sharing the rage.

But she was too wound up to devote much thought to that now. She'd had an epiphany of sorts back in Nathan's room.

Sam's subconscious was protecting a blocked memory all right — a memory of abuse. It was as mundane and tawdry as that.

Julie thought of that kraken; something more horrible lay buried deep in Sam's mind. A memory so awful that Sam's subconscious had walled it off, relieving her consciousness of ever having to deal with it again.

But what if Sam had made an end run around her subconscious, the way her memories seemed to be doing now? What if, through her art, she'd accessed the memory and then . . .

God, that had to be it.

That was why it was such slow going in Sam's memoryscape. The key memory had been repressed all her life, so even now, even after her consciousness had been ruined, Sam's subconscious was still guarding it, blocking Julie, throwing other memories at her as distractions.

But a memory of what? What could have happened, what could be so awful that merely reliving the memory of it could devastate her consciousness like that? Maybe it was a combination of the memory and some sort of instability in Sam's brain as a result of Nathan's experiments.

That had to be it. If Nathan hadn't toyed with Sam's internal wiring, she probably could have handled reliving the repressed memory. She might have suffered other repercussions, but she wouldn't be in a coma now.

Damn Nathan Gordon! Did he do something worse than dose them with neurohormones? Sam had a deeply buried memory. Most so-called repressed memories were fiction, but Julie felt she was dealing with the real thing this time. And what repressed memory would be most deeply buried?

Sexual abuse.

A wave of nausea swept over Julie. Was there no end to this?

She wished she knew how to cry. It would bring some relief. But she couldn't cry. Nathan Gordon had seen to that.

Only one thing to do. Go back into the 'scape and scour that third level for a clue to the whereabouts of the hidden memory. She'd have all the answers then, and maybe the key to Sam's recovery.

But she was too tired now. She needed rest.

She headed for her bedroom. Just a few hours and she'd be okay . . .

2

The sun was high when Julie opened her eyes. She snapped up to a sitting position and grabbed her bedside clock. Eleven A.M. She'd wanted only a couple of hours. The morning was practically gone. She leaped out of bed and headed for the hall. She didn't have to get dressed — she was still wearing yesterday's clothes. A shower would have been heaven but she didn't have time.

She spotted Clarice in the hall.

"Where's my uncle?"

"Oh, he's out, mum," the maid said. "Been out since early morning."

Julie hurried down to the dining room and found a note on the table:

Julia,
Had to go to London for the wake. Will be back tonight. Do NOT do anything with Sam until I get back. Very important that I talk to you first.

Love,
Eathan

Put off going into Sam's memoryscape until tonight? Not a chance.

Julie got a cup of coffee from the kitchen and hurried upstairs. This was perfect. She could make two trips into the memory-scape before Eathan returned. Maybe then she'd have proof enough to make even Eathan admit that his brother truly had been a monster.

And maybe she'd even have the answer to Sam's condition.

Thirty

Children under age 8 are especially sus-
ceptible to false memories because their
frontal lobes are immature, and that's
where the time and place of a memory
— its source — are stored.
            — Random notes: Julia Gordon

You enter the memoryscape and find yourself
in the gallery, but this is a strange one — inside
the hollowed-out stump of a shattered redwood. It's empty save for the large canvas —
Sam's last work. More detail has been added.
You now see that the bright yellow-orange
light radiating from behind the central darkness is fire, flames roaring into the night, reaching for the full moon. And that central darkness
now has a shape. Unquestionably a human
silhouette. But whose?

Liam? In Sam's memory he'd been silhouetted against the flames from the Branham Bank
fire.

Could be him . . . and it could be someone
else.

You go outside and scan the upslope of the

volcano. Smoke, black and toxic, still drifts from the ragged maw, streaking the clouds with red from the sputtering fire in its belly. The dead trees that littered the slope yesterday are all gone now, the last sign of life removed like a stubble scraped away by a giant razor.

You look up. The moon . . . no — no longer a moon, just a cluster of glowing rocks floating in the sky — shattered. Even the moon isn't safe from the progressive deterioration of Sam's mind. The fragments provide scant illumination.

It's the most hopeless place you've ever seen.

Hopeless . . . because you realize you haven't much time left — *Sam* hasn't much time left.

But there's got to be something here, planted on the slope between the flatland and the fire above. A clue to the ultimate memory . . .

Propelled by the growing terror that you'll lose Sam if you don't find something, you start up the slope, searching. What else can you do?

Nothing catches your eye, nothing at all. It's all dead here.

And then, to your right, about halfway up the flank of the volcano's cinder cone, you see a tiny streak of light.

You hurry toward it and find a crack in the cinder and ash-strewn crust. Not a volcanic side vent, for there's no heat coming up. More like a cave or tunnel that's been reopened by the eruption. The faint light is leaking from within. Deep within.

You enter and, like a moth, you float toward the light.

Or perhaps "lights" is more accurate. You see them far ahead. They seem to be in motion, swirling like lightning bugs in a midsummer field.

Your heartbeat kicks up its meter. Is this the way to the lost memory you're searching for? Obviously whatever's down here has been buried, hidden away.

Abruptly the tunnel ends and you find yourself in a huge, seemingly limitless cavern. It's as if you've passed through the volcano and emerged on the other side. But you sense this is a pocket world, completely encased in stone even though the living rock gives way to a field of golden grain, with dark green cypresses undulating sinuously as they reach toward the stars.

And — God — what stars. They twirl deliriously above like flaming pinwheels. The night air is alive and awhirl with light. You laugh. You know this place. It's Van Gogh's *Starry Night*. You and Sam had a running argument about it for years, Sam insisting the phantasmagor- ical scene sprang from Vincent's imagination, and you infuriating her by saying it was the result of some neurochemical aberration, that this wasn't artistic vision, this was psychosis — this is what the poor mad artist actually *saw.*

God, how you could drive each other crazy.

But now, to *live* in the painting, to see the stars swirl and the cypresses dance, it's . . . it's wonderful.

But where are the village and the steepled church of the painting? This landscape appears uninhabited.

No, not completely uninhabited. There's one house there, nestled among the trees in the background. It looks like —

Oh, no. Not that house again. Not the Millburn house. You don't want to go in there again. It's too painful. You start to turn away, then stop.

Why else are you here? Certainly not to be comforted. You're supposed to be exploring all the memories you can find. Isn't that what this is about? And you've learned that the associated pain seems to be directly proportional to their importance.

Clearly, knowledge has a price in this memoryscape.

Your insides coil with dread as you turn and start toward the house.

You try to keep from wondering what you will find within; you study the writhing cypresses that seem to be made of green-brown flame rather than vegetation, and you marvel at the twisting shadows cast by the whirling stars, yet you cannot shut out the raised, angry voices filtering through the night air from somewhere nearby. Men's voices. You follow the sound around the side of the Millburn house.

And there —

Nathan and a young Eathan face each other like two prizefighters waiting for the bell, separated by half a dozen feet and a redwood picnic table. You feel the thickening tension between them. Nathan has a pair of work gloves folded in his right hand. Twenty feet away is the vegetable garden with rows of corn and tomatoes and eggplant. A rake and a hoe lay where Nathan must have dropped them upon Eathan's arrival.

Even in the wan starlight you can see that Nathan's cheeks are flushed with anger; small droplets of spittle fleck his mustache. Eathan seems calmer, but only marginally so. His expression is difficult to read through his beard, but his rage appears to be calm, cold.

You look around. No children about. How could . . . ? You glance up and see a little face peering through the screen of one of the upstairs windows, watching with wide, wondering eyes. Sam with her games of surprise and boo.

Abruptly your perspective shifts. You're looking down on the scene from above, through the aluminum screen on your bedroom window. You're Sammi and you're wondering why your father and uncle are so mad. *You* know now that Nathan's not your father, but to little Sammi he's Daddy — and you can't separate her feelings from your own while you're here. Everything is turmoil.

"You had no right!" Daddy shouts. "No damn right at all!"

"*I* had no right?" Uncle Eathan points to the experimental journals that lay scattered across the picnic table. "You play God and then have the nerve to stand there and complain about someone snooping through your file cabinet?" He throws up his hands. "There's no talking to you, Nathan. You're insane!"

"I left those papers with you for safekeeping. I expected you to respect my privacy. I thought I could trust my own brother not to break into my files!"

"Trust?" Uncle Eathan says. "How does that word even pass your lips?"

Daddy looks as if he's about to explode. He jabs a finger at Eathan's face.

"And how does it pass *yours*, brother? It appears that nothing of mine is safe when you're about. Isn't that right?"

"What . . . ?" A guilty look sweeps across Uncle Eathan's face. Suddenly he seems on the defensive, unable to meet his brother's eyes. "I don't know —"

"You know *damn* well what I'm talking about. . . ." His leer is all bitterness and fury. "Don't you."

Uncle Eathan refuses to take the bait. He draws himself up and glares back at his brother.

"Don't try to change the subject. And for

the record, I did *not* break into anything. You left the cabinet unlocked."

Daddy kicks the picnic table. The journals jump and one tumbles to the grass.

Those journals — they're Nathan's. The ones you spent all last night reading. What are they doing here? Just this morning Eathan told you he didn't discover them until *after* the fire. And yet here he is, confronting Nathan with them. The shouting draws your attention back to the picnic table.

"Damn you, Eathan! You could have left *your* papers scattered on my floor and I never would have so much as glanced at them!"

"Well, I *did* glance at these. I was curious where your work was going. I . . . I was aghast. . . . I can't believe what you've done! It's criminal."

"And I couldn't believe what *you* did!"

"Nathan, you're incredible! Don't even attempt to gain the moral high ground here. You're a monster. I . . . how could you? Your own *daughters*, Nathan!"

"Skinner used his own child —"

"He didn't use *drugs* on her!"

Daddy waves his hands between them. "Shut up! You'll do no one any good by opening your mouth about this." He lowers his voice and it takes on a placating tone. "I've made a mistake, Eathan. I acted rashly and I regret what I did. But what's done is done. I can't turn back the clock. And there's been no harm, as you can see. They're both perfectly healthy, normal children. Perfectly normal. So let's keep this between us — for the girls' sake."

But Uncle Eathan isn't buying any of it. He shakes his head. "Too late, Nathan. I already told Lucy — for the girls' sake."

In a heartbeat Daddy's angry flush fades to ashen shock. His voice is hoarse, barely audible as he sways and clutches the edge of the table.

"No! You're lying! You wouldn't hurt her like that!"

Shaking his head in disgust, Uncle Eathan gathers the journals from the picnic table, picks up the one in the grass, and shoves them into his brother's arms.

"Maybe you'd better read those again — then tell me about hurting."

He starts toward the corner of the house and Daddy chases after him. In an instant they're around the corner and out of sight.

And suddenly Mommy's got you by the hand and she's hurrying you downstairs. You hear Daddy's voice from the front porch.

"Stay out, Eathan," he's saying in a low voice. "You're not welcome here. You can't come in. I don't want to see you on my property again. If you even —"

"It's too late, Nathan!" Mommy says as you reach the bottom.

"Lucy!" Daddy rushes inside. "Lucy, you can't believe him!"

Slowly, hesitantly, Uncle Eathan comes in behind him.

Little Julie runs in from the rear of the house and Mommy grabs her hand.

And now you're an observer again. You see your mother standing in the center hall by the foot of the stairs. She's flanked by her daughters and clutches one of their hands in each of hers. The look in her eyes . . .

You've never seen your mother like this. You have pictures, and she's always smiling, always looking so soft. But this woman . . . the cold fury in her eyes is a frightening thing. It stops you in your tracks. For she's more than Mommy now. She's all mothers, and someone has harmed her children.

God help whoever did it.

Suddenly the perspective blurs and shifts again and you're little Julie now, clutching your mommy's hand and feeling very confused. Mommy's angry with Daddy and little Julie doesn't know why.

"I don't have to believe him," Mommy says in a cold, scary voice. "He didn't have to say a thing." She points to the journals clutched in Daddy's arms. "Your own words,

444

written in your own hand, were more than enough."

"But it's all a misunderstanding." He holds the journals out before him. "This . . . it's all fiction. A novel I'm writing."

But Mommy's eyes only grow colder. "Don't insult my intelligence."

"Lucy!" Daddy's voice sounds like he's whining. "You can't believe I'd do anything to harm my own daughters."

Her eyes bore into his. "We both know the truth about that now, don't we, Nathan. And pretty soon your brother will know that truth as well." She starts toward the door, dragging Julie and Sammi along. "I'm leaving. I'm taking the girls with me. And, so help me, if I see you within a mile of them I'll shoot you dead."

"No!" Daddy's voice rises to a scream as he hurls the journals against the wall and runs toward the rear of the house. *"No!"*

Then Julie cowers back against Mommy's leg. She sees Sammi doing the same on the other side. It's late and she's tired, and never in her life has she heard a sound like that, especially from Daddy. Where'd he go? She's confused . . . and she's scared.

Uncle Eathan stands just inside the door, a dazed look on his face.

"What truth?" he says. "What are you talking about, Lucy?"

Mommy tries to smile at him, but it misfires. She looks ready to shatter into a million pieces.

"I — I'll tell you about it later. Right now I want to get out of here. Eathan, will you help me?"

He nods. "Of course."

"There's a bag at the top of the stairs. . . ."

"I'll get it."

As Uncle Eathan runs up the stairs, little Julie looks up at her mother. "M-Mommy, are we going on a trip?"

"Yes. A long one."

"And Daddy's not coming," Sammi says, not sounding too upset about it. "He and Uncle Eathan don't like each other anymore. I seen them . . . I seen them fighting."

"Why?" Julie asks.

Before Mommy or Sammi can answer, Uncle Eathan reappears, struggling with a huge suitcase on the stairs.

"What's in this? Everything you own?"

"Just about."

As Uncle Eathan lugs the suitcase toward the door, everyone freezes. . . .

And suddenly you're standing apart again as everyone fades.

You're in an empty house now. You rush from room to room but no one is here. You stumble back outside, into the Van Gogh night, and search the yard. You even pry among the cornstalks in the garden.

No one.

After one final look at the deserted grounds, you drift away from the house, looking for the tunnel back to the surface.

But you're bothered. Why don't you remember any of this? You were there. Your parents never separated. You saw yourself in that memory — at least in Sam's mind you were there. So you should remember. Or . . .

. . . is this same memory buried in its own rocky niche within your memoryscape?

But doesn't what you've just seen seem too innocuous to be repressed? No hard trauma there, just loud voices and non sequiturs.

And when did it happen? You and Sam looked about five, but you could have been four and a half.

You spot the wide, dark mouth of the tunnel to the surface ahead. And off to your right, another narrower, darker opening. Where does that go? From its position it appears to lead to the heart of the volcano.

Whichever path you choose, it's time to leave the *Starry Night* grotto.

You glance over your shoulder for a last look. And as you watch, a tendril of fire writhes from one of the stars and snakes toward the house. It touches the roof, and suddenly —

Flames burst from the windows, the front door.

"Oh, no!" you cry aloud.

Not the fire! You can't bear to watch the fire. You've relived it so many times in your own mind, why should you have to suffer through it in Sam's memoryscape too? You can't do it.

Wait . . . *Sam's* memoryscape. Maybe Sam has a different take on the tragedy. Maybe she saw something you didn't — or remembers something you don't. After all, you don't remember anything of what you just saw in the house. And thank God you didn't see yourself with matches. . . .

You hurry back, and as you do, the cypresses change to oaks and maples and elms. The sky changes too, the stars shrinking to pinpoints of light, and the moon turning full and round and staring.

You swing too close and the heat backs you up.

The fire has taken command inside, shooting jets of flame from the basement windows, running through the first floor, licking at the upstairs windows. It's fast, alive, terrifying.

And then there's a figure in the front doorway, silhouetted in the flames. Carrying two bundles in his arms, he leaps from the front porch and dashes onto the lawn. He runs directly toward you, stopping only a few feet in front of you. Nathan. He drops to his knees and deposits little Sam and Julie on the grass.

You know the next words.

"You girls stay here. I'm going back for your mom."

And still the scene affects you. As much as you hate this man for what he did to you, and for what he did to your mother as well — pretending you were his own daughters when he knew differently, getting even with her by using you as guinea pigs — you can't help but feel the same surge of love and trust you've felt every time you've remembered this moment.

He saved you from the fire.

You watch him rush back to the house, raise his arms across his face against the heat, and charge back into the flames.

And now the worst part. The waiting. You watch reflections of the flames dancing on the tear-stained faces of Julie and Sammi as their fear grows. Where's Daddy? Why isn't he bringing Mommy? And then the terror. Daddy! Mommy! Where are you? Don't leave us here!

Suddenly both girls are screaming in horror. Why? Nothing has changed — unless they've both realized simultaneously that their daddy and mommy aren't coming out of that fire.

No one responds to their screams. No one comes to comfort them. Only the pitiless full moon witnesses their plight. The stupid, grinning moon.

And suddenly all is black — no house, no fire, no moon. Utter darkness, utter silence.

Panic threatens for a moment, and then you hear — *feel* — the crunch of leaves underfoot. Light begins to filter from above. You look up.

It's day now. Sunlight coming through the trees. You look around and see your sister, Sammi, beside you. Neither of you is crying — you're both cried out by now. But you're so cold and so hungry.

Suddenly there's a man ahead in the trees, wearing a flannel shirt and dirty jeans. He stands frozen, staring at you, then he starts forward.

"Don't be afraid, girls," he says in a hoarse voice, holding his hands out as if approaching a skittish puppy or kitten. "I'm not going to hurt you."

You slip your arms around your sister and she twines hers around you. Mommy always warned you about strangers and how you should stay away from them, and run and scream if one tries to touch you, but you're both too tired and weak to run. You stand quaking against each other, waiting for this stranger and hoping he's not the kind Mommy told you about.

Finally he's standing before you, towering over you. His face is all stubbly and he smells like he needs a bath. He reaches out his hands. They're trembling. He lays one on your shoulder and one on Sammi's.

"Are you the Gordon girls?" he says.

You're too frightened to speak. You can only nod.

"Thank God," he says. He turns and shouts into the woods. "Hey! Over here! I found them!

They're over here!" A half-sob wavers in his voice. "And they're all right!" He turns back to you and drops to his knees before you. You see tears in his eyes. "You're safe now, girls. You're gonna be all right."

And then the man fades away, and little Sammi and Julie fade away, but the woods remain. So do the chill and the hunger. You sense it could take you hours to find your way out of these woods. You don't have time for that.

You click EXIT.

Thirty-One

T. S. Eliot:
  "Footfalls echo in the memory
  Down the passage which we did not
    take."
        — Random notes: Julia Gordon

1

Julie rubbed her eyes as she leaned back in the recliner and waited for her mind to slow its chaotic whirl.

So many questions — *too* many questions.

But first — see to Sam.

Julie got up, turned off the VCR, and then removed Sam's headset. She paused and stared down at her sister's pale, relaxed features as a rush of tender feelings almost overwhelmed her.

"We've been through a lot, haven't we, sis? Been through hell, in fact." She touched Sam's cheek with the backs of her fingers. "Dear, dear Sam. If only I'd known then what I know now . . . if only Eathan had told us. . . . It would have been so different. Maybe —"

Her throat constricted.

I think I'm going to cry.

What an odd sensation. Was that a sob building in her chest? And tears pressing against the backs of her lids?

She swallowed and the feeling passed. *Don't want to break my mold.* No, she wasn't going to cry. She never cried.

But it left her wondering. Was she somehow incorporating a bit of Sam into her own psyche during each trip into Sam's 'scape? It seemed crazy . . . but if so, was she leaving a little bit of Julie behind?

An exciting possibility. If true, it might be a way to undo some of Nathan's meddling. But it would take a *long* time. And time wasn't something they had a lot of.

Julie called in the nurse to see to Sam's IVs and feeding tube while she stretched her legs by wandering the halls.

Questions assaulted her — about Nathan, about Eathan, about Sam's memory of that terrible night.

First, Nathan. Julie had hated him, utterly and completely, since reading his experimental journals. But reliving the night of the fire in Sam's 'scape had left her with mixed emotions about Nathan Gordon.

When she stood back and considered everything, she couldn't deny that he'd been horribly wronged by his wife and brother. No matter how brief their affair, or how true Lucy had remained to him after it was over . . . imagine how Nathan must have felt each time he looked at the twin daughters he was raising and realized they were his brother's.

Maybe that had unbalanced him. It didn't excuse what he did to those two little girls, but at least it provided an explanation. And the fact remained that despite whatever monstrousness he'd committed during his life, Nathan Gordon died a hero.

No question of that.

He could have run out alone and watched his house burn, collected the insurance money on his unfaithful wife, and lived out his years as a millionaire. But he'd carried the girls out and died trying to save that unfaithful wife.

Did guilt drive him to it? Was he trying to atone for what he'd done to the twins? Maybe he hoped that if he saved their lives, Lucy would forgive him.

Which brought up another question: Sam's buried memory of Lucy learning of Nathan's experiments and leaving with the girls. When did that happen? The memory ended with Eathan, Lucy, and the twins headed out the door. Yet the next memory was the fire.

How long between that incident and the fire? Had Lucy and the twins returned to the house? Had there been a reconciliation of sorts?

And there were more inconsistencies.

Only hours ago Eathan had sat in his bedroom and told her that he hadn't found Nathan's experimental journals until *after* the fire. That was what he said, but if Sam's memory was at all accurate, Eathan *did* know — *he* brought the journals to Nathan's house the night of the big fight.

Obviously he hadn't known the twins were his — not yet — but he'd certainly known about the journals. Yet he'd lied to Julie about them. Why?

Unless . . .

The thought stopped Julie in midstride. She had to lean on the newel post at the top of the stairs and wait for the cold, sick feeling to pass.

Unless Eathan had something to do with the fire.

No. That wasn't possible. Not Eathan. Anyone but Eathan.

But he had lied to her about the journals. She couldn't ignore that. Eathan wouldn't lie to her unless he had a reason.

But must that reason have anything to do with the fire?

And what *about* the fire?

The most disturbing aspect of what she'd just seen was that Sam's memory of that night had the same blank spot as her own.

When she was older Eathan had told her that the generally accepted theory at the time was that the horror of the fire had propelled the pair of them into a fugue state that left them wandering aimlessly through the woods.

But what happened between the fire and when they were found in the woods?

And what happened in the interval — however long it was — between Lucy walking out on Nathan and the fire?

As much as she hated thinking about it, she had to ask herself: What if Mom told Eathan he was the father of the twins, and then, knowing what Nathan had done to them, Eathan went a little crazy.

That didn't answer all the questions — not even close. Eathan wouldn't jeopardize his own daughters. No way would he start the fire.

But what if Nathan and Lucy tried to work things out? What if she moved back with the twins? Wouldn't that have made Eathan even crazier?

And with them all dead he'd have been left with two million dollars free and clear.

Julie shook herself. *What am I thinking?*

Not Eathan. Anybody but Eathan.

But she'd never really know, would she?

Not unless . . .

I have to go back in.

She glanced at her watch. Still too early in New York to link up with Dr. S.

Damn! Every hour meant there was less of Sam to find in the memoryscape.

But she didn't want to go back in alone. Things were becoming too *physical* in there. She wanted a lifeline to the real world.

She sighed. At least the nurse would have time to tend to Sam's various tubes; and the physical therapists were due in for their daily routine of chest PT, sensory stimulation, stretching, massage, and passive range-of-motion exercises.

They worked like hell to keep her outside in good shape, but inside she was all but gone.

2

"How do you know about this tunnel?" Dr. S. was saying.

His face filled the monitor screen and his expression was a study in suspicion.

Might as well tell him — but only about this morning's solo trip.

"I went in alone."

"Dammit, Julie! I told you —"

"I didn't have time to wait for you and I haven't got time to argue with you about it.

457

Sam's whole 'scape could shut down anytime now. I went in, I came out, I'm okay. I'm going back in and you're going to be with me this time, so let's not make a federal case out of it."

She realized how she sounded but she was tired and anxious and didn't want Dr. S. going on and on about the dangers in Sam's memoryscape.

Because he didn't know the half of it.

When he made no reply she glanced at his face. Suspicion had been replaced by hurt. Damn.

"Sorry," she said. "I haven't had much sleep lately. But I can't stop now. I'm getting to the heart of the matter and —"

"What matter?"

"Everything. The last secrets. I'm sure that the other, smaller tunnel I saw leads into the heart of the volcano, and I have a feeling that's where all my questions will be answered."

She couldn't tell him that those questions weren't strictly about Sam. They pertained to herself as well — because back in those days the two of them were practically joined at the hip, and whatever happened to little Sammi happened to little Julie as well.

This is no longer just about Sam. It's about me too.

But she couldn't let Dr. S. know that.

"Why the volcano?" he said. "Couldn't

what you seek lie buried somewhere else?"

"Possibly. But we tend to forget — at least I know I do — that the memoryscape is a symbolic landscape. We've got to ask ourselves what a volcano represents in real life. It's the release point for an uncontainable pressure that builds up within the earth's crust. What does it represent in the memoryscape? Something very similar, I think. Why couldn't it be the blowout point for a cataclysmic memory that got too close to the surface and was simply too hot to handle? It broke free and blasted everything around it."

"I don't know, Julie. . . . How could any memory, no matter how awful, wreak the devastation we've seen in your sister?"

"I told you what was done to us."

She'd given Dr. S. some of the details, but had skipped the paternity mess. She'd fill him in on that some other time. Later. Maybe.

"Yes, but still . . ."

"It must have left her vulnerable in some way."

"Well, doesn't that leave you vulnerable too?"

Damn! She knew immediately she shouldn't have said that. Dr. S. didn't miss a trick.

"No," she said, fabricating on the fly. "Because I'm so unnaturally left-brained,

I'm actually *less* susceptible."

I hope.

"I don't know how you know that, but I certainly hope you're right. In a very real sense you'll be entering the belly of the beast. A beast that's waiting for you. Are you ready for that?"

No, she thought. But she said, "Yes. And I want you with me."

"I'll be right here, watching over your shoulder. I want you back."

"Why?" she said teasingly. "For the Bruchmeyer grant?"

Christ, she'd forgotten all about that. Strangely enough, she found she couldn't care less.

"You know better than that," he said.

She took a breath. "Yeah. I do."

And for the first time, she wasn't bristling at the thought of someone monitoring her every move. She had a feeling it was going to get hairy in there this time.

I could die, she thought. But this was something she had to do.

"All right," she said. "Here we go."

Thirty-Two

You can understand how easily false memories can be implanted in a susceptible person when you realize that the act of imagining the look of an object utilizes the same area of the cortex involved in actually seeing an object; the act of imagining a touch utilizes the same area of the cortex involved in actually feeling a touch.
— Random notes: Julia Gordon

Even the gallery is gone now. Under the shattered moon you strike out immediately for the right flank of the slumbering volcano.

You enter the crevasse, travel down through the fissure and along the tunnel until you reach the *Starry Night* grotto.

But instead of smoking ruins nestled among the trees, you see the Millburn house intact and unscorched. Waiting to replay the fights and the fire?

No, thank you. You'll pass this time.

You spot the smaller tunnel off to the side. You enter that and follow it deep into the hill.

461

As you glide this way and that along its dark, tortuous path, you sense the growing heat, a sure sign that you're nearing your destination. But you can't mention that to Dr. S. — you're not supposed to be able to feel anything here.

And then you see the red glow ahead. You're almost there. Soon you'll have the answers to all your questions.

Your stomach knots. Do you want those answers? Will you be able to handle them? Look what happened to Sam.

But you're different from Sam.

You never took things as hard as she did. You could always reason your way through, and you don't see why this should turn out to be any different.

At least you hope it won't.

No. You'll be okay. You're steeled for this. You're ready for the worst. You can handle anything this memoryscape can throw at you.

So why won't your stomach unknot?

You push on and soon you see flames ahead. The heat grows as you move toward them. Hot, but not unbearable. Yes, you have a physical presence here, but not a substantial one. You're a gossamer-thin curtain, and most of the heat passes through you.

And then you're at the tunnel mouth, staring into the heart of the volcano. The chimney is a flaming well, with a pool of magma bubbling and belching a dozen feet below you and the well's narrow walls disappearing into a red haze as they stretch toward the night.

And there, maybe twenty or thirty feet above you, a bridge. Or at least what once had been a bridge. A narrow span, no more than three feet in diameter, that must have arched across the gap when its middle section was intact.

But that's gone now, blown away by the blast of the eruption. All that remain are two truncated protrusions from the chimney wall, like two lovers reaching across the fire, separated by no more than seven or eight feet, yet never to touch again.

You search about for the event that triggered this cataclysm but see nothing that could possibly be a memory.

You notice the Window button blinking and click it. Dr. S. appears in the drop-down screen.

"This is frightening, Julie," he says. *"You've found the locus of the memory, but there's nothing left. Whatever was here has been utterly destroyed. The memory's gone."*

"That's the way it looks," you say, yet you find it difficult to accept. "But how could a memory be so volatile that it not only destroys the entire memoryscape, but itself as well?"

"I couldn't say. I've been disturbed by the utter devastation of this memoryscape since you first set foot in it. This scene is even more distressing. There is something deeply wrong here."

"I think that's obvious."

"No-no. I don't mean just what we see. I think it

goes deeper than that."

"Explain."

"I wish I could." His face looks troubled, his expression almost embarrassed. *"I'm responding to that time-honored scientific tool that nobody talks about: intuition."*

"Never ignore intuition," you say. "I'm going to explore what's left of that bridge."

You click Dr. S. away, then glide up to the sundered bridge. You stop near one of the stumps of its span. The heat is relentless. You realize that your body, reclining in the cool of Sam's bedroom, is probably flushed and bathed in sweat. You hover above the bubbling lava and try to make sense of this.

Why a bridge? Did the final, awful memory take place on a bridge? Was someone thrown off? Into what? The Seine? The Thames? The Hudson? Dammit, you need a clue. Just one clue!

That's when you notice an irregularity in the surface of the opposing stump. More than an irregularity — actually the truncated end is stippled with countless fingertip-sized protrusions. Except at the center where a somewhat smoother, roughly oval dome protrudes.

You glide toward it. Close up, the dome has a wrinkled look, slightly puckered here and there, as if scarred by the heat. And now that you're this close, you see that the thousands of finger-sized protrusions are moving, twisting, stretching, toward . . .

You turn and approach the other stump and find it's exactly the same. A low, wrinkled central dome surrounded by thousands of fingerlike papillae, more active here, wriggling, reaching . . .

And then you realize: They're reaching for the other side, reaching for their other half, their severed counterpart across the divide.

The Window button is blinking again. You click Dr. S. into view. He looks excited.

"Lord, Julie, I just realized something. After you entered the crevasse on the flank of the volcano, the direction you traveled was downward."

"Right. Far down."

"Sure, but listen — when you traveled the second tunnel, the direction was lateral, correct?"

"Correct. But —"

"Then this isn't a bridge. You understand? Unless both our senses of direction are completely off, this structure was underground — under the memoryscape's virtual surface — when the eruption took place."

Mentally you retrace your path to this spot.

"You're right. Of course. How could I have missed that?"

"Ah-ha! Now you see the benefit of an off-site observer. What else did you miss on your solo trip, eh?"

You could tell him you've soloed more than once, but why add fuel to his fire? It's already hot enough in here.

And unfortunately, his observation doesn't

help you. In fact, it only adds to the mystery.

"So what was it, then?" you say. "A subterranean structure . . . but what?"

As you speak you look more closely at the wrinkled dome in the stump. It reminds you of something. You touch it —

And snatch your glove away as the dome's surface ripples and bulges. The disturbance subsides immediately, so you touch it again. This time the response is more dramatic. The dome ripples, then contracts into large folds as its surface slides up, revealing . . .

An eye.

You gasp and dart back. You stare at the huge blue iris set in the glistening white sclera. And in the center of it all, a pupil as deep and dark as interstellar space.

"My God! Do you see?"

"*I see,*" Dr. S. replies. His voice is hushed, awed. "*But does it see?*"

"I don't know. . . ."

You move to your left and the eye follows you. Back again to your starting point and it tracks you all the way.

"It can see. But what in the name of heaven does it mean?"

A polite beep from the physiologic readout strip across the bottom of your visual field informs you of a change in one of the parameters.

Sam's resting pulse, usually a uniform seventy to seventy-two beats per minute, has kicked up to eighty-six. Still well within normal. No problem.

You turn and approach the opposite stump of the bridge — or root or conduit or whatever it is . . . was. You touch the corresponding dome. Its surface ripples, but barely. Another touch, with a similar response, but no more. No matter what you try, this lid will not open. You turn back and find the other eye staring at you, watching your every move. It's eerie.

"I've got an idea," Dr. S. says. *"It sounds a little crazy, but I have a feeling this broken structure connects Sam's cortex with her reticular activating system."*

"No way," you say. "The RAS isn't an anatomical structure. It's a functional unit. More of a network. There's no direct trunkline between it and the brain."

"But this isn't the brain, Julie. This is the memoryscape. As you said only a short while ago, it's symbolic."

"And this is a symbolic link . . . ruptured."

"Yes . . . exactly . . . ruptured. And that means the repressed volatile memory was buried here, right under the RAS-cortex link."

"Talk about lousy luck," you say.

"Was it just bad luck?"

"What else could it be?"

"Maybe it was hidden here for a reason."

"What? To wreck the RAS-cortex linkage when it was accessed? That's practically suicidal. The brain wouldn't do that. It makes no —"

And then you stop. Sam *was* suicidal. More than once, most likely. But this? How could she ever manage this?

You say, "So you think this memory was so awful that she'd rather die than remember it?"

"Or perhaps someone else preferred that she die rather than remember it."

The remark strikes you like a blow. "Someone else?" You're shocked. You can't think for a moment. "Who? Why? How?"

"I have no idea. Just trying to cover all the possibilities. The strategic location of this memory — or I should say, of this former memory — disturbs me to no end."

"What disturbs *me*," you say, "is the finality of what we see here. These two ends here will never be rejoined. It's hopeless. If this symbolic representation is a true reflection of Sam's neurophysiologic condition, then . . ." That tightness in your throat again. You can barely speak. "Then Sam will never regain consciousness."

The realization hurts you more than you ever thought anything could.

She's going to die. Hell, she's as good as dead now. And you can't help her. You've failed her.

Again.

You feel a sob building. But you can't allow yourself to break down. You close your eyes, swallowing hard, collecting yourself.

"Julie? Are you all right?"

468

"No," you say, and the word sounds choked. "No, I'm not."

"Then I think it's better you exit. After all, anything of interest here has been destroyed, and her pulse is – well into the nineties now."

You glance at the readout strip. Pulse up to ninety-four; respirations up from six to eight.

You're as edgy as Dr. S. And hot. You'd like nothing better than to run to someplace cool where you wouldn't have to feel so damn ineffectual and powerless.

But you pull yourself together. You're loath to admit defeat.

"I'm curious," you say, meeting the eye's giant stare. "Which end do you think is which? Where's that eye looking out from? The cortex or the RAS?"

"If the condition of the memoryscape is any clue to the condition of the cortex, I'd say that eye has got to be looking at you from the reticular activating system."

"Exactly what I thought. The midbrain is fine. It's the cortex that's out cold."

"And it will remain that way unless contact is reestablished. I don't see that happening. Like a ruptured tendon, like a severed nerve, it won't heal, the ends won't knit unless approximated."

You can't see any way to bring the two severed ends together, but . . .

"Maybe there's some way to bridge that gap."

"How? What will you use? Whatever was in that

span has been vaporized."

A wild thought flashes through your mind.

"Why not me?"

"What?" Dr. S.'s stare from the window is almost as wide as that of the giant eye before you. "Exit now, Julie. I think you're losing your mind."

"No, I'm serious. Sam and I are made of the same stuff. Identical twins, remember? Why not use myself to bridge the gap?"

"But that's impossible. You have no physical presence in the memoryscape. You're immaterial, a ghost. And without any substance, how can you bridge anything?"

No way you can keep it a secret any longer. You remove the data glove and hold your virtual hand before you where he can see it.

"What's that?" he says. "Did you scan your image into the program?"

"No. It's me."

Stunned silence for a few seconds, then Dr. Siegal's voice, shaky, barely audible, trickles into your earphones.

"Dear Lord! Julie . . . when − ?"

"I first noticed it on the second level." She remembered the bruise from the kraken.

"You soloed there as well?"

"Yes, I had to."

"Dear Lord! I warned you, Julie. I knew the genetic link between you and your twin was too close. Now look what's happened! Do you know what this means?"

470

"Yes. It means I might actually be able to do something here."

"It means you can be hurt here, dammit!" You've never heard Dr. S. so angry. Or frightened. *"Get out, Julie. I order you. Exit immediately."*

"Not yet. I have to try something. I can't call it quits yet."

"You exit now or I'll cut the satellite feed."

You've been expecting that threat, and you're ready for it.

"Then you'll be pulling the plug on both of us. I'm Sam's only hope. Do you want to deprive her of her only chance to regain consciousness? Is that what you want?"

"No, of course not."

"Then give me a chance here. Just one. Please."

A very long pause. *"I don't like it. I haven't liked any of this."* Another pause, then, *"Go ahead."*

You shut his window and approach the open eye. You run your hands over the surrounding fingerlike projections. Their tips undulate back and forth in response to your touch, like the tendrils of a sea anemone, tickling your palms. You glide to the other side. This eye remains closed and the papillae here are much less responsive. Which confirms your worst fear.

Sam's cortex is failing . . . almost gone.

You wrap your arms around the trunk and try to move it, pull it farther out of the volcano wall. But you might as well be trying to uproot an oak.

So much for trying to make ends meet. You never had much hope of that anyway. But if you can bridge the gap with your virtual self, maybe you can act as a conductor. Maybe you can send a wake-up call to Sam's cortex.

And maybe you can't. But you've got to try.

You place your hands against the papillae on either side of the closed eye, straighten your arms, then stretch your feet toward the other stump.

You don't reach. You extend to your fingertips and point your toes, and still you can't reach the other side.

Damn!

Frustrated, you rotate until you're upright, suspended between the stumps.

You need help, and there's only one person who can give it.

"Sam?"

You call out the name and it echoes in the volcano's chimney. You know that beyond your earphones, in the real world, your voice is filling the bedroom. Your words are entering Sam through her ears and via the memoryscape. She's got to hear.

"Sam! Sam, can you hear me? It's me, Julie. I don't know if you've been aware of me, but I've been traveling your mind, trying to bring you back."

You wonder how Sam, if she can hear you, will react to those words.

"Isn't that a laugh . . . me wanting to do

something for you? But it's the truth. I'm here to help you. I've been trying for weeks but haven't found a way to do it until now. Trouble is, I can't do it alone. You've got to work with me. Just a little. Do you hear me, Sam? Please . . . give me a sign if you hear me."

You watch the closed lid. Not even a twitch. And on the other side . . . an unbroken stare.

"Sam! Listen! Can you hear me or are you ignoring me? I know I've got no right to think you'll trust me. I know I've hurt you time and again, and I know I've crushed every olive branch you've extended until you ran out of branches, but this time is different. I'm here as a friend, Sam. As your sister, ready to act like a sister for the first time in our lives."

A beep from the physiologic ribbon. Sam's pulse is up to 118. Her respirations are 10. Damn . . .

Is that the sign? No. Can't be. Her pulse was on the rise before you began talking to her. Then why is this happening? You haven't been in the memoryscape all that long. Is it because of *where* you are?

Whatever the reason, it's not good. The program will automatically exit you when her pulse hits 130.

You hear a rumble. The walls of the volcano tremble. What was that?

And is it getting hotter, or is that just you?

"Listen to me, Sam. There's not much time. Some way, somehow, you've got to

473

let these words through. Between the two of us, you were always the one who could love, and I know you loved me. And I know I killed that love over the years. If you hate me, Sam, you've got every right. But that was the other Julie. This is a different Julie talking. For the first time in my life I'm here for you, Sam. As a sister. As the missing part of you. I —"

Another beep. Pulse now 125.

And a louder rumble. The lava is bubbling more, and appears to be rising . . . slowly, perhaps, but you know its roiling surface is closer than before. No question — it's definitely hotter.

And you're almost out of time. You press on.

"We were betrayed, Sam. We were warped by a madman. The result is, neither of us is complete. You've got the rest of me, Sam. And I've got the rest of you. We can beat this, but neither of us can do it alone."

The WINDOW is blinking. A click brings Dr. S.'s worried face into view.

"Give it up, Julie. There's some sort of reaction going on. Get out before you hurt her and yourself as well."

"No. Not yet. I've got a feeling I'll never get this chance again. Please, not yet!"

"It's not up to me. The program will —"

"Override it."

"I can't. There is no override. And even if I could —"

"Type in 'P-H-Y-S-O-V-R-D-dot-E-X-E.' "

"What?"

474

"Now! Do it now! It's an override program I wrote. Just in case. And this is that case. Please. I'm begging you!"

"Very well." A few seconds later: *"It's asking me for a password."*

"E-I-L-U-J."

"What? Oh, I get it." Another pause. *"There. It says 'Override Executed.' "*

"Thank you!"

"I hope you know what you're doing."

I have no idea what I'm doing, you think. But it's getting too hot for thinking.

"I've learned a lot in here, Sam." You're shouting now, hoping it makes a difference. "I learned a lot about you I never knew, and a lot about me. Most of what I learned about me I don't like. But I've changed, Sam. Because of you. You're responsible. So don't leave me hanging here. Help me help you, Sam. All I need is a little. Stretch a little, Sam. You see these two cut ends on either side of me? Move them just a little closer together so I can bridge the gap. Come on, Sam! Just a little!"

"Give it up, Julie," Dr. S. says gently. *"Her pulse is one-forty. You gave it your best shot, but, damn it, she's too far gone."*

He's right. It's no use. The eye on the cortex side remains closed. Not even a twitch there. The heat sears you and the rumbling and shaking are beginning to rattle you.

This isn't going to work. You've got to get out.

Your throat constricts and a pressure builds again in your chest. But you don't fight it this time. This time you let the sob burst free.

With your eyes squeezed shut against the tears welling inside your goggles and your arms stretched to either side like a crucified martyr waiting for the last nail, you wail unashamedly into the heat and noise. Because you've got to let her know and you may not get another chance.

"I love you, Sam. . . . I hope you can hear me. And I'm sorry for all the hurt I caused you while we were growing up, but I . . . I never knew. I didn't understand. Couldn't understand. But I do now, and I do love you, Sam. I want you to know that, and I want you to take it with you wherever you're going. Maybe you *want* to go, and if that's the case I beg you to reconsider. You've given me something, Sam. You've given me back a bit of my missing part, and it's made me hunger for more. And I can give you back some of what you're missing. We're two cripples, Sam. But together we can help rebuild each other. I've got the tools right here. So come back to me, Sam. Let me make it up to you. I'm not a monster . . . really I'm not. Don't give up on me, Sam. I just learned that I love my sister. Please don't leave me now."

And that's all you can say. You're sobbing uncontrollably now. Part of you feels like a damn fool, but another part, a newer part, doesn't give a damn. If only —

Something clamps around your left index finger. You glance over, and through the blur of tears you think you see . . .

No. Can't be. You blink, and blink again, and you see that it's true.

One of the papillae from the open-eye side has stretched out from the stump and *reached* you. Its tip has taken the shape of an infant's tiny hand . . . and its stubby, pudgy fingers are holding on for dear life. Others too are stretching toward you, undulating in the heat, reaching. . . .

"Yes!" you cry and your voice sounds choked and you're afraid you're going to start sobbing again because the emotions surging through you are almost overwhelming and you can't allow yourself to be overwhelmed because you've got to keep a straight head here, got to stay focused and help Sam make this connection.

What about the other side, the cortex side?

You turn and see a single, blunt-tipped papilla reaching out from below the closed eye, stretching in your direction but not very far — no more than eighteen inches at best. So feeble, and already it appears to be weakening, sagging with the heat.

You stretch your arm toward it, but you're still a good six inches short.

"Come on, Sam! You can do it! Come *on!*"

But the papilla sags farther. Desperate, you

wrap your fingers around the little hand from the other side, and pull it toward you, stretching the tendril behind it. As it elongates it begins to thin along its midsection.

"Don't break," you whisper. "Please don't break."

You give it a moment and it seems to thicken, or at least redistribute its mass, but still it appears dangerously thin.

You can't wait any longer. You stretch it farther, all the while extending your right arm toward the closed eye, just inches now.

"Come on . . . just a little farther . . ."

And then almost as if sensing your presence, the papilla rises and stretches and —

Contact is like an electric shock, a nerve-jittering, jaw-clenching, muscle-spasming jolt running up your left arm and down your right. You scream in pain but you won't let go, won't pull back. You must hold on.

And then the pain subsides to a tingle. You relax and open your eyes. The cortex eye is still closed but the papillae around it have sprung to life. They move with new energy, some of them shooting out toward you. On the other end, farther away, the same thing: hundreds of tendrils snaking toward you.

It's working! You've bridged the gap and you're conducting the impulses. They're flowing through you to Sam's cortex!

You can only hope it's enough.

You hear a loud, shuddering sob and realize

it's you. Not again! Where's your fabled control? You haven't cried since you were a baby. What are you going to do, make up for all that time in one day?

The new tendrils from each side reach you then, their tips morphing into hands as soon as they make contact — baby hands, little-girl hands, teenager and adult hands, all the hands of Sam's life — and they grasp you and crawl up your arms, and clutch at you, stretching to your shoulders and then to your chest and your breasts, the ones on the left pouring their impulses into you and the ones on the right drinking them up, and, God, you're crying like a baby and you feel like a mother nursing her firstborn, and some new hands move to your face to wipe your tears while others caress your hair before sliding past you to fuse with the members from the opposite side, and suddenly they're proliferating in a frenzy and you're engulfed in tendrils, almost smothering in conducting fibers that don't need you anymore so you struggle from the wild tangle, wriggling downward, extricating yourself from the snarled mess. And just before you pull free you glance at the cortex eye and see that it's open now, its iris as blue as the other eye's, as blue as Sam's, and it's watching you.

You smile and you know it's a tremulous, wavering thing. You can barely speak through the torrent of emotions cascading through you.

"Welcome back, sis."

And then you're half a dozen feet away, watching the connections thicken and multiply. You can almost see the impulses surging through to Sam's starved cortex. Her EEG readout is going wild.

You've done it! And it feels *wonderful.*

But then . . . there's another rumble − the loudest yet. It cuts off your little celebration. A different rumble, deeper and longer than any before. The others seemed to come from the volcano itself. This one originates elsewhere. And suddenly everything is shaking.

You check the readout and see that Sam's pulse is 162. Is that the cause of the quake? Have you stayed in too − ?

Something dark blurs past you on the left and splashes into the lava below. You look up and see other chunks of lava rock tumbling from the chimney wall as the rumbling continues.

"No!"

Your shout echoes in your headphones. Not now! This can't happen now. Sam's just got her chance to rejoin the living and now the whole mountain is collapsing on her. You've got to stop this, find some way to −

Pain lances up your arm as you're knocked back by a falling chunk of lava. You look at your virtual arm and see the skin is torn and bleeding. And it *hurts.*

The Window button is beeping and blinking.

You know what he's going to say. And he's right. You've got to leave. Now. Or you'll both suffer.

Damn! Damn everything! You want to scream.

Instead you click EXIT.

Thirty-Three

People have asked if the memoryscape programs could be useful in treating or identifying False Memory Syndrome. I haven't 'scaped an FMS patient yet, but it's a fascinating challenge. To the sufferer, false memories are indistinguishable from true memories, but the memoryscape might offer clues.
— Random notes: Julia Gordon

1

Julie tore off her helmet and lay there gasping, drenched in sweat. And her arm was killing her. As her breathing slowed she heard an insistent pounding somewhere in the room. She sat up and looked around.

The afternoon sun had been swallowed by rain clouds, turning the room dim and gloomy. To her right the monitor beeped. Its flashing icon said Dr. S. wanted to talk.

Fine, but that awful racket . . . where — ?

The door. Someone was rattling and banging on the door.

Julie pushed herself from the chair, wiped her tears as she crossed the room, and unlocked the door.

The nurse stood in the hallway with cook and the maid clustered behind her. She stared at Julie in shock.

"Great heavens, miss! What's happened in there?"

"Why . . . nothing. Just —"

"We heard terrible shouting and crying. We thought you were struggling with someone and —" She gasped as her wide-eyed gaze came to rest on Julie's right arm. "Oh — look at your arm! What happened to you?"

Julie stared at her sleeve. The fabric was intact but glistening with blood. She rolled it up and stared at the inch-long tear in the skin beneath. It was much smaller than the wound to her virtual arm in the 'scape, but still . . . a wound.

She swallowed. "It's nothing. I'll be okay."

The nurse squeezed past her and hurried into the bedroom.

"I'll help you with that in a minute. Right now I've got to tend to my patient. She should be — oh! Great heavens! What's happened to her?"

Julie reached to the bedside. "What's wrong?"

"She's soaked!"

True enough. Sam's flannel nightgown was drenched with perspiration and plastered to her skin.

Julie removed Sam's headgear, then lifted her wrist and counted her pulse: 140. Down from a few moments ago. Her face, though, was as slack and expressionless as ever.

"Sam?" She grasped her shoulder and shook it. "Sam, can you hear me?"

No response. Not even a twitch of an eyelid.

She pulled up one of those lids: The blue eye within stared back at her, unseeing.

Crushed, Julie sank onto the edge of the bed, gazing at her sister.

"Sam?" she said plaintively. "After all that, aren't you coming back to me?"

What did I *do* in there? she wondered. I thought I brought you back. Why aren't you back?

"She must have run a fever," the nurse said.

"No . . . no fever."

"Well, *something* must have happened."

"No," Julie said, still gazing at Sam's face. "I'm afraid nothing happened . . . nothing at all."

The monitor beeped again.

The nurse said, "I've got to change her immediately before she takes a chill."

"Sure." Julie pushed herself up from the bed. "Go ahead. I'll be over here."

She dropped into the wooden chair by the monitor — Alma's old seat. And inside she felt as dead as Alma. Outside she felt like hell: damp, exhausted, and her arm throbbing with pain. She stared at the blood. Dr. S. had been right. She'd been in real physical danger in there. So what? It had all been for nothing.

She hadn't accomplished anything.

You failed her again, dammit.

She hit a couple of keys and Dr. Mordecai Siegal's face filled the screen.

"Finally!" he said. "I was worried something had happened to you."

Reflexively Julie pulled her bloody arm behind her before remembering he couldn't see her.

"I'm okay. I was checking Sam."

"How is she? Any sign she's regaining —"

"Nothing," Julie said. "No change at all, other than a sweat."

"A sweat?"

"Yeah. She was drenched."

"Hmmm." Dr. S. tapped his fingertips against his lips. "A burst of autonomic activity. That *could* mean something. How's her EEG? Her cortex showed such a tremendous response when you bridged that gap. Which, I must say, was a truly heroic effort on your part. You've changed, Julie.

485

I don't know if you realize it, but —"

"Yeah, well . . . looks like it was all a waste of time. She was back to her usual eleven- to twelve-Hertz when I removed her headset. Which means . . ."

She couldn't finish the sentence. She was filling up again.

"Easy, Julie. You did everything humanly possible."

"But not enough!" she yelled. "What happened in there, Dr. S.? I found the problem, repaired the connection, and that should have been it. Sam should have been on her way back to consciousness. Why did everything start to fall apart at the end? At first I thought the volcano was going to erupt again, but then came that earthquake or whatever it was . . . the connection must have been torn apart again." She let out a great breath. "I'm missing something."

Julie squeezed her eyes shut, remembering the wonderful touch of those tendrils, those little hands, the impulses surging through her.

"We had her fixed! And now we're right back where we started. No, we're *worse* than when we started. Because after the cave-in, that chimney has to be completely choked with rubble. We won't get another chance to reconnect her. She's a goner."

"Wait, now," he said. "You don't know for sure that the repair was cut. That quake may have been her own doing, a way to block up the volcano chimney and bury the connection. Remember, it started off subterranean; maybe your sister wants it underground again."

Julie looked over at her limp, motionless twin.

"If she's still connected, why isn't she responding? Why isn't there *some* sign of improvement? I don't expect her to get up and start painting, but I was hoping maybe she'd move a toe or twitch a finger or blink her eyes. God, I'll take anything. But there is no change. Nothing. Nada."

Julie realized she sounded angry. And she was. Furious, in fact. Furious that she'd tried everything she knew and had come up empty-handed.

Good. Hold on to that. It's better than the crushing despair of a moment ago.

"Maybe even a twitch is too much to expect so soon. Who knows? It may take a while for her cortex to repair itself, for her consciousness to reorganize after such a catastrophic assault."

Julie barked a harsh laugh. "Usually I'm the optimist and you're the naysayer. How'd we get switched around?"

"Because I've never heard you sound so defeated. It's not like you."

"Well, as you said a moment ago, I've changed."

"You're giving up, then? Should I close the satellite link and call it quits?"

"No." She sighed. "Not yet. I'll go back in tomorrow for another look at her memoryscape. If it shows signs of healing, we'll hang in. If there's been no change, I'll try to get back into the volcano. If I can't, we'll . . . dammit, Mordecai, I can't stand the thought of abandoning her!"

"You've done everything possible."

"But I *didn't* bring her back. And I didn't find out what caused this. *What* was that last memory?"

"We'll never know. Apparently it self-destructed when your sister accessed it. It's gone forever, I'm afraid."

A thought struck Julie with the force of a blow.

"Wait a second. It's gone from Sam's memory . . . but what about mine?"

"What do you mean?"

"As much as we fought, Sam and I were rarely out of hailing distance throughout our childhood."

"So?"

"So, there's a good chance that whatever awful thing happened to her also happened to me. I could very likely have the same bomb buried in my own memory."

"Yes . . ." he said slowly. "It's possible, but hardly probable. Even if you both experienced the same horrible incident simultaneously, the probability that both of you would completely suppress the memory approaches zero, I'd think."

"But we're identical twins, remember?"

"But you're *not* alike. Your reactions would be completely different from Sam's. Sam might suppress it, or deal with it in her art. You would find a rational way to handle it. No. Not possible."

He had a point. Still . . .

"I guess the only way to find out for sure would be in the memoryscape. Too bad I can't explore my own."

"Don't even think of such a thing! That could be catastrophic! You could get caught in a closed feedback loop and end up like your sister if you broke it. Or you'd wind up trapped in your own memoryscape forever. Thank God it's not possible, because I'm sure you'd be reckless enough to try it."

"Right," Julie said. "I probably would. Maybe I'll work on that when I get back."

"You will *not!* And that's my final word on that."

"Only kidding." She sighed. "Look, I'm going to get some sleep. I'll call you first thing tomorrow — eight o'clock your time — and we'll take another look into Sam."

"Okay. But no soloing in the meantime. Promise?"

"Promise: No trips into Sam's 'scape till tomorrow."

"Good. See you then."

No. No more trips into Sam's 'scape.

But that doesn't mean I won't try to peek into my own.

She rose and headed for the bathroom. A shower . . . not only did she need one, but she did her best thinking in the shower.

And she had a lot of thinking to do.

2

Julie spent the late afternoon in Sam's room, pounding on the computer's keyboard.

The shower had worked its usual magic. As she'd lathered her body and shampooed her hair, the solution had floated to the surface of her mind. If she looped the outflow from her own headset through Sam's empty headset, she could fool the program into thinking it was reading someone else's 'scape, and make it feed it back to her.

The changes would allow her to enter her own memoryscape.

Sounded logical. At least she hadn't yet found a reason why it wouldn't work.

The question was, Would it work without destabilizing the rest of the program?

Only one way to find out.

Julie knew that even under the most controlled circumstances, this was one hell of a risky experiment. To try it alone was downright reckless. Some might even say stupid. But the only one she could go in with was Dr. S., and he'd never permit that. She could threaten to quit, to jump off one of the World Trade Towers, to immolate herself in the center of Washington Square, and he'd still refuse to allow it.

With good reason . . .

So she was going to go it alone . . . *if* she could successfully alter the program. And if she could complete the trip before Eathan arrived. He hadn't returned from his previous trip to London until 7 P.M. or so. She hoped he'd be running on the same schedule this time.

Because by then she hoped to have the answer to the final question: What awful secret was buried in their minds?

Her fingers ran across the keyboard and she hit ENTER like a pianist ending a concerto.

There. The last patch of altered code blocked the audio-video feed to New York. It wouldn't do at all to have Dr. S. stroll by a monitor and see Julie's memoryscape flowing by.

With that entered, she was ready to give it a try.

I should feel scared half to death, she thought, but she was curiously exhilarated.

The nurse gave Julie a funny look when

she asked her to wait outside. A new shift had started at 4 P.M., but undoubtedly the day nurse had given her a blow-by-blow description of the strange goings-on behind the locked door, and how she'd had to bandage a mysterious laceration on the patient's sister's arm.

"This will only be a brief equipment test," Julie said in her most reassuring tone. "Samantha's not even going to be involved in this, so there's absolutely no cause to worry. Twenty minutes, tops. Then she's all yours for the rest of the night."

The nurse looked unsure. She'd probably complain to Eathan when he returned.

But every word Julie told the nurse was true. She didn't need Sam for this. The only reason Julie was using Sam's room was because this was where the hardware was set up.

She locked the door behind the nurse, then hit the Record button on the VCR. She most definitely wanted a record of this.

Minutes later she was gloved up, goggles and headphones in place, ready to go.

But she hesitated.

Okay . . . I'm scared, she thought.

Yes, more frightened than she'd ever been in her life. More than when she'd almost tumbled off the cliffs outside. A different kind of fear. Not visceral . . . almost intellectual.

One thing to venture into someone else's unknown, but to wander your own memoryscape. . . . It was almost like examining your own soul, or your karma.

That could be the ultimate horror.

For what could be riskier than digging into your own memory, looking to unearth buried secrets, secrets interred for a very good reason: because they're dangerous.

Only a fool pokes through a toxic-waste dump.

Then again, if she didn't clean up the toxins now, they could eventually pollute her whole countryside.

Look what happened when Sam's dump sprang a leak.

Of course, poking around also risked *causing* a leak. She could precipitate a catastrophe.

Still, she had to know. She couldn't go through the rest of her life wondering if she had a ticking bomb in her brain. If it was there, she wanted to find it and defuse it.

If she could.

Julie bit her lip and adjusted her goggles. Enough vacillation. Do it.

Thirty-Four

Fascinating results from U.C. at Irvine. A group of volunteers was shown a movie about a series of traumatic events. Before the film, half of them were dosed with propranolol to block the effects of adrenaline on the brain; the other half were not. A week later, the group that received the beta-blocker remembered significantly fewer details about the traumatic events in the film, but had excellent recall of the nontraumatic events. This might lead to a means of preventing post-traumatic stress syndrome.

— Random notes: Julia Gordon

You've become so used to the night land within Sam that the clear blue skies of your own memoryscape come as a shock. You rise and hover, gazing at your own peaceful inner panorama.

At first glance you're reminded of Lorraine's memoryscape, or any of the dozens of other normal 'scapes you've wandered. Towns and villages dot the countryside all around you, and directly below, an island city of skyscrapers — your own Manhattan.

But not like any Manhattan you know. This city is clean and well ordered, laid out completely in a neat grid; even the lower city, where Greenwich Village and Wall Street would be, are methodically gridded.

You drift over the perfectly laid out suburbs, and then out to the countryside, where each farm is perfectly square and neatly bordered with rows of trees.

God, you think. This is so embarrassing. Am I really such a compulsively ordered nerd?

Off to your left, deeper in the countryside, you see smoke rising from a stand of trees. You start toward it, then stop. You can guess what's burning in those woods. The last thing you need is another replay of that scene.

You look down at yourself and notice that you have a body here, a much more substantial model than you had in Sam's 'scape. And that makes sense — this is *your* place, after all. In no other memoryscape will you have a more physical presence.

You head back toward the city.

So far so good, right? Not so bad, really. Of course, you haven't been down to ground level to observe the nitty-gritty, but you've no time for that now. You've got to find that buried memory — if it exists here.

You wish you'd been able to browse Sam's

'scape before the cataclysm, and seen if there'd been any surface clues to the location of her deadly memory. You don't care how deeply it's buried; a memory that toxic has got to leave traces on the surface.

You start above the center of your city and begin moving outward in a widening gyre, searching the terrain below for something, anything, out of the ordinary. One good thing about this anal-retentive layout is that the slightest warping effect will stick out like the proverbial sore thumb.

But the cityscape remains perfect: clean streets, smoothly flowing traffic, a subway stop every ten blocks, a verdant, mugger-free Central Park. Even the South Bronx has been tidied up.

Your concentric circles take you over the suburbs. You note with approval that your subways continue out here as elevateds. How convenient. Tight-ass Julie hasn't missed a trick. And out here in suburbia the story is the same as in the city: nothing out of the ordinary.

It's a mathematically perfect world.

Which isn't all bad, you think. If you don't find anything amiss, you'll never know what Sam was hiding from, but at least you won't have to worry about a ticking bomb inside your own mind.

You increase your speed as you leave the populated areas and hit the countryside. You notice that the tracks of the elevated subway once again disappear into the earth at the outer edge of the 'burbs. Is that their terminus? Or do they continue under the countryside? Below you lie farms and fields in varying shades of green and gold, with corn and wheat and soybeans filling field after field. You're getting bored. You're beginning to feel safe.

And then you see something ahead that looks a little out of the ordinary. The color is off, and it doesn't have the sharp right angles of the rest of your 'scape.

Your gut winds into a slow knot as you zoom toward it, then pulls tight as you recognize what it is.

A bare spot.

Neatly laid out grain fields and orchards surround you on all sides, but here in this roughly circular patch, maybe two hundred feet in diameter, nothing grows.

Nothing. Not even a weed. No hint of green mars this dry, cracked expanse of sterile earth.

Poisoned, you think. Poisoned from below. Bad soil. Bad earth. Bad bedrock.

Something wrong below.

You fight the sick, weak feeling that threatens to overcome you. Here is what you were looking for. Here is what you'd hoped you wouldn't find. Here lies the secret that can leave you like Sam. And now that you've found it you can't walk away.

You're going to have to deal with it.

But how? How to get it? Dig it up? With what? You have no virtual tools. And you'll have to be careful — extremely careful. One false move and you'll be a vegetable. But there has to be a way.

You turn and see the spires of your city. Maybe there . . .

As you glide over the outlying suburbs you notice the tracks again. One set runs in the direction of the bare spot. Is it possible?

Deciding it's worth a try, you descend to the northbound platform outside the tunnel and check the train map. Yes, the tracks run for miles under the countryside with regular stops along the way. But not forever. They stop at a place called, appropriately enough, End of the Line.

You don't like the sound of that.

You turn and the sight of a waiting train startles you. The doors are open. As you step into the front car, they slide closed behind you and the train lurches into motion. And into the tunnel.

The well-lit, clean, neat — of course — train car hurtles through the subterranean darkness with a minimum of noise and wobble. Every so often an empty subway platform flashes by, but the train never stops. Why should it? You're the only passenger.

Finally it slides to a halt at a station and the doors hiss open. A voice announces, *"End of the Line. All passengers off, please."*

This may be the end of the line, but this isn't your destination. You look out the front window and see that the tunnel goes farther. A line of widely spaced incandescent bulbs curves off into the darkness. You knock on the engineer's door.

"Hello? Is anybody in there?"

The door swings open and you gasp at the sight of Eathan sitting at the controls.

"End of the line, miss," he says officiously. "All trains stop here."

You shake off the shock, reminding yourself that anything can happen in a memoryscape, even yours.

"Can't you take me farther? I need to go —"

"End of the line, miss," he repeats. Then his features soften and he looks at you. "I've taken you as far as I can, Julie. You'll have to finish the journey on your own."

You nod. On your own . . . you should have known this is how it would end.

You exit the train, hesitate a moment on the platform as you contemplate the dark maw of the tunnel, then you glide toward it and begin the last leg of your journey.

As you follow the trail of bulbs, hurrying from one pool of light to the next, the cool dampness seeps through your skin and chills you. The thought of the unknown terror you are approaching sets off an even deeper chill.

You pass an abandoned train stop, exit gate bricked up, platform strewn with trash, walls marred with graffiti.

No question about it. The environment is deteriorating.

Farther down the tunnel, the tracks disappear. The lights are spaced farther apart, and dimmer, and soon there are no lights at all. You're moving through perfect darkness. And as you push on, you notice a foul odor, a mixture of mold, mildew, and putrefaction.

Death is here.

And fear.

Where is all the orderliness now? This is like something from Sam's 'scape. You fight the urge to run, reminding yourself of that wonderful Exit button that's always available. You can bail out anytime you feel too threatened. So you press on.

And suddenly there's a sharp turn in the tunnel, and dim light leaking around the corner. This could be it. Taking a breath, you make the turn . . .

And find the tunnel blocked. Twenty feet away, a seamless wall of granite. And seated before it in a cone of light, a man at a desk, writing furiously in a notebook. As you take a step forward he stops his scribbling and looks up. You freeze.

Nathan.

The man you thought of as "Daddy" until yesterday, looking just as he did twenty-three years ago when he ran back into the burning house. And suddenly you know that he's behind it all. Nathan did something to you and Sam, something worse than the neurohormones, something horrible.

And now he's here, guarding the memory of it.

"Couldn't stay away, could you, Julie," he says, his tone a mixture of contempt and amusement. "Couldn't leave well enough alone." He *tsks* and shakes his head. "Too bad. I had such high hopes for you. Now you're going to be left with the intellectual capacity of a cabbage. What a waste."

You begin to back away, begin to reach for that blessed Exit button. You'll come back some other time and face this. With Dr. S. You're not ready for this now. You —

"Don't run off," he says. "It will do you no good. You've already set the machine in motion." He points to the digital clock behind him as it begins counting down by seconds from one hundred. "That's all the time you have left, so you might as well stick around and see if you can buy yourself some more."

You stop. Is he lying? But this isn't really Nathan. This is an image constructed from your own mind. And you wouldn't lie to yourself. Would you?

"Come closer," he says, gesturing to the straight-back wooden chair before his desk. "Have a seat and we'll play a variation on our little game. You remember our game, don't you?"

Trembling, eyes fixed on the spinning dial of that clock, you approach the desk. And as you do, you shrink . . . or he becomes larger. No, it's you. You're a little girl again. Four or five years old, and Daddy's going to play the math-quiz game. You climb up on the seat and glance briefly at him before returning your attention to the shrinking total on the wall.

"Pay no attention to the clock, Julie dear. It will only distract you. Listen well. Here's how our little game works: When I ask a question, the clock stops. If I give the right answer first, it starts again and continues until I ask the next question. If *you* give the right answer first, it stays stopped until I get one right again. Fair enough?"

You have to ask: "What happens when it reaches zero?"

Nathan smiles. "You lose."

"I lose what?"

"Your mind."

An icy hand grips your heart. You know this is no joke. You've seen what happened to Sam.

Another glance at the clock. You've lost forty-two seconds already.

"Can we start? Now?"

"Of course. First question: Compute five thousand seven hundred and twenty-one multiplied by twenty-one."

The clock freezes and so does your mind.

You always scored well in the game as a child, but that was simple addition or subtraction. And who does math in their head any-more? Nowadays you'd probably use a damn calculator to count your toes.

Suddenly Nathan is tapping keys some-where on his desktop. A buzzer sounds. The countdown resumes.

"The answer," he says, "is one hundred twenty thousand, one hundred and forty-one."

The number flashes in red across the front of the desk: *120,141 ... 120,141 ... 120,141....*

"Let's try another, shall we?" he says. "How about, oh, I don't know: Why don't you com-pute two thousand one hundred ninety-eight times fourteen?"

God, you can't think. If you could only see the numbers you might have a chance, but —

"Got it!" Nathan cries and starts tapping his desktop again.

The buzzer sounds and the numbers on the clock resume their relentless downward spiral as *30,772* flashes across the desk front.

"Julie, dear," he says in a solicitous tone that sets your teeth on edge. "You've got to do better than this if you don't want to end up a drooling husk. Let's try a different type of calculation. Compute one million, eleven thou-sand, seven hundred and fifty-two divided by fourteen."

The clock stops again and you try to picture the number in your mind: Fourteen into one-oh-one is seven ... into thirty-one is two ... into thirty-seven is another two ... you hear

Nathan's keyboard — *No!* . . . Into ninety-five is —

The buzzer again — that damn buzzer — and suddenly *72,268* is flashing across the desk front.

And oh, God, you've got only twenty-one seconds left. A cold, sick sweat is pouring out of you. This sham of a contest is fixed. He knows the answers before he asks the questions. It was always fixed. Never had a chance.

How can you hope to compete with him? You can't win!

And that's the whole point.

"Time for just one more," Nathan says. "Let's see —"

Fixed . . . even as a kid, you didn't know the real game, what was really being done, as a little girl sitting there, playing the stupid —

But wait. You're not a little girl anymore. . . . Nineteen seconds. Eighteen seconds.

And he's not even your real father. . . .

"Wait!" you say. "Stop! This isn't your house — this is *my* house, *my* turf. I'm not your little girl, and I don't have to play your goddamn game."

"Time is fleeting, Julie. You know the rules."

"Fuck your rules! They don't apply here. In my place you play by *my* rules, and *I* don't want to play."

You rise from the chair and as you do you grow in size, returning to your adult height. Your knees feel spongy, barely able to support you. You look down at him. And you realize that for the first time he looks scared.

His mouth moves as though he's trying to ask that last question, but nothing comes out. With a surge of triumph you realize that you were right. He's not in control here — you are.

At that instant the desk bursts into flame and the heat flash drives you back. When your vision clears you see that Nathan's jacket is ablaze. The fire spreads quickly until he's engulfed in flame. You want to turn away but you can't. You watch in horrid fascination as his flesh bubbles, smokes, and hisses, his limbs begin to twist and contract.

A voice screams from within the flames.

"Damn you, Julie! Now you've done it! You wanted to see? You've got your wish! I hope you enjoy it. And damn you, Julie! Damn you . . . to hell!"

Seconds later the fire burns itself out and you're faced with a blackened, twisted corpse, an exact three-dimensional replica of the photo you found in the coroner's report.

You feel your gorge rise, but there's no time to be sick. The fire has spread to the stone wall behind him — and the stone is burning.

No. Not stone. Canvas. A trompe l'oeil mural that blazes furiously for a few seconds, then sputters out, leaving a pall of smoke . . . and an open passage.

You stand on the threshold of that passage,

aching to flee but knowing it's too late. You've freed the beast and now you must face it — here or in the real world — but you *must* face it. Now. The memory is uncaged and you have no choice.

A breeze brushes against your back, billowing the smoke ahead of you. It rises swiftly to a gale, then a howling tempest, propelling you forward, into the smoke, into . . .

. . . the front foyer of the Millburn house.

Your mother is standing in the center, holding you and Sam by the hand. Your uncle Eathan is hurrying up the stairs. Instantly you recognize the scene. Yes, you were here only this morning. Eathan and Nathan have just had their fight, and Mommy's said she's leaving and taking you girls away where Nathan can never get near you again.

Suddenly you're no longer watching the scene — you're part of it. You're little Julie again, just as before.

As Uncle Eathan runs up the stairs, little Julie looks up at her mother. "M-Mommy, are we going on a trip?"

"Yes. A long one."

"And Daddy's not coming," Sammi says, not sounding too upset about it. "He and Uncle Eathan don't like each other anymore. I seen them . . . I seen them fighting."

"Why?" Julie asks.

Before Sammi can answer, Uncle Eathan reappears, struggling with a huge suitcase on the stairs.

"What's in this? Everything you own?"

"Just about."

As Uncle Eathan lugs the suitcase toward the door, everyone freezes at the sound of Daddy's voice.

"Stop!" he shouts, running from the rear of the foyer. He has a wild look in his eyes. "Don't take another step!"

Uncle Eathan glances over his shoulder, but doesn't break step or even bother to reply. As he reaches out to push the screen door open, Daddy lurches by Julie and her mother and sister.

"No, damn it!"

Julie notices something in his hand. Something with a needle on the end, like one of the shots the doctor gave her at her last checkup.

Daddy leaps on Uncle Eathan and *jabs* the needle into the back of his shoulder. Uncle Eathan cries out and drops the bag. The two of them begin to struggle, shouting incoherently, growling like animals.

"Stop it!" Mommy cries. "My God, Nathan! Please! This won't change anything!"

Julie is terrified. . . . Daddy is acting like a crazy man. Uncle Eathan seems to be weakening, gasping for air. Julie screams as Mommy peels her and Sammi off her legs and rushes forward.

"Leave him alone!" she cries, trying to pull

Daddy off Uncle Eathan.

But Daddy rears up and grabs her and shakes her like a toy. His bared teeth and blazing eyes make him look more beast than human as he hurls Mommy across the foyer with terrible force. She caroms off the wall and tumbles against the stairs.

The back of her head strikes the edge of one of the wooden steps with a loud *thwack,* and she goes limp.

Julie and Sammi scream, "Mommy!" as one and rush to her side. Instinctively Julie cries out to the other most important person in her life.

"Daddy! Please, Daddy, help her!"

But even as the words pass her lips she knows that Daddy is not going to help Mommy. Daddy the protector stands panting over his brother, who is now as limp as Mommy.

Suddenly Julie is close to panic. The foundations of her home, her family, her life, are crumbling. She looks to her sister for help, but Sammi is sobbing uncontrollably with her face buried between Mommy's breasts. She has never felt so afraid, so helpless, so alone. . . .

And Daddy is coming toward her with murder in his eyes.

She screams in terror as he grabs her arm and yanks her away from Mommy. He does the same with Sammi and pushes the two of them into the dark living room.

"Stay here!" he says through tight-clenched

teeth. "Don't move until I tell you to!" He pulls the French doors closed behind him.

Moaning, sobbing, shaking, Julie and Sammi cling to each other in the dark. Through the glass panes of the doors they see Daddy moving back and forth in the foyer.

A moment later he returns. He grabs Julie's jaw and forces a pill into her mouth.

"Chew and swallow!" When she doesn't, he smacks her and gives the order again. "Chew and swallow!"

Julie bites the tablet. Bitter taste floods her mouth as he moves on to Sammi.

"It tastes awful!" Sammi cries, and Daddy slaps her on her behind.

"Eat it!"

When Julie and Sammi have swallowed their pills, he leaves them again. They huddle there in the darkness for what seems like forever.

Suddenly Julie smells something burning. Smoke begins to seep into the living room. Like the fireplace smell, but stronger.

Sammi screams, "Fire!" and points through the French doors.

The living room fills with smoke. Julie struggles to her feet, pulling Sammi up with her. They've got to get out of here. She drags Sammi to the French doors. The whole foyer is full of flame. She grabs the door handle. It's hot but she holds on and twists it.

A blast of heat pushes the doors open, singeing her hair. The flames roar toward them. She turns away, crying —

They can't escape.

Suddenly a strong arm wraps around her. She and Sammi are lifted from the ground. It's Daddy! Daddy the protector has shaken off whatever evil spell possessed him and has come to rescue his little girls. He'll save everyone now.

She sees Mommy still slumped by the stairs and Uncle Eathan still on the floor. Daddy steps over their inert uncle and carries them into the cool, clear night air.

He carries them safely away from the heat and smoke and deposits them in the damp grass.

"Stay here," he says. "I'm going back for your mother."

And so they wait, watching the flames move through the house, waiting for Daddy to save their mommy and bring her to their side.

And suddenly they see him, barreling through the flames at the door with a wet towel wrapped around his head. He's carrying something in his arms. . . . Yes, something —

But it's not Mommy. It's a duffel bag and an armful of books. The same books he threw down in the foyer a few moments ago. Important books, like his important papers. He trots up to the twins' side and places the books on the ground nearby. Then he turns and stares at the fire.

"Where's Mommy?" Julie asks. "Didn't you save her?"

But Daddy doesn't answer, doesn't even glance her way. He seems entranced by the fire. He walks away, moving closer to the flaming house. He stands with his hands on his hips and watches the flames.

Suddenly Julie sees movement in one of the side windows near Daddy. Movement . . . and someone is there, pounding against the screen. A woman — her dress is smoldering, her hair ablaze.

"Mommy!" she screams and Sammi joins her. *"Mommy!"* They stand up, screaming. Mommy's there, she's okay, she's getting out.

Daddy sees her too. Her weakening efforts manage to knock the screen out of the window frame. As it topples to the grass she sags against the sill, half in, half out, reaching toward him, pleading for help, for rescue.

Daddy quickly looks around, rushes to the edge of the garden, and returns with . . . the hoe. He braves the heat and stretches it up to her.

Julie holds her breath. Daddy can do it! Daddy can save her!

But as Mommy reaches for the hoe —

Daddy rams it against her body and Mommy topples back into the flames.

Julie and Sammi wail their horror into the night. Won't somebody come to put out the fire? Won't a fireman come save their mommy?

But only the unblinking face of the full moon is witness.

Daddy waits by the window a while longer, and when Mommy doesn't reappear, he starts toward them, a black form silhouetted against the flames, coming closer, looming larger, blocking out the house and the fire until there's only the fire-lit trees and the moon and his shadow.

The fire colors everything.

Even the moon . . .

No. This makes no sense. This isn't what happened.

You tear free from little Julie . . . and watch.

Dazed, numb with shock and horror, you see Nathan scoop up the hysterical twins and toss them like so much baggage into the backseat of Eathan's car. Then he retrieves his journals and the duffel bag and places them in the front seat.

A siren begins to wail in the distance as he speeds away.

You don't absorb much of what follows. You see him take the girls to the basement of Eathan's home. He forces more pills into them while they cry. He flashes lights in their eyes and tells them over and over to imagine their father running back into the house and never coming out . . . running back into the house and never coming out . . . telling them they will remember nothing of tonight except their daddy carrying them to safety, Daddy telling them he's going back for their mother, and then running back into the flames.

Somehow, the girls stop crying.

And then Nathan reappears, only now he's wearing a beard exactly like his brother's, and telling the girls over and over that they will call him Uncle Eathan from now on, only Uncle Eathan, and all they will remember about tonight is . . .

It goes on and on, but then he begins adding a new twist to the message:

If they ever remember anything else other than what he has said, they will die.

They will die. The memory will kill them, so if they wish to live, they must never, ever remember what happened tonight.

And then he's driving them into the woods, walking them in among the trees, and leaving them with only the man in the moon as guardian.

They huddle together, cold and miserable, wondering how they got here. . . .

Suddenly the scene goes blank. More than blank. Dark. No blue screen, no button bar, readout. Dead. A system failure. You grasp your headset and —

Thirty-Five

Quintilius: "A liar should have a good memory."
— Random notes: Julia Gordon

1

Julie pulled her head free and looked around. Night had fallen but someone had turned on the room light. She looked toward the monitor. Dead. The VCR too — no power. For a minute she'd thought she was trapped in there, in her own mind. But it was okay, only a —

She started to rise from the recliner, and a hand gripped her shoulder.

She gasped and looked up.

"Eathan!"

No — not Eathan. She knew that now. *Nathan.*

A tsunami of rage surged through her, overpowered her, launched her at him, clawing at his face, reaching for his eyes.

Roughly, he shoved her back into the recliner.

"Stay right where you are, Julia."

He restrained her until she realized that he was heavier and stronger, and had enough leverage to hold her in place indefinitely.

She stopped struggling and lay there panting, glaring at him as he moved around and sat on the edge of the recliner, facing her. His eyes were cold, his expression unreadable behind the beard. But he knew where she'd been, knew what she'd seen. She was sure of that.

But she could find no hint of remorse in his face.

She closed her eyes as bile surged into her throat. What he did, what he *did!* Murdered her mother, and her real father. And all these years pretending to be the brother he murdered. And she all these years loving and respecting and admiring him.

She was going to be sick. No. She couldn't be. Not in front of this man. She swallowed, waited for the nausea to pass, then opened her eyes and stared at him.

God, the sight of him repulsed her. And the thought of being alone with him terrified her.

"Help!" she shouted. "Nurse! Help! Get in here!"

"Don't bother," Nathan said. "The cook

and the maid are gone for the day, and I fired the nurse."

"You're lying."

"No. I found her sitting outside the door, made a big scene about abandoning her patient, and fired her on the spot." His smile never got near his eyes. "I'm a *most* concerned uncle."

"You're a monster."

"I believe we've already had that conversation. It bored me the first time."

"You'd better get used to boredom," she said through her teeth. "You're going to spend the rest of your days behind bars. I only wish New York had had the death penalty then. I'd love to see you fry!"

Nathan laughed. "Oh, I don't think so."

"I've got evidence. I remember now. I know who you are. I know what you did. God, I've even got it on tape!"

Nathan shook his head slowly, and something about the ease of gesture sent a bolt of cold fear through Julie. He was too relaxed, too confident for someone who'd just been exposed as a double murderer.

He said, "Sorry. That tape won't exist by the end of the night, and —"

"There's another in New York," Julie said, blurting the lie and hoping he'd buy it. "Dr. Siegal saw everything."

"Julie, Julie." Nathan sighed. "You're a brilliant young woman — and you shouldn't forget how much of that brilliance you owe to me — but I've been ahead of you all the way. If I'd let you rummage through the bird's nest of wires and cables you've got behind the cabinet with the monitor and the VCR, you'd find a small RF video transmitter. The receiver is in the basement, hooked up to my own VCR."

Another chill rattled through Julie. "So you've been watching all along."

"Not all along. Only since before my London trip earlier in the week. I became suspicious when you said you'd 'forgotten' to record a session. That wasn't like you. So I decided to install my own safeguard against any further lapses in memory. It came in quite handy today. By the way, I never did get to London today. I called cook a little while ago and told her I'd be late and not to fix you dinner — I was taking you to the Bay Hotel. But I came back as soon as she left and reviewed the tape. I can't tell you how relieved I was when I saw that the blocked memory was destroyed, how you failed to reconnect Samantha. I thought I was home free. But I've got to hand it to you, Julia: You are one persistent little devil."

"*I'm* not the devil here."

"Whatever. As for the missing tape, I eventually learned its contents from Alma. I do wish I'd known sooner. I could have headed off this nasty scene."

"Alma told you?"

"Yes. She was an exceptional woman. She'd gained a handle on the imagery of Samantha's memoryscape, reading into things I'd seen but thought nothing of. She thought Samantha was suffering from a delusion that Nathan was still alive. That concerned me no end, because I feared Alma would begin talking this up, and between the two of you, and with more information from the memoryscape — especially all that recurring back-from-the-dead imagery — you might determine that it wasn't a delusion. That perhaps Nathan had somehow risen from the ashes."

"*You* killed her!"

He shrugged. "Quite regretfully. I suggested we take a walk in the night air to discuss these things. And you know how treacherous those cliffs can be."

Another wave of nausea. *Three* murders. And Julie had implicated Liam in Alma's death.

"Why?" Julie whispered.

"I believe I just told you —"

"No. Why everything? Why this whole elaborate . . . ?" Her voice failed her.

"Charade? It's not so elaborate, really. It just seems that way. It began when I couldn't get permission for human trials of my neurohormone protocol, and couldn't get grants for the necessary animal studies to qualify for the clinical trials. The proverbial Catch-Twenty-Two. I was in a terrible state, swinging between dark depression and manic agitation. No money, too. I didn't know what to do.

"And then your mother, my wife, true-blue Lucy, announced she was pregnant. Now this puzzled me. After years of trying, we'd never been able to have children. We'd just about given up hope, and frankly my sex drive had fizzled during the stress of that past year — so much so that I couldn't remember the last time we'd had sex. And my dear brother had been hanging around an awful lot lately. Puzzlement turned to suspicion, but I refused to believe that my wife and my own twin brother would betray me like that. It took me almost the entire duration of the pregnancy — a somewhat shortened term because you were twins — to find the nerve to get a sperm count. Well" — he smirked — "you know the results."

Julie nodded. "Sterile."

"Yes. I raged privately, and that was when I decided to kill them both. But before I could conceive a plan, your mother went into labor and delivered twins. Identical twins."

Julie gripped the armrests of her recliner. "And suddenly you had the raw material for your human trials."

"And the ultimate revenge. I don't believe in God, but can't you almost see the hand of divine retribution in this?"

"No," Julie said. "Not at all."

"Yes, well, perhaps not. No matter. I seized the opportunity and began dosing you and Samantha according to my protocol."

"But you could never publish the results."

"That didn't matter so much as proving to myself that I was right. If you two worked out according to plan, I would continue pursuing grants. If you failed, I'd know I was on the wrong track and go back to basic research."

"Well," she said grimly, "you succeeded."

"Oh, yes. Beyond my wildest dreams."

"But Eathan found out and you had to kill him."

"Oh, I'd already decided to kill him and Lucy. I'd been laying the groundwork for years. I took out the insurance policies on both of us — that looks much less suspicious than to keep one on your wife only — and drew up the will and the trusts. The only question was when. Sooner or later? My precarious financial situation was forcing me to act sooner. It was deteriorating as quickly as my marriage. The bank was threatening to foreclose . . . a terrible thing. I loathed your mother for what she'd done.

I only stayed married to her to be with you two. But I knew that when I lost the house, I'd lose Lucy and her twins."

"Your two little experiments."

"Exactly. I had the plan in place — the fire, switching places with Eathan — everything was ready to go. The time was now, but I lacked the nerve to do it. I imagined so many things that could go wrong and trip me up. . . . I delayed for months. I might never have done a thing if Eathan hadn't found my journals and read them. By telling Lucy, he forced my hand. Not only would I lose the twins, but I risked exposure, arrest, and even jail. I had to act immediately."

Julie's head whirled. Her father was her uncle who became her father but was really her uncle. A flesh-and-blood matrioshka doll.

"But the coroner's report," she said. "The dental records proved without a doubt —"

"That the corpse was Nathan?" His grin was genuine now. He really seemed to enjoy telling his tale. "I'm very proud of that one. You see, I made sure that I went to the same dentist as Eathan. When I decided the time had come to put my plan into action, I sneaked into the dentist's office — no big deal, really; Millburn was a homey little town in 1972 and the idea of a security system back then was utterly absurd — and switched the first letters on our names. Close inspection might show evidence of an alteration, but the coroner and the insurance inspectors all worked from photocopies. They never even had a clue. In one fell swoop I'd solved all my familial and financial problems. My only worry was you two. I'd dosed you with propranolol —"

"A beta-blocker. Of course . . . to dull the memory-enhancing effects of adrenaline."

"Quite. I was way ahead of my time. I hypnotized you and instilled a false memory of the fire. But no plan is foolproof. If one of you ever remembered what happened that night, I could lose everything."

"So you got us out of the country."

"Yes. The move solved a number of problems. Eathan was a physician, an internist. I was not. I could not take over his practice, nor could I risk one of his friends catching on to my charade. Fortunately he was a bit of a loner like me. He made a brief, distraught appearance at the funeral, then shunned what few friends he had — he took it so hard. Soon my own beard filled in but I knew I could not carry off the role indefinitely. I had to leave Millburn. But the move also served to remove you two from the vicinity of the trauma. If I'd kept you in the Millburn area, there would be an ongoing risk of one of you coming across something that might trigger the true memory. England seemed perfect. No language barrier, and the dollar went a lot further over here then than it does now — I got this place for a song. And with the two of you all to myself here on the North Yorkshire coast, I could continually reinforce the false memory, make you relive it —"

"All those 'ventilating' sessions!"

"Yes. I couldn't kill the true memory because the false memory shared a piece of it. Every time I strengthened the false memory I was preserving the true memory as well. So I had to keep the false memory so fresh and alive that there'd be no way you could get to the truth."

"No way?" Julie said, pointing to her memoryscape headgear.

Nathan's grin broadened. "Isn't the irony delicious? I made Samantha perfectly right-brained, the compleat artist. But she used her art to unblock the memory of that night. Poor Sammi was catching glimpses of something in her art. She got close to the truth . . . too close . . . and when she released it she didn't die as I had hypnotically suggested — Samantha never did do as she was told. But it did disrupt her entire memory system and she fell into what looked like a coma."

"Bastard!"

"But the irony continues. I made you the ultimate left-brained scientist, and what do you do? You unblock the memory with a computer." He actually laughed and clapped his hands. "Hoist by my own petard!"

"But why did you risk letting me go into her memory at all?"

"Did I have a choice? You were so damned insistent. And as Samantha's loving, concerned uncle, how could I refuse you at least one look? I was utterly terrified at first, but after I saw what her memoryscape looked like, I relaxed. I knew the true memory was gone and you weren't going to find anything." Another laugh. "I never guessed you'd travel into your own mind. Bravo, Julia!"

"But why continue the charade all these years? Why devote so much effort to playing a loving uncle to your orphaned nieces?"

"The experiment, remember? I wanted to provide a stable environment that supported you in whatever direction you wished to take. I nurtured your differences. I wanted to see how far each of you would go in your divergent interests. The farther apart the better — the more it confirmed the success of my protocol. Because this has been an ongoing experiment." He took a deep breath, a resigned sigh. "At least until now."

Something in his voice gave her a crawling feeling in her gut. She wanted to keep him talking.

"So that's why you've got all our accomplishments tagged and filed in that cabinet. An ongoing record. For what?"

"For eventual publication."

Julie searched Nathan's face for some sign that he was joking. She found none.

"You can't be serious."

"Posthumous publication, of course."

"But even then, this monstrous toying with children's minds will . . . the whole world will —"

"Revile me? I certainly expect so. But I also expect them to finally take a good look at my protocol. It works. You and Samantha have proved that. And so along with the widespread opprobrium will come a certain grudging respect for my genius. Yes, they'll revile me, but at least I won't soon be forgotten." His eyes got a faraway look. "I wonder what they'll say."

"You'll never know."

"Oh, don't be so sure. I've been thinking of writing up the details and leaving them here with all the hard proof of the experiment's success, and then just . . . disappearing. How wonderfully entertaining to sit back in the safety of a new identity and watch the firestorm of controversy over my experiment. Yes . . . I might find a way to die a second time." He reached into his pocket and withdrew a syringe. "You and Samantha, unfortunately, will only get to die once."

Julie pushed back, trying to shrink into the fabric of the recliner.

"What's that?"

"Succinylcholine. I used it on your uncle — excuse me — father. I don't have to tell you what it does."

Julie knew. The ultimate muscle relaxant. The right amount would leave her limp as a dishrag. Too much would paralyze her muscles of respiration and she'd suffocate. God, what was she going to do? Think! *Think!*

"And then what? Another fire? You don't really believe you can get away with this twice, do you?"

"Why not? The first fire is ancient history. In another country. But I never would have even toyed with the idea if you hadn't turned in a suspected arsonist to Scotland Yard. *That* made the decision for me. Oh, I'll be heroically fighting the blaze when the firemen arrive from Bay. I'm sure we can confine it to this wing . . . sparing my study."

Julie's mouth was so dry she could barely speak. "They'll know it was you."

"Their loving uncle? I hardly think so. Not after you betrayed Liam O'Donnell. How awful that this known terrorist decided to make an example of you and your sister, a fiery warning to anyone else who might be of a mind to talk to the police." He glanced across Julie to where Sam lay inert under her covers. "I wish there were another way, but since half of the experiment is already as good as gone —"

The syringe caught the pale light of the room. Nathan brought it close.

Julie kicked with her right leg and caught him in the chest. *"Bastard!"*

She'd seen her chance and had aimed for his throat but didn't get her foot high enough.

Nathan grunted and fell back off the recliner. Julie slipped forward and aimed another kick at his face but he got his arm up — so quickly — and blocked it.

She rolled off the opposite side of the recliner, bumping against Sam's bed as she headed for the door.

But Nathan was up and stretching across the recliner. Julie screamed as he caught her arm and shoved her back onto Sam's bed. The back of her head knocked against Sam's knees.

Julie tried to roll away but Nathan flung himself on her and pinned her to the bed. Her left arm was trapped between them but she flailed at him with her right. He had the syringe in his right fist, holding it like a dagger, his thumb on the plunger. His eyes were wild.

Julie kept beating at him but he barely seemed to notice. She closed her eyes and screamed in an agony of fear, anger, frustration, and horror as he raised the needle over her shoulder.

This was how it would end, all the secrets leading to her own death.

And then Nathan stopped. He said, "Uh?"

Julie opened her eyes and saw Nathan staring wide-eyed at his hand. At first she thought he'd accidentally stuck himself and her heart lifted. But then she noticed what had captured his stunned attention . . .

A hand was locked around his wrist.

She thought her heart would explode with joy. It was impossible. It was wonderful.

Julie screamed, "Sam!"

And from behind Nathan she heard Sam's voice — hoarse, dry, cracked, after long disuse — a sepulchral whisper.

"Ju-lie."

New strength burst through Julie's limbs. She shoved Nathan back and managed to slip free of him. His left hand made an awkward snatch for her but he still seemed distracted, stunned by the fingers wrapped around his wrist.

Julie stumbled to her feet and turned.

She glanced at Sam's face and saw her blue eyes open and staring at Nathan.

Nathan looked up and was caught by her accusing stare. He froze for an instant — and in that instant, Julie acted.

She grabbed the straight-back chair and lifted it over her head. *Do it!*

Nathan broke free of Sam's gaze and yanked his wrist from her grasp. He was pushing himself up from the bed, scrambling now, disoriented, when Julie swung the chair. She brought it down hard from somewhere near the ceiling and caught him square across the back.

And it felt good, oh God, it felt so damn *good* to let the son-of-a-bitch have it.

He cried out in pain and sagged, then slid to his knees on the floor. Groaning, he started to straighten from there. Julie didn't hesitate. She swung the chair again —

"You sick" — she slammed the chair down — "bastard!"

And this time, aiming for his head, she put everything into it, every bit of anger at everything he had done to their lives, everything he had stolen from them, the years she and Sam could have known each other, loved each other.

One of the legs caught him square across the back of the skull.

And that felt even better than the first shot.

This time he didn't make a sound as he slumped to the floor and lay still.

And nearly giddy with the act, Julie slammed the chair against his head a third time, just to make sure he wasn't faking.

He was so damn good at faking.

She watched him a moment, ready to give him a fourth shot, almost hoping he'd move, but he was out. She dropped the chair. She looked at the bed.

And saw Sam, looking up at her.

Gingerly, Julie stepped over Nathan to get to the bed.

Sam was watching her with her sunken, luminous eyes. She lifted her hand — her arm muscles were so weak — and Julie grasped it, clutching it between both of hers. Her fingers were cool, damp.

"Sammi! You're awake. You've come back to us."

"Jule," she said in a voice as dry as the heather out on the moors, and weakly squeezed Julie's hands. "Jule . . . I had the weirdest dream. And you were in it."

Julie felt that pressure building up in her chest, felt her eyes filling. Oh yes, she thought. Let it come.

"Was I?"

"Yes. It was an awful dream, but in it you said you loved me. Isn't that weird?"

"No. That's not weird, Sam. And it wasn't a dream. It's true. I do love you."

And then she couldn't hold back the tears any longer. She wrapped her arms around her twin, clutching her tight. She buried her face against Sam's shoulder and sobbed. "You're my sister, and I love you. . . ."

"You're crying, Jule," Sam said. "You never cry."

Julie tried but couldn't answer. She felt Sam's free hand start to stroke her hair. Like those other hands . . .

"Does this mean we're friends now?"

Julie could only nod against her shoulder. *Oh, yes.*

"Good. I always wanted us to be friends, but . . ." now Sam's voice started to catch, "you never seemed to. Twins should be friends."

The simple truth of that only caused Julie to cry harder.

"Don't cry, Jule. We're gonna be all right."

Finally Julie found her voice again.

"Yes, we are, Sammi." She sat up and wiped her eyes. "We're going to be better than all right. We're going to be the best. The two of us. I'll see to that. *We'll* see to that. But first . . ."

She turned and sat on the edge of the bed, looking down at Nathan's still form, sprawled on the rug. She had to pull herself together now. Something had to be done about Nathan. She had to call the police but there was no phone in this room. What if Nathan came to while she was out calling?

Only one way to solve that: Take him with her. Drag the monster down the hall by his ankles.

She knelt beside him, got her hands under him, and flipped him onto his back.

"Oh, God!"

"What's wrong?" Sam asked from the bed.

Julie stared at Nathan's white face and open, unseeing eyes. Then she noticed the empty syringe protruding from his chest wall. He wasn't going anywhere.

Relief swept through her.

"What's wrong, Jule?" Sam asked again.

"Nothing, Sammi," she told her. "Nothing at all. Everything's fine now."

And they sat there together, with so much to say and yet — saying nothing.

Because they had plenty of time now.